Slum City Africa

Slum City Africa

"A Very Bad Place With Good Teachings"

by
Warren Elofson and Jonah Weyessa

ANTHEM PRESS

FIRST HILL BOOKS
An imprint of Wimbledon Publishing Company Limited (WPC)

This edition first published in UK and USA 2022
by FIRST HILL BOOKS
75–76 Blackfriars Road, London SE1 8HA, UK
or PO Box 9779, London SW19 7ZG, UK
and
244 Madison Ave #116, New York, NY 10016, USA

British Library Cataloguing-in-Publication Data
A catalogue record for this book is available from the British Library.

Library of Congress Cataloging-in-Publication Data
A catalog record for this book has been requested.

ISBN-13: 978-1-83998-579-9 (Pbk)
ISBN-10: 1-83998-579-8 (Pbk)

Cover credit: Image of Life in The Kibera Slum In Nairobi
By Jan Hetfleisch @ Getty images

This title is also available as an e-book.

CONTENTS

INTRODUCTION

Following is a story based on the experiences of a family forced to abandon an agrarian life in Ethiopia and move to Kibera, Kenya, one of the world's dirtiest and most dangerous city slums. The central characters are representative of many who made that transition in the twenty-first century. The characters themselves are not true to life, but all the events described happened. We have confirmed them by extensive research and, most importantly, the recollections of a mother and her son who experienced the journey themselves.

This story is also about facing and eventually finding means to overcome a multitude of life's challenges. What we learn as we go is that when people have to face significant trials in their everyday lives, they become very creative. We focus mainly on the experiences of Mahret during a period when she shelters her two children, Gamado, five, and Berhanu, eight, while adjusting to a massive urban shantytown. Before husband Barisso can join her in Kibera, Mahret finds herself struggling with incredibly difficult surroundings. Rape, murder, and rampant diseases, she discovers, are a threat, and some desperate adults allow young children to be drawn into sexual exploitation even before they reach puberty.

When Mahret learns to face up to the harsh realities of slum life, she must rely on and trust individuals of a variety of cultures and walks of life. And she becomes much more accommodating and accepting than she could ever have been at her previous home in an ethnocentric farming community. She learns as well that women generally must be more assertive in dealing with a wide array of critical social and financial issues than she ever thought possible. When Barisso finally joins her and the kids in Kibera, he, like most everyone else living around them, goes through a similar process of personal development. However, for him, the transition is much more difficult as it compels him and other men to relinquish authority they previously took for granted.

Chapter 1

ETHIOPIA: A FRAGILE LIFE IN THE COUNTRYSIDE

Barisso and wife Mahret farmed in the wheat country of Oromia, Ethiopia, some fifty miles southeast of Addis Ababa. They and their two young sons, Gamado, five, and Berhanu, eight, lived in a small round house with a grass roof and stick walls. To this point, their life had been reasonably satisfying if not always as secure as Barisso, in particular, would have liked.

It was about to change for the worse.

As usual, Barisso was outside this morning looking over the crops in the little fields surrounding the house. Anyone who saw him might have guessed that he was older than his thirty-two years. Recently, his appearance had begun to show the effects of the sun's rays, the dry wind, and his constant worries about the future. His slim, straight build still suggested youthful stages of life, but subtle lines had appeared in his dark brown facial skin, and grey patches were showing in the curly black hair below the turban-like wrap he wore on his head.

Barisso loved the farm he had inherited after his *abbaa* and *haadha* had died years ago in a government denied epidemic. Still, his concerns about the future were not unfounded. So far this crop year, the rains had been less frequent than in the past, and he knew that if they did not come soon, the wheat and maize would be severely damaged. He realized too that there was a longer-term problem. The soil itself was losing its power. He used to be able to bolster it with manure from the communal pasture, but these days the dung was disappearing as fast as the oxen and goats could produce it. Everyone in the area was using it, and the pasture was beginning to look as tired as his cropland.

Barisso worried too that he, himself, had been guilty of abusing the soil. Before every planting season, he had worked it over and over again with his ox-drawn plow to make it receptive to the wheat and corn seeds, which he and Mahret planted by hand.

"What else could I do? The land bakes under the hot sun when the rainy season ends. It gets hard like a gravel road. Sometimes I even have to chop it up in places with my ax so the plow can cut through. If I don't work it and work it, I wouldn't get no crop at all."

Barisso had heard there was a way to bolster the soil with a product one of his neighbors was using.

"What was it called?—'phospheris' or something like that."

But it was expensive. The neighbor, Badhasso, was wealthy. He inherited twice as much land as Barisso—over six full acres—because his wife had no brothers or sisters. As a result, he was able to grow more wheat than his family needed for flour and to sell enough to purchase whatever it was he was using.

"My only hope," Barisso mused, "was if I could have talked the merchants in town into letting me have it free till after the crop is harvested. The wheat and corn too would be better, and if it improved the crops a lot, I would have extra to sell and pay them back."

But the merchants told him this would be like lending him money, and he had no credit rating.

"It's not fair, Badhasso's crops have been better than mine, and I worked the land more than he did. I can't get credit because my land is not good, and the only way to make it better is by getting credit. It's all luck, that's all it is. If my farm was bigger, I wouldn't be in this situation. I wouldn't need no [...]"

Mahret's voice cut into his thoughts:

"Barisso, come, breakfast."

Mahret was outside as usual too. She was working over a wood and charcoal fire boiling *shaayii* and mixing flour into a pot of hot water for the morning staple of *marqaa*.

Mahret was used to spending most of her time outdoors as well, not just with domestic duties, but also helping Barisso with the fieldwork and the animals. Even so, her looks had changed little since their marriage some eight years ago. Her hair was still black under the brightly colored *shashi* she wore on her head, her facial skin was still smooth, and her dark eyes still sparkled as if to deny the impact of a relatively strenuous existence.

While she worked, Mahret hummed to herself, something she had developed a habit of doing over the years as she went about her daily routines.

She loved the farm as much as Barisso did. She had married Barisso when she was in her fifteenth year, and she had always helped him out of doors. But she took special pride in her domestic contributions. Among other things, this was evident in her efforts to keep the family neat and clean. She regularly scrubbed her floor with fresh water from a stream some 200 yards from the house that flowed into the Ter' Shet' River. She made the soap herself from *goraa* growing wild in the valley, and from wood ashes mixed with water and tallow. She hand-washed Barisso, Berhanu, and Gamado's clothes in the stream every week. And, if weather permitted, she took both the boys for a swim most Saturday afternoons. When the elements were uncooperative, she used a bucket system for bathing them. She also kept a pail of soap and water by the doorway so the boys could wash their hands when they came in from play, and after using the smelly dugout toilet behind the house.

Mahret was disappointed that she and Barisso had not had more children.

"*Waqaa* wishes us to have a small family," she told her husband, "he knew it would be hard enough for us to live on what we have."

Her close relationship with God rooted in her upbringing at home and in the little grass-roofed church and school she had attended in the village, gave Mahret the strength to face life's major challenges. Lately, Barisso seemed to be warning her that there was something wrong with the land, and she also knew that two families on the other side of the village had to abandon their farms.

Mahret firmly believed, however, that it would be their destiny to spend the rest of their days on the farm raising their children until they were old enough to take wives of their own.

"*Waqaa*," she was sure, "will show us the way."

Chapter 2

THE LAST HURRAH

Barisso and Mahret sat cross-legged on the worn rug in front of the house, sipping their morning *shaayii* and eating bite-size bits of *daabo*. The latter they would break off with their fingers from a little ring-shaped mound on a wooden plate and then dip it into a mixture of butter, flax, and sunflower seeds in the center of the ring.

"Everyone is in the same condition as us," Barisso said, "some might hold on till next year and others maybe two years, but they are all worried like us."

He looked out at the other five grass-roofed farmhouses clustered around theirs with their nearly identical small fields of ripening wheat and corn.

"These will all be gone. They will be taken over by huge companies that they tell me are buying up all the land in other districts. Their crops, like ours, will be replaced by the huge open fields of rich farmers with expensive machinery. Us common folk will all have to move away, move to the city for work."

Mahret refused to accept this.

"But Barisso, there must be something you can do! We have to find an answer! How long till you know for sure about our crops?"

"When the wheat and corn are in the bin, we'll know. No matter what, we'll have enough food for quite a while. But if it's not gonna get us through to next year's harvest, we'll have to do something before it runs out. We can't let the kids go hungry."

"For now, then, we can do nothing but pray. We must pray to Waqaa with all our hearts!"

"Yes, that's all we have left. This is the greatest challenge of my life. I hate this, and I'm scared to death. All we have ever known is farming. I don't want to leave. I don't even know how to leave. Yet, I don't know what else to do. *Waqaa* help us, please help us! We will do anything you ask, please show mercy on us."

Without another word, they both performed three full prostrations to the Trinity, with their faces down flat on the earth. They would repeat this twice more during the day—once to the Virgin Mary and then to the cross of Jesus.

Mercifully, while they were waiting for their crops to ripen, Mahret and Barisso had something much less serious to divert their attention for a short while.

That was the Enkutatash, a preharvest festival celebrating the end of the rainy season.

Locally, the Enkutatash stirred considerable interest and excitement.

Most of the men in the community shared Barisso's fears for the future welfare of their families and, thus, like him, welcomed the break from reality this year even more than usual. They appreciated most of all the access it allowed them to alcohol. In their minds, the critical component of the Enkutatash was a drink they all prepared at home in the weeks before the event.

Making the drink was a complex undertaking, and each had his precise formula.

Barisso first picked the leaves from the gesho bushes growing along the banks of a nearby stream. He dried the leaves in the sun and pounded them into a powder. The powder he blended with a malt he had made by sun-drying and grinding up kernels of barley, a small patch of which Mahret always cultivated for him in her garden. After allowing the mixture to ferment for several days, he combined it with maize flour. After fermenting this concoction for a couple more days, he filtered it and mixed it with honey. Then, finally, he poured the mixture into a rounded vase-like *berele*.

The end product was his own special brand of *daadhi*. And it was considerably stronger than any sold in stores.

Mahret and the other women enjoyed the preharvest celebration too. However, they were normally not quite as pleased with it as the men for two reasons. Firstly, it was a waste of resources. The *daadhi* required using up a bit of their all too precious maize and a small piece of land for growing the barley. Moreover, Barisso and his friends would randomly get together before and during the celebration to sample their wares. At such time times, invariably, they would come home tipsy, and often not in the best of moods.

Mahret was normally not afraid of her husband. Like all other husbands, her husband saw himself as the boss of the family, and she never wanted to seem to be threatening his position. During each drinking session, however, his demeanor might darken. At such times, he would get angry at the slightest irritation, and a couple of times in past years, he had got aggressive. Mahret sometimes wondered if this was because he was trying to live up to an image he got from his *daadhi*-fueled conversations with the other men. His outbursts were not severe: he slapped her once or twice, and it was over. However, Mahret did feel pain, and she worried that with time, it could get worse.

However, the Enkutatash was a welcomed opportunity for the women to get together too and exchange pleasantries and gossip. That part of it they all relished.

On the morning of the celebration, all the families attended church. Then they gathered together to share a traditional meal of *daabo* and *wat*. Later in the day, young girls in the neighborhood would pick daisies and then, singing New Year's songs, present each other with a bouquet.

The main gathering took place in the evening on the low-lying flood plain that reappeared each summer as the water along the stream receded. The women donated the food they would have fed to their families for supper.

They brought the food in baskets and set it out on the old wooden table the men carried over from storage on higher ground.

After that Barisso and his friends started a bonfire to keep everyone comfortable while the evening air cooled. The men then got together off to the side of the table next to the stream, basically just to get drunk and entertain each other with jokes and tall tales.

This year, just as they were working on their first drinks, something momentarily interrupted their fun. Gamechu, who was in a small group standing around Barisso, saw a man in military garb walking towards them on the riverside pathway.

"Hey," Gamechu said smiling, "looky here, the soldiers are coming."

When Barisso and the other three men around him looked up, they could also see two parked jeeps with soldiers standing next to them, holding what looked like rifles.

They watched as the one man came toward them.

He was a short man with a scruffy beard and a protruding belly that, along with full battle fatigues, gave him an almost surreal appearance.

"*Nagaa jirtann?*," he said as he drew close, "how are you, fellows?"

"We're okay," someone answered.

"Hey folks," he said in a louder voice, "I am Colonel Mashad and I have a message for you from the OLF. We want to help you make your life much better. We can pay you good money."

The word money got their attention. Everyone closed in around him.

"The OLF, what's that?," Barisso asked.

"The Oromia Liberation Front. You have to know we are the militia that has been fighting for years now to liberate Oromia. The bastards in the government, the EPRDF, the so-called Ethiopian People's Revolutionary Democratic Front are our oppressors. They're the lowest of the low, the *haadha rawoch* of the human race. They are not democratic like they pretend, they're dictators, and they're taking the whole country prisoner."

"I know there's been fighting," Barisso told him, "but I don't know what it's about. Around here, we stay out of that kind of thing."

"Well you better start paying more attention. They're not just trying to take us prisoner, all of us, they're murderers, mass murderers; you and your neighbors will find yourselves threatened, many will be imprisoned for no reason and even killed if these people are allowed to hold power and impose their rule. They want to enslave Ethiopia, especially us in Oromia, and they're committing genocide. Their political party, the Oromo Peoples' Democratic Organization is a combination of small, ruthless political groups. They're all trying even by their titles to sound like freedom fighters; the Amhara National Democratic Movement, the South Ethiopian Peoples' Democratic Front, and the Tigran People's Liberation Front. When you hear those labels, don't be fooled.

What nonsense! They're all criminals. All of them think nothing of killing anyone who disagrees with them; their object is to control the whole country. Their leader, Meles Zenawi, is crazy with power lust, we have to stop him. He has implemented policies such as land redistribution. It has brought Zenawi mass support in some areas. He wants our land, your land, to redistribute to his followers. We recognized this and broke away; we're spearheading an insurgency against him."

"I can't follow all that," Gamechu said, "all I get from it is you don't have much chance. You can't beat all those groups, they must have lots of soldiers, and guns. How're you gonna defeat that?"

"We can if we all pull together. Oromo are sixty percent of all Ethiopia's population. Some from other provinces, Tigray, Mathare, as well as many from Somalia, and Eritrea are fighting on our side."

The colonel paused as if catching his breath (or trying to remember his lines).

He continued.

"They call us bandits because they want to draw international attention away from what is obviously ethnic cleansing.

They have even been planning to make it illegal to speak Oromo in public. They're driving us from our lands and subjecting our people to torture, imprisonment, forced conscription. They execute any who resist, without even a trial.

I'll give you an example.

They sprayed flammable chemicals over an Oromo valley in the south. Then they brought in jet fighters launching rockets to ignite the chemicals. They destroyed animals, buildings, and crops. More than 2,000 Oromo died, and more than 20,000 had to leave their homes. The recent wave of refugees fleeing to Nairobi is not from drought. It is genocide. A million and a quarter Oromo have been driven out of the country. The junta have not got to your region yet but they're coming, and very soon, they will kill your children, and they will rape your women just for the fun of it. Many of our brothers are now joining us in the Oromo Liberation Front. You must too. You must be brave; you must stand up for your family and your country—like a man."

Barisso and others were skeptical. Who was this guy really? How much of this was true, and how much was just lies to draw in supporters?

"What can I do," one of them said, "a poor farmer trying to feed his family? I have no power; I just want to stay on the land—mind my own business."

"The best way to make sure you can't stay on the land is to ignore the problem. The farmers all tell me their soils are failing. They, like you, have no chance of improving their condition. Every generation adds to the tract of desert that was once fertile wheat land; every generation sees villages and churches abandoned, and no others taking their place. If this continues very much longer, the Oromo farmer will be, like his elephant, a thing of the past."

"What can you do about that?"

"When the OLF gets control, we'll see that everyone has the resources they need to make a go of it. We will be fair. You should come with me now, join us, take up arms for the cause to protect your farm, your wife and children."

"If I did, how would my children and my wife live without me?" Barisso asked, "we are running out of food now. Do you want my children to starve?"

"We will feed them; we'll provide food for them. All your wife has to do is come to our headquarters at the church. We have teff flour, corn, and a great variety of vegetables. We even have powdered milk and some meat. Tell your wives, we collect produce from the farmers in the north who have extra, and we have lots of food to keep our soldiers healthy and our families too."

He opened a bag to show them not just flour and powdered milk but, potatoes, assorted other vegetables, and a small amount of *shonkora*.

"The government is trying to turn our land and farms over to corporations. This means we would lose everything. We can win this war. I give this to you now."

He handed the bag to Barisso,

"There will be much more to come. Once you join us, you can tell your wives to go weekly to your local church for more food. We have access to farms all the way through to Eritrea and Somalia. The land up north is still good; they have had rain."

"But I'm not a soldier. I don't even know how to shoot a gun."

"My friends, we will teach you all you need to know. We will teach you to fight for your family, to be a soldier, a man who defends his family, his people. Some Oromo joined the EPRDF, and we are calling on them to come back to us. Many are. As they do, we will defeat the enemy for sure. You must help them.

Listen to me, all of you. We are asking you to think it over. What have you got to lose? Before I go, I will just say that we will look after you; we have planned this carefully. Our headquarters is in Jijiga near the Somalia border, but we also have a secret liaison agent, a *lubaa*, Father Jerome, at the Ethiopian Orthodox Tewahedo Church in Shashamane. You must know where that is. Just turn up at the church and your life will change. Go to him, and he will tell you what to do next. Be careful though, do not talk to anyone else; most Oromo are on our side, especially the farmers, but we can't be sure who to trust."

"Why is the church involved?"

"Because they care about their people, they know *Waqaa* is on our side in a fight against evil.

We will expect to see you at the church. We will welcome you. You will have comrades in arms, fellow Oromo, brave men who care about their country as well as their families.

You do not want to be caught on the wrong side. This is a bloody war. You do not want to be seen as a traitor to your own. Come join us like men."

With that not so thinly veiled threat, the colonel turned and headed back down the little trail, got into one of the vehicles waiting for him, and disappeared with his crew.

Barisso and the other men went back to their booze. The Oromo Liberation Front (OLF) and the EPRDF were just two of the many subjects most of them broached during the rest of the night.

The wine they loved so much tended to render their conversations rather jumbled anyway. Much of what they discussed, they would not remember even the next day.

The women and girls gathered on the other side of the big table with the smaller children, so they could access the food while talking and keeping their distance from the men. They caught up on quite a lot of news:

Nuritu and Safayo had introduced themselves through a friend to the parents of a young lady in the next district named Guye, whom they were hoping their young son, Amos, would wed. It looked good. They tried to get Amos to follow up by going over to the girl's home to ask her himself. But he was too shy, so his younger brother went over to sneak into the house and leave the traditional coffee bean in a *nono* bowl. The two families then proceeded to the regular negotiations over coffee at Safayo and Nuritu's house. The parents gave the usual assurances of their daughter's sexual innocence, and Safayo agreed that when he died Amos, as his eldest, would have his land. The negotiations to be sure were not all that easy. Both sets of parents were farmers, and the dowry would have to be small.

"We have so little left," Nuritu said. "Our crops look bad too this year. We have six goats and can maybe give one or possibly two. But it is hard. We need them so badly. We have three other children to feed, and two are still growing. What can you offer when you live in fear of losing what you have?,"

There were a host of other stories too.

Two of the men at the party had recently taken a second wife.

"How can they possibly afford it?" one woman asked.

"They can afford it if the new wife comes with land," another said. "A husband dies, and the widow becomes valuable. She can sell herself like a cow at the auction. 'I don't know what to do, so many offers who will buy me a new dress? or a nice bracelet?'"

[Scores of laughter]

On another, more serious, note: Manu and wife Sophia, who had always attended tonight's celebration in the past, were noticeably absent. Manu beat his wife so severely that she almost died. The couple's oldest son came home to find his mother in a very bad state and warned his father that he would kill him if he ever hurt her again.

While both the men and the women continued their conversations, the kids turned to sport. As usual, Berhanu and some friends organized a game of soccer—and this year with a real store-bought ball that a government guy from Shashamane had given to Galgallu's dad.

Without adult supervision, the game could get out of hand. Galgallu body checked little Gamado as they went for the ball, knocking him down.

Berhanu would have none of that.

He walked over to Galgallu and, without a word, grabbed him, wrestled him to the ground, and then proceeded to slap him lightly in the face, basically just to humiliate him.

"Pick on somebody your own size!" he yelled. "Next time I'll put a *qamis* on ya. You fight like a girl anyway."

"Eat shit," Galgallu yelled.

The other kids pulled Berhanu off and then kept the two combatants apart until the play resumed. After that, there was no further trouble mainly because all the boys on the opposing team kept a healthy distance from Berhanu (and Gamado).

When darkness set in, the boys had to give up their game. At that point, they sat in a circle, a comfortable distance from the fire, and took turns scaring the daylights out of each other with ghost stories.

The end of the Enkutatash celebration began in the early morning hours when the women, their conversations finally waning like the fire, started one at a time to head back home. Mahret was one of the first to decide to leave. She went to tell Barisso, but when she got close, she could see he had a rather vague and distant look on his face, and he was arguing heatedly with a couple of his friends. She turned away and went to summon her boys.

As the three of them made their way toward home, Gamado and Berhanu stayed very close to their mother.

An hour or so after they had gone to bed, Barisso staggered home. Mahret woke up when she heard him. He stumbled across the floor, lifted the bed cover, and more or less fell on top of her. Pulling up her nightshirt, he rolled between her legs only to discover that he was unable to perform. When he had to give up the quest, he angrily pushed and kicked her off the mattress.

"You can sshleep on the kround tonight," he said, "it's yer fault, you don't know yer place—like a man."

As she rested on the edge of the cowhide that underlay the mattress, Mahret felt a sharp pain in her back where Barisso's foot had contacted it. She was sure there would be a bruise there in the morning. But she had been through episodes like this before, and she knew better than to argue with him. She waited a few minutes until she could hear his irregular snore, and then quietly rolled back onto the mattress and went back to sleep.

Chapter 3

FUNDAMENTAL ISSUES

It was over breakfast two mornings after the Enkutatash—when Barisso and Mahret were on speaking terms again—that they managed their next serious conversation about the future. The boys, having gobbled down their meal, were playing on the little pathway connecting the main trail to other farms and clusters of farms in the area.

Barisso glanced over at the kids and smiled. Then he turned to Mahret.

His tone was grim:

"Uh, I have to tell you what I've put off for too long, there is no way to avoid it."

Mahret had a pretty good idea what was coming.

"Yes?"

"Well, I'm worried. The signs are very bad—worse than I thought; if *Waqaa* does not answer our prayers soon, I don't think we will have enough flour and corn to see us through to the next harvest. This is the worst it has ever been for us, and it looks like we have no choice but to make our plans to leave. I thought maybe we could get by, but I see now we are in the same position as so many others. I'm afraid ours will soon be just one more of the empty fields scattered around the country."

The fact that Mahret had foreseen this moment did little to soften the impact of hearing the actual words. Her natural reaction, as always, was to call upon her Christian faith.

"No," she pleaded, "no, it will be okay. It must be; we must trust *Waqaa* to look after us. He will if we ask him, it will be alright. He wants us to be here. We will always be here. Please, you must try to find another way! Our crops will be better than you think."

Though Barisso was a man of faith too, his view of life was more directly affected by the pragmatic concerns of a farmer trying to feed his family.

"I trust *Waqaa*," he told her, "but he must be angry at us for cropping the land for so long and stealing its power. Like the government man told us, we should have put more back into the soil. It seems it's already too late. Even if we could afford to buy the stuff Badhasso is using, Sheva is not strong anymore. She is getting old, and she might not be here next year. Since we killed her brother for the meat, Sheva has to pull the plow herself, over and over again to get the land ready for seeding. She is very tired. If she dies, we can't afford to buy another Ox, not now. We will have to work the land ourselves with a pick and hoe. That would humiliate us with our neighbors, and, anyway, it is an impossible task."

"But our garden is good; I have weeded it and given it water. It will be as good as ever. Look at how big the lentils are. And we still have sweet potatoes, banana, cassava, peanuts, eggplant, cucumbers, beans."

"That's not good enough; if we run out of flour from the wheat and maize, we can't make enough *daabo*. Everything depends on the *daabo* and the *marqaa* too. The kids won't have enough; they will suffer, and they won't grow the way they're supposed to. I don't know what to do. I don't want to leave, but I don't know what else to do. The neighbors can't afford to help us either; we'll starve if we stay."

Barisso said he wouldn't make the final decision until after the harvest.

"But, if things are as bad as they look now, I'm afraid this will be our last harvest. This will no longer be our home. We will have to follow others to the city—Shashamane or Jimma or Dire Dawa—to find work and start a new life."

"But this is our home; this is all we have. We are farmers, not city people. We have to find a way."

It was a sad comment on the precarious state they were in that the food the man from the OLF had given Barisso provided the best meal the family had had for some time. That evening, Mahret fried up four round loaves of fresh unleavened *daabo*, and she and *abbaa* and both boys filled their stomachs. There was more food than they could eat in one sitting. It tasted delicious. Along with everything else, the *shonkora* was a rare and tasty treat.

Barisso and Mahret continued to pray for rain at home every night and, along with the other farmers, at their little church on Sunday. But *Waqaa* showed no mercy. One morning clouds appeared on the horizon, giving hope. The clouds slowly moved inward and then overhead, covering the sky with a thick gray blanket. It actually started to sprinkle. Even as it did, however, ports of light began to show in the blanket, and too quickly it broke up into several pieces.

The rain stopped.

"It's too late anyway," Barisso said, "the moisture would have helped next year's crops, but ours this year are too far gone. *Waqaa* is teasing us. He doesn't care anymore."

"You must not say that; *Waqaa* is our only hope. Do not anger him; we must continue to ask him to forgive us, to provide an answer. We are helpless without him."

"I think he has already answered us. He has no mercy. I'm afraid we're finished."

Several days later, it was with a sense of fear more than hope, that they both turned their attention to the harvest. For this, they used the system they had inherited from their ancestors. He first cut down the stalks of wheat with a sickle. She collected them and laid them out on the small threshing space by the house that generations of Barisso's family had "paved" over and over again, by spreading ox and goat dung on it and letting it bake and harden in the sun.

The grain was so dry they needed to let it sit for just one day before harvesting it.

Then, Barisso ran Sheva back and forth over it for hours, trampling the stalks to break the kernels loose. He next scooped up the straw with a pitchfork and threw it into the air to coax out any remaining kernels. After that, he and Mahret swept the straw to the side and stacked it for livestock feed before gathering up the grain remaining on the pavement into baskets and dumping it into the large wicker storage container in the house.

All the families in the district were engaged in the same business. Consequently, there were no disruptions other than from Gamado and Berhanu. The two kids could be a handful. They had to be fed, of course, but that was not a big challenge. Mahret had just weaned Gamado from the breast, and the boys both ate at meal-time with their parents. Otherwise, they mostly just played soldiers and other games around the house. At one point, Berhanu decided to get his brother to play hide and seek in the cornfield. He let Gamado go first, finding him within a couple of minutes. When he took his turn to hide, he went into the cornfield and watched Gamado from a distance as he searched for him.

Berhanu stayed just out of his brother's sightline by shifting from one row of corn to another.

Gamado got flustered. He was pretty sure his brother was trying to torture him.

Tears started to trickle down his face.

"Berhanu, where you are? Where you are? Not funny, where you are?"

No answer.

Gamado screamed.

"Berhanu! Help, help! This not funny, help! Haaaaaadha! Help! Berhanu's gone!!"

Mahret had just dropped an armful of wheat on the pavement when she heard her younger son's shouts. She went over to the cornfield to rescue him, shouting as she went.

"Berhanu, stop it, get out here right now!"

Berhanu knew better than to defy *haadha*.

"I'm here," he said as he pushed his way through the stalks. "I was just playing. Gamado is such a baby. He's got to grow up. He's a fraidy little kid."

"Berhanu, *abbaa* and I are very busy bringing in all our food! I don't have time for this. You have to look after your little brother, not scare him to death. Now you grow up and help us or I'm going to call *abbaa*. Do you understand?"

"Okay, okay, I'm sorry."

It was noon, so Mahret took both boys back to the house and made lunch.

Later that afternoon, she and Barisso finished up cutting the last of the wheat and started on the maize. They worked separately, breaking the ears of corn off the stocks, unsheathing them, and collecting them in sacks. They emptied the sacks into the other large wicker storage bins in the house. Later days, they would allow Sheva and the two goats to graze the cornfield until all the leafy matter on the thicker stalks still sticking about a foot out of the ground was gone. Barisso would normally plow these under before the next seeding.

The reality that Mahret and Barisso could not now avoid was that their crops were, indeed, not going to be sufficient. The containers were not bursting as in previous good years; they were barely more than half full. The flour Mahret would ultimately get by grinding up the wheat and maize would, they could both see, be too little to produce enough *daabo* and *marqaa* to sustain the family.

"We're in trouble," Barisso said. "Even the straw for Sheva and the goats is less than I hoped."

"Should you kill the goats so we could have the meat?"

"No woman! Think about what you're saying, the kids need the milk. How would you replace that? Killing the goats would give us only a little extra food anyway; the animals are both small and thin, and they have little meat on their bones."

"What about Sheva? Couldn't you butcher her and rent an animal to work the fields next year? I know Genemo's husband did that. They rent from one of the farms across the valley by giving them some of their harvest. They're getting by. Maybe the weather will be better next year."

"No way, we can't afford to do that. It would cut into our crops too much. Even if the weather's perfect, we'd be worse off next year than we are now. Is that what you want?"

Mahret had no answer.

But she was not giving up. They had to find a way.

"We must pray more earnestly. We must be better people."

Chapter 4

THE CALL OF DUTY

During the years she attended school in the little local church, Mahret had learned to read and write, and to speak English at a fundamental level. She started taking classes when she was ten-years old.

There had not been much reading material at the school. Still, she was captivated by the scriptures, especially the stories of Jesus, his early life with Mary and Joseph, his later years with the disciples, his betrayal, and, finally, his crucifixion.

Mahret was intrigued too by the thought of reading about all sorts of other subjects, distant places, distant people, and earlier times.

When contracted to Barisso, however, she agreed at his insistence, to give up her education to concentrate on her duties as a wife and then mother.

"Book learnin is not for women," he told her.

Mahret had always felt some guilt about taking time away from her family duties to go to school. She also thought Barisso must be right about the danger of being drawn away from her proper wifely roles. And she did not like to resist his will. He would be the head of the family, and that was that.

Barisso did not, at all disapprove of Mahret's religiosity, and he allowed her to coax him and the children to church on Sundays. He also supported the evening Bible readings she often carried out with the children. To him, the fact that she was close to *Waqaa* could not hurt them in their struggles with the land.

The signs that the Great Ruler of the Universe had disserted them now, both Barisso and Mahret instinctively felt, were a trial of their faith.

But what else could they do to demonstrate their commitment?

The afternoon after the harvest was complete, Barisso called Mahret outside to show her the sad state they were in. He had a handful of wheat from the basket.

"Look at these kernels, they're shriveled, it will take many more than usual to make up the same amount of flour we've had in the past. And we have fewer kernels than we used to too. The wheat and the corn will only last us a few months at best. That will not get us through to the next harvest. If we can't find a way to get more food before it runs out, there is no way we can stay here. I'm telling you, we will have to leave!"

"How would we live?" she asked. "We have no money and no income. Where would we stay in the city?"

"Listen, Mahret," he said. "It kills me to even think about leaving the farm. I grew up here, our boys were born here, I love the land, and I love the country, our neighbors, our friends. It's driving me mad. I think about this all the time. Sometimes I feel like I can't take it, like I want to die.

End it all.

But, I can't, I can't leave you to face this on your own."

Mahret looked directly into his watering eyes. She could see the emotion, the pain.

"I'm sorry," she said. "I know this isn't easy for you either. I know it's your whole life."

"I keep trying to come up with a plan," he said. "Badhasso tells me the government is buying up the land so they can lease it out to big foreign companies. Believe me, it's not what I want to do. But maybe I'll have to sell and get some money so we can get a place in the city.

I can get a job."

Barisso astounded Mahret by adding, "you know, you might be able to find work too."

Chapter 5

MORE WAYS THAN ONE?

As the days rolled by after the harvest, Mahret could see the family food supply was slipping away. It was a frightening situation, and now, suddenly, Barisso's determination to do something about it waned. It was as if he was dealing with it by just putting it off indefinitely.

Mahret had seen him do this once before. She remembered when he took a sick sheep to the government veterinarian who was traveling through the area, trying to give people advice about their livestock.

"The animal's got IBR," the vet told him, "Infectious Bovine Rhinotracheitis." Bovine means cattle, but it strikes sheep and goats too. It really is infectious; if this animal's been mixing with others, they very possibly all have it."

Barisso had a small herd of six sheep at that time emanating from a ram and ewe he'd inherited with the farm.

When he told the veterinarian the animals had all been together, the vet warned him, "they may be okay now, but they might well all get sick. If so, I'll have to condemn the whole lot. It's probably too late to vaccinate and, anyway, at the moment, we're shit out of vaccine."

He advised Barisso to butcher all the sheep right away, "before the disease gets a chance to develop. At least then, you don't lose the meat."

Barisso was heartbroken. Besides the regular supply of mutton, the herd provided the money that he got each year by selling one or two of the animals at the market along with the sweaters that Mahret wove with the extra wool. And the milk the sheep produced was crucial for the baby.

"It doesn't matter," he told Mahret. "I've got to slaughter them. We can't take a chance on losing everything. We'll at least salvage one final cache of lamb and mutton."

For the next few days, however, he did nothing. He was unable to act on his decision.

"It's simply easier to avoid the issue," Mahret thought, "than give up the hope that if the animals don't get sick, we'll have so much more."

The next morning, another animal lay on the ground in the little pen, dying. The vet happened to come back to check on the sheep later that day. He condemned them all.

Barisso had to take them to the local dump and cut their throats.

Now, Mahret suspected he was in the same frame of mind he'd been in during that catastrophe.

"He believes we have to leave, but he can't follow through. The decision is too big. Another way might come along. It's easier not to think about it. I understand this. It is hard to be the head of the family with all decisions. I'm glad it's him and not me."

She, herself, continued to pray for a way out. But she knew that the worst approach was to let the time slip by.

"We can't just sit, we'll starve to death; we can't let the kids go hungry. What can I do? I feel so weak, so helpless. Barisso has no plan, no plan at all!"

She tried to talk to her husband.

"What do you think? What are we going to do about the future, about food for the kids?"

"I'm thinking about it," he would tell her. "Leave it to me, I've always made sure our lives are good, and I'll keep on doin it. You have to trust me."

When he thought she was pushing him too hard, he would get angry.

"Stop it now! You're just making it worse. Back off! It's not your affair!"

He would then, by all appearances, remove himself from the challenges at hand by retreating to a simpler world inside his brain.

Mahret thought seriously about killing the goats herself and maybe even Sheva. That would give them more food at the very least. But she was afraid, afraid to appear to be trying to take over, fearful of Barisso, afraid to step outside the limits of her role, afraid to take such a step on her own.

Then, one Sunday morning, the *lubaa* at the little church the family attended in the village seemed to offer what appeared a glimmer of hope, a small one, but hope nonetheless.

The *lubaa* trumpeted a powerful message of resistance. He claimed it came directly from *Waqaa* and that, therefore, every Oromo must heed it. He spoke in-depth and from a Christian point of view.

He sounded both genuine and convincing.

"The Church possesses a real feeling for the Oromo people, and it is strong in countering the dictatorial power in the government's hold over us. The Amhara control the government and the EPRDF, and they arrogantly look down on all of us; they call Oromo things like, 'backward, heathen, filthy, deceitful, lazy, and even stupid.' Every human is equal in the eyes of *Waqaa*. Oromo political consciousness has been strengthened by persecution and mistreatment. Our relatives, friends, church elders, pastors, all have been victimized by the EPRDF, their police, army officers, and judges.

Our cause is to resist the work of the devil. This is a valiant struggle. The junta follow the devil and oppose *Waqaa*, and they fear the growth of Christianity. We have injected force into resistance. Christianity, both in the past and at present, has encouraged us to take pride in our true identity. It has fostered self-consciousness and equipped us morally to confront our oppressors. Those who stand for the peace and unity of our church, including the clergy, organized orthodox groups, and the faithful in Ethiopia, are all threatened. It is time to react, time for you as ordinary everyday believers to take a stand."

The *lubaa*'s assertion that the hated Muslim population in the country was on the side of the government really hit home.

"The ruling junta have been cultivating the dreaded Islamic community in this country. They are prepared to embrace the very people who will want to stamp out our faith. Those people have much better support in their areas than in Christian areas. What will come of those of us who hold our traditional Christian values, who love *Waqaa*, who are prepared to die for *Waqaa*? They are embracing the very people who hate our faith. Do you think we should just let them do that?"

Mahret, herself, had heard some of the neighbor women, whose husbands had been to Shashamane, repeat serious concerns regarding the rising influence of Wahhabi extremists. They told her as well that more and more women in the town were covering their faces with the hijab.

When Barisso had told her about the OLF guy who appeared at the Enkutatash she had agreed with him that he could never join that fight. Now she thought that might be wrong.

Finding a way out of her family's predicament was suddenly more than just a practical or secular challenge. Siding with a Christian sense of brotherhood, and of justice, to defend a persecuted minority in the name of the Almighty had a heroic tone to it.

"How could it be wrong to defend ourselves against infidels who threaten our religion and way of life, people who want to kill the only true religion? Aren't they the greatest threat to all of us, not just our men, our soldiers, but our families, our children? We have to stop them. They love Satan; *Waqaa* wants us to stop them. It's a holy crusade."

Mahret put this to her husband one evening after sending both the children to bed. She proceeded cautiously.

"The recruiter who came to the Enkutatash that time, you know a few weeks ago, you sure figured him out in a hurry. He was a promoter, trying to sell something, and we have to be suspicious of what he said, isn't that right?"

"That's right, that's what I said."

"I was wondering if he was telling the truth about the food. Do they really have more than they gave us? If they did, it could save us, right?"

"I don't know, but I don't want to be a soldier. I don't want to shoot anyone."

"You know a lot more about such things, but I was kind of wondering, if the OLF did have food as he said, would some men join in part to get it; like your friends I mean, would they join the OLF for a while, you know to support *Waqaa* and our religion and get more food too? The men could go to that church the recruiter talked about and enlist, and then their wives could get food from the OLF at the same time. The recruiter told you they had lots of food and milk. We, I mean they, could get as much as possible and store it too for later. Then, after a while, maybe a month or two, the men could come home knowing they had saved their families while doing their share for *Waqaa* and good, against Satan and evil."

This made Barisso angry.

"You back off woman! I know what you're trying to do. I'm not taking orders from you. I don't want to talk about this. I'm not a soldier, I could get killed. Then what would you do? How would you and the kids survive? I don't want to talk about this anymore. Now stop!!"

Nonetheless, Mahret soldiered on.

"If you fight for *Waqaa*, He will surely protect you, and He would be happy to see you feed your family too. Gamado is five-years old. I have stopped nursing him. The milk powder will be precious. The man gave you the food to get your wife to support the cause. They could hardly say no to me if you were one of their own."

"Back off, woman, I know what you're trying to do. You're willing to risk my life to save yours. I'm warning you if you don't stop this right now, I'm gonna teach you the lesson I should have given you years ago."

Mahret obeyed.

"For now."

She said, "okay, I'm sorry, I was just trying to help you. I know you love *Waqaa* as I do, and you want to save the farm as much as me."

"The discussion is not over," she thought, "this could still be a way out. At least it's a chance, some hope. We are desperate. We have to try anything that might work."

A few days later, she tried to put other ideas to Barisso.

"You first told me the land was failing. You showed me the dried-out wheat kernels. You were right too. I see what you mean. We are in trouble. Can we try cooperating with our neighbors to save us and them at the same time? Could we pool all our animals, use some to work the land, and kill some for food? If we get together, could we use more of our own labor to work the land by hand? I'm just asking you, that's all."

She also suggested that they could plant a second crop of wheat now that the harvest was over.

"Even if it doesn't have time to ripen properly, wouldn't it provide enough for the extra flour we need to get through the year?"

Barisso was still unmoved. He insisted that everyone needed their own livestock and everything they could get out of their crops and that another crop would ruin the land altogether.

"We have already taken too much out of our soil. Do you really think the answer is to push it further?"

"Anyway, it is none of your business. If you'd just keep your mouth shut and let me handle things, I'd be able to work something out. Leaving for the city is still the only answer. I need to think about that. I need to go to Jima or Dire Dawa to find the people that's offering to buy the land."

But, in the following days, he continued to do nothing.

To Mahret, the challenges—the drought, Barisso's inertia—were seeming insurmountable.

As much as anything, the fact that she, herself, had tried to push him into the army showed just how distressing things were. She felt her husband was not strong in that way, not really a fighter; he might just wilt trying to be a soldier.

"I'm so bad at this. I don't know how to handle it. I'm a woman trying to think like a man, trying to push a man. I don't know what I'm doing."

Yet, the possibility of Barisso fighting seemed no less realistic than anything else she could think of.

"Maybe he's right, we have to leave. But if he doesn't do anything about it, we'll starve first. We have no money.

So hopeless."

Chapter 6

SAVING THE WORLD?

Mahret tried to economize. She scrimped on the amount of flour she used to make *daabo*, and she consistently added ground maize to the wheat flour to make it go further. She and Barisso also ate less of everything than they had. They were losing weight, and still, it was not a permanent solution. The children were not going hungry now, but she feared she would soon have to start feeding them less, and they would stop growing and might even get sick. She was haunted by the image of Alucia, her only sister's first baby growing sickly during the drought two years ago and succumbing to the excruciating aches and fevers of malaria. Could it be that the maize Merla had mixed into the wheat flour at that time had made the food she was eating too weak and damaged her milk?

Mahret woke up almost every morning now with such thoughts. During the day, she no longer sang while she prepared meals. She no longer found her heart was really in it when she played with the boys. She lived in constant tension, in unrelenting fear. And that fear was only partly relieved one day when Barisso came home from a meeting at the church and announced that he'd found a solution. He'd had a complete change of heart and was now enlisting in the OLF.

He spoke in a monotone, sounding as though he was reading from a script someone else had laid out for him.

"There comes a time when a man has to do what he has to do. I'm going with Mundu and Shabede to the OLF training center in Somalia. The Eritreans have sent loads of arms there, and the OLF now has a huge army with many soldiers. We will win and keep our land, and we will be free. Abdata Basire, the commander in chief of the Southern Front, is a brave man and he tells us we must fight with courage because we're surrounded by the enemy.

All OLF fighters are giving a voice to the Oromo; their dedication to the struggle is unlimited. We are in a war for the people."

Mahret was stunned and, suddenly, all too bluntly aware of her own naivety.

What worried her most was that Barisso sounded so deeply committed, as if he was prepared to fight to the end, to give his life if necessary. She should have foreseen this. He wasn't soldier material anyway. She had just wanted him to get involved temporarily, fight the glorious fight for the Almighty, but for a short time, join for a while, gain access to the food, and then come home.

"I know," she told Barisso, "there is a real threat, and it scares me too. These people are very bad, especially, the Muslims. They must be stopped. But you must be careful. You have two children; we need you here on earth."

"I have to do my part. It's my fight; it's everyone's fight. We love our religion, the only true religion. We must stop them no matter how long it takes or how hard it is."

Barisso had now learned impatience with Oromo brothers who were refusing to take up arms.

"They must all join us. They have to do their part; or, maybe, they deserve to lose their land."

Barisso had never before shown interest in any political or religious rights. Mahret suspected that someone had offered him more than he was telling her. It was a good thing that she would be able to get some extra food, if what the military guy said was not a lie. But she now felt there was a greater chance than she wanted to take, that the kids would lose their father.

She said nothing, however. She had other worries, she needed the food, and she knew that once Barisso made up his mind, she would not be able to dissuade him.

After breakfast the next morning, he packed some things into a bag and prepared to head off down the road for the training camp in northern Somalia. The last thing he told Mahret was that he would eat well at the camp and that she should go to the church and get as much food as she could.

Meanwhile, she and the children could dip into their supplies of flour, maize, and vegetables without worrying about the future. Everything would be alright, and he would bring back more when he returned in a couple of weeks.

"I will come back. I will stay here for a while before I go back again to fight. This is a fight to the end, and we will win. Then our own family will have a better life. The OLF will see that we keep our land."

"Be careful, if something happens to you, we're all dead. Remember your children."

"You worry too much; no matter what happens, you will have enough to eat. That's what counts most. You know *Waqaa* supports us against the government. He hates the Muslims who support them as much as we do. We will win. We can't lose."

The only thing Mahret thought she could not lose was her sense of guilt about being the one who first suggested that he join the OLF.

When he left, she also felt afraid and alone.

"How long will the OLF continue to be generous if he is killed? They may feed families of soldiers, but what about families of dead soldiers?"

Chapter 7

ONLY LITTLE FOOLS

Barisso started out as dawn broke; a cloth bag with some vegetables, and *daabo* and basic clothing slung over his shoulder. In a few minutes, he got to the junction in the path where he was to meet his two friends. He waited in vain for them. After an hour or so, he decided he should go alone.

"Bastards were just pretending to care about our fight. When we come back here to liberate our people, we'll be throwing both of them in the clink."

To get to northern Somalia, he was to go first some thirty miles northwest to a church in the town of Shashamane. There, he was to be met by someone who would drive him the entire distance to the eastern Ethiopian border and, from there, to the OLF camp.

At dusk, he found himself walking along the side of a major road with cars and trucks speeding past him in both directions.

It was then that it happened.

A jeep pulled off the road in front of him and stopped. A door opened, and a man jumped out.

Barisso could see he was carrying a gun in a holster on his one hip.

"Hey, you, you're not from around here. What're you doin? Where do you think you're goin? You been talking to any of them crazy insurgents around here."

"I'm heading to Shashamane. What's an insurgent? I don't know what you're talking about."

"I think you damn well do know. What're you gonna do in the city? What's your business there?"

"Looking for work."

"Carrying any arms?"

"Arms?"

"Yes, arms, you know what I'm talking about. Are you carrying a gun?"

"No sir. I've never had a gun. I don't even know how to fire one."

Barisso was scared mainly because he had the map to the church the OLF man had left with him. It also had the *lubaa's* name on it. If this guy found it, he could figure things out.

"Why don't I believe you? Where're you coming from?"

"My farm, to the south."

"Farmer? Crops bad?"

"Yes sir."

"Not enough for the family?"

"No sir."

"How do I know you're not an OLF traitor?"

"What do you mean, what's that?"

"You know what it is!"

The man grabbed Barisso by the arm, swung him around, and pushed him face-first against the jeep. Then he began patting him down.

Barisso held his breath as the man's hand moved across his left leg and over the pocket that contained the incriminating piece of paper.

"Hey, what's this?" he said, "there's something here."

Barisso readied himself to break and run into the small clump of bushes beside the road, hoping he might be able to lose the guy before he could get a shot off.

The man spoke again.

"Okay, it's just a lump of some kind in the cloth."

Barisso realized he was not feeling the piece of paper, but a tear Mahret had sewn up in his pants.

"Okay, carry on," the man said. "I'm an Oromo farmer too, at least I was. I've got no quarrel with you."

As he went back toward his jeep, Barisso quickly headed the other way. He heard the jeep start up and the squeak of tires as it did a U-turn and took off in the opposite direction.

Barisso's legs were shaking. He felt dizzy as if he were about to pass out.

But he managed to carry on.

"*Waaqayyo galatom* to Waqaa," he whispered, "he sent one of our own."

When he got to the outskirts of Shashamane, he found himself basically in a slum. He had seen it all before, but it never failed to astonish him. People seemed to be living wherever they could, some in one of a large number of ugly little huts with tin roofs and walls of mud mixed with wood and cardboard, some in run-down derelict buildings, and some, out of doors, under a bridge or in one of the narrow walkways haphazardly threading their way through the settlement.

There was garbage strewn everywhere, and a very bad smell in the air. Barisso noted that some people were burning dung apparently for fuel for cooking. Animal bones and carcasses and food waste were rotting in the streets. Also, cows and horses roamed through the settlement, leaving their shit everywhere. He saw people, both male and female, defecating in the filthy little streams that flowed down the middle and edges of the street.

Past the outskirts, the town looked better. The houses and a few local stores spaced among them had glass windows, mostly tile roofs, and sidewalks. The buildings were of brick, concrete, and timber. And the roads were wider and much more regular. Signs identified the streets with names or numbers.

Barisso was anxious to avoid any more authorities. While generally following his map, he managed, for the most part, to stay off the main roads with the heavy traffic. When he got to the church, he could see some taller looking buildings in the skyline further on that he knew would be the city center.

From the outside, the Ethiopian Orthodox Tewahedo Church appeared much more impressive than the little grass-roofed Jehovah's Witnesses Church the family attended in the village at home. The exterior was rock with brickwork around the windows; there was a prominent bell tower above, and large pillars on either side of the massive wooden front doors.

Barisso was a bit intimidated; when he got up to the church, he paused.

"Can I just walk in?"

What else can I do?"

He pulled open one of the doors and entered. The interior of the building was as impressive as the outside. The ceiling was very high, and the walls looked grand with huge murals depicting Jesus, Mary, Joseph, and the Apostles.

The recruiting officer had told him to talk to a *lubaa* named Heeran, who would be expecting him.

He called out:

"*Akkam, akkam*, your worship, are you here?"

No one answered. He could see some stairs behind the altar. He climbed the stairs, walked down a hallway, and knocked on the first door he came to. The door swung open. He could see a man wearing vestments sitting on a chair on the other side of the room. The man was staring straight ahead, his eyes wide open.

Barisso thought he might be in a trance.

"*Akkam*, my name is Barisso, I am sorry to interrupt. I was told you would advise me how to find some people in Somalia that need [...]"

As he drew closer, he could see a wound on the lubaa's forehead. Then he saw the back of his chair was covered in what looked like dried blood.

"He's not in a trance. He's dead!"

Barisso froze. His brain refused to work; it couldn't process the moment. He steadied himself by holding on to the back of a chair.

He bent over, took some deep breaths, and then turned and ran. He went back down the stairs two at a time, raced across the ground floor and exited the church through a side door.

When he got to the street, he heard a voice.

"Hey, you, quick in here."

A man was waiting in a small truck.

Barisso had no idea what to do, so he did as ordered.

The vehicle was running, the man immediately threw it into gear and took off.

"Who are you?" Barisso said, "where are you goin? I'm not an insurgent."

"I believe you must be. They told me to pick you up here and take you to Somalia. You're the right guy, aren't you? If you're the enemy, get ready to die."

He pointed a pistol at Barisso's head.

"Okay, don't shoot, you're right, I'm trying to join the insurgency, the OLF, please don't shoot."

"I thought so."

"I'm scared. They almost caught me, just a few hours ago. They must be everywhere."

Don't worry. This truck has a big engine, they can't catch us. It's a four-wheel-drive too. I can go off-road, leaving any goof dumb enough to chase us, in the dust."

"What happened, do you know who shot the *lubaa*?"

"I'm not sure. When I arrived about an hour ago, he was like that. It must be the EPRDF. They're getting ruthless, trying to put us down. Some of their soldiers are crazy and taking things into their own hands."

The driver told Barisso that it would take them longer than usual to get to the border.

"Normally I can do it in six or seven hours, but today we'll have to stay on the side roads and paths. If they see us, they'll probably try to kill us both. Keep your eyes peeled for roadblocks. If there is one, we'll be okay as long as we spot it soon enough. If they try to go after us over the bumpy fields, their shots will miss."

Barisso fixed his eyes firmly out of the front window.

"How did you know to pick me up? I didn't tell anyone I was coming here."

"I went in to see the *lubaa* just before you did. When I saw he was dead, I left by the same door. I went back around to the front of the church to get my truck and saw you go in. I figured you would come out that side door too. It's the shortest way out. They told me if I saw anyone else arriving to give them a lift to the training camp. You're the only one I've seen.

I'm Tolessa, and you?"

"Barisso."

"Okay, hold on, this is gonna be a rough trip."

It was a long and eventful trip. At one point, on a stretch of country road, Barisso thought he saw a car parked some distance ahead of them.

"Roadblock, roadblock," he yelled.

Taking no chances, Tolesso crossed a farmer's freshly harvested wheat field. On the other side, he turned down a footpath and continued east. A short while later, he drove back up onto the road just in time to see a military vehicle in the rear-view mirror. He stepped on the gas.

"Hang on," he said again, "we'll outrun them. Just pray, they don't have a special engine too."

Barisso was scared; as they raced along, he grabbed a hand bar above the door and held on for dear life sure that the truck would flip over and kill them both. However, Tolesso maneuvered the curves in the road like a professional.

Soon, the gap between them and the pursuing vehicle began to widen.

"Looks like they've given up," Tolesso finally said, "close call."

Hours later, they approached the Somalia border.

"How will we cross? The guards must be government men?"

"Don't worry. We have that covered."

When they got to the border, Tolesso handed the officer who came up to his window an envelope.

The man glanced inside and immediately waved them through.

"Everything has a price," Tolesso said, grinning. "The boys on this shift are workin for us. They're makin money too."

Tolesso had another envelope for the Somalian border guard.

Chapter 8

OFF TO "WAR"

Barisso expected that when he got to the OLF training camp, he would find a well-equipped, highly professional fighting machine. He was to be disappointed. They first showed him to an empty cot in a large tent where he bunked in with a dozen other recruits and got his first night of sleep. After an ample breakfast in the cook tent the next morning, a supervisor sent him out to an open area beyond the camp for target practice. He found himself with a group of young men and two young women, all of whom, like him, were farmers. His commander was sergeant Salibaan, whose main claim to the title seemed to be the month he had spent in the militia before coming to camp. No one else had any military experience at all.

Salbaan gave each of the recruits a rifle and two bullet clips.

"This," he said, "is a semi-automatic rifle, which means it loads and reloads automatically after you insert the clip into the magazine chamber. Watch me as I load my rifle, and then practice doing it yourselves. Place the clip in the magazine like this and then take it out and do it a couple times more."

When he felt they had got the hang of it, Salbaan directed them to some targets with stick-soldiers painted on them and showed them how to aim the guns and shoot at them.

"Just place your cheek on the butt, like this. Then align the target with the sites on either end of the barrel. When the clip is in the gun, it will fire once for every time you pull the trigger."

He then had them take turns trying to hit the face or the approximate heart of the stick-soldiers.

"I want three of you to shoot at each target from one of the logs we've placed here about forty paces back from each one. Get down on your stomach and hold your rifle with your elbows on the ground. Use the log to support the rifle, shoot once, and then wait your turn to shoot again."

Barisso, at first, was startled by the loud noise his gun made.

Otherwise, he and the other recruits rather enjoyed target practice. His only complaint was the limited number of shots he could fire as the two clips only held six cartridges each.

The recruits returned for target practice twice per day during the next four days. Then, the morning after that, they found themselves standing in the covered back of a truck heading toward real-life combat in Ethiopia.

Most of them, including Barisso, did not have a uniform.

The truck stopped and dispatched them in some rough country back on the Ethiopian side of the border. Salbaan then gave them the most basic instructions, the intention of which seemed to be to invoke passion, paranoia, and hatred of the enemy.

"We are targeting foreign companies that support the government in stealing land from our people. Many countries that import most of their food have begun planning the development of further large tracts of Ethiopian land. We have to wipe out the ones already here to show the others they can't succeed. We will attack these companies and look for any government troops we can find and kill them too.

Surprise is important, but you should always consider how you're going to escape if things don't go your way. Try to stay close to forest cover or on a hillside where you'll be above the enemy."

Salbaan also told them that they could take heart from the fact that they were winning the war.

"The companies the government has brought in to take over our land are planning to leave Oromia because of our resistance. We have attacked ninety percent of the flower farms in the corridor between Ziway and Hawassa, as well as textile and agricultural processing plants. The owners are getting totally discouraged because we keep destroying their facilities."

Barisso could feel some pride in the mission. They were liberators, and they alone could save the people, the farmers in particular.

They marched for the rest of that day into East Haraghe province and set up camp in a remote hilly area from which they hoped to conduct raids.

After following Salbaan around for two more days, they came to the huge greenhouses of the Dutch flower company, Esmeralda Farms, and the processing buildings of the Dutch-owned fruit company, African Juice BV.

"Between them," Salbaan told the troops, "they employ as many as 3,000 people.

These companies want to take the food from the mouths of our children. If we take them out, we will be doing a lot of good for our country. The people who work for them now will all be given shares in new Oromo companies. They will be owners, not just workers. Our farmers will have their land back, and this time they will have the capital they need to do a proper job."

Barisso wondered if the OLF could have been as destructive recently as Salbaan told them. The companies did not seem to be doing much at this point to protect themselves. There were only two guards on duty at each site. Barisso was disappointed too that after all the bravado, they attacked like hooligans instead of soldiers. Salbaan had his troops wait until dark, and then he designated four of his un-uniformed men each to walk up to one of the guards, greet him "*akkam jirtuu*," and put a bullet in his head.

That accomplished, he set all the troops loose on an orgy of destruction. They smashed row upon row of flowers in the greenhouses of the one company and thousands of jars of fruit in the other. Then, they set the establishments ablaze.

After that, the troops returned to the bush and set up camp again.

Unfortunately for them, their first encounter with the government troops occurred the next morning when they were having breakfast.

"Enemy approaching," one of the men on guard duty shouted.

Barisso heard marching soldiers. He and all the others hit the ground stomach first and, as the enemy approached, began randomly to take shots at them. A few fell, but the others immediately began firing back with fully automatic assault rifles and machine guns.

It was soon all too clear that the enemy had vastly superior firepower.

Salbaan ordered a retreat.

He need not have bothered. By then, all his soldiers still able were heading through the trees in sundry directions, the enemy on their heels.

A lad running beside Barisso took a bullet in the back and fell to the ground. Barisso hesitated, but he had to leave him lying there as the enemy was approaching too fast. He sprinted through a dense thicket of low-lying bushes and then down the side of a ravine and into a flat forested area. After about a half-hour, he sensed that he was out of immediate danger. He continued to run at a reduced pace until he came to a stream, which he followed until he found himself on the outskirts of a city.

"This has to be Dare Dawa."

Barisso threw his gun and munitions belt into a patch of tall grasses and proceeded down a suburban street through a slummy area more or less like the one in Shashamane. He continued until he came to a marketplace in a slightly better part of town with crowds of people milling around.

He slipped into the crowd, trying to blend in.

The OLF had given him and the rest of the soldiers each 300 birr, a paltry amount, but it was enough to buy a snack here and there. He ordered a cup of *shaayii* and some *daabo* from a cook stand and sat down at one of the tables.

A few minutes later, he saw them – two men in uniform carrying rifles with ammunition belts slung over their shoulders.

They were heading his way. He got to his feet and slowly moved off in the opposite direction until, at the periphery of the eating area, he was penned in by a wire-netting fence. He sat down again at an empty table.

An older man and a boy having lunch at a table several yards to his left were watching him. The man glanced over at the two soldiers and then back at him. He pointed to an empty chair and motioned to Barisso to join them.

Realizing that once again, a man had his life in his hands no matter what he did, Barisso complied.

The two military men came closer. Barisso was terrified. He had to make a run for it, climb over the fence, and hope they would be afraid to fire at him through the dense crowd.

Just as he was about to bolt, the man at the table stood up and began yelling loudly.

"There! Over there, they're getting away. Stop them; stop them!"

When the soldiers looked his way, he pointed behind them.

"I just saw a guy run out of that tent over there. He looked like one of those OLF guys! Carrying a gun!"

The soldiers turned and ran around the cook stand and out from the eating area.

The man sat down again. He spoke first.

"That was close if you're who they were looking for."

Barisso reached over and shook his hand.

"*Waqaa* blesses you. *Galatom*, sir! You took a big risk. If they find out you were just faking it, they'll punish you for sure."

"I know, but I've had it with these people. Those of us who are not helping to fight them have to help those of you who are. This is our duty as your countrymen.

I read one of the reports that are circulating here that describes many cases of abuse in the government's villagization program, including forced displacement, arbitrary arrests, and torture. They're sending people to new settlements located far from water sources where the land is dry and arid. And they're lying to them too. More than a year after they forced people to move to some of these places, they've provided virtually none of the promised basic services.

They say that to prevent resettled farmers from returning to their original homes, soldiers have been destroying everything in the old locations, bulldozing their houses and crops, and killing their animals.

Yeah, and they've been abusing the women too. The report tells of three women and a girl who were arrested, detained, beaten, and then raped. One woman I know said her husband had been arrested after the attacks because the soldiers said he knew where the rebels were. When she went to the prisons to try and find him, soldiers followed her back to her home and had their way with her.

Another woman I heard about was arrested in Wancarmie. They took her to the military barracks in Gambella. One night they pulled her out of the cell and demanded she show them where her husband was. When she told them she didn't know, they raped her.

I have three young daughters. I can't stand this stuff. My wife and I even worry about our son. They're prepared to fuck anything that moves. The report said the government's own figures show that out of more than 10,000 rape cases last year in this country, over twenty percent were young boys, some two-years-old."

Barisso shook his head.

"I know, I've heard the rumors. I am in your debt for your help."

He got up, bowed to his rescuer, and, moving slowly to avoid drawing attention, withdrew from the cook stand and the marketplace. He made his way down city side streets again for a good part of the rest of the day until he found himself alone under a bridge at the edge of a river.

Barisso was tired, scared, and disillusioned; never had he felt more defeated. He felt even worse when he read in a discarded newspaper that blew over the bridge that full OLF units were retreating across the southern Oromia border to Kenya. Their leaders claimed they were just regrouping and would soon be back with greater force than ever. They also said that the OLF was organized militarily as a conventional army, with platoons, battalions, and regiments.

"Nonsense, imagine calling a bunch of farmers who don't even have uniforms an army. We're no army, and we can't defeat them. We're just a bunch of desperate farmers. We can't win. The EPRDF are trying to commit genocide, and they have the power too."

Barisso longed to be back home on the farm with Mahret, Gamado, and Berhanu.

That night, exhausted, he slept with his back against a concrete pillar bolstering the bridge over the Dechatu River.

Chapter 9

SELLING OUT

When Barisso came to, it was dawn, and the darkness was fading. Two little boys and a little girl were standing up to their knees in the shallow water at the edge of the river, looking at him.

Self-consciously, he got to his feet, smiled at the kids, and went over to the river and washed his hands and face.

The kids went about their play.

When Barisso finished cleaning up, he decided to go back to the second marketplace he had found the day before.

He knew it was not far, but it took him some time walking unfamiliar streets to find it. By the time he got to the square, life was starting as people were beginning to assemble their wares in stands and spaces. Barisso bought a cup of *shaayii* at a little concession catering to the traders and then sat down.

Slowly consuming what he knew could well be the only sustenance he would have this day, he tried to come up with a new plan.

As he contemplated the very limited possibilities, two men began assembling a stand next to the eating area. They set up a counter and placed a sign on it with a message in big black letters.

Farmland Anywhere in Oromia
Fair Market Price

It took a moment, but the message eventually registered in Barisso's distracted mind.

"Whoa! They're the people, the ones I heard about.! They're the ones who're buying farmland!"

He hesitated to react, however, afraid this might be a "con job."

"They might be looking to help the EPRDF find and round up insurgents."

But, again, he had to take a chance. He would just act as he was, a desperate farmer who needed the money to feed his family, and uninvolved in any ongoing civil war.

He went over to the stand.

"You guys want to buy farmland. That what you're looking for?"

Instead of answering the question, one of the men challenged him.

"You're with the OLF, aren't you? I can tell the look of fear in your face, your dirty clothes. You're on the run from the EPRDF. There've been a lot of you guys around; the OLF is a terrible force, no match for the government; you're all on the lam."

When Barisso turned to leave, the man's tone quickly changed.

"But don't worry; we do want your farm. I've [...] that is, we, have noticed that your fight is hopeless, and the government is waging war on your families. We want to show you a way to get out of this mess. If you are farming the land, we can offer you a way to get yourselves and your family some money and leave the country if you want. We can help you right away and pay you in full. You can use the money to move to the city or go north to Libya or across the sea to Europe, or south to Nairobi or east to Eritrea. You'll have the cash to make sure your family is fed and protected."

The man assured Barisso that if he turned over his land to their organization, he would have the government's blessing. That way, he wouldn't have to worry about the EPRDF anymore. The family would be safe to take the money and run.

"There are several agricultural companies that are close to the government. They're foreign companies, and the Ethiopian government owns a big part of them. It has spent millions investing in their stocks and now has a lot of control over their policies.

Our own organization represents two of these companies in particular—Africa Juice and FV SeleQt—both are Dutch. The government owns ten percent of the one, and the other is run by people very close to the government.

You'll have their blessing and enough to live for years."

Barisso knew the companies taking over farmland were in government hands, and he feared them for that reason. But he also wanted to hear what the man had to say just in case there was a chance he could help get him out of this mess. He, Mahret, and the kids were going to have to leave anyway. Was it possible that he could get some money first?

"This is crazy," Barisso told the man, "trying to get money out of the same companies farmers in the OLF have been trying to burn to the ground."

"I know, you're right, but it's not your fight. This gives you an out and a chance to start over. Do you understand what exactly is going on with the government taking over the land?"

"I just know they're renting it cheap to foreign companies. How are you ever gonna determine which land belongs to which farmers and what the real price should be?"

"It's not that hard because the government doesn't have to buy the land from you. It already owns it all. You realize, do you, that in the late 1970s, Ethiopia nationalized all land, and private ownership was outlawed? After that, all the millions of small-scale farmers like you have been working under license from the state. All the state is doing is paying you to hand it back. There is no legal property exchange. We just give you money to leave."

"You telling me the land me and my family have been working for generations isn't really ours? That's bullshit. If we'd known this was going on, there would have been a farmers' revolution a long time ago. And I would have been a leader too!"

"I think there already is one. It's called the OLF. I understand your feelings, but remember we're prepared to pay you full market value for it now. You get paid just as though legally you own it all. So, what's the problem?"

"Why are they doing this? Aren't they afraid people will turn on them once they see these foreign companies own every stick in the country?"

"They don't think so. They believe the big companies they lease your land to are going to make big profits and provide good-paying farming jobs for all the farmers currently in financial trouble."

"What if the companies don't make it?"

"The government believes they'll do fine because they're giving them great deals and at the same time bringing in millions in foreign investment. The agriculture ministry is advertising well over a million hectares in various regions to companies from places like Holland, India, and Saudi Arabia. Saudi Star Agricultural Development is growing 10,000 hectares of rice in Gambella. Firms from other Arab countries and China, Japan, and the US are also looking into leasing land.

These companies are getting good deals too. For its farm in Bako, Karuturi Global, the Bangalore-based rose company, is paying no rent for six years and then only 135 birr per hectare per year for the remainder of the fifty-year lease. In Gambella, the rent is only fifteen birr per hectare."

"They're just giving our land away!"

"Yes, but you can't deny they're bringing in a tremendous amount of capital. Karuturi plans to invest nearly 1,000,000,000 US dollars in Ethiopian agriculture. Within eight years, it hopes to be producing 3,000,000 tons of cereals—mostly maize and rice—each year on the Gambella farm alone, as well as palm oil and sugar."

"Okay, but if this doesn't work, there'll be an uprising for sure once people find out their money is gone, and still, they have no way of making more."

"Maybe. You might be right. The government might have to answer to the people for this in the future. We know they've done some pretty awful things to make farmers leave their land. Human Rights Watch is keeping a close check on it, and they're not happy with what's going on.

But you can see there is no point in resisting the government's plan. Thousands of farmers like you must find a way out of this crisis. We can get you fair compensation for your land now. That's the only way you have of coming out of this chaos with something for your wife and children."

Barisso realized these guys were conceding this to convince him to sell out. But they were not covering up the truth. They seemed to be telling it the way it was. Principles no longer mattered. He could not go back to his land, having fought for the pathetic OLF. The government was much stronger and would be after him for sure. He had no choice but to give up the fight, find any solution he could. If the offer was fair, at least it was now, and payment would be quick.

"What if I do have land? How much is it worth to you? You say your people will pay market value?"

"Yes, we have to. The government has insisted on a fair compensation payment. They are desperate to demonstrate that they're helping the country instead of stealing from it. Come to our office here in town, and we'll make you an offer. We'll look up your property and settle with you in a few minutes."

"You will pay me in cash?"

"Yes, cash, American dollars in cash. I promise we pay you what the land is worth. Fair market value."

"That's what they all say."

"Come see us. What've you got to lose? If this fighting keeps on, you'll never be able to relax now that you've chosen sides. They'll kill you and probably your family too. If you come to us, we'll give you a chance, the only chance you have."

Barisso was still afraid they were going to try to steal his land. He tried to put on a brave front.

"Listen," he said, "I might come to see you, but I'm warning you, if this is a hoax, if you're just crooks, if you try to rob us, we'll make you pay. We have guns, and we know how to use them."

The man smiled.

"From what I've seen, you're a pretty poor excuse for a military. Don't worry, if you come to our office, we'll help you out. We want the land, but we also want the best for you and Ethiopia. The government wants to look credible and caring. Do yourself a favor and your family. It's the only way."

"Where is your office? I will come today."

"We can go together. Here, I'll buy you a proper meal, and then we can both go over and get this finished."

And that was that.

After Barisso finished eating, he followed the one man over to the modern new office of the Africa Juice company where a government agent got him to describe exactly where his land was and how much he was farming. He also took his name and those of his father and grandfather (the official occupiers in the records). He then searched through a huge book, found the record he was looking for, and offered Barisso 2,500 American dollars. That was a lot of money to Barisso, but about half what he, talking to his neighbors on the farm, had decided it was worth.

"You're robbing me," he said. "Pure and simple, you're trying to steal my land."

"Listen, buddy," the agent said, "we're the only ones gonna give ya anything. This is enough to save your worthless ass. If you don't want it, fine. We'll just kick ya off by force and then take it for nothin."

Barisso knew he could not win. There was no one else. $2,500.00 was all he could hope to get. The cash should at least pay their way to a new place in the city. What else could he do?

"One day, you fucking bastards will pay us properly," he said. "We'll take it all back and throw the whole criminal lot of ya in the slammer, or the ground."

"Yeah, right. Sign here."

Barisso signed some papers, collected the cash in crisp new bills, and left for home.

"I've never had so much money, and I feel like I just lost everything I have!"

Chapter 10

LIVING IN FEAR

Things continued to go badly for the OLF. At no time was the ragtag operation able to mount a significant threat to the EPRDF. The government used the specter of an ongoing OLF "armed uprising" to justify further widespread repression. Regional security officials routinely accused any of their critics, and anyone who opposed them politically, of being OLF "terrorists" or "insurgents." The penalty was death, often by gun on the streets or in the fields.

Mahret remained on the farm, waiting to hear from Barisso. She felt defenseless and very much alone. And she had no way to know if her husband was alive or dead, or if the family would be held accountable for joining the OLF.

One morning when she was preparing breakfast for the two boys, some of her worst fears seemed to be coming to pass. Two uniformed men approached via the path in front of the house.

She quickly told Berhanu and Gamado to go inside.

The men were intrusive and discourteous.

"Where is your husband? We want to speak to him."

"He's not here. He went to Shashamane to get supplies."

"Do we look that stupid? We know what's going on. He's joined the uprising, hasn't he?"

"No, he would never do that. He is loyal to Ethiopia. He has gone to Shashamane for powdered milk. He will be home tomorrow."

"Why should I believe you? Oromo are all liars. Your husband's in the OLF, tell the truth."

Mahret was terrified, but she continued to insist that Barisso was away shopping.

While the one man interrogated her, the other went into the house, apparently looking for evidence. The two boys came running out and straight to their mother's side. Gamado was in tears.

After a couple of minutes, the man came back out, shaking his head at the interrogator as if to say he found nothing. The two then left with the warning they did not believe a single word of her story and would be coming back.

It was in the evening, two fear-filled days later, that Barisso appeared in the doorway.

The second she saw him, Mahret let out a scream.

"Barisso, you're alive! I've been so worried; you're back! Thank *Waqaa*."

After embracing her husband, she stepped back to look at him. He looked worn out. When he spoke, it was in hushed tones as if he thought someone could be listening.

He told her the OLF had collapsed.

"The government has taken over much of the land and arrested thousands of people and killed many others or chased them out of the country under suspicion of being OLF members. Nearly half the southern arm of the insurgency has surrendered. I have to lay low and stay out of sight. They want to recruit all men into the EPRDF. If they see me on the loose, they'll arrest me for sure.

Then he told her he'd sold the land.

"Oh, Barisso, how could you?"

"I had no choice. It was either that or die. I couldn't come back here. I chose the wrong side. They'd a killed me.

You and the kids have to leave the farm, leave Oromia and Ethiopia. I will join you later when I can. But we can't travel together. The government does not care about innocent bystanders. They murder women and children, too, if they think the husband isn't on the right side."

He showed her a stack of cash.

"Dollar bills from America. I sold the farm, I had to. The amount isn't right, but it's more than I could get anywhere else. The man told me it's 'market value.' He's a dirty liar.

The companies are rich, and they can buy it all, but at least now we have enough to get out.

You three can go to Eritrea or Somalia, and I will join you later."

To Mahret, neither the farm nor the role of obedient wife now mattered so much. The main objective had to be the safety of the children.

"No," she said, "we should not go to Eritrea or Somalia; we should go to my cousin's place in Nairobi."

Her temerity angered Barisso.

"What do you mean by that? You do what I say. You will take the kids east; Nairobi has nothing for us."

"Yes, it does, you forget, my uncle in Australia has been sending my cousin, Dawit, fifty American dollars a month. When his letter got through to the church last year, he told me the money is to be shared with us if we go there. We will have twenty-five dollars every month. It might save our life when the farm money is gone. It's regular, comes every month. Uncle says it might even be enough to pay the rent."

Barisso paused, looked at her, and then reached over and opened the door, beckoning someone to come in.

"This man is a businessman, an agent for a company that will help you and the children get out of Ethiopia by bus."

Mahret was stunned to see a total stranger walk into her home. She thought he looked too scruffy to be a modern businessman. His shirt was frayed and soiled, and there was a tear in one knee of his trousers.

Still, she managed to find words quickly.

"Can you take us to Nairobi? What about it? Do you have a connection there too?"

"Yeah," he said, glancing at Barisso, "I can get them to Nairobi too. It is farther and will cost you a bit more, but I can do it. I will ride with them to make sure everything is good."

"How much?"

"500 dollars."

"Okay, but no more."

"Alright, Nairobi, it makes no difference to us which country. I will take them to Shashamane tonight and then get them on the right bus early tomorrow morning."

"That's an awful lot of money," Mahret thought.

But this time she kept it inside.

Once again, Barisso was in control. He told the man to leave them for a moment.

"You can trust him," Barisso said when he was gone; "he knows what he's doing. I've given him 300 dollars. When you get to Nairobi, you must pay him 200 more."

He handed her some bills.

"I have 2,500 American dollars from the land compensation. I am giving you $1500. That should be enough until I can join you. The rest I will keep, for now; I can protect it from thieves better than you."

"Yes, you're right. I'm scared to take this much. It will be a terrible worry. But I know I'll need it for the boys. I'll guard it carefully."

"It's not nearly as much as it should be, but it's more money than it looks," Barisso explained. "They tell me American dollars are highly valued everywhere in Africa. They have a power of their own. Don't let anyone know you have them. You must hide the money in your crotch or something?"

"I have a pouch I found in the village. It will hold this much. I can tie it to my leg above the knee. No one will find it there."

"Go to your cousin's place then. Don't worry; this man is an agent of a group that specializes in moving Oromo out of trouble. He is trusted in our village, and he has done this before. He knows what he's doing. Hurry, the government is coming here, probably in the morning. We have no time; pack some food and other things you and the kids need into your bag. Then wake up the children. You must go tonight."

That agreed, Mahret found it almost impossible to fight off emotions of fear and panic.

"Can't you come with us now? I don't know if I can do this alone with two little kids. It's a long trip and dangerous. How will I ever be able to find Dawit's place? I have an address, but I don't know what it means. Barisso, I'm scared. Why can't you come with us? We might never see you again. We need your help!"

"I can't. Mahret, if the EPRDF sees a man my age on the bus with his family, they will take him for sure. They'd either kill me or force me to fight for their army. They have spies out everywhere, and they'll be watching the buses for sure. I want to come, but I can't."

"But I'm just so scared."

"So am I. I'm sorry, this is goodbye for now."

He kissed her on the forehead and slipped off into the night.

Mahret regrouped.

Along with everything else, she disliked setting off with this strange "businessman." She thought she felt his eyes focusing too closely on her.

She heard her voice speak, but she was unsure of its origin.

"I carry a knife, and I have used it before. One wrong move and it goes straight into your heart."

She hoped he did not hear the tremor she, herself, detected in her voice.

He did not seem to. He was not a big man. Indeed, he was shorter than her.

And he shook his head with a facial expression that quite clearly avowed, "you don't have to worry about me."

Chapter 11

THE TRIP OF A LIFETIME

Mahret pushed the wicker bins over, spilling most of the contents on the floor. She picked up several hand scoops of maize and an assortment of vegetables and put them into a cloth sack along with two bottles of water and two loaves of *daabo*. She also got a change of clothes for herself and the boys from an old wooden cabinet and packed them in her bag.

Then she turned and took her last look at the home she almost certainly would never see again. To her, it had always been a source of pride and comfort; indeed, of love. It also reflected a considerable part of what for years now had been her personal life. She focused on the wood floor Barisso had installed after acquiring the lumber from a merchant in the village in trade for a goat and a jug of *daadhu* wine. Covering the dirt, it had made her life so much easier. She glanced at the sturdy set of shelves against the one wall for the pans, pottery, utensils, and basin she used for preparing meals, serving them to the family, and the washing-up. And she viewed the two beds positioned head to toe along the opposite wall—blankets over a straw-filled mattress resting on a cowhide rug—and bulging with memories. In the one, she had surrendered her virginity on her wedding night and then conceived and given birth to their lovely little boys, both now soundly sleeping in the other.

Mahret wanted to cry.

Instead, she shook the boys to wake them up.

"Berhanu, Gamado, we have to go on a trip. Get up and get dressed. We have to go right now."

Neither was happy.

"Stop it, mom," Berhanu pleaded. "We don't want to go anywhere. We just want to go back to sleep."

"Berhanu, you will be my big boy now. *Abbaa* can't come with us. You have to take his place. I can't do this on my own. You must help me with your little brother. We're going to do this together. Do you understand? *Abbaa* will come later."

"Ah mom."

"No argument! We're going to a new home for a while in a big city in Kenya. We will be safe there, and we will have lots of food, and you will have new friends. But I need your help. We have to go whether we want to or not. And I'm counting on you to help me just the way *abbaa* would if he was with us. You help Gamado; help him follow this nice man and me.

Now! Do as I say! Okay?"

"Okay! Okay!"

Once she got the boys dressed, Mahret pulled the rope tight around the opening of her packed bag and lifted it up and over her shoulder. She spotted the knife hanging on the wall that Barisso used to castrate goats. She took it down, shoved the blade into a leather holster, and put the knife in the pocket of her *qamis*.

Finally, taking Berhanu and Gamado by the hands, she nodded to the agent and followed him out of the house and into the night.

"That's it Berhanu," she said, "you and me, we will start a new life when we get to Kenya. You and *haadha*, the two of us, we won't hesitate, we will be strong."

"Where's Kenya? What's hesitate mean?"

Mahret didn't answer. The only emotion she felt now was deep sadness—the grief of love lost—the farm with all the memories —her home, her life. These feelings came back briefly, almost but not quite, overpoweringly.

The tears welling up in her eyes made her glad for the darkness.

She wiped them away with her hand.

The half-moon was just bright enough to help them follow the agent across the fields behind the house and down a winding trail.

It was a long journey. Mahret thought they must have walked for at least an hour when Gamado started to complain. He was getting tired; she urged him to be strong.

"It won't be much longer; we will soon be on a bus to our new home in Nairobi."

They came to a dirt road, which they followed until they came to a huge rock glistening in the moonlight.

"This is our landmark," the agent said, "we will wait here for the bus."

Mahret sat down on the side of the road with her back against the rock. Gamado laid his head on her lap and fell asleep. Berhanu sat beside her, leaning on her shoulder. She hoped he slept some too.

Several minutes later, she heard engine sounds in the distance and saw the lights of a vehicle approaching.

As the bus pulled up to the rock and stopped, she was just able to make out its green and white colors. The side door opened. The agent climbed in, spoke to the driver, and handed him some money. After a quick count, the driver looked out at Mahret and the kids and nodded. Mahret picked up Gamado, slung her bag over her shoulder again, and, with Berhanu, climbed aboard.

The driver was a man about fifty-years old, heavily bearded, and in ordinary clothes rather than a uniform. At the start, there were no other passengers. But the bus stopped several times after that to pick up mostly women like Mahret with children, and some older men, older women, and older couples.

The leathered faces of most told Mahret who they were.

"Farmers, like us, all of them."

The agent seemed to be in control. He helped people in and directed them to their seats.

When they got to a garage on the outskirts of Shashamane an hour or so later, several buses were waiting for them. The agent directed people to each bus according to their intended destination. He got Mahret and the boys on theirs last and then got on himself and sat across the aisle from them.

"Your husband promised me extra to stay with you to the end of the journey."

"How long will it take to get to Nairobi?"

"It is a long journey, at least ten hours, maybe more. It depends on how many times they stop us."

"Who?"

"The officials."

Mahret resisted asking which officials? The very thought of being interrogated by men in uniform terrified her in part because she had no documents identifying her or the children. She was worried they could be pulled off the bus at any time.

Some fifty miles down the road, exactly that appeared to be happening.

The bus slowed, and she could see two uniformed men through the side window, waving the driver over. When he opened the door, the men came aboard. They started demanding documents from the passengers in the first seats.

The agent intervened.

"Hey fellas," he said, "the people on this bus are just taking a trip to the south to see their relatives. They don't need no papers for that."

"Says who?" One of the officials snapped.

"Uh, listen, let's go outside for a minute, and I'll explain."

He showed the officials something in his hand. They followed him outside. Mahret could see them talking, but she could not hear what they were saying. They just seemed to be arguing or, perhaps, negotiating. Finally, the agent handed one of them something and climbed back into the bus.

"It's okay," he said to the driver. "Let's go."

"I wonder," Mahret thought, "what will happen when he runs out of money."

On the road again, some of the other dangers that might lie ahead flashed through Mahret's mind. She thought about how bitter some must feel toward Oromo who supported the OLF. Men who backed the EPRDF might well consider why the people on the bus were traveling, and they could decide to intervene. She knew too that here in the southern part of the country, a radical Islamic group had a large following. There were Ethiopian Jews in parts of Oromia also. Stories abounded in the neighborhood back home, about these people, and the hateful things they had done in the past to persecute Christians. She and Barisso had also heard on their transistor radio about some of the regular crimes that had beset people traveling through Ethiopia or Somalia—robbery, murder, rape.

Also, the bus was old.

"What if it breaks down? I have only enough food to feed us for two or three days. How horrible it would be to watch the boys starving here in the dust and heat."

However, the bus continued on without incident for quite a long time before the driver stopped for people to stretch their legs and take a toilet break. Mahret woke the boys up and led them outside. She gave them some *daabo*, and then played a bit of tag with them in hopes they would use up some of their energy and go back to sleep when they were underway again.

The driver, a large, relatively thin younger-looking, stubble-faced man, who also did not have a uniform, stayed in his seat scanning the horizon.

Suddenly, he jumped to his feet and ordered everyone to get back on board.

"Hurry," he shouted, "people are coming. Hurry."

In the minute or so it took everyone to climb aboard, a dilapidated van with five or six men in it pulled up in front of them. One of the men got out. He walked over to the door of the bus and signaled for the driver to open up. Four other men took positions in front of the bus. Mahret could see they were all holding rifles.

The driver opened the door.

"You guys get out of the way," he shouted, "you have no right to stop us. These people are Ethiopian citizens. They ain't harming no one."

As he started the bus forward again, Mahret heard a loud bang and the sound of glass breaking. She could see a hole among the cracks in the front window.

The driver suddenly hit the gas, pulled off the road to the right, and started across the flat open field.

Shots rang out; thud, thud, thud bullets hit the back of the bus.

Someone screamed.

"Ahh, help, Nandene, no Nandene, no, no, no! Help, help! My son, my son, he's hit, he's hit bad!"

Mahret quickly pushed her two boys to their knees on the floor between the seats.

"*Haadha, haadha*, they're coming," Berhanu shouted, "they're gonna kill us, they're gonna kill us."

Gamado cried.

"No boys," she said, "we'll be alright."

With her hands, she cradled both heads in her lap.

Mahret could see the headlights of the van through the back window. It appeared to her to be closing on them.

But then, the lights suddenly twisted, rolled to one side as if the vehicle had hit a rock or something, and disappeared in the darkness.

That was the last they saw of it.

"They're gone now. There is no danger. Berhanu, watch your little brother, I'll see if the people in the back need […] if I can help them."

"No," Berhanu said, "no, don't go, I'm scared."

She put Gamado on his lap. "Hold him until I get back. I mean it now, Berhanu, do as I say."

When she came back, she took Gamado.

"It's too late. There's nothing I or anyone else can do."

The cries emanating from the back gradually faded into an almost constant heart-rending moan.

Mahret could only pray.

"Almighty *Waqaa*, please help them.

And all of us!"

Chapter 12

A LONG WAY FROM HOME

For several hours, there was no further trouble. While both boys slept, Mahret nervously pondered matters she had not had time to think about earlier.

"What will happen when we meet the Kenyan customs officials?

Can we really get through without papers? Or will they throw us all in jail? If we do eventually get through to Nairobi, will I know what to do? How do we find cousin Dawit? Where do we stay when we get there?"

An older lady in the seat in front of her turned to her for help.

"Excuse me," she said in Oromo. "Could I have a drink of your water? My water spilled on the floor during the shooting. I am dying of thirst, and I see you still have some."

"Yes, okay, but only a sip. I need this for the boys."

The woman was very thankful.

After she drank, they struck up a conversation. Among other things, the woman told Mahret that all the other people on the bus feared they would end up in one of the Dadaab refugee camps in Kenya.

"Many who go to Dadaab, the 'death camps,' starve or die from a disease. The whole place is filthy. People can't get food. They starve and their kids too. The death rate is worse there than in the violent places most of these people are trying to escape. Children, particularly the young ones, are dying like flies. Refugees get there and then find themselves desperate to get out, even to go back home.

Most of us agreed to pay extra bribe-money to the agent to avoid Dadaab. He's gonna get the money when we are safely through to Nairobi. You can bet he won't let anyone off till he gets what we promised. I'm pretty sure the cost for everyone is an extra thousand shillings. Everything is for sale. Do you have the money?"

"Uh, yes, I think so."

"Good."

Then, it happened again. As the bus rattled over a small rise, the driver abruptly pulled over and stopped. There were two armed and uniformed officers waiting by a jeep parked at the side of the road. There was no escape; the road was hemmed in on both sides by small but steep bluffs. The driver opened the door, a man climbed in.

"You move this bus before we tell you to, we'll kill you and everyone on it," he yelled in Swahili.

He screamed something else at the passengers that Mahret did not get. He yelled angrily again and pulled out a revolver waving it threateningly. Gamado and Berhanu were seated between Mahret and the window. She shifted her body forward and turned toward the aisle to shield them.

No one on the bus did anything. Everyone just sat where they were, frozen.

"They know what he wants, but they have nothing to give him."

Mahret glanced at the driver. He also was not moving.

She quickly placed cash she had kept in her bag for incidentals in Gamado's pocket and put a finger to her lips, indicating a secret. The man grabbed one of the younger-looking women near the front of the bus and dragged her toward the steps.

"Shut up bitch," he yelled, trying to quash her screams.

When that didn't work, he hit her hard in the face.

That did it.

Outside, he hauled her around the jeep, unbuckling his belt and holster at the same time.

He pushed her to the ground out of view and then disappeared, ostensibly, on top of her.

Another man climbed onto the bus. He took hold of his crouch, menacingly looking up and down the aisle. When his eyes came to Mahret his face broke into a smile. He went straight to her. He grabbed her by the hand, pulled her into the aisle, and pushed her toward the front. Gamado screamed, and Berhanu leaped to his feet to defend his mother. The man hit him with the back of his hand, knocking him to the floor.

Berhanu jumped up again and hit him back.

"You're a tough little guy, aren't you? I'm beginning to like that. Maybe I'll change my diet this morning."

The man pushed Mahret into the seats on one side, grabbed Berhanu, and pulled him down the aisle to the steps, and outside.

Berhanu screamed, kicked, and fought.

Mahret was right with them.

"Stop," she yelled as she pulled on the man's arm, "I can give you money."

"Is that so? Let's see it."

"I can give you twenty American dollars."

She showed him the one bill she kept when she gave the rest to Gamado.

"Not enough," he said, "but I'll take it."

He smiled and snatched the bill from her hand.

"I have more money; I can give you a lot more, hundreds of dollars."

"Good, I'll get back to you when I'm finished."

"I can give you a special prize."

Mahret sucked her finger and slowly worked it in and out of her mouth.

"That's not enough," he laughed, "I'm gonna fuck your boy here."

She put her hand on the man's genitals.

"You can have me. I am much better. I love to fuck. Do you want to do it in your truck?"

"You bet, but I feel like a boy this morning."

Mahret removed her hand and kneed him in the testicles with a blow that had the combined force of rage and terror behind it.

He let out a loud howl and bent over and away from her. She took hold of the knife in her pocket, pulled it out of the holster, and rammed it into the side of his chest.

"You dirty fucking bitch," he screamed, holding his chest with one hand, and fumbling for his handgun with the other.

Mahret had no choice; she stabbed him again, this time in the neck.

He fell, desperately gasping for air.

He did not get up.

There was blood on the part of Mahret's *shashi* that covered her shoulders. She took the *shashi* off, used it to wipe the blood from her knife, and then threw it away.

She heard another voice coming from the side of the jeep and looked up to see the other rapist, rifle in hand.

"You've killed my friend, you dirty fucking *shallee*. I'm gonna kill you and your kid and the other one too."

Mahret wrapped her arms around Berhanu and turned away. She heard the shots that would kill them both.

"Bang, bang."

But she felt nothing; they were still standing—there was no pain!

Mahret looked up again. Another military man by a second jeep in front of the bus was lowering his rifle.

She looked back at her would-be assassin. He lay on the ground, blood spewing from his face.

The new guy spoke.

"Hate to admit it but these bastards are my soldiers. They're a disgrace. We've warned them about this. We execute all rapists, but the ones that really piss me off are the ones that's supposed to be fighting on our side. They're idiots, animals."

He glanced over at the poor woman still lying on the ground behind the jeep.

"You better help your friend."

He got into his vehicle and drove off.

Mahret was stunned; she stood where she was, unable to move, her arms still clamped around Berhanu.

When she heard the bus engine start up, she snapped back to life.

"Wait, wait for us," she shouted through the open door.

The driver ignored her and shifted into gear.

A woman sitting directly behind him stood up, lifted her backpack into the air, and brought it down hard on his head. The bus lurched forward and stalled. The woman reached over, turned the key off, pulled it out of the ignition, and threw it to Mahret.

Mahret lifted Berhanu back onto the bus.

"Go to your seat."

She went back to the young mother, still sitting in the dust. She helped her up, pulled down her *qamis*, brushed the dirt off the back of it and then picked her *shashi* off the ground, and draped it around her shoulders.

"*Galatom*," the woman sobbed, "*Galatom*, you're an angel. Please, please don't tell anyone. If my husband finds out he will hate me, he will throw me away like an old shoe."

"Don't worry," Mahret told her as she helped her into the bus, "he did nothing. You fought him off. Everyone here saw that."

When she got back to her seat, Mahret found Gamado on the floor in the fetal position.

She picked him up and cradled him on her lap.

"It's okay. Everything will be okay."

She hugged Berhanu too.

"You get us to Kenya," she shouted at the driver, "I've still got a knife in my pack if I need it."

She handed the key to the woman in front of her.

"Give it to him."

The woman complied, and the driver started up the engine again and pointed the bus back down the road.

It took several more fear-filled hours to reach Kenya.

When they finally pulled into the town of Moyale on the border between Oromia and Kenya, there were only two uniformed officials at the stop beside what looked like a makeshift guardhouse. The agent got off again and spoke to them. The officials turned their backs and disappeared.

When the agent got back on board, the driver suddenly announced that he would not be going any further.

He also demanded the agent give him the final payment.

"But the journey is not over," an elderly man said. "We're not in Nairobi."

"You're in Kenya. I've had it with you people. I can't stand it anymore. I want the the rest now!"

"No one is going to pay you anything," Mahret told him. "You want the same fate as those guys back on the road?"

"Burn in hell; all of you."

He got up from his seat, descended the stairs, and disappeared like the guards.

The agent demanded his final installment.

"You didn't do the job. You got your first payments. Either find us another bus or get out of here," Mahret said.

The agent spat at her and followed the driver.

"Up yours," he said.

Chapter 13

MOYALE

To the other passengers, Mahret was the strongest person in the world. She was master of their fate. She had taken control in the face of incredible danger, and apparently, without flinching. They did not realize that as she shepherded her little flock into the town of Moyale she was shaking like a leaf and pleading under her breath to *Waqaa* for assistance.

"Help me. I'm so afraid. Please help me! And please forgive me for the terrible things I have done!"

Moyale, a town of some 25,000, turned out to be a thoroughfare for refugees fleeing either the Oromia violence or conflicts that had recently erupted in Somalia. On this northern Ethiopian side, the town had a suburb of white, plastic-looking tents that the United Nations had erected to house and help feed transients.

UN officials were watching as the passengers left the bus. When one spotted Mahret carrying what looked like a heavy bag and leading two young children, he came over to her.

"If you need a place to stay," he said, "we have a tent for you. You are allowed to stay for a week while you arrange for something more permanent."

"I appreciate your help. We are so very tired. We really do need to rest for a while."

The man led Mahret and the kids up a small rise into the tented area. He first showed them the washroom facilities, a large tent with male and female toilets—really just separate holes in the ground, privacy provided by canvass walls. There were also fresh water taps over drains. Mahret and the boys used the toilet, got a good drink of water, and had a bit of a wash.

"We can do a better job in the morning. Right now, let's get some sleep."

The man led them to a tent with the number 747 on it and opened the flap. Mahret threw her bag inside, and Berhanu and Gamado flopped down onto one of the two mattresses laid out on the floor.

"*Galatom*," Mahret said again to the man, "we will sleep now."

"You have a good rest; we'll talk to you about your future plans tomorrow."

The tent was small, and Mahret had to kneel to get inside. She gave the boys the last of the food and then got them to bed on one mattress, covering them with a blanket that had been rolled up at its head. It looked clean and new. She took another blanket from the other mattress for herself.

They were all asleep in minutes.

Hours later, when Mahret awoke, it was dark in the tent, but she could make out the figure of Berhanu sitting next to her. He was sobbing quietly.

Mahret knew what was wrong. She reached over and pulled him to her.

"It's alright. No one is going to hurt you now. No one will ever try to do that to you again. If they do, I will kill them."

Berhanu cried.

"What was that man gonna do to me? You killed that guy; you knifed him! I'm scared, I'm really scared."

"Berhanu, that man was very bad. *Waqaa* will punish him, and he will help me keep you safe now. We are all safe now, and, as you saw, I am very strong. I will protect you. Let's go back to sleep, and when we're settled in Nairobi, we will talk some more. I can't explain it now. Just remember you are safe, and I can protect all three of us until *abbaa* gets here. Everything will be alright."

She kept him cradled in her arms. Berhanu shut his eyes. The night closed back in on both of them.

When Mahret woke up the second time, the light of a new day was just beginning to break. Seeing the boys were still asleep, she crawled out of the tent and went to the washroom.

Afterward, she discovered that amid the tents, there was a small market with United Nations management acknowledged by a large sign. People were just beginning to stock up at the fruit, vegetable, and rice stands. When Mahret browsed, she found the men who were serving very friendly.

"Good morning, madam," the one in the bakery shop said in Oromo, "I hope you had a good sleep last night. Can I help you with anything?"

"Yes, I feel much better today, I'll have a loaf of the white."

She went to another stand and bought some slices of ham and to another where she got milk and rice.

There were a lot of people beginning to mill around when she started back to the tent. Most were shopping for provisions, but a few were just sort of standing back and watching everyone else.

"They have no money," Mahret thought, "I wish I could help them."

Then she noticed that officials with UN badges on their arms were approaching some of these people. They would talk to them briefly, and then lead them to a very large tent, marked "United Nations Headquarters."

"They'll help them get food; surely they will. That's their job. They can't let people starve."

After breakfast on the second day, Mahret learned that Moyale was more than just a refugee camp. It was also a racial time bomb ready to explode.

As she and the boys were sauntering through the marketplace they heard a deafening noise.

"What on earth was that?" She asked one of the merchants.

"It's almost certainly another flare-up in the never-ending fight between the Garre and Oromo. They absolutely hate each other, and no one can do much about it."

"Garre people, who are they?"

"They're mostly from Somalia; a big clan from Manderra County, mostly farmers I think."

Mahret found out later that an explosion had killed a Garre couple along with their twelve-year-old child.

Everyone was tense.

Then, when Mahret and the boys were walking back toward their tent, gunfire erupted. Within seconds, the sound was deafening.

Mahret grabbed both boys and ducked down behind a large garbage can. When a bullet creased the top of the can she picked Gamado up, and, with Berhanu, started running down a path leading out from the tented area.

Berhanu fell hard to the ground.

Mahret ran a few more steps and then stopped, put Gamado down in a small ditch beside the path and ran back to Berhanu.

His face had turned to one side. She looked at it closely; the eyes were open.

"Are you hurt? Are you wounded?"

"I'm okay."

"Get up."

Berhanu got to his knees. She grabbed him under one arm and pulled him to his feet.

The gunfire was loud again. Hand in hand, they ran and dived into the ditch next to Gamado.

Sheltered from the bullets, Mahret took Berhanu's face in her two hands, inspecting it closely.

She shouted above the roar.

"Tell me, are you hurt, are you hurt?"

"I'm okay; I tripped is all."

"You didn't get hit by the bullets?"

"No, no, I'm okay."

They stayed where they were until the shots stopped. Mahret saw a group of very frightened-looking people hurrying past them on the road. She recognized some of them from the bus.

"Come on, boys. We go too."

They joined the convoy as it hurried down the road and turned to follow a narrow path across a rough, hilly area. They stayed with it until, finally, they were in a new section of the town.

"This is Moyale, Kenya," someone said. "We're in Kenya now."

They found themselves in another UN tent city. It looked less well organized than the one they had just left. Tents of various shapes, sizes, and wear were spread around an open area strewn with garbage.

An elderly woman in one of the bigger tents reached out to Mahret.

"Come," she said, "I have room. You can stay with me tonight."

Mahret was afraid.

"I have no money," she said, "I can't pay you."

"I don't want your money. I'm a refugee just like you. This tent was left to me by people who stayed here for a while and then went to Nairobi. I want to help you the way they helped me."

Mahret looked around. The tents all seemed to be full.

"Okay."

"You're in Kenya now, without going through customs," the woman told her when they were inside. "If you had stayed in Oromia, you would have been held up for weeks by those guys. They are supposed to process people properly and make sure they have papers. If you want to, you can just sneak away from here and head down the road to Nairobi. The numbers are too many for the officials to handle. They won't stop you. They're relieved when people leave. I'm going daylight tomorrow."

"How're you gonna do that? They told me it's still over 400 miles to Nairobi."

"There's a bus. It's not expensive like the ones in Oromia, because it runs a regular route. They told me a thousand shillings. I must pay before I get on."

"Do you have that much?"

"No, I had to get away quick. One of my neighbors was shot and killed during the day as he came from a school meeting in Moyale. The following day, another neighbor was strangled when he went to the shops in the evening. I was really scared, so I decided to cross the border for safety. I didn't have time to scrape together no money. But one more for you to pay for won't be too much? I give you shelter; you pay for the bus for me too."

"I knew there must be a hitch," Mahret thought. "That's just ten American dollars, forty dollars for all of us and maybe less because everyone likes American money."

"Okay, it's a deal. You take us to the bus in the morning, and I will pay your fare too. I just barely have that much. What have you been eating?"

"I have a few shillings left. I have to buy a little food each day, one piece of daabo, an apple, a bit of maize. It's not enough, but since the numbers got so big, Kenya Red Cross and the UN have been helping—food and shelter, blankets, a kitchen, medicine too, and good water. One group called World Vision, and another called Concern are helping too. They keep me from starving."

Later, Mahret found out from a woman in a tent beside theirs that the Ethiopian army had killed at least nine civilians and wounded fifteen others and in the mayhem she and the kids had just escaped.

"Ethiopian soldiers see enemies everywhere, and they don't do much investigation before they start shooting," her roommate told her. "Some people who went to the Oromia part of Moyale are going back home.

In the beginning, a few years ago, about 3,000 people fled Oromia to the Kenyan side with nothing but the clothes on their backs. At first, Kenyans took most of them in, aiding them in any way they could. But the UN had to take over when, practically overnight, refugee numbers shot up to almost 10,000."

Exploring, Mahret saw a lot of women, many bare-footed, lining up to gain access to a man sitting in a chair inside a tent. When she asked one of them what was going on she learned that they had to register so they could qualify to receive rations.

In their hands, the women were carrying United Nations International Children's Emergency Fund jugs and empty bags.

Mahret got her own jug and bag from an official in another tent, and then joined the line. Once processed, she was able to collect free vegetables and water from a UN stand.

By the time she got back to the tent, swirling campfire smoke was giving the atmosphere a gritty look and smell. In the background, Mahret could just make out a lush green mountainous area with a road running through it.

"I wonder if that is our one hope—the road out of here?"

She and the boys got their chance to leave the next day when their tent-mate led them to a line of people boarding a bus to Nairobi.

It was then that Mahret discovered American dollars did, indeed, have a power of their own.

A man handing out tickets demanded she pay the forty shillings.

"I don't have quite enough," she told him. "I do have some American money. I give you twenty-five American dollars."

The man shook his head.

"No way, you pay full amount, or you don't ride."

"Okay," she said, "we can't go. We stay here."

The man's voice softened.

"I guess I could let you on for thirty-five dollars. How about that?"

"No, I give you thirty American dollars for the four of us, that's all I have."

"Okay, okay, you drive a hard bargain. Here, four tickets."

"*Galatom.*"

Chapter 14

A DAUNTING NEW LIFE

The trip along the rough, gravelly part of the road that covered two-thirds of the distance from Moyale to Nairobi was uneventful for a change. The two boys slept most of the way, and Mahret dropped off for moments here and there as well.

It was when they hit the paved, multi-lane A2 superhighway at Isiolo about a hundred miles from Nairobi, that the sleepy drive turned into something much more exciting. There seemed to be no traffic control, and cars kept racing by the bus in both directions at incredibly high speeds. At the Nanyuki bypass, there was a bus, an old one, tipped over on the side of the road with a smashed-up fancy-looking sports car beside it. Some attendants were lifting people into an ambulance on stretchers. Three, what appeared to be bodies, were laid out on the ground covered by blankets.

Further along, two newish looking cars, obviously racing, came speeding up to the bus from behind. Mahret watched them out of the back window as one car nicked the corner of the bus when the vehicles tried to pass it and each other, at the same time. The car careened off the bus and flew into the steel railing on the edge of the road. It flipped over and landed in the ditch.

"They must be dead," Mahret thought, "so unnecessary, what's wrong with these people?"

The bus driver seemed unperturbed. He just kept on going.

"He must have seen it all before."

They eventually came to the northern suburbs of Nairobi. The houses looked modern, and there were what looked to Mahret like skyscrapers in the distance. The bus did not stop, however, until it pulled into Kibera—the world-renowned shanty town that had mushroomed on the south side of the city, in the last couple of decades.

The driver parked behind some other buses.

Once in the muddy street outside, most of the travelers at first just stood where they were, seemingly bewildered. Mahret had no idea where to go other than the address for her cousin written on the piece of paper. She pushed on into the settlement anyway. When she tried to ask local people she came across for directions; they just ignored her. She thought maybe they couldn't understand her Oromo tongue. She tried English and Swahili.

But still no luck.

She saw an attractive and well-dressed young lady standing on the street corner.

"She looks rich. She won't want to have anything to do with me."

But Mahret had to do something. So, hesitantly, she dragged her little party over to her.

"Good afternoon."

To her surprise, the woman smiled and responded.

"You can use your own tongue," she said. "I'm from Oromia too."

Mahret showed her the piece of paper with her cousin's contact information."

"Do you know where this is?"

"Well, yes, I know approximately where it is, it's the Western Union office by Mashimoni. It's quite a long way from here. Head down the main road that is about three streets over that way."

She pointed.

"Then head east, uh, to your right."

"Would we be able to walk that far tonight?"

The lady looked at Mahret and then the two children.

"It's too far for that. Your kids will get awfully tired, especially the little one, and you'd probably get mugged after dark. It's too risky; I wouldn't do it if I were you. You must be new around here?"

"Yes, we just got off a bus. I want to find my cousin. The address is his."

"Well, it's not an address; it is a place where people send and receive cash payments."

The lady's voice took on a sympathetic quality.

"You all look very tired. Do you have a place to stay? Do you have any money?

Mahret lied: "no, we had to leave Oromia in a hurry."

"I know what that's like. I had to leave like that too. As I said, I'm Oromo like you. At least I was."

Mahret was astounded when she heard herself ask, "can you help us?"

The young woman seemed to understand.

"Well, I'm working at the moment. I can't give up a night's work."

She looked pensive, though.

"Look, come to my place. It's just up here. You can stay with me tonight. I can give up the trade just one night, and in the morning, I'll send you on the right path to find the Western Union office where, I believe, your cousin must do business."

It was Mahret who hesitated now, cautious about going into this stranger's home.

"Do you live around here?"

"Yes, listen; I know how you're feeling. You don't know if I intend to harm you. Please, I want to help you because I was once in your place. A couple years ago I had to leave Oromia like you. I didn't have anything either. It was hard. I almost died. I can't leave you on the streets with two little kids. Come with me, I just want to help."

Mahret was desperate, it was getting dark. It would be more dangerous to stay on the street.

"Okay, I, that is, I trust you, *Galatom.*"

"Follow me, it's not far, my name is Rekik."

"I'm Mahret, and my boys are Berhanu, and Gamado.

"How old?"

"Eight and five."

Rekik led them down a path and through an area that, to Barisso, would have looked very much like the growing slums he had witnessed in Shashamane and Dire Dawa— only he would have thought it was even more crowded and much bigger.

Rekik's was one of the numerous small, dark, and dilapidated shanties attached one to the other on her street. All had tin roofs and mud walls. Her pale blue door stood out from others on the street; the floor inside had no covering, just hard-packed dirt. There were, however, some furnishings, a rickety table with two chairs, a small settee, and a television.

Rekik brought out some *daabo*, jelly, eggplant, and three apples from a box on some shelves, and a knife, and placed them on the little table.

"Here, eat, you all look very hungry."

She cut off some pieces of *daabo* and began spreading the jelly on it.

Mahret was overwhelmed.

"You are too kind," she said, "I can't believe it, you take complete strangers into your home. I will never be able to thank you enough."

Rekik smiled as she spread the jam.

"Go ahead," she said to the boys. "It's okay; you can sit down and have something to eat."

They each climbed up onto a chair and started gulping down the food, and some water Rekik poured into glasses for them.

They had both been apprehensive like their mother to come into this stranger's home. But they were hungry. Questions they both had for their mother would wait until they were alone.

Mahret felt sick when Rekik took her to the holes in the ground in the horribly smelly hut a short walk from her place that constituted a toilet. Rekik told her that for some women, this was one of the most difficult parts of living in Kibera because, at night, rape was such a constant danger.

"In most of Kibera, there are no toilet facilities. One latrine, a hole in the ground, shared by up to fifty shacks. Some women have to walk too far after dark to get to them, and they live in fear. They try to do their business before nightfall, but that's not always possible. Here though, the toilet is close. And everybody around here knows that my business partners and I, we have bodyguards. No one bothers us."

Rekik seemed to have a much higher and intelligent view of life than Mahret expected of a woman living in such a settlement.

"The lack of sanitation is a reliable example of how the poorest in this country are doing. But although it's the poor who overwhelmingly do not have toilets, everyone suffers from the contaminating effects. A lot of people just pee and shit in the garbage piles and the run-off that streams from some of the plugged ground toilets. So, everyone should have a sense of urgency about addressing this problem. They don't, and they should. Disease seems to strike the slums first, but it spills over into the rest of Nairobi too. Lots of people have died out there.

We have some portable toilets, but many of them are privately owned anyway, and a lot of people won't use them for that reason—they charge three shillings each time a person goes. As you can see, the streets are also full of every kind of animal that people keep, and, of course, rats. You can see why the smell is so bad. On top of everything else, people here all burn wood or kerosene for cooking. Both give off a strong smell.

But you will get used to it. All the rest of us here have. I don't even notice it anymore."

When they got back, Mahret took the two kids to the facility; and then Rekik showed them the bed in the little room adjoining the one they had eaten in. Minutes later, both boys were asleep.

"It's a big bed," Rekik said, "lots of room for all of you. You could wash them if we took them to the water tap down the street, but maybe it's better just to let them get some rest. Surely, one more night won't matter."

"Yes, I won't worry about it; they've been through a terrible ordeal."

"You'll have to tell me about that. I have a pretty good understanding of the reality of the so-called 'trip to the promised land,' as some people have sarcastically tagged it. I experienced it firsthand too."

Mahret did tell her the whole story. She described even the most traumatic events, including the rape and the knifing (though she did not tell her who exactly it was who did it).

Mahret did not understand why she found herself confiding so much in this lady.

When she finished telling her story, she began to have difficulty staying awake. Rekik could tell.

"Listen," she said, "I'm going to go to work. I will see you in the morning."

"Where will you sleep?"

"Don't worry about me. I'll have no difficulty finding lots of places.

Oh, and I wash my sheets every day. Today was no exception. See you in the morning."

When Rekik left, Mahret joined the boys in this lovely lady's very comfortable bed.

Chapter 15

LIFE FRIENDS

The next morning, when Mahret got up, she found her new friend sitting at the table.

"Good morning," Rekik said. "Did you sleep okay?"

"Yes, okay; I was beat. I fell asleep fast and only just woke up."

She sat down at the table.

"I learned a lot from you last night, and I appreciate you telling me how it is around here. You're being kind. I will not forget this. So, you are Oromo too? What are you doing here? You are so young and pretty."

"That's very kind of you. Yes, I came here several months ago after they killed my husband in Addis Ababa. The government troops took him from the street and tortured him to death. It was so cruel, and he had never been in any insurgency like they accused him of. I had no way to live, and the government was taking my friends too. I had a little money, and I used it all to get some men to smuggle me south and across the border. I left in the middle of the night."

"How could you trust them? Didn't they try to rape you like the girl on our bus?"

"They raped me a few times. I couldn't fight it. It was that or stay and die in Oromia."

"How awful!"

"Yes, it was horrible. I was a poor helpless girl. The only man I had ever been with was my husband. I felt dirty, used, alone, and so afraid. I thought for sure they would kill me when they got enough fucking. Part of me hoped so. I felt I would never be able to go on with life anywhere."

"You poor thing, were you afraid of getting, you know, the disease from those men?"

"Of course, but I was lucky. If I had stayed, the Oromo police and guards would have raped me. One is just as bad as the other."

"You have no children?"

"No, we had just married. My husband sold fruit in the marketplace. We had a stall. We bought from farmers and sold in the market. We made enough to live. It was okay. I had a little cash when I left, but it didn't last long."

Mahret resisted asking her what she was doing now for a living.

"It very dangerous here?"

"Yes, but it's okay as long as you keep to your own."

"What do you mean?"

Rekik instinctively now saw Mahret as herself when she first arrived in Kibera – an Oromo girl, unaccustomed to the world around her, afraid and very naïve. She felt she had to provide her with all the information she could to equip her for life – to keep herself and her children safe and healthy.

It was time for a crash course on slum life.

"Okay, first, I'm gonna tell you the truth about me. I work with a group of young people who sell ourselves for sex. Most are women, but some are men. When I came here, I had no choice. There is no work. Most people here don't have a regular job. My money was gone, and I was starving. And after being violated so many times, it didn't seem that difficult to do it for a living. What the heck, I thought, I'm used goods, I might as well get paid for it. The other girls I work with are in the same boat. That makes us care for each other. We work the bars in Kibera, and we watch out for each other. We keep closest to one bar; we have some men we pay to help us find clients and who protect us. They take a part of our pay, but they're not pimps. They work for us, and not the other way around."

"Really, you hire the men?"

"Yes, and they do as we ask too. They're poor like everyone else, and they're happy to have a job. We pay them quite well considering."

"That's incredible. It would never happen back home."

"No, not on the farms or the country towns, but maybe in Addis Abba or Dire Dawa."

"Do you make much money?"

"We do better than most men who work. The girls feed their children well."

"They have children?"

"Yes, most of them have lost their husband. They're single mothers, and they do this like me, to survive. So many husbands here have died mostly from disease. We make sure the men use condoms. Two of the girls were reckless and sometimes didn't insist. Both died."

"Did they have children?"

"Yes, the one did, two little girls. We took them to live in the back of the bar. We all look after them. We have to help each other. We see they have food and a bed, and we make sure they bathe and keep themselves clean; the oldest is going to school this year."

"Are there a lot of prostitutes in Kibera?"

"Yes, they say about three times as many as in other parts of the city. And most of them aren't like me and my friends. We keep it civilized. Treating the children properly is part of it. We keep them out of the trade too while they're just children."

"When you say you keep the children out of the trade, do other children get into it a lot?"

"Working mothers, I think, try to keep their young ones out. They lock them up when they go out to look for clients, so they're safe. But, unfortunately, in some parts of Kibera, mothers intentionally bring their girls in."

"That's awful. How could they, their own children?"

"In a lot of cases, I'm sorry to say; the mothers are drunks who neglect their kids and spend their money on alcohol. They're desperate for the money. But some just have no husband and too many children to feed, and when their oldest reaches puberty, they get them out on the streets to help pay the bills. They rationalize: 'is this so bad, all the young girls these days give up their virginity anyway. My own will soon, too, no matter what I do. Helping to pay the bills is a better reason than most have.'"

"I can't believe what I'm hearing! How could they?"

"These mothers think in practical terms instead of moral ones. Also, of course, some young girls get into the business all by themselves once they get mature enough."

"You mean for food and clothes their parents can't give them?"

"Well, yes, but they're also desperate for pads, you know when their monthly comes. When they get their first period, they don't know what to do. They bleed for four or five days, and they don't have any way to control it. If they're in school, they have to stay at home, and they can't go out at night. When they quit bleeding, they sleep with some old guy for money so they can buy the pads for the next time. They take the risk. And some get the sickness and some, the lucky ones, maybe don't."

"This is so sad. What do *you* do about bleeding?"

"I can afford pads because I have regular work.

The main way to keep kids like ours out of the trade is by making life better for them than it is for almost anyone else in Kibera."

"What else do you do?"

"We pool our resources. We always have someone who can look after the kids when mom is on the streets. One of us takes a night off every week to help share the responsibility. When the kids are old enough, we tell them what's going on, but we also tell them to work on their school studies so they can find something better when they grow up. Also, if one of our sisters gets partying too much, the rest of us pull her aside and help her dry up and get off the booze and the drugs."

"Are any of the working girls still living with their husband, you know, a husband who hasn't died?"

"Actually, yes, and those guys mostly understand their wive's business."

"What do you mean?"

"Believe it or not, they help their wives look after the children, and they help our guys protect them, and the rest of us too. Some of them we even hire. They make sure their wives always have condoms too. They don't want to get the clap."

"Holy, my husband would kill me if I even thought about, you know, doing anything like this. He'd just kill me."

"Maybe not if you were desperate for money to live. It's amazing how much that changes people. If it made you comfortable, if it took the worry, the fear, out of life, if it fed your kids, don't be too sure."

"The demand for sex here must be really high?"

"Yes, it is, in Kibera, because we sell it cheap, 150 to 200 shillings a pop. A lot of men in other parts of Nairobi who stray from their wives come here to fool around.

We even have live sex shows. A lot of the girls who have children prefer to have sex in public, or on a video, rather than go out on the streets. It's safer, and the shows charge about the same as the prostitutes."

"You mean they make their own picture shows?"

"That's one way to put it; picture shows with more sex than story."

"How do you live when your charges are so low?"

"The main thing is that Kibera has the lowest cost of living in Kenya. Nobody here has a lot of money. And lots are in some sort of business catering to everyone else's needs.

That means the cost of living must be low. Also, of course, those of us in my business, we take on three, four, or even sometimes five clients a night."

"My Gosh! You must have to wash yourself a lot?'

"Oh, yeah, even though they use condoms, I carry soap and a douche, and I clean out good after every 'event', and I take bucket baths."

Mahret was as curious about life in general in Kibera as Rekik was anxious to inform her. She was naturally most concerned about how it would be for her boys.

"You said something about education. Is there a school here?"

"Yes, the best one is the Harmony Child Rescue Centre, but it is too far from here for the kids to go, especially with the danger of rape. We have made a little school for our girls' kids and a few other kids in the home of one of the girls who used to work with us. We each pay her a little out of our earnings. She gets about what she used to make on the street, and the kids are getting a basic education. It isn't perfect, but they at least are becoming literate."

"Hmm, but do you know any schools close to Mashimoni that my boys could go to?"

"I don't really know which ones will be close to you and what they're called. But you can inquire when you get settled. What you'll find is that there are schools around that are what we call 'informal schools,' most started up by individuals who get financial support from charitable organizations—churches, the International Children's Fund, the United Way, and so on, I think. Most schools don't have much to offer, their facilities are basic, but they're better than nothing and the kids have a chance to learn to read and write.

There are also several government schools, but they're all full and have long waiting lists. You can put your kids' names on one of the lists and try to enroll them in an informal school while you wait."

Mahret thought she would probably do that.

Her most powerful emotion at this point was amazement. How helpful this woman of the night was to her. And how cooperative she and all her "sisters" were with each other!

"I don't understand," she said, "all these people in such an awful business, but you are kind and caring. I would have thought it would be the opposite. You're better to each other than the people in my own neighborhood back home. We helped each other sometimes, like when there was a flood or a hurricane, but we were selfish too. When we got a good crop, we kept it for ourselves, for our own family. We would shut others out even if they needed help."

"Yes, I know, you live closely with your kind here, or you can't live at all. That's the difference."

"It's kind of instinctive?"

"Yes, it is. We all understand. We do it for survival. For me, it's first of all the other women in the business, and the men we pay, but it's also the families and others living close around us. You must find your relatives and get to know the people living near him. Usually, this will be just a few families, maybe ten or, at most, fifteen. I'm sure your cousin will have a good relationship with them, or he couldn't stay there; you have to trust the other people in your little area, we call the area compounds. The people in yours help each other, and they will help you because they know the alternative. Bad people are living outside the compounds: drug dealers, addicts, thieves and rapists, and all kinds of people with deadly diseases. And there is little or no police protection. For that reason, the good people who live in each little compound—Kibera is divided up into hundreds of them—look out for each other. It's the only way. They're like me and my sisters in the business."

"I can't believe it; I always thought most people in slums were just bad, like animals, fighting each other for every mouthful of food, no morals, no character."

"The words 'bad,' or 'good' for that matter, have no meaning here. A better word is 'desperate.' We're all just trying to live. This is far from heaven, but I sometimes wonder if life isn't in some ways better here than it was at home simply because people pull together so much. Most are family people who eke out an existence any way they can. In all our minds, it's us against the world. We kinda start to think of ourselves as one big family. We can't help it, we really have learned a vital lesson for survival, and in a way, it's made us better. I wish I could find better words to explain it. Do you understand what I'm saying? I trust people because I have to, and they do the same for the same reason."

"Yes, okay, I guess."

Mahret did think she understood at least somewhat; after all, here she was in the same situation Rekik was describing.

"I have to trust her, rely on her; there is no other way. I just have to. But I feel very close to her too. Like I would want to do anything I could for her if she needed it."

She felt very naïve, though. She was leaning on someone she would in her previous life have written off as just a dirty slut. She liked this person, even admired her.

Mahret thought she would never do what Rekik was doing for a living, but she grasped that people have to make decisions here. It is a matter of life. Her new friend would be her friend, no matter what. She was a good person, she had gone out of her way to help her and the boys get through their first dreadfully scary night in what she believed could be one of the most dangerous places on earth.

"What really matters? That's what really matters!"

Chapter 16

THE FACTS OF LIFE

Mahret knew Rekik's advice and information would help her in this scary world but she was still not confident in her ability to adjust.

"I have to admit, I'm afraid," she told her, "I have never been in a place like this. I'm afraid for my children. I'm afraid I can't cope. On the farm, everything was so much simpler. We didn't have much, but we knew the air was good, and there were no drugs or rapists or smelly sewer streams. Until the government troops came, there was no reason to fear any of the people around us. I know I must be strong, but right now, I don't know where to find the courage."

"You'll be alright," Rekik assured her. "I didn't have kids, but I felt much the same way the first few days I was here. The feeling goes away. You just struggle on until you know what you're dealing with. If you can find clean drinking water, the kids should be alright. That's the secret. The water we have here is not pure. It's okay for washing, but we always boil it before we drink it. You must!"

Mahret felt a little better when Rekik took her down the street to get a pail of water from an outdoor tap so she could wash thoroughly for the first time in the last few days.

She felt a little less so when Rekik explained in full how the water system worked.

"Until recently, Kibera had no water, and it had to be collected from the Nairobi dam. The dam water is not clean and causes typhoid and cholera. Recently the municipal council and the World Bank brought two water mains into Kibera. We, me and the rest of the girls in the business, get it free. With our own protectors, we've managed to stop anyone from claiming the taps and charging money for it. In other areas, though, gangs have taken control of the taps. Most people pay about three shillings for twenty liters of drinking water. They pay it. They have no choice.

The tap water is the best we have, but I worry about it too. The pipes are plastic and cracked. During heavy rains, latrines overflow. The overflow forms streams that eventually end up in the reservoir or the river. They flow across the water pipes on the way. The cracks allow dirt and sewage in. It's criminal, but when the dry season comes, they'll increase their price to fill a jeri can, up to seven shillings or even ten. They tell me that some water mafias are forcing people here to pay higher prices for water than wealthier Kenyans in better neighborhoods of Nairobi."

"But they're not all like that, overcharging whenever they can?"

"No, they're not, not all. When you find a home of your own, try to make sure it's in a compound where the water is good and reasonable. Just don't agree to rent until you know that for sure."

"You boil all the drinking water though?"

"Yes, just get a little kerosene burner; we all have them. They're not expensive. Don't ever take a chance. We'll make sure you all have a good big drink before you leave today, and I'll give you some water to take with you in a plastic bottle. When you get to your cousin's place, they will have a pail-full in their house, and you'll be able to get water from the reservoir, or a tap, and boil it.

Will your cousin help you with money?"

"Actually, I do have some money. I didn't know I could trust you when we met last night, but I do have enough for a while. If necessary, I'll get my own cooker. Thanks for telling me all this. You've adjusted so well to your life here; do you think you'll ever be able to leave Kibera?"

"I don't know, I dream of getting another job in a better area, but it's difficult. I don't have any training and very little education."

"Aren't you afraid you'll get killed by one of your clients or a disease?"

"Not really, I told you last night we have men to protect us. They're tough, and clients know about them. Also, I buy condoms myself. I can afford it, and I make all clients use them. I am well protected."

"But everyone is so poor, and the streets are so dirty. Don't you want more?"

"Yes, I do want more, but for the time being, I'm not so unhappy. I eat well, and I have enough money to live on. I have friends who care about me, and I care about them. In time, I'll probably want to get married again but for now, I'm satisfied. This life is not so bad."

"I see."

Mahret was certainly impressed with the cohesion that Rekik talked about among the groups in Kibera, but she still could not believe that she, herself, would ever be happy here.

"It's so dirty, and housing is so bad. In comparison, we lived in luxury back on the farm."

On the way back to Rekik's place to get the kids, she asked about all the wires attached to wood and metal poles protruding from many of the tin rooftops and running helter-skelter down the street from one little shack to another. Rekik told her they were electrical wires and that even though they seemed to be everywhere, electricity was hard to get.

"Some people get it through illegal hook up, which they use mostly for lights at night or a radio or even a television or a telephone.

Most of the wires are in the hands of local cartels that steal electricity directly from Kenya Power Corporation's transformers; others are controlled by people who legally buy the electricity from Kenya Power and then share, for a fee, with their neighbors. Neither system is very safe. But people can't afford anything else. The lines you see running along the ground are dangerous. Tell the kids to watch out for them. The danger is really great when it rains. Goats, dogs, and occasionally a small child, get electrocuted when they step on the lines."

The whole business of electricity was foreign to Mahret. The family had not had electrical service on the farm in Ethiopia, and she did not know anyone who did. Rekik's information just added to her fears about life in Kibera.

And there was more bad news.

"The wires sometimes short out and cause fires. Fires can be scary. They spread very fast here. The houses are so close together, and none of them even have ventilation. All the mud walls have paper and wood lining them.

The worst fire ever in Kibera destroyed hundreds of houses. It started one evening in a village about three miles from here in wiring they stole from the public grid. It burned through the night. About 30,000 people were left homeless. Can you believe it?"

All of this, naturally enough, added to Mahret's misgivings. She felt her one consolation was her money. If she could keep the kids away from dangers like fires and protect them from dirty water, the filth, and the diseases, she would have enough to see them through many days ahead. She still had most of the 1,500 dollars Barisso had given her, and that clearly could go a long way, maybe support them for the next whole year, maybe more. One dollar was worth about a hundred Kenyan shillings. So, the amounts Rekik was quoting her for water and toilet were really quite low in comparison. Barisso had a lot more cash too, and he would bring it to Kibera someday soon. She also felt solace from what Rekik told her about people in neighborhoods looking out for each other. Hopefully, that would be the way it was in her cousin, Dawit's, compound.

The other advantage she would have was the money her uncle was sending to Dawit. Twenty-five dollars a month was supposed to be hers, and it would be a big help.

"One thing Rekik," she said, "as you noticed before, all I have here for an address for my cousin is an office where he picks up the money my uncle sends him. It says 'near Mashimoni.' Do you know how I can find my cousin's home?"

Rekik scanned Mahret's piece of paper again.

"First, you have to get to Mashimoni. Kibera is made up of a bunch of districts or villages, about fourteen, I think. Mashimoni is one of them. Most of them connect by a main road. To get to it, you make your way down that road over there. As you can see, there are no street names or numbers here, like in other cities. Your cousin must pick his mail up at the closest Western Union (WU) office to Mashimoni. Once you get to the village, you can ask someone where the office is. A lot of people use it here. Someone will know."

"How far is Mashimoni?'

"It's the third village from here. There're two others in between. You follow the main road through this village, Gatwekera, and then onto Kisumu Ndogo, and Kambi Munu. There are crowds on the streets too. It will take you a couple of hours to get to Mashimoni.

When you do get there, you'll have to go to the WU office and just wait until you see your cousin coming to collect his money. I see your uncle has given you very clear instructions about the when. He obviously knows that this much money means an awful lot here, and he wants to be sure you get it. It says that he sends it on the first Tuesday of the month, late in the day—six o'clock—and it arrives in a few minutes. He says it would be here just after eleven our time on Wednesday, because of the time change.

You'll have to go into the WU office in Mashimoni and watch for your cousin."

"Yes, but what if he doesn't come for the money on Wednesday?"

"He will come the minute he thinks it's there. Even though the WU is dependable, he would worry about his money. The amount is an awful lot for around here. He must worry it could get lost or something. It's too much to take a chance. It's probably his whole life. Your cousin probably doesn't have much else to do anyway, no permanent job or anything. He will come to start checking right at about eleven, or soon after. Today is Wednesday. His money will be in before noon. He'll be there waiting for it. If you start out early, you'll get there in time to see him.

Him and his wife, they'll both be anxious about the money, one of them, but almost surely him, he'll be there for sure."

"I see," Mahret said, "if you can give me directions, I'll head out as soon as I can get the kids up."

"Actually, I don't work during the day. I'll go at least part of the way with you just to be sure you don't get lost."

"Really! I don't know what to say. You're so wonderful. I'll owe you my life."

"No, you'll owe me nothing, at least not in the way you think. One day I might ask you to return the favor. That's how it works around here. I'll be happy to have you in my debt."

"You'll sure have that. Forever too!"

Mahret hurried to get the children up. Rekik helped her strip and wash them.

Afterward, they all had a breakfast of *daabo* and *shaayii*.

Then they set out down the road to Mashimoni.

"Here we go," Mahret said to herself, "on to a new adventure.

I'm scared to death."

Chapter 17

"PUBLIC TRANSPORT"

Mahret told Rekik it was not necessary for her to come along with them, that she, Mahret, had some money, and she could use some of it for public transport.

"We could take the train. I saw a track over there that looks like it's running through the village."

Rekik talked her out of it.

"It's called the Uganda Railway. But it's run by the Kenya Railway Corporation. We also know it as the 'lunatic express.' It passes through some of the villages, including, I believe, Laini Saba, Kianda, Kisumu Ndogo, Kambi Muru, and also Mashimoni. Most Kibera who live along the rail lines use it as a commuter train if they have to go long distances out of here for work or something. The fares are quite cheap, thirty shillings, which most people here can afford to spend when they have work. The problem is that it's apparently in very bad condition. It's very old, it breaks down, and is often off schedule; and, in Kibera, it doesn't stop in enough places. You might end up walking even more than if you just went on foot from here.

The railway has been a disaster from the beginning. One of my rich clients from Nairobi once told me that when they were building the railway line over a hundred years ago, some lions snuck into the construction camp one night and ate like twenty-five or thirty of the Indian workers.

That's one reason people call it the lunatic express. The other is that the train just gives outsiders a good view of our life. You can see them staring out the windows at us as they ride through. Wealthier people find us interesting, even amusing."

"What about the little buses I saw on the street?"

"They're called *matatus*. They're not very dependable, and they don't make a lot of stops in Kibera either. You might not get as close to the Western Union in Mashimoni as you'd like on it either. Their charges can vary too from twenty to a hundred shillings."

"Still," Mahret said, "a hundred shillings is just one dollar, and I wouldn't have to put you through any more bother. You've done enough, and the kids will get very tired if we have to walk the whole way. They've done enough walking in the last week to last them a long time. It must surely get us at least a little closer than walking all the way from here; and the bus driver should be able to tell me where the closest Western Union office is."

"Okay," Rekik said, "I'll take you to the *matatu* Kibera office to get tickets. It's just a little way from here. The buses go there before they continue on through the poor areas. Just be very careful when you're on the bus and try not to draw attention to yourself. I know you wouldn't do that, but just keep the kids quiet if you can and blend in with the others. It's best if no one notices you. And don't let anyone know you have any money.

I have to say, after the long journey you've been on, you don't look like you have any."

As they made their way toward the *matatu* office, Mahret showed the kids the wires in the streets. She warned both boys that they could get "really badly hurt," if they ever got too close to them.

"You must stay out of the dirty, filthy streams too. They'll make you really sick. And don't ever go near any strange men! I guess now you know that."

When they got to the office, Rekik stayed outside with the kids while Mahret joined a line of three people to buy the tickets. She could hear the lady at the front of the line arguing with the clerk behind the wicket.

"A hundred shillings? No way. I can't pay that. Yesterday it was thirty shillings. You can't raise the price like that overnight."

The clerk was unmoved.

"Lady, pay the price or get outa here. I've got others to deal with."

The guy behind the lady in the line cut into the conversation.

"Listen buddy," he said, "people are getting tired of this. We don't have that kind of money. We're not gonna pay three times as much today as it cost yesterday. We have a family to feed."

"Then go feed your family and leave me alone; the price is one hundred shillings, and that's it."

Two hefty looking men appeared, one on each side of the clerk.

"Trouble?" one of them asked.

"Nah, these two don't want no trouble, do you?"

They both turned and left without saying anything.

Mahret was next in line.

"How many tickets do you want, or are you a troublemaker too?"

"Four tickets to the Mashimoni Western Union."

"That will be 400 shillings."

Mahret was too intimidated to argue. She handed over four American dollars and went back outside.

The *matatu* had arrived, but she couldn't see Rekik and the kids.

"Mahret, watch out, we're over here [...]"

It was Rekik's voice.

A shot rang out, and a man fell on the street in front of the *matatu*. Mahret heard other shots. They were loud and close.

She ran across the street toward Rekik's voice. When she got to her, kneeling on the ground behind a small ridge shielding the two kids, she dropped down beside her wrapping her arms around all three of them.

The shooting was constant for just about two minutes. After it stopped, Mahret and Rekik kept the kids still for a few more minutes until fairly sure it really was finished. When they peered over the edge of the ridge, they could see six or seven young men. They all had guns. Two of them were dragging a limp body away from the front of the *matatu*. The clerk and his backup came outside with their hands in the air. They took off down the street, fast.

Still kneeling in the dirt, Mahret scrutinized the boys.

"They're alright," Rekik said. "They're not hurt."

They were wide-eyed and pale. Both stared at *haadha*.

Rekik repeated the message:

"They're okay, don't worry, they're okay!"

The four waited a little longer and then cautiously got up. Several feet away, the woman who had been trying to buy a ticket did the same, with some difficulty.

"What's happening?" Rekik asked her. "These buses, they must be terrible dangerous. What the heck is going on?"

"It's gang warfare; they must be fighting for control of the *matatus*; I only use them because my legs aren't good. I guess a new gang must be taking over in Kibera. They want a cut of the fees for protecting them. The gangs make the buses pay for protection, and the buses make their passengers pay, that's one reason the price keeps changing."

"They're not safe then?"

"Are you kidding? We call them 'death traps' for a reason. I'm old, I have little to lose. I wouldn't take kids near them. The buses sometimes get hijacked by one of the gangs, and when the people on them refuse to pay them off, they get beaten up, robbed, sometimes even raped. Once when I was trying to get to see my son in Nairobi, the driver started speeding like a crazy man, and he hit one of the big buses. They called a truck to come to tow the *matatu* away. We all had to get off. A lady passenger was hurt pretty bad, and they just left her on the side of the road."

"That's the end of that," Mahret told Rekik. "We're not ever taking one of those things. They can keep my four dollars.

This is so discouraging. The kids will never get over all the violence they've seen since leaving the farm. They're gonna be maimed for life. And me too, I think. You keep telling me we can find a decent life here, but all I'm seeing is danger, fire, gangs, violence, disease. Everything is so scary."

"I'm really sorry," Rekik told her. "I said the *matatus* weren't very dependable, but I walk the streets, I've never taken a bus. As for everything else, I need to say it again. If you keep your kids in your little compound within Mashimoni and get to know and work with your neighbors, you'll be okay. It's when you venture outside your little area where there is no one to help you, protection breaks down and things like this happen."

"I believe you. I guess we'll walk to my cousin's place."

"I guess you'll have to. If you stay to the main road, you'll be okay. When you're between villages, go quickly, don't stop, don't talk to anyone, and make your way into the next village as quickly as you can.

You'll be okay on foot while it's still daylight; there's danger, but no one is going to bother a mother with her two children while everyone else can see them. The boys can make it too. Don't worry; you can buy some food for them as you go along. One thing you learn here, once you have enough to eat, there's lots of time. It's quite a long walk, but you should still get there before noon.

Now that we've decided you're going to do it on foot, I think I'll go back to my first plan and come part way with you."

"You don't have to."

"Oh, yes, I think I do. Suddenly, I can't help it; I'm starting to feel like I am you. Or maybe you're me!"

Chapter 18

LEARNING TO LOVE: (EVEN THE HATED)

The first part of the walk turned out to be almost as disheartening as the *matatu* episode. As the morning slipped away, the day grew hot, the air became smoky, and the smell got worse. They walked along and past stagnant looking little streams full of garbage, plastic bags with waste in them, and dung (both animal and human). Rekik told Mahret that the plastic bags were called "throw or flying toilets."

The housing looked even cruder than it had.

"The shanties are tiny," Rekik told her, "and some have as many as eight people living in them—most sleeping on the dirt floor. The tin roofs almost all leak when it rains."

There was, though, one positive quality Mahret detected about this society as they went. Most of the children playing in the streets looked like any others. They seemed carefree and happy. Some were just laughing and running around as kids do. Some were kicking a ball made out of a plastic bag Rekik said was filled with paper and would have a small stone in it for weight. Others were swinging from a rope tied to the branch of a huge, ancient-looking tree growing at the side of the road.

Ugly realities kept popping up, however. Mahret saw some kids wading up to their knees in a little pond of dirty brown water.

"I can see those kids are having fun," she said, "but oh my heavens, that water looks filthy."

"It is. The pond is fed by the streams you see around here. The streams are fed by the water flowing from the underground sewers. They're not what you'd call clean, but the kids seem to get immune to them after living here for a while. It's amazing how tough they are. I don't know where they get their energy; many of them don't get more than a single meal a day."

"One meal? My kids couldn't live like that. How do they do it?"

"Food is scarce because parents often don't have the money to pay for it. So, they'll forego food to feed their children. You may have noticed there are virtually no fat people around here. But that's often not enough to keep the kids' stomachs full."

"I can relate to that. We were beginning to face the same problem on the farm."

Mahret noticed too that some kids looked much less content than most. They weren't playing with the others. Instead, they seemed to be just standing around. Thy looked low-spirited, even grim. One boy, about Gamado's age, came up to Mahret and Rekik with his hand out.

"He wants food or money," Rekik said, "don't give him anything. If you do, we'll be swarmed. You can't help them."

She told Mahret that many children like this one were orphans.

"Their parents die because they don't know how to get tested or treated for diseases like AIDS. These children are a big tragedy here. Waterborne diseases like typhoid and diarrhea kill a lot of them. They kill other children too, but the orphans more because their nutrition levels are even lower.

The HIV/AIDS scourge has hit them the hardest. When their parents die, they're on their own. Many go into prostitution to support themselves. Then they're very likely to catch it."

"You mean they catch the sickness when they sell sex to get money for food?"

"Well, yes, that's one reason. Many of the orphan kids sell themselves to men who like children—boys as well as girls. They get the disease from the men. The biggest problem, though, is they also share the needles the men use for their drugs. They get it that way."

"What do you mean? I don't understand."

"There are a lot of drug addicts, mostly men but women too. They drink cheap liquor when they can get it, but they prefer heroin and any other hard drug types they can find. There are a lot of dealers preying on them. The orphan kids who sell themselves to men are likely to contact seasoned drug-users who convince them that drugs will help them cope with their tough life. Injection needles are just another expense, so they share them, passing the disease from one to the other. Then they die. They also inject themselves with the left-over needles that still have some drugs in them when the men who fuck them overdose and pass out, as they often do.

The used needles are everywhere; if you look closely, you'll see them; they litter the ground in places, they're in the garbage and the sewer streams, everywhere. So, make sure your kids know to stay away from them.

The orphan kids who don't die are often the toughest and most streetwise of them all. They become leaders and often head up crime cartels as they age. They're nasty too. They've learned to get by on their own by fighting for their life, by taking what they can when they can, sometimes even stealing from the drug and sex addicts who exploit them. Some eventually even murder their exploiters and take over their jobs as gang leaders or pimps or drug traders."

Rekik wanted to tell Mahret the truth so she would grasp what she was up against, but she also felt bound to keep enforcing the message that there were reasons for hope.

"Listen," she said, "you can still make a decent home here. What you have to do is become part of the community life where you settle. Talk to people, help them too, and they'll help you. Everybody knows it's necessary to support each other. Chances are you'll find that the little neighborhood you settle in is safe because everybody acts to ward off danger. If not, you have to move to another neighborhood. In a good neighborhood, and most are good, those people living around you, even those you would have considered enemies in the past, will pitch in. Even non-Ethiopians—Eritreans, Somalis, Muslims, Jews too; they all know that everyone has to help each other to some extent to get by. They'll work with you and you with them. When that happens, life will be okay, and you'll be okay too."

Mahret shook her head in a way that said she understood.

Kind of.

"How," she asked, "do the kids who only get one meal a day get by?"

"Many of the kids are pretty good at supplementing their food supply in the streets. They get overripe fruit and stale baked goods that the dealers throw in the garbage cans, and they scrounge through the dumps too; to be honest, I think they also steal from the market stands when the crowds are thick. As much as anything, though, they get hand-outs."

"Hand-outs?"

"Yes, a lot of rich people come here, many of them on tours, just to see how poor people live."

"Tours?"

"Yes, there are some people from Nairobi who bring tourists here. They're businesspeople who charge money to curious rich people who want to see how awful conditions are. The tourists often bring candy bars for the kids. It makes the wealthy people feel good about themselves—superior is probably more like it. But they almost all bring something, money too, the kids use it to buy snacks.

One girl who used to be my business sister has made enough money conducting these tours to get out of the sex trade altogether. Up to five years ago, Awino made a living selling fresh food in Mombasa. She dealt with tourists who came for the sandy beaches of the Indian Ocean. She moved back to Kibera because her aunt, who lived here, was dying. She started working with us and then saw the camera-toting tourists again, but not on the beaches; right here on the streets. So, she started going to the big hotels with a sign advertising trips to slum city. She's doing quite well; she quit us and says she's not coming back."

"Imagine making money by showing people poverty, gloom, sadness?"

"Yes, it's quite something. But the tours also show hope, the kids playing happily in the streets, the good nature of the merchants selling things, the people chatting with each other just like they do in wealthier places. The visitors buy stuff that people are selling too because they're so cheap. I think, overall, the touring business is highly competitive, though. Several companies are showcasing us.

On the other hand, curiosity seems endless."

"Don't people here object?"

"Some do. They don't like the tourists. They don't like being treated like objects. I keep telling them we should tolerate them as long as they help us feed the kids.

Some rich people come through on their own, too, without a tour. And they're often quite generous.

You see that guy over there?"

A well-dressed man across the street was surrounded by children with their hands out, all screaming "me, me, me."

"This happens all the time. Guys like that love to feel they're helping the poor, so they give out money or goodies when they see a hungry child, a shilling here, a shilling there, or whatever. Probably depends on how guilty their conscience is about some of the things they do back home to make their money."

As they watched, the man tried to break away, but the kids stayed right with him until he ducked into a taxi waiting for him on the side of the road. He then leaned out the window and threw out handfuls of candy. The kids went after them like a flock of seagulls for breadcrumbs.

"You see why I warned you about swarming?"

"I do now."

Rekik believed at this point that she had done her duty. She had taken her fellow Oromos in hand, and she had given Mahret tools she needed to set up a home in Kibera

"We've now passed through the village of Gatwekera; Kisumu Ndogo is next, then Kambi Munu, and then Mashimoni. I need to go. I have to report to the business; I can't be late this afternoon after getting there late last night. You should be okay. Just remember to stay on the main road until you get to the district beyond the next one. Then, ask someone for the closest Western Union office and go straight there. Your cousin will likely turn up around noon. If he doesn't, you can come back to my place today and try again tomorrow. But he will come for his money, and I'm pretty damned sure it will be today. No one here would ever neglect a free fifty dollars, not even for a minute.

Good luck now. If I don't see you tonight, I'll check on you in a few weeks."

Mahret felt a ting of panic returning. She would be on her own again. But all she could do was let her new friend see how grateful she was.

"You saved me and my children. I will never forget this. You are in my heart forever."

Rekik just smiled and headed back down the street, waving as she went.

All sorts of other emotions were again floating through Mahret's mind. Incredulity was at the top of the list. Once more, all her previous convictions about right and wrong were looking fuzzy.

"Can this be real? At home, we looked down even on some Oromo outside our neighborhood whose skin was darker than ours. Now a prostitute, we've been saved by a prostitute! In some ways, she's more like the Virgin Mary!

Oooh, I shouldn't say that.

Forgive me *Waqaa*."

Chapter 19

THE EVIL COUSIN

Mahret picked up some *daabo*, raw vegetables, and candy snacks at a grocery stand in a local marketplace and fed the boys as they walked along. The journey tired them both out, and Gamado started whining and complaining. When Berhanu seemed to be encouraging him, Mahret had to speak to him. She reminded him again that he was the man of the family until *abbaa* could be with them, and that *abbaa* would be very proud of him for taking his place.

"You must help me look after your little brother. We have to be strong. Okay?"

"Yeah, okay, okay! Gamado, grow up, you're such a baby!"

"Berhanu" Mahret thought to herself, "I know you'll try, even though you're still just a baby yourself."

Having become a little more acclimatized to the filth and poverty, Mahret started to take notice of all sorts of other things. There were large crowds of people milling around the villages. She noted how so many were trying to eke out an existence.

"They're selling everything at makeshift stands or on mats they've just laid out on the ground."

Some were selling fruit, some vegetables, some baked goods, others second-hand sandals, rolls of cloth, scarfs, used books, used toys.

She saw one woman selling second-hand clothing. Her sign read: "Cheap from Nairobi, Freshly Washed."

The woman had some men's and some women's clothes: three or four pairs of trousers, a few skirts, some shirts, and two or three blouses.

People were examining them carefully, as if they were interested.

There were handcraft artists too, mostly women, selling jewelry, purses, beaded pens and letter openers, scarves, dolls, hand-sewn animals, and greeting cards made from banana leaves.

The other thing Mahret noticed was how cheap everything was:

a man's shirt for fifty shillings, apples for five shillings, enough milk powder for a whole family for a day, two shillings.

"At a hundred shillings to the dollar, the American money will last a long, long time."

She noticed too that many of the buyers were not from the area. They looked too well dressed. None she saw at this point were with a tour; most seemed just to be Nairobian citizens from outside the district.

"They must come to buy stuff too when they can because it's so cheap."

After moving on past the market, she saw two men digging nails out of the dirt with their hands in one area along a garbage-strewn ditch and laying them out on the edge of the road.

"Rusty nails, they're gonna try sell rusty nails."

When they got to the far edge of the one village, the road widened slightly for fifty meters or so as it went through a low spot that had a tiny, filthy looking lake on both sides of it. When they got past it, they were back in another settlement, more or less exactly like the previous one.

"We're in the second village that Rekik mentioned. What did she say it's called? Oh well, I know the one that Dawit is in is Mashimoni, it's the third one, oh yeah Kambi Munu."

Their pace through the crowds was slow. It took them until late morning to get to Mashimoni.

"Rekik thinks it's about the time of day when cousin Dawit should be looking for his money."

Mahret stopped a young woman walking along the road.

"Western Union? Can you tell me where is Western Union?"

The woman replied in Swahili.

"I don't understand you."

Mahret switched languages.

"*Pesa*, where people collect *pesa*—Western Union, Western Union?"

She motioned with her fingers to suggest shuffling a handful of bills.

"Oh, *pesa*" the woman said, "Western Union, *pesa*, you must keep going. Go that way, follow the road (she pointed), and go until you come to another road, turn right. Keep going, you will come to Western Union."

"Is it far?"

"Fifteen minutes."

Mahret bowed her head in a motion of thanks.

When she followed the woman's directions, she discovered the Western Union was not really in the shantytown through which they had been walking. It was in a two-story, dull grey concrete structure across the road from the shanties. Instead of metal-roofed shacks beside it, there were several small office buildings and regular storefronts.

Inside, on the ground level, Mahret surveyed a large single room with a teller behind a long counter and three men in the lineup.

She had known Dawit back when they were kids on the farms in Oromia. He would be older now, of course, but, like her, he should still be distinguishable.

She was quite sure none of the men were him. So, she took Berhanu and Gamado back outside and sat them down in a spot directly across the road from the building. The building offered shade from the direct rays of the sun. She pulled a half-loaf of *daabo* out of her bag and broke off a large piece for each child. The boys were hungry again, and they were tired too, but now neither complained. They seemed to sense that what their mother was doing was important and that the moment was somehow serious. Gamado put his head down on the food bag and closed his eyes. Berhanu sat by his mother and watched the people with her as they walked by. A number approached the Western Union office, but they all passed it.

Then a tall man with a slim build whose medium brown skin suggested a family trait entered the street about a hundred meters away. He headed straight for the building, pulled open the front door and went in.

"Watch your brother," Mahret said to Berhanu, "I'll be right back."

She crossed the street and entered, as well.

Inside, she watched the man line up in front of a teller who was finishing up with a client. When his turn came, he handed the teller a piece of paper. The teller left the room through a door in the back. When she returned, she gave him a document, which he signed. She then got some money out of a drawer, counted out some bills, and handed them to him.

Mahret looked closely at the man's face as he turned to go back outside.

"No mistake, it's him, it's Dawit."

She had decided not to approach her cousin at this stage. She knew he was unlikely to be at all pleased to see her and might not want her even to know where he lived. So, when she went outside herself, she moved slowly. Keeping an appropriate distance, she and the boys trailed Dawit home. They did not have to go far. He led them back into Mashimoni, down a narrow side street with typical shanties on both sides, to a taller building that looked to be of better construction than most of those around it.

After Dawit went inside, Mahret took a deep breath, walked up to the door, and knocked.

"Dawit, you remember me, your cousin, Mahret," she said when he reappeared.

"Yes?" he replied.

"We had to leave Oromia because of persecution by the government. We have come a long way. We are very tired."

She gripped both boys by the wrist and pushed passed her cousin into the house.

"Can I help you? What do you want here?"

"We need a place to stay until we can get settled."

"But you can't stay here. We are four people already in three rooms."

He towered above Mahret.

She stood her ground.

"Listen, I'm too tired to argue with you. My children are exhausted from a very long, hard journey. I know from our uncle's letters that he's been sending you money from New Zealand *for both of us*; fifty dollars a month. He said you would share it with us if we had to come to Nairobi too. He could not send money to the farm because there is no Western Union within many miles. You've been lucky to have it to yourself, but now it is time to help us too."

Dawit knew he was not in a position to say no, and not just because Mahret had a claim to half the money from New Zealand. He, too, had come from a farming neighborhood in Ethiopia, where people of the same skin color and Christian religion helped each other whenever they felt it necessary; to battle illness, floods and drought, and the government. Mahret was one of his own, and he knew it. He had dreaded the day she and her family might arrive, knowing full well that the moral high road would be hers. There was little he could do about that.

"Okay," he said, "I will let you stay for a while, but you must find your own place soon."

"Yes, I will do that when you give me half the money our uncle sends."

Dawit glared at her.

"We'll see about that. I don't think you know what you're talking about. I have had all the responsibility you have had none."

"It's been a tough day," Mahret thought, "and what a very stupid thing to say."

"I'll tell you what, Dawit, if the responsibility is too great, give me the money. I'll look after it for a while, and you can rest your weary soul."

"Not on your life."

"Okay then, let's get some lunch ready for the boys."

Chapter 20

LIFE IN THE COMPOUND

In the days that followed, Dawit and wife, Baredu were, to say the least, not particularly pleasant. They were short with Mahret and the boys and impersonal.

"They have enjoyed uncle's money by themselves for too long."

Mahret was uncomfortable, but she was determined to care little. She was going to be impervious to their bad vibes. She had no choice. The challenge for her now became adjusting to life in the slums of Kibera.

Dawit and Baredu had not felt a need to form close bonds with their neighbors because they had a steady income. On top of the uncle's fifty dollars monthly, Dawit had a clerical job on the other side of the road separating Kibera from the better parts of Nairobi. The couple was financially able, therefore, to live independently, and they chose to do so.

Mashimoni had its own little local market on the edge of the Nairobi River just a few blocks from Dawit's home. Mahret went there later on the first day and bought some used blankets, a cowhide rug, and some straw-filled mattresses to make a bed for her and the kids. She bartered with her American money and managed to get it all for 8 dollars. She laid the new bed out on the floor in the second room in Dawit's house, where his two daughters had slept when they were home from the Goodwill Charity Boarding School.

This arrangement would do for a while.

When, a few days after their arrival, Dawit tried to encourage Mahret to look for another place she bristled.

"I can't find another place right now, I have little money, and I'm afraid to take the children into an abandoned sheet metal shack. It is much better for us all here. We are safe here and have a good water tap, so we can at least clean ourselves, and a toilet right next to the house. When Barisso arrives, we will have more money, and we will feel secure enough to live on our own."

She could not help reminding her uncle once more that, figuratively speaking, they were "tied at the hip."

You're getting fifty dollars meant for both families. If you still really want us to go, give me twenty-five dollars each month, and I will try to find a smaller place. Otherwise, we do the smarter thing and share these rooms; and you stop pushing me."

That ended Dawit's resistance for the time being. He was beaten, and he knew it. He moved his daughters' mattresses out of the room Mahret and the boys were using, and into his and Baredu's bedroom.

The atmosphere in the place did not suddenly improve, but Mahret's claim to settlers' rights would for the time being, go unchallenged.

"For now, just for a while," Dawit promised Baredu.

In the neighborhood, Mahret put Rekik's advice to practical use. Daily, she would take the children out among the people on the streets in the area and try to befriend as many as she could. She discovered that the settlement she now lived in was, as her friend had described, a small compound composed of families that worked together for survival. The people living in the compound had erected an old rusty metal fence around their neighborhood to augment their sense of unity, mutual support, and protection.

There were twelve families all told, including Dawit's, with two to five children each. Only four were two-parent families. The rest had just the mother. A few families also had a grandparent living with them. It was convenient for Mahret that most of the adults she met could at least understand her Afaan Oromoo language, either because it was their original tongue or because they had learned the basics of it from Ethiopians here in Kibera. There were four other Oromo families. The rest were Kenyans, Somalis, or Eritreans. One of the Kenyan mothers Mahret met had spoken only Bantu Swahili when she arrived in Mashimoni just two weeks earlier. Kirmeet had already picked up a smattering of Oromo terms, which she practiced and used to connect with her neighbors, along, that is, with her version of sign language.

Mahret discovered there were a plethora of reasons why people were here. The Kenyans were generally just too poor to live in better parts of Nairobi. The Somalis and Eritreans were escaping ethnic rivalry of one form or another. Some of the Oromo were wanted by the police back home for teaching their language in village schools. Others had been jailed and tortured on suspicion of belonging to political organizations or the Oromo Liberation Front.

Recently, Mahret learned, stepped-up military action by the Tigran/Amhara dominated EPRDF had brought a new influx of refugees. The junta was actively working to suppress not only the OLF but also the Islamic Front for the Liberation of Oromia and the Ogaden National Liberation Front (fighting for the rights of Somalis in Ethiopia), and other ethnic/religious groups.

An Oromo Jewish woman about Mahret's age told her she was arrested one night and taken to a military camp. She was held in solitary confinement in total darkness and repeatedly raped in her cell. They pulled her out of her cell several times and interrogated her about involvement in resistance groups, and the whereabouts of others, who the interrogators insisted were promoting revolution. She said that when they finished abusing her, they taunted her husband with it, and then shot him.

Mahret soon realized that Rekik was correct in her assertion that it was mostly universal need that drew this diverse group together. People she talked to stressed this. The knowledge that they had faced the same sorts of persecution at home helped many to bond in the newer Kibera environment.

Mahret determined that in the future she would continue to reach out to all of them.

A few days after their arrival, she met a woman named Milka at the big Toi market in Makina about an hour's walk from Dawit's place. They were both standing in line to buy fruit.

Milka was multilingual. Her background was Swahili, and she spoke English as well as Oromo fluently. Once she discovered that Mahret was from Oromia she conveniently slipped into her original language.

Milka spoke with a rather peculiar posh accent that Mahret found both amusing and attractive.

"You're new here, aren't you?" Milka asked her. "I've seen you a couple times looking around. I think you must be planning to stay for a while. Some people think they'll be getting out soon after they arrive. Almost none ever do."

"Yes, we'll probably be here longer than suits me. At the moment, I have no idea where else to go."

Mahret and Milka continued to talk while they purchased provisions and then, afterward, as they walked around the marketplace. Mahret found herself telling her friend almost the entire account of her life in Oromia and her hasty escape.

When Milka told her story, Mahret could see that she must be a rare species in Kibera. She told her she had an education in social welfare from the University of Nairobi.

"What did she say? A master's degree, I think."

Her husband, a university professor no less, had died suddenly of a heart attack almost a year earlier. When the autopsy showed that he had AIDS, Milka was shunned by "polite society." She was also let go from her work as a social statistics analyst at the university and could not find another job.

She was lucky in one way only. She had not contracted the disease from her husband.

"We quit having sex. I think he played himself out, taking advantage of his students."

Milka and her husband had saved up some money, which she now lived on, but it was dwindling fast in greater Nairobi, so she had no choice but to uproot and move to Kibera with her two kids.

She said that she had enough savings to survive for quite some time without taking a menial job, given the reasonable cost of living in Kibera.

"I'm trying to find something in Nairobi that recognizes my credentials. It's not easy, I'm tainted by my husband's disease; they think I'm a miscreant too."

"A what?"

"A cheating bastard."

Milka was to provide vital life support for Mahret. Her education gave her an advantage over most other women as she could and did read fluently any printed sources that came her way. She maintained a broad interest in public and political affairs she had developed in her previous life. And she could speak to many subjects, including how to deal with most challenges relative to life in Kibera.

She also helped Mahret connect more closely with all the other women who lived in their compound.

"People seem so nice here," Mahret said after meeting several of them. "It's amazing; everybody must be worried about how they're going to keep life and limb together, and yet they're so nice to me, and to each other too."

"They have to be," Milka told her, "we all have to be. I've only been here for six months. The first glimpses I had into the life of a working mother in Kibera were staggering. When I first arrived, I spent a lot of time talking to Janet, who had lived here for more than twenty years. I immediately adopted her attitude, and so far, it has worked out. She sees her duty as bolstering her three kids with every shilling or birr she can get her hands on. Janet would scrounge for money to buy food while taking care of domestic needs. A pile of laundry that I used to toss into the washing machine and ignore took her a full day to clean—fetching water for the tubs and bending over for hours scrubbing the dirt off.

But she never complained.

The day after I met her, Janet found herself short of school lunch money for her kids. She took a day off from her part-time job at a baker's stand and spent the last shillings she had on second-hand clothing in Nairobi, which she then brought here to sell. She was lucky that day; someone came along and bought her whole supply; she managed to make a small profit.

Her kids got to eat."

"Doesn't she ever worry that sometimes she won't be able to provide for her children?"

"I asked her that. She said, 'No, I don't worry. I know *Waqaa* will provide.'"

"I immediately emulated her attitude towards life, and her spirit."

Milka admitted though that she had some "significant advantages" over Janet. She told Mahret that her daughter, Hilani, at twelve years of age, was able to help her with household tasks, so she didn't have to work as hard as Janet at those things; and that both Hilani and her son, Evra, thirteen, looked after their own personal hygiene and even washed their own clothes when necessary and hung them up to dry.

"They're both getting self-conscious about their looks, so they tend to stay ahead of me when it comes to their wearing apparel."

"Their what?"

"You know, their clothes."

Milka stressed too that people here could never afford to forget certain realities. There were dangers in slum society that no amount of communal spirit and cooperation could overcome should they not take essential precautions. She warned her most of all of the risks from men coming in from outside the area at night.

"They look for something worth stealing, or sexual prey or they sell drugs."

Milka sounded much like Rekik when she emphasized the importance of accepting everyone no matter their background.

"You must get to know them all, not as other religions or other races but as individuals who share your challenges, your fears, your quest for survival. You will soon see they do not fit any preconceptions you have about them. They are men, women, and children. They have individual personalities, and most want to help you if you help them."

"This is so different from my life back home," Mahret told her. "On the farm all the people were the same. We were all Oromo farmers. We all spoke the same language. Most of us even attended the same Church. We prayed and worshipped together. And we celebrated together too.

We didn't like any people we considered different. In our area, we had lighter skin than most other Ethiopians. We thought we were special, reason enough not to trust outsiders. How could we have been so narrow?

I still can't get over the fact that, here in Kibera, I even befriended a real live prostitute—and it will be for life!"

Milka just laughed.

"You're learning fast, my dear friend, I have so much more to teach you."

Chapter 21

SETTLING IN

What Mahret was most relieved to discover in her new neighborhood was that all the adults took responsibility for all the kids. The mothers and fathers, but especially the mothers, combined their efforts to watch over them. Some of her neighbors worked, and on any given day, others spent much of their time hunting for work or digging through the garbage dump looking for things to sell or eat. The rest, those who stayed on the streets of Mashimoni, were a sort of tribal village, a huge extended family.

When one of the younger children got hurt playing football or falling out of a tree in the field by the river, someone was always available to help them. An adult would comfort them, clean their wound, if necessary, and treat it with one of the cheap disinfectants the "doctor" at the drugstore prescribed. When they could, someone with a little extra food might also feed a kid left without lunch because a parent failed to make it home by noon.

Knowing this helped Mahret feel more relaxed than she had been. She felt more so again after Milka told her about the role a local youth gang played in keeping the peace in the village.

"We defend ourselves against outsiders; we all donate a tiny bit of money. It's not much, but it adds up and makes a difference. We employ a group of tough young men who help protect us and all the other compounds in Mashimoni. They're able to keep all the derelicts, thieves, and druggies out at least during daylight. Because of them, as long as the sun is in the sky, your kids can play unattended. They'll normally be perfectly okay.

Most districts have these gangs. Mashimoni's gang is led by a young man named Hashu, who formed the group three or four years ago. He started gang activity a year or two earlier under a leader in Log Ganga. He got caught up in some kind of group warfare and decided to move to Mashimoni to get away from it. Apparently, he's still only twenty-one-years old. Members of his troop can almost always be seen standing guard on the corners of the streets in Mashimoni.

They're a kind of police force, and we need them."

"Are you saying we don't need the police then?"

"Well, it's not quite so simple. In the so-called 'temporary settlements' like this, people report crimes to both the regular police force and their gang. It depends on the type of crime. Murder and very violent rape usually go directly to the police because those crimes are so serious and might bring in interference from the justice system outside. The police here are afraid not to seem to be dealing with them, but things like muggings, theft, break-ins, drug trafficking, and let's call it 'regular sexual abuse,' we bring to Hashu, or to one of his trusted officers. There's no point going to the police for such matters because they do nothing about them. They don't even try to recover property that gets stolen.

The level of corruption in the police force is a huge impediment to local community crime enforcement as well. We just do not believe the police are an honest law enforcement agency. They take bribes, and they kill people who would inform on them. Yes, and they're likely to shoot anyone they suspect of a crime."

"I see," Mahret said. "We never trusted the police at home either. They're controlled by the EPRDF, and they do all those terrible things, all of them! When people try to stage a protest about anything the government does, like take our land, police just shoot into the crowd and kill anyone who gets in the way. I think they shoot anyone who either opposes what they're doing or who might get off in court for a crime they, maybe, didn't even do.

But here, most of you see Hashu's gang as a necessity, is that right? They're the ones who make sure the amount of regular crime is kept to a livable level?"

"Yes. When they take a criminal, the gang might hand him over to the police, but they might just beat him up and leave him lying on the street as an example. If he deserves to die for his crime, though, they're more likely to turn him over to the police. If a guy who commits one of the crimes comes from this district, they might banish him too. This keeps our area clean and civilized. Everybody likes this; we all feel safer."

"People in these areas want their gang then?"

"Yes, but there is sometimes resentment against them too. First, they are known to shoot people they see as criminals too, although I must say they have a much better idea than the police about who's guilty and who's not. And they tend to be fairer when dealing with local suspects than with those that come in from outside.

The gangs are resented by some though for taking over control of vacant shanties and electricity and water lines. They charge for these services, and when times are tough, people think they charge more than they should. The gangs argue that they need the money to protect the communities."

"They act like these things are theirs?"

"Yes, and on top of those charges, Hashu makes every house pay a fee per month for security, and since you don't want to have problems, you just pay it. You have no choice.

Even though they pose as security providers, they also engage in some criminal activities. If a man refuses to pay their fee, Hashu's men might break into his house, beat him up, and tell people it was a criminal that did it, and that they would have prevented it if he had paid like everyone else. Drugs are a huge problem outside the fences, and there is a feeling that Hashu's guys themselves are involved in that trade too."

"So, you're kind of scared of them?"

"Call it nervous. On the whole, we see that these guys are a necessity. The police sometimes start to see them as a threat, and they have shot individual members on the street just to remind them of their power. We protect our gang by helping to hide its members from the police when they come after them – let one of them stay in one of our homes, keep him off the street until the police stop looking for him, things like that.

Gang members sometimes hide individual Mashimonians too when they think the police are being unfair or are just trying to extort money from someone.

Gangs and police cooperate to some degree, however. Sometimes they get together to fight certain crimes. The police also take money from them, you know bribes, to not interfere in their business."

"What about gang warfare? Isn't that sometimes a problem here?"

"Yes, in some districts, gunfights break out when the local group gets challenged by another one that wants to take its business."

"Like when they try to take over the *matatus*?"

"Yes, this happened recently in another village."

"I know. My boys and I almost got caught in it."

"As you already know then, this kind of warfare is sometimes deadly, and people can get hurt. But it has not occurred in Mashimoni. Hashu is too strong. Besides fear, he uses race and religion to keep his group together even though the rest of us manage to overlook both. All the families of the kids in Hashu's group are Eritrean Christians. None are Islamists even though there are lots of them around."

"So, are you saying they work against racial and religious acceptance here? They don't understand our ways?"

"No, that's not what I'm saying. Hashu is a sort of enlightened despot. He keeps his group together and strong through race and religion, but he seems to understand that acceptance is a key outside his group. He treats us pretty much all the same."

Milka told Mahret that she, herself, got Hashu to promise to make sure the children were safe and that he told her not to worry, his guards were vigilant.

"They watch out for strangers.

He said, 'no one will touch them,' and I believe him. He's a real dictator, he keeps close control over his men, and they're scared to death of him. Most people here would say that it is vital to have loyal and trusted people from the neighborhood who will voluntarily provide security, so we don't have to rely on external forces."

Mahret managed as a result of her discussion with Milka, and her growing confidence in the local security system, to leave both of the kids to play with other kids for relatively long periods when necessary. Though, she was still not assured enough to leave them all day long as some did.

The main reason she would leave the area was to get a greater variety of goods at a lower price than available in her compound. Many of these goods were available at the central Toi Market in the village of Makina, a good hour on foot from Mashimoni. Toi was big, and it attracted people from all over Nairobi for the great variety of foodstuffs it provided. It also brought in wealthy Kenyans and foreigners looking for all sorts of low-cost goods.

Besides food, Mahret found a cheap source of clothing for herself and the boys at the big market. A reformed and repentant criminal was running an initiative with a group of transformed youth from the slums who, out of past hard life experiences, wanted to give back to the community in the most practical ways possible. The initiative targeted the vulnerable children, widows, single mothers, and old people living in any

Nairobi slums. It provided used, but perfectly acceptable blouses, skirts, dresses, shirts, and trousers free if the need was great enough.

Having brought little more with her than the clothes on her and the children's backs, Mahret was pleased she was able to convince the owners to let her have some things she and the boys needed. She was careful, though, not to push their generosity too far. She took what she felt they would make good use of, and she always contributed a dollar or two as well.

Mika told Mahret about another amenity outside the fence that she considered essential. There was a little Jehovah's Witnesses Church south of Mashimoni near the junction between the Southern Bypass Freeway and Langata Road. Mahret began taking the boys there every Sunday for one of the services.

Often Milka and children would accompany them.

After one service, an inspirational appeal for human compassion and brotherhood, Mahret felt a rare moment of hope.

"I think maybe, with *Waqaa's* help, we might be okay living with all the different kinds of people in this horrible place—at least until Barisso gets here.

Or maybe I'm just losing my mind?"

Chapter 22

SURVIVAL

Mahret learned a lot from Milka, and she loved having her as a regular companion even though her friend sometimes made her feel she had embarrassingly poor knowledge of the world around her. They met randomly on the streets and in the marketplace, and they always got along very well. Somehow their personalities matched.

Mahret's one concern about Milka was that she might possibly be too educated for her own good. This thought first occurred to her after a particular conversation during which Mahret told her how disgusted she had become with the men who roamed Kibera districts committing every possible sin.

"If they aren't trying to abuse little children, they're shooting other men to steal their business or they're selling drugs or robbing people who're just trying to survive. *Waqaa* will punish them, I'm sure of that."

"Oh, I don't think so," Milka told her. "They're wicked but I've come to realize they're also blameless."

Mahret was startled.

"Blameless, how can you say that? They do awful things, and they know better. They're just bad and that's all there is to it. You can't argue with that! What are you saying?"

"Oh, never mind. I have a theory about people, but no one thinks I'm right. You won't either."

"You have to finish what you're saying. I want to hear your whole story."

"Okay then, it goes like this: people can't be blamed for their actions because they have no control over who they are."

"What do you mean?"

"I mean, everyone is a certain type of person at birth. Their brains are made (some would say programed) in a certain way to make them who they are and that is what determines how they respond to the conditions they encounter in life. Some will respond violently to slum life and/or by breaking the law; others, who are by nature less volatile or more empathetic, will work with the people around them to make life more bearable for us all. It all depends on the type of person they are, which depends on the brain they inherit when they are born. Over that they have no control. There is no free will. People are doomed to be whoever nature has made them. Everything they do in life is governed by forces beyond them."

"That's silly, by that reasoning there is no good and no bad and no one has to answer for it. Everyone goes to heaven no matter what they do on earth. You can't believe that!"

"I do. I think we need to update our image of God and judgment just as we should take a more realistic look at mankind.

But I told you, you wouldn't agree. Let's talk about something else."

"But you're just guessing. You can't prove any of this."

"I've seen it here in Kibera where we live so close to each other in our compounds. Amongst all these terribly poor downtrodden people, I see the same traits as I did in some I knew well at the university. Mildred's man Garbo is narcissistic. Always showing off his muscles, always bragging about what a great footballer he was, and always obsessed with self. The head of my husband's department was just like that. He constantly had to tell people how many books he had published. He posted his books behind the glass in the main office for all to see. At times, he would come right out and tell people how smart he was. I knew a woman just like Marsi next door too. Outgoing, they talk constantly. In two days after she and her son arrived, Marsi knew everyone in our group. Hilli down the street also has a twin gene with one of my previous friends—shy gene. She seldom ventures outside our fence. When people talk to her, she can't even look them in the eyes, she looks away to avoid it. Mildred is another; like someone I've known, she's by nature endlessly caring. She constantly keeps an eye on the children, helps them organize games, and she looks out for unpopular or shy kids and makes sure they're included—no one is left out.

I'm convinced people have their personal characteristics by nature —they are who they are, and they can't help it. And it's the same everywhere. Marsi's oldest son seemed deeply thoughtful, almost from birth. He was withdrawn, seldom talked to anyone. You would never see him laughing gleefully like the other kids when playing in the streets. At age twelve, he stole off by himself one night, attached a rope to a rafter in an abandoned hovel, and hanged himself. He brought terrible pain to his family, but he couldn't help it. He was born with what psychologists call a suicide gene, a powerful program inside the brains of people in all societies that pretty much makes it certain that one day they will kill themselves. And there seems to be nothing anyone can do to stop them. They don't do it because they want to; they do it because they have to. Like everyone else, these people really are doomed to be themselves."

"But someone who rapes a child. That person knows better. He's just consumed with lust. He doesn't care who he hurts, the child, the mother [...] How can you let him off the hook? How can he be innocent?"

"There is always an explanation, even for him. He has a faulty gene or something that makes him lust after children. He's also narcissistic, in that he can feel only his own urges, and he can't feel the pain he causes to others. He was born devoid of empathy, and he's bound to go through life that way. That's why there are child abusers everywhere. We studied this problem in our sociology class years ago when I was an undergraduate. It is in all countries, from first to third world. They cover it up better than we do but cases keep coming up in the press in countries like Britain and the United States. Think of all those holy men in the big churches in Europe who have molested little boys. They're in a situation where they're relatively free to express their evil impulses (or at least they used to be). It's the lack of restraint that turns that type loose and it will do so anywhere like it does here.

Mahret, you and I share a gene of our own. Despite the fact we're separated by race, education, and background we get along famously. We've known each other only a few weeks and yet we both like to be with each other more than almost anyone else. Somehow our brains are aligned; and we had nothing to do with making them that way."

"But I like you! That's all there is to it."

"I agree, I like you too. We like each other because somethings in our mental makeup match; somethings we had no role in creating, that we don't control.

I think everything you do in life is pre-determined by the type of person you are, and the type of person you are, is pre-determined by the qualities you inherit. We are who we are not because we want to be but because we have to be. That's all there is to it. The longer I live here and watch the people around me, the more I'm sure of it."

"But people change, alcoholics stop drinking sometimes, and people who get in trouble stop doing bad stuff sometimes. People change because they want to take control. Doesn't that prove you're wrong?'

"The only ones who change are those who were born with the ability to change. They have no control over whether they have that quality or not. And most of them don't."

It was Mahret who wanted to drop the conversation now. She wasn't sure of some of her friend's words but felt she got the basic drift; and she was pretty sure it was just the case of someone trained to question things, going too far.

"I see," she said, "I have to go now to get some things at the Toi, I'll probably see you there tomorrow."

Milka smiled as they parted.

"I told you."

When Mahret got to the market, she took a big step toward solving one of the day-to-day problems that plagued all young women and older girls in Kibera. A Somali woman about her age named Malmet had invented a washable, and, therefore, reusable, menstruation pad by hand sowing thick pieces of cotton together with a foam rubber filler underneath. She found both materials in the dump. She sold the finished product to other women living in the community for a hundred shillings. When Mahret came across her stand, she promptly bought four of them.

"What a relief. These will keep me supplied for months."

She told Milka about the pads and she also bought a few.

Cooking arrangements eventually also reduced tensions in Mahret's life. At first, she would do her cooking for both breakfast and lunch each morning after Dawit and family had finished using the kitchen area. However, Baredu was almost unbearably difficult. She had ruled the house previously and seemed to see Mahret as a threat to her authority. She refused to leave the room with Dawit after meals, and she openly complained to him about the way Mahret did things.

Baredu did her best to make sure that Mahret heard her too.

"She's not cleaning up properly after herself. The dishes are always sticky. The whole house smells awful after she cooks. These people have very strange eating habits. She keeps so much food in the cooking area, there's no room for mine."

One morning Milka took Mahret to the Mashimoni community cooker that had very recently been installed as a charitable project by some white people who came in from outside the district. It had a large stovetop for cooking and heating water and an oven for baking *daabo* and other staples. It was something of a modern-day miracle. The only fuel required was a portion of the tons of plastic bags, bottles, and wrappings scattered on the ground and in the garbage streams and dumps all over the district. People were required to contribute a certain amount of "trash" before using the facility.

The cooker provided an opportunity for Mashimonians to make some money. They could bake *daabo* or cakes or muffins in the oven, and then sell them in the marketplace. The system was not perfect. People got to fighting over who should be able to use the cooker at what time and that sort of thing. The managers were going to have to draw up some rules.

But it was a real asset. A private group soon took it over and made a little money for the community by selling time on it. The charges were meager and only applied to the people who utilized it for business. The group did not turn away the impoverished.

"The majority of people here live on less than a shilling a day," Milka said. "They can't afford to be buying charcoal and paraffin. The community cooker is more affordable, and they tell us that it burns at such a high temperature that it eradicates the pollutants. We're seeing a little less trash on the streets too, though obviously, we could still do a lot better on that score."

The cooker allowed Mahret to pretty well stop using Baredu's kitchen. She bought two cooking pans and a very basic set of tin plates and dishes. Now she could cook a whole variety of foodstuffs for the boys whenever she chose, without worrying about complaints.

And she loved the idea of cleaning up the district.

"Anyway," Milka said, "this system has got to work, it's too good to fail."

Mahret's breakfasts were much the same as they had always been—*shaayii, daabo* and *marqaa*. Her central concern for the main dish late in the day was always cost. One that became her favorite was *autée wiki*, a Kenyan stew to which Milka introduced her.

"Kenyan cooks like to make it out of greens sautéed with garlic, diced tomatoes, and broth. The name means 'stretch the week,' because it makes other foods go further."

Mutura, a traditional sausage made of onions, seasoning, and meat was the only pre-cooked food Mahret ever bought. It, too, was a very reasonable and poplar traditional Kenyan dish. When she did buy it, she would use the cooker to heat it up.

After meals, Mahret would wash her dishes and utensils in soap and boiled water.

At first, the only time the cooker was not convenient was during the rains. However, the group controlling it solved that problem by erecting a canvass roof.

If the new facility significantly improved Mahret's life, something that materialized soon after it came along absolutely thrilled her. The only disadvantage was that it required her to leave the compound in Mashimoni a good deal more. And that, of course, required her to put more and more faith in the security system.

It was Milka who introduced her to it.

"I am going to give you some information that will make your life easier still," she said one day. "I'm telling you this because I know you're going to be in trouble if your husband doesn't arrive for a long time. You must keep this secret, it's between the two of us; do you promise?"

"Yes, of course."

"There are several Christian churches in Kibera."

"I know, you showed me our church, and we go every Sunday."

"What I think you don't know is that they and some other churches provide groceries as a charity. Three are the best, Anglican, Catholic, and our Jehovah's Witnesses church. They rotate weekly. I go regularly to them all and usually get enough food to last my three kids and me for two or three days at a time."

"Wow! Will you take me with you?"

"Yes, that's why I'm telling you."

"This is great news, but how do the churches manage? They sure don't get enough from the Sunday offerings."

"There's an organization called Feed the Hungry, a church-to-church charity responding to the scriptural call to care for the destitute. It secures guarantees from the appropriate government agencies, obtaining the right to distribute food through local churches. They have a program called 'Every Child, Every Day.' If you have children to feed and you're poor like us, you qualify. I understand they're now feeding a total of about 150,000 children daily."

"This is wonderful. It could solve all my worries. When can we go?"

"We can go tomorrow. I should warn you that two of the churches are quite far away, and the groceries get heavier when you have to carry them so far; it takes most of the day, and you need to come by yourself. Can you leave the children for a few hours?"

"Yes, I think so. I'm learning to trust the security system more all the time. I've lectured Berhanu about staying inside the fence. He looks after his brother, and since you told me about them, I've been noticing Hashu's guys are on the job every day."

In the afternoon, Mahret went over to the security guy stationed in the area at that time and gave him five dollars.

"My children are Berhanu and Gamado," she said, "I know you've seen them playing with the others. Please tell Hashu I am making this contribution because of the fine job you guys are doing protecting our children."

She was quite sure Hashu would get the message and the money. If Milka was correct about his authority, none of his men would ever betray him.

The next morning, Mahret got up early, filled a bucket from the water tap, and gave both kids a thorough washing outside in the street. Once they dressed, she put some supplies together for their breakfast, and for later in the day, and then set out to meet Milka at the cooker.

Despite the early hour, the village was, by that time, filling with people. In the alleyways and streets, night shift workers were coming home to their shacks. Women who had a little money to spare were going to the market. And a great number of both men and women were setting up in the market to peddle everything and anything from bottled water to pots and pans and plastic flowers. Numerous children were already begging or heading to school or just gathering with their friends for play.

Largely because of the milling crowd, Mahret got rather confused about the streets they initially took outside the compound. However, she felt she had a good enough picture in her mind to find her way on her own if necessary, later on.

"Hopefully, we'll go together most times."

It took nearly the entire morning to get to the Catholic Church.

There, the two ladies found themselves at the end of a line up about thirty feet long, leading to a side door. It took at least a half-hour for them to get inside where they moved along a big table laden with produce. They were not allowed to take all they wanted; just a small bag of rice and one of flour and a few scoops of peas and beans, a small sachet of milk powder, and a can of lamb.

Still, Mahret was thrilled.

"This is so good," she said when they were back outside. "It will make it possible for me to keep my children healthy. My money won't last forever, I've been so worried."

"Yes, I know. I told you about this because you have two children and no other means. I do not tell everyone. If they have any other means of support, they should rely on it. I'm afraid too many will come, and there will not be enough left at the churches for those of us who need it most. From now on this will be our secret. We should only tell close friends we can trust and only those who might otherwise starve."

Mahret had no problem with that.

"You, Milka, are like someone else I met after coming here. You're a very good person and very smart. I will learn from you. The other one, by the way, was a prostitute."

Milka laughed.

"Really?"

"Yes, but a very nice one, and smart like you."

Over the following week, they visited the other two churches, with similar results.

"I will be okay now." Mahret told her new best friend, "Berhanu and Gamado will be alright. We have a way to live and stretch what we have until Barisso comes."

During their third church excursion, Milka happened to ask Mahret where her cousins get their food.

"They buy it from the market. Dawit has some kind of job in Nairobi. I don't think it brings in much, but it helps. They also have some money; we get fifty dollars a month from our uncle in Australia that he says just pays the rent."

"Fifty dollars for rent? Five thousand shillings. That seems an awful lot. You told me they have quite a good place, but that's high for around here."

"Oh, I didn't know that. I haven't tried to rent on my own. I've no idea what it should be."

"You must look into that."

Chapter 23

GETTING STRAIGHT

One of Mahret's major worries now was Berhanu's mental health. Through the settling in period, she had been concentrating on all the practical challenges of everyday life. But she was not unaware that her older son could still need extra help. He had always seemed to be a tough enough little character. Mahret knew, however, that the many incidents they had encountered since leaving home might well have harmed him mentally. Hopefully, in time, his memories, and with them the fears arising particularly out of that one terrible episode on the road, would fade. But she had no way of knowing how deep the scars were.

She also felt guilty inside that she had not done much of anything for him.

"He's only a little boy; he's faced way too much."

Should she talk more to him about it? Should she ask him if he was living in fear? Did he sometimes feel very angry? Was he waking up at night? Did he have bad dreams?

Or would it be better just to say nothing rather than revive and re-kindle awful memories?

To complicate matters, Mahret's worries about Berhanu merged with concerns she suddenly also had about herself. In her sleep one night, she saw vivid and all too palpable images of the one man pulling Berhanu down the aisle of the bus, his pants down, his penis out and erect. She desperately tried to get to them, to stop him, but something was holding her back; her arms and legs were like lead, she could barely move. She did not know she was asleep, but she understood she had to wake up.

She screamed as loud as she could.

"Berhanu, Berhanu, no, no!"

Her voice was muffled, not clear, not forceful.

Then, suddenly, she did wake up, sitting in bed. Berhanu was beside her, shaking her.

"What's wrong *haadha*, you have a weird dream?"

She hugged him.

"Stop *haadha*, you're hurting me. What's wrong with you?"

"Nothing's wrong, my darling, nothing, I'm okay because you're okay. *Sin jaladah!*"

"Yuk *haadha*; stop talking like that. You're acting like a crazy person."

"Oh *Waqaa*," Mahret thought after sending Berhanu back to bed, "what if that man had raped my precious boy? What if I didn't kill him? How terrible, how incredibly awful? I would much rather die.

Galatom Waqaa, I am so grateful to you for protecting the boys. Please forgive me; please understand what I can't understand myself. Please don't make me go to hell for this terrible thing I did."

Mahret just barely managed to contain her sobs.

She got up, dressed, and went outside to try to distract herself. It did not work. All that day, alternating images kept coming back of the incident and the two men lying on the ground in pools of blood.

"I can't believe it. I was cold-blooded, and out of my mind, and I took a terrible chance. They could have killed me and then Berhanu and Gamado too!"

Mahret feared that Oromo authorities would investigate the case and eventually trace it back to the bus company and then hand it over to the Kenyan authorities. She now knew the Kenyan police were not particularly efficient, and, thus, might well never figure it out, and she thought the bus company might want to cover it up to avoid scaring the public and damaging its own business. The possibility, however, that she could get off free after killing an army officer seemed outrageous.

That day was tough, all day, and long into the following night.

After that, though, other demands forced her to relegate images and fears left over from the past to a psychological storage compartment. Fearful thoughts would break loose from time to time, but mainly in short flashes, which she, herself, would find the strength to control. She had to do this. Two young boys were dependent on her.

Worries about Berhanu did not fade, however. At times his behavior did seem odd. Sometimes he would act sulky and withdrawn. He would become sort of listless, and she would see him gazing into the distance as if in deep thought. At other times, he would fly into a rage over something Gamado did like spilling his milk or wetting their bed.

Berhanu's sense of humor also seemed to wane. He used to laugh about things Mahret did to cheer him up. She would make a funny face or tickle him or put Gamado on her shoulders and prance around like a horse. But this sort of thing no longer worked. Nothing she could do any more seemed to give him joy.

"He's growing up," Mahret rationalized, "perhaps that's part of it. Childish foolishness doesn't appeal to him so much anymore."

Nonetheless, she decided she had to try to talk to him:

"You know what happened that time on the bus trip wasn't your fault," she said one morning when Gamado was still asleep. "That man who grabbed you was just very evil. He was sick in his head. He deserved to die."

"I know that."

"I had to stop him from doing bad things to us. I would never have done it if I didn't think we were in danger. I care so much about you boys, you know that."

"Yeah I know."

"Is there anything you want to talk about, you know, about what happened?"

"No!"

"Are you sure, Berhanu? I hated what happened too. It scared me too. Sometimes I think about it, and I'm scared, really scared. I don't even understand why because we're okay now. I don't understand my own feelings."

That did it:

Berhanu did something he had rarely done from infancy. He started to cry.

Momentarily, he stopped being Berhanu.

"What was that man gonna do to me?" He sobbed. "He was gonna hurt me, and you killed him! Dead! My friend Gamechu said a man once stuck his *tambo* in his bum! Is that what he wanted to do to me? Why did he want to do that? He was crazy! There's lots of crazy grownups. Do all men want to do that? I'm not big enough to stop them! I [...]I [...] don't know what to do!"

Mahret took him in her arms and hugged him.

This time he hugged her back.

She stroked his forehead and kissed him.

"I will never let anyone do bad things like that to you. I will protect you, and when *abbaa* gets here, he will protect you too. He is very strong. He will be here soon. Most men are good, like your father. Only a few of them are like that awful man on the road. Here in Mashimoni, Hashu and his guys keep those types away. We're safe, and we will be even safer when *abbaa* is with us."

Then, just like that, Berhanu went back to being himself. He stopped crying, pulled away from his mother, wiped his eyes, and headed for the door.

"It's okay. I'm alright."

"Remember how much I love you."

Berhanu just kept going.

"Please, my husband, come home. I can't do this on my own. We need you. I need help."

Chapter 24

A PLACE OF OUR OWN

One thing Mahret knew was that to attend appropriately to both her children's emotional needs, she would eventually have to find a place for the family to live by themselves. She had thought she should wait for Barisso before doing this, but now, after her talk with Berhanu, the urgency seemed more pressing.

"We need a place where I can talk freely to both boys whenever I want. I have to know who they are and where they are inside. And they have to be able to talk freely to me too."

She decided that to put an end to the present living arrangements, she would have to write to her uncle in Australia.

When Uncle Hagos had written her a couple of years ago, he had told her that Dawit knew the money was equally hers should she be forced to join him in Nairobi.

"So, there should be no problem."

She would tell her uncle there was, indeed, a problem.

Mahret still had the envelope with her uncle's address on it.

Writing a letter was not all that easy for her, however. It required a pen, a piece of paper, an envelope, and the right amount of postage. One of Mahret's new friends, Anna, had told her there was a post office a morning's walk away and that if she ever needed it, she would be glad to take her there.

Mahret went to Anna's home the morning after her conversation with Berhanu and asked her if she would be free to make the journey soon.

"I can go today," Anna told her, "this morning I have to help my husband in the market, but later I can take you."

She told her to meet her at the entrance to the marketplace right after lunch.

"Just be careful," Anna told her when they set out, "we have to go through an area just about exclusively inhabited by a small ethnic minority of Kenyans. There has been a lot of violence there. It's usually at night, but maybe not always. A couple of women were raped, walking through the area a few weeks ago. I think it was at night; they should have known better. But it was really nasty; six or seven men, I think."

This bothered Mahret, but she knew that Anna was what people in Kibera called "streetwise." Hence, she felt reasonably secure with her.

"Yes, I remember. Milka mentioned an ethnic group that is very unhappy here. She said that when the Egyptians built a dam or something, they forced thousands of these people who lived in the way to leave their homeland. I guess quite a lot came here."

"All I know is they're bitter. Some are Muslims, but that's not the reason. They're unhappy because the government has refused to give them property and citizen rights, and they're even poorer than the rest of us. A lot are crowded together in certain areas, separate from everyone else; one area we're going through. They're bitter, and they don't mix with the rest of us. They can't. They don't work with people like us partly because they don't get hired. They don't get to know or give a damn about us, and the vice versa is true too. They feel like second-class citizens. They must think we live better than they do—no question we do. Landlords charge them more for rents than others and also more for water and toilets and so on. The best is to ignore them if anyone says anything and don't look at anyone, just keep moving."

They followed the main street for some time and then when it branched off to one side, they took a winding pathway that had the usual stagnant, garbage-strewn stream running down the middle. When they came to a fork in the pathway, they veered to the right, then, on coming to a junction, pushed straight on through.

At that point, they noticed men looking at them, and not in what seemed the friendliest way.

The men had grouped ahead of them on the other side of the pathway.

One of them whistled.

They kept walking.

"I wonder if this happens every time women leave their little area," Mahret whispered.

"Pretty much," Anna said. "But most of these guys are not as tough as they want us to believe. Ignore them."

"Hey there ladies," one of them shouted in Swahili, "why you don't come over here? We gonna treat you right. Come on, we like Ethiopians, we help you."

Two of the men crossed the path and stopped in front of Mahret. As she tried to push her way past them, one grabbed her by the arm.

"Hey, beautiful lady, you want to make some real money? Buy your kids all the good food they can eat, send them to school. I have a job for you; night work. What do you think?"

Mahret twisted her arm loose and pushed past him.

He persisted.

"Don't ignore me, my lady, you better think about the offer; if you work for me you live in luxury. No more hunger, no more worry. What could be more natural? All you have to do is use your beautiful body for a living; show them your lovely tits and ass, and they'll go mad. You'll make lots of money? You'll be like a queen compared to your friends."

A female voice emanated from somewhere in the distance.

"Jamal, you leave them alone, or you don't come home, you hear me, you don't have no family no more!"

Mahret and Anna didn't look, but they could tell the men stopped following them.

"I wonder how far they would have gone if the wife wasn't so tough," Anna said.

"I wonder too. The good thing is women in these parts have learned they have to be tough. Thank *Waqaa*! I used to carry a knife. Why did I stop?"

About thirty minutes later, they came to a street just out of Kibera that had an assortment of retail shops with a small building in their midst marked "Postal Service."

When they went into the building, Mahret found a pen chained to a little ledge. There was also a pad of forms. She tore off one of the forms, turned it over, and wrote on the blank backside in English.

Dear Uncle Hagos,

Galatom for sending money to help us in Kenya. We are all grateful. The money has done so much to keep us alive. Cousin Dawit always take all the money and he say that it all gone on the rent. Can you please send me half as Dawit does not share and I am have trouble to get enough food for my boys? Rent in Kibera much lower than $50.00. You reply to Post Office in Kibera, and so I get your answer.

Galatom.

She printed her name at the bottom, purchased an envelope and a stamp, addressed the envelope, and gave the letter back to the clerk to mail.

"How long it takes for mail to New Zealand?"

"It varies, but I would say about a week."

"If a letter comes for me, can you send it to the Jehovah's Witnesses Church south of Mashimoni near the junction between the Southern Bypass Freeway and Langata Road?"

"Yes, it will cost you five shillings. Just pay me and give me your name. And write down the address for the church."

When they finished at the post office, Mahret told Anna that she needed to pick up some flour for the next day.

"Do you think we could go home by the Toi?"

"Yes, I know the way, and I can take you," Anna said, "but we better hurry. We don't want to be on the road when it gets dark. I don't think those guys have the guts to bother us again, but who knows for sure."

When they got to the market, they found a stall with large barrels of grains—wheat, barley, teff.

"How much for a kilogram of wheat flour?" Mahret asked the man behind the makeshift counter.

"Sixteen birr."

"But sir this is so expensive."

"Sorry ma'am, but that's the price. I have to buy it in the country. Crops are poor because of the drought last year. There's little supply. You should be happy to have any. Pay the price or move on."

"Alright then, I will take a half kilo. But this is robbery."

"Okay a half kilo is ten birr."

"You mean eight birr."

"No mam, you pay extra for being so cheap. You want a better deal, you give me a better deal."

Mahret sighed and handed him ten birr and then opened her bag for the man to pour in the grain.

"Hey, that's not a half kilo. That was not a full scoop, give me some more."

"Move on mam, you're making me angry."

"Hey mister, you're cheating her," one of two women standing behind her shouted, "give her more. You cheat us all the time, too much. Give her a full scoop."

Other women began to gather around the stall.

"Okay, okay, you're taking advantage of me but here, here is some more. Now go away from here."

Mahret closed her bag and then moved behind the two women and watched closely as they too purchased wheat flour. They had no trouble. When he had served them, the man looked over at her.

"What's the matter with you? I don't cheat; you're a troublemaker, go away from here."

"Gladly," Mahret told him. "But don't worry, we'll be back."

At that point, Anna rejoined her.

"It's getting late, we better go."

The first part of their journey was uneventful. They were apprehensive when they got to the place where the men had caused the trouble.

"Looks like they're not still hanging around here." Anna said.

"I hope not."

At that moment the one who had bothered Mahret before came up behind her, grabbed her, and pulled her into a sheltered spot between two shanties. Another followed with Anna.

The one holding Mahret started touching her. She struggled and tried to pull away, but he was too strong. He kept right at it.

"Stop," she yelled. "Leave me alone."

Mahret felt hands on her breasts, his penis against her bottom.

"Hey lady, let's fuck. Fuck me, and you'll find it a lot easier to get into the business. Ya just have to get started. I'll give you fifty shillings. Your first client is always the hardest. After that it gets easy, life too."

Mahret twisted loose from his grip, and relying on what had saved her before, turned to face him and kneed him in the groin. When his hands dropped, she slapped him in the face as hard as she could.

But then another man grabbed her from behind.

The first assailant straightened up. He turned back toward her, pulled up her *qamis* and stuck his fingers in her vagina.

She screamed; he screamed louder.

"You, fuckin bitch. Now we're both gonna fuck the hell out of you."

The two men threw her to the ground.

One held her down while the other pulled his pants down.

"Fun time!"

At that moment, a voice emanated from somewhere above. It sounded forceful and angry, and it seemed to be heaping wrath on the two men. The men hesitated, but they didn't stop.

Then something amazing happened. Mahret saw a hunting knife appear against the throat of the man on top of her.

She heard a female voice.

"You bastard, did ya think we wouldn't be watching you? Get off, or I kill you!"

A woman was holding the knife against the man's neck with her one hand, and she had her other hand around the back of his head. When the man tried to pull away from the knife, it moved with him drawing some blood.

"You go home now, say goodbye to your kids, then you get out. You don't come back no more. We're gonna keep your type out of here for good."

"Okay, okay," he yelled, carefully getting to his feet, the knife still at his throat.

"Go on, bitch," he screamed at Mahret as he pulled up his pants. "Go back where you came from. We have no room for you here. I see you again, no more fucking, I kill you."

The woman let the man go keeping the knife at the ready.

"You get out of here."

He turned and defiantly walked slowly away. The man who had held her down was backing away from two other women.

Another man got off Anna, pulled up his pants, and followed his friends.

Anna's top was torn, and she had a large scrape on her forehead. One of the women helped her cover-up by tying some of the torn strips together.

Mahret fought the urge to cry as she turned to the three women who had helped them.

"*Galatom*," she said in a weak voice. "*Waqaa* will thank you. You are very strong."

"Are you okay?" one of them said to Anna. "They hurt you? If you come to my house, I can wash your head and put a bandage on the cut. I'm so sorry, our men are pigs."

"I'm alright," Anna said, "I'll be okay. He hurt me; he got his *tambo* inside but just barely. He didn't manage to finish."

"We'll be alright," Mahret added.

"Are you sure?"

Mahret turned to Anna. "Are you sure?"

"Yes. Let's go."

They both bowed in thanks to their rescuers.

As they headed toward home again, they could hear a masculine voice yelling obscenities at them.

But that soon stopped.

Mahret felt weak, and her legs were shaking.

She reached over and took hold of Anna's arm. She was shaking as well.

They continued to prop each other up as they made their way down the road.

"The fence is our shelter," Anna said when they were finally back in their compound.

"Yes, I know, it certainly is. Life itself has made that clear to me."

"I must find my knife and keep it with me from now on."

"Me, I'll get one too."

Chapter 25

SECURITY

Anna and Mahret met at the cooker a few days after their harrowing experience. They sat down together over *shaayii* at one of the tables.

At first, they avoided talking about what had happened. They broached all sorts of other subjects, the weather, the price of food, the kids, but not that.

Finally, Anna said, "it's amazing how much a woman changes when she has to live in Kibera. If what happened to us the other day had ever happened back home on the farm, I wouldn't have got over it for a long time. I would have been mentally sick. What's the word?"

"I think Milka would say something like traaaumatized. She would tell us that on the farm, a thing like that would have traaaumatized us."

"Yes, well, whatever, but look at how fast we get over it now. Here we are so soon, carrying on just like we did before. We're back to looking after our homes and kids as if nothing much happened. Back on the farm, I would have wanted to kill myself."

"True, and we would deny that those guys touched us because we'd felt like spoiled goods; we'd have been lying to ourselves. We'd have been afraid our husbands wouldn't understand, they'd hate us some; yeah and we would have thought maybe they had a reason. Now we just carry on with life. We don't really want to talk about the attack. We're pissed that those guys got their dirty hands on us, but we don't go crazy. Even if they'd totally raped us, we'd be able to go on with life. They only hurt us, our pride, not our family, our kids."

"The reason is that we've been through so many serious things, life and death things, times when we thought we were afraid we would see our kids starve or get hurt or abused or killed by murderers. I think we all know the threats are just about always around us. We've changed our minds about what's serious."

"We were so lady-like back home," Anna added. "We thought we had to be. We've changed. All of us women here have changed. And in some things, we'll never go back. We've got our worries lined up straighter."

And that was the last they ever spoke of it, or even gave it much thought.

"We can't afford luxuries like anxiety or depression," Milka later told Mahret.

"Only rich people can afford such things."

Most mornings after breakfast, Mahret's first task was to divide up the *daabo* she'd made the day before between her sons. Then she would go to the cooker and prepare some food and boil water for their mid-day meal. She would give Berhanu charge of Gamado, with strict instructions about how he had to keep a constant watch on the only brother he had. Her more specific directions were straight forward. Make sure they stay within the fenced area and away from the streams of garbage, the throw toilets, the wire, and, most of all, the poisoned needles. And they should not under any circumstances drink water from one of the outside taps.

"If you get thirsty, either go home and get water from the pail or ask one of the adults you know watching you boys play, or just wait for me. I should be back pretty soon."

Increasingly, her faith in the security system in Mashimoni grew. And she began to take whatever time she needed to do what she'd set out to do before coming back home.

"Berhanu seems okay without me, and he and Gamado don't want to come with me even when I'm not going far. They prefer the company of their friends over their mother. Who could blame them? They love playing outside with so many other kids, let them be kids. Maybe that's the best way to heal."

One Monday morning, an incident both shook Mahret's faith in the security system in Mashimoni and, at the same time, strengthened it. It also underlined the fact that children could, at times, be subject to the same dangers outside their compound that she and other women faced.

And in broad daylight.

When Gamado and Berhanu were on their own, they would play in and around their home street. One day, when several kids were playing hide and seek, Garfield, who was about Gamado's age, went off on his own to find a place where no one could find him. He got to the rusty fence, crawled under it, and then under a big empty box a fruit merchant had left turned upside down on the ground.

Ostensibly, out of nowhere, a stranger appeared and lifted the box off him. He picked the boy up, threw him over his shoulder, and started down the street with him. The man was laughing, and he tickled Garfield as he went as if he were just playing a friendly game. The boy giggled and did not struggle or scream.

Berhanu was "it," which meant he had to close his eyes, count to a hundred, and then try to find the other kids. As he finished his count, he caught a glimpse of the man hurrying off with Garfield.

He immediately sensed something was wrong.

"Hey mister," he yelled, running after them, "put him down, leave him alone."

The guy tried to run, but the extra load slowed him, and Berhanu managed to catch up. He was terrified, but somehow, he found the strength to make a flying leap at the guy's legs, causing him to stumble and drop Garfield. A Muslim man named Muktar, heard Berhanu yelling. He jumped the fence and ran over to help him. When the predator got up, he knocked him down again and started punching and kicking him.

The guy just lay there in the dirt with his arms clasped around his face and head. Then, two of Hashu's henchmen arrived to finish the job.

"This will teach you to stay away from our kids," one of them yelled.

"I have money," he said, "please, I will pay you."

Impervious, they beat him repeatedly in the torso and face. The three men then took Berhanu and Garfield back to the fenced area, leaving the guy lying in a bloody heap on the ground.

Later that evening, the man (or body), disappeared, and no one ever saw it again.

When Berhanu told his mother about this incident, she grabbed Gamado and hugged him hard.

He didn't like that sort of thing any more than his brother.

"You're hurting me!"

"It's just the pain of love," she told him.

"What's that?"

"You're so dumb!" Berhanu said.

This incident bothered Mahret, but it also provided some sense of sanctuary. There were people on the watch that they could trust and who really would be around to protect everyone. The key, once again, was obvious.

"Stay inside the fence."

The policing system, both citizen and quasi-professional, had worked.

Mahret stressed this to her sons.

"We're safe here. Your little friend should have known that if he had stayed in our area, this wouldn't have happened. Our people and our guys protect us, but they don't expect you kids to go outside the fence. Hashu's guys are strong; our neighbors care about us. They'll stop anybody from doing bad things around here. You won't have to protect yourselves. They will."

However, she asked Berhanu if he wasn't terribly scared when he went after the bad man.

"Yeah, I was, I threw up when I was running, but I couldn't help it. I kinda thought Garfield was me. I had to save him! I think I thought I was saving me."

The next time Mahret saw one of the gang members watching over the street, she approached him.

"Hi, my friends here tell me what a fine job you boys are doing. I have two children; you helped my oldest, Berhanu, stop a child rapist. Anyway, I donated to your cause once before, and I want to again. Can you see that Hashu knows about this?"

This time, she handed over an American ten-dollar bill.

For Berhanu, the incident naturally revived the memory of what had happened on the trip from Oromia. He hated the fear that was constantly in his mind, but he, like his mother, also gained some faith that life in the compound was quite safe.

"The fence protects us," he would tell the other kids. "Hashu and those guys too, and no one can do anything to us when they're around here.

They wouldn't dare."

Chapter 26

A KID'S LIFE

Berhanu lectured the other kids about security inside the compound, perhaps as much to emphasize it to himself as to them. He did feel an anxiety that he would not gain complete control over for years. His feelings were both rational and hysterical. However, he managed, for the most part, to keep them at bay mainly because over and above the security issue, there were some very good features about life for kids in Mashimoni. On the farm, he and Gamado had only a couple friends around their age close by on any given day; now, there were always at least a dozen. The kids they played with here were more than just playmates. They were their comrades in life. Like them, they all had at least one parent and lived outside without adult interference most of the time. They plotted, experienced, and enjoyed their days together.

Each morning they would all get up after their parent, or parents, had left, find and devour whatever they had or could get for food, and then head out to join each other. They not only organized their own forms of entertainment, they also made up their own rules for everything from the sports and games they played to the way they treated each other. In the process, they fashioned their own value system concerning right and wrong, and they gained their own sense of identity as the kids of Kibera.

Their passion turned out to be football. For a playing field, they at first used the middle of the street behind Milka's shack, which was normally less crowded than most of the other streets. The adults who lived along the street cooperated by staying off it as much as they could when the kids were playing.

Berhanu and another bigger kid named Wasco usually acted as captains. And they took turns picking their players, one of them going first one day and the other the next.

When Berhanu had to pick his brother, he would belittle him.

"Okay, Gamado, I guess I got no choice, I gotta take ya. Try not to embarrass me, ya little spoof."

When Gamado would hang his head and look like he was about to cry, Berhanu would back off.

Nonetheless, the next time he got him, he would demean him again.

But if anybody else seemed abusive to Gamado, Berhanu would threaten to beat his brains out. In a short time, everyone understood that, and no one did.

An aspect of life the kids liked besides football was that various charitable organizations appeared from time to time to bring them great new adventures. One morning, a group of young men and women from outside Kibera came through the area with a camera, evidently doing a program on the living conditions. They interviewed adults walking through the area, and when they came across the kids' playing football, they stopped to videotape the game. Two days later, a man appeared while the kids were playing and gave them a real soccer ball, with a tire pump, adapter, and air pressure gauge so they could keep it properly inflated. The kids were thrilled. Berhanu instantly became the unofficial keeper of the ball. From that point on, all the boys and some girls too played with more enthusiasm than ever.

Berhanu took the ball home every night and serviced it meticulously.

The regularity with which the kids played football after that brought concerns from some adults who needed to navigate the one street.

"It's great to see the kids playing," one of the men said, "but it's getting impossible to visit outside with our neighbors when their games are on. The tiny ones on our street who aren't old enough to play can't go outside at all. Since they got their new ball, the older kids want to play all the time."

In a community meeting, the adults agreed that when any one of the men was at home and available, he should accompany the kids to a grassy area along the Nairobi River. It was beyond the fence, and he should therefore stay and watch over them while they played.

The kids felt safe enough under adult supervision, and they all preferred the grass field to the street. It was a softer surface for falls, and it seemed much more professional. They played in an area between two sewer streams flowing across the field to the river. Their playing ground was also a hundred yards or so from the heap where locals commonly dumped their garbage.

"This can't be healthy," Milka told Mahret. "But I suppose the air's not much different than on the street."

One Saturday morning, a group of young adults known as the "slum watchers of Nairobi," appeared with roller skates for the kids. They gave them each a pair, erected moveable baskets on the street where the ground was hard, and coached them in a game of roller basketball. The kids played for a couple of hours before the group took the skates back and left with the promise they would return when they could on Saturdays.

The kids loved the game, and most Saturdays, the slum watchers kept their word. The kids played at most once a week, so there were few complaints about them taking over the street.

Also, a group associated with the Red Cross enlisted Berhanu and Gamado and a few other kids to clean up the neighborhood. They picked up garbage and painted the exterior of some of the shacks in their compound in fresh colors. The kids enjoyed this too in part because the description a member of the group read to them made them feel they were participating in something extraordinary—almost heroic:

"When we can change the environment, we can change people's minds. The community begins to see the common interest in keeping their neighborhood clean and safe. Many neighborhoods can be turned into much nicer places, and you kids can play a huge role in making it happen."

The kids were even more thrilled with the little bit of money the group paid them— change of their own to purchase candy and other treats.

To their great disappointment, the program had to shut down after three weeks, ostensibly, for lack of funds.

However, with soccer, roller basketball, games like hide and seek, and just goofing off, the shantytown provided a reasonably satisfying existence for kids; at least, that is, for those who were able to get enough to eat.

And the communal approach saw that in this compound, most of them normally did.

Chapter 27

HOME AND SCHOOL

Ironically, considering Mahret's determination from the beginning that her boys would never go hungry, two of the kids who sometimes missed a noontime meal were hers. Most days, when she went to one of the churches for food, and occasionally, when she went to the Toi Market, she would leave in the morning and be away beyond the mid-day period, sometimes well beyond it.

On those occasions, Berhanu and Gamado would leave the house in the morning, play vigorously with their friends, and by lunchtime, they would invariably be very hungry. Sometimes, however, when they went back home for the food their mother had left for them, their uncle would refuse to let them in.

"Go away," he would say, "there's nothing here for you."

Usually, they would not go hungry because one of the other kid's parents would step in and see that they got at least something to eat. The amount was usually meager, but it got them through the day. However, once when no one seemed to notice their dilemma, or, perhaps, some who might have, had no extra food in the house, they were left without anything.

On that occasion, Gamado got really upset. He flopped down on the road in front of the house and cried.

"I'm hungry. I'm starving hungry!"

Berhanu decided he had to do something.

He left his brother with the other kids and then closely following two unaware mothers he recognized, he went beyond the fence to the relatively safe confines of the local market on the Nairobi River. He crowded in amongst several adults at the first baker's stall he saw, quickly reached over, and grabbed a couple of fresh buns and took off running.

Unfortunately, the baker noticed him.

"Hey, stop thief, stop now. I'll have you locked up [...]"

The baker made chase, but Berhanu was able to lose him in the crowd. Fearful every step of the way that he was about to be mugged, he ran as fast as his legs would carry him back to the compound.

After that, he lived in fear the baker would find out who he was and bring Hashu's guys to the house. Luckily for him, the man did not connect him with his mother, and she never heard anything about it.

Berhanu felt like a fugitive, but he was unrepentant. After all, what he did was exactly what was necessary to save his little brother.

"If I ever need to do that again, I will. People cheat me and Gamado, I fight back."

Berhanu did not tell Mahret about any of the times when their uncle came between them and their lunch. He had two reasons. First, Dawit was a big man who scowled a lot, and he didn't want trouble with him. Secondly, he was not sure *haadha* had left anything for them to eat on those occasions. Uncle Dawit told them there was nothing there for them, and Berhanu was afraid that perhaps she just couldn't bring herself to admit that she had run out of money for food.

However, Eden, one of the women who fed the boys once, did tell Mahret. One afternoon when she stopped to talk to her on the street, she told her that she felt sorry for the boys when they were left without something to eat while she was gone.

"They get hungry, and they don't have anywhere to go. I give them what I can, and others will too, but something isn't right."

"What do you mean?" Mahret said, indignantly, "my kids always have enough to eat at home. They don't need charity."

"They sometimes do if I don't give them something or one of the other mothers. It only happens once in a while, but it does sometimes, I think when you're gone shopping."

Mahret went straight back to the house and then out to the street to find Berhanu.

At first, he refused to come clean.

"What happens to the food I leave you boys?"

"I don't know what do you mean? We eat it."

"Listen Berhanu, I've been talking to some of the other mothers, and they tell me that you and Gamado have even gone hungry sometimes when I'm gone. Now tell me the truth. Why does this happen?"

"Okay, it's like this. Sometimes uncle won't let us in. He says there isn't anything to eat and tells us to go away."

"Really? Often?"

"No, just sometimes. When you're gone, we never know for sure if there's gonna be food or not."

Mahret went straight inside to confront Dawit.

"Tell me something, why are my kids left outside with nothing to eat when I'm away?"

"I don't know what you mean. What're you talking about?"

"I think you're lying; of course, you know. When I leave for the day, I always leave lots of food for the kids. But the neighbors tell me that sometimes they have to feed them. Or else they'd get nothing."

"Maybe sometimes they're just having so much fun they don't want to come home."

"That's ridiculous; when boys get hungry, they always want food."

Mahret was angry. She raised her voice.

"Don't you ever do that again. If you do I will write to uncle in New Zealand and tell him that you're not trustworthy, and I will have him send all the money to me. Then I'll decide how much, if anything, you get."

That ended the problem for the time being. It also made it plain to Mahret that her cousin was a cheat, and it convinced her more than ever before that she had to find a home of her own, now, even before Barisso got here.

Soon after the confrontation with Dawit, Mahret received a letter at church from her uncle, replying to the one she had sent him. He told her that since they were all now in Nairobi, he would split the offering and send twenty-five dollars a month to each family. She should go to the Western Union office outside Mashimoni on the fifth day of the month, and her money would be waiting for her.

Dawit was furious when he only got twenty-five dollars. He knew exactly what had happened.

"How could you write to uncle behind my back? We let you into our home, and you do this. You should be ashamed of yourself."

She was prepared for the outburst.

"You let us into your home because you had no choice. You were spending money that was rightfully ours for a long time and living well on it. You told me it was all going toward the rent. You lied. You're the one who should be ashamed!"

She also told him he wouldn't have to worry about them living with him much longer.

"Believe me, we don't want to. We will leave as soon as we can find a place of our own. I'm looking all the time."

Mahret had, indeed, been watching for any shanty that might come available in the compound, and a few days later, she got a chance to make good on her promise. When heading over to visit Milka she noticed a shack that one of the Oromo families had been living in that seemed possibly to be empty. The door was open, and she could see no one inside.

Cautiously, she went in to check it out.

There was no sign of human life, no furnishings of any sort, no beds or covers, no food or equipment.

The house had two rooms, but it was nothing special, a sheet metal roof, dried mud over wood and paper walls and a dirt floor. Mahret could see daylight through a crack in the ceiling where two of the tin sheets came together.

However, she wanted it. She checked to make sure there was a water tap and a toilet close by. Then she went and found Berhanu and Gamado playing in the street. She brought them back to her cousin's house to help collect all their belongings and simply moved the family in.

"This isn't that nice," she admitted, "the floor is just dirt, but tomorrow I'll get some more blankets, and another hide from the guy at Toi and you guys can have your own bed."

Mahret had been in Kibera a total of eighteen full months now, and she was quite thoroughly adjusted to its ways. The following day when she saw one of Hashu's young men at the marketplace, she approached him.

"*Akkam waaritan?*" she said, smiling.

"I am fine," he said. "Is there something you want?"

"Yes, I want to move my family into an empty house behind that first row of houses you see over there. Can you let Hashu know? Perhaps he can help me."

"I will talk to Hashu."

"*Galatom.*"

One of Hashu's henchmen arrived later that evening.

"Yes," he told her, "you can stay here. It will cost you a hundred shillings initial payment, a hundred shillings for connecting both electricity and water, and then 650 shillings for security each month."

"You can hook up the water too?"

"Yes, you will have a tap inside that no one else can use."

"And no monthly charge?"

"No, as long as you use it only for your family. If you try to exploit it by selling water or giving it to others, we'll charge you more, maybe much more."

Mahret thought this was a bargain. The other water tap she had seen was about a half-block away. It was "privately owned," and people had to pay the three shillings to fill a pail.

Her total first payment would amount to eight and a half American dollars.

"Okay," she said, "but you must fix the roof."

"Oh, no, we don't do that sort of thing. We're not repairmen."

"You have to fix it. You can't charge this kind of money if you don't look after the place. When it rains, water will spill all over the floor. Tell Hashu I will give you another 400 shillings."

"Yes, okay then, I guess. I can fix it myself. I'll get some tar and seal it."

"We have a deal then. Can you take American dollars?"

"Yes, of course."

Mahret retrieved a ten-dollar bill and a five-dollar bill from her bag and handed it to him.

"You won't get change; it will cost us money to exchange it for shillings."

"Hmm, a lie, they'll get extra for it at the bank. That's okay."

"You'll be connected this afternoon."

In the days that followed Mahret and the boys were much happier on their own. The place was small and ugly, but they could come and go with ease, and they were far more relaxed.

They felt like a real family again.

"This is the dumpiest place we've ever lived in," Mahret told her boys.

But it's ours."

Chapter 28

OFF TO SCHOOL

Mahret had told herself after coming to Kibera that she would get her boys enrolled in a school once she could deal with the necessities of life. She hoped too that, somehow, whatever school she found, it might offer more than just a basic education for the boys. It might also provide some support for Berhanu's emotional well-being.

Her fountain of all knowledge, Milka, told her that she had enrolled her kids in an organization called the Miracle and Victory Children's Center (MVCC). A Kenyan woman named Monica Akinye had started it up, first as a charitable facility to feed starving kids. Slowly, she had managed to take more and more kids, and despite major obstacles, she was determined to help them get an education. Akinye kept the place running without tuition fees by appealing for donations in the United States, Canada, and England. Her school was not what anyone would call a highly efficient institution, but Milka believed her kids were at least learning the basics of literacy.

The bowl of *marqaa* the school provided each student at the beginning of the day was an extra blessing.

"It's all free." Milka told Mahret, "the opportunity for an extensive, well-rounded education in Kibera is rare, but the MVCC provides over a hundred children a chance to learn to read and write. They choose students because of their living conditions; all come from extreme poverty. For some, the porridge they receive in the morning is their only meal.

You should talk to Monica, she might say no to you, but what have you got to lose? Just make sure you tell her you have no regular earnings."

Mahret did not like the idea of putting on any kind of an act. She struggled with the rationalization that the twenty-five dollars she now received from her uncle was really a handout, not an income, and that she was dependent on charity.

"But okay," she said.

The following Monday morning, she went with Milka to the MVCC. It was about two miles from home.

"The kids have to leave the compound," Milka told her, "but in broad daylight, both there and back, and I always escort them. If your boys get in, you and I can take turns."

What Mahret discovered when she got there was not exactly what she had hoped.

Mostly, the school was just so incredibly under-endowed. It was extremely crowded. It was in some large, interconnected shanties—mud walls, tin roofs, and flimsy plywood doors. It did not even have electricity. The children received instruction in classrooms for which light was provided mainly by taking the cardboard down from the window openings. A lot of the plastic desks and chairs were cracked and broken and propped up with bricks and piles of tattered books in place of missing legs. The toilet for each room was a bag in a bucket outside the entranceway.

Still, Milka believed in the school.

"At the MVCC, teachers have almost no support, but they give it their best, and there are virtually no discipline problems. The conditions are horrible, but the students do learn. They are well-behaved because they know how lucky they are, compared to a lot of other kids in Kibera. They are thankful for the food as much as anything. Achieving focus in a room where three different teachers are teaching three different courses at the same time is not easy, but they do try, and my kids are starting to read some of the books I got for them before we had to move here."

As they walked back to their compound, Mahret told Milka that she was at a loss whether to put the kids in the school or not. First, she was still struggling with the idea of claiming poverty when, in fact, she and the boys were better off than most people in Kibera.

"This will change when your money runs out," Milka told her. "You need to get ready for that. And what if your uncle stops sending money? He could even die. That could realistically happen at any time."

The other thing she did not like was, of course, the condition of the facility itself.

"It's so dark and dirty, and so crude, and those toilets, how awful! The kids could get really sick."

"I think it's no worse than living in greater Kibera," Milka insisted. "And when I talked to Monica while you were looking around, she told me about a new program she is about to instigate. It's about to start to make a significant difference for poor people like us.

She's applied to have the school enrolled in a government initiative called the 'School Feeding Program,' which I read all about in the *Nairobi News* last week. It will give the kids a free lunch to go with breakfast. I think she'll get it too. The Kenyan government started the program specifically to fight childhood malnutrition, increase primary school enrollment, and to give more educational opportunities for girls in particular. Kenya couldn't do this on its own. The excellent news is that there is outside support. It's getting money from the World Food Program (WFP), one of the most extensive and longest-standing school feeding programs in the world."

"Wow, it's hard to believe," Mahret admitted, "this could solve all our money worries. With what we get from the churches, we would both be feeding our kids basically for nothing."

"Yes, that's right. I'm sure Monica will be successful. WFP and the government of Kenya provide a hot lunch to a million and a half children in schools across the country. Why would they turn her down? They give priority to the most food-insecure districts with the lowest overall school enrolment and completion rates. Trust me, that's us. Right now, they've agreed to help the schools in informal settlements in particular.

Again, that's us."

"You're right, I agree. That would be a great help to feed the boys even if Barisso never gets here. I could go on for quite a while on my own."

"Yes, and the extra food will help to strengthen your boys' health. That's the best thing you can do to fight off diseases. You've managed to keep them fed to this point. This will help you cover any possible deficiency in the future."

"I see what you're saying. I'll just have to quit worrying about other things. I'll come back with the kids tomorrow."

"There's something else you might care about, coming as you do from a farm family. A big part of what they're trying to do is stimulate local agricultural production through the purchase of food from smallholder farmers here in Kenya. The problem is that this country's agricultural sector isn't up to the demand. People don't realize that though roughly eighty percent of Kenyans live in rural areas and eke out a living as farmers, poor land quality, chronic water shortages, and severe droughts have put the whole country in a constant state of food insecurity.

The extra demand created by this WFP program they hope will help stimulate changes, including massive irrigation programs that the government is considering. Other countries might benefit as well. What about Ethiopia, for instance, our next-door neighbor? Greater demand for Oromo wheat, corn, teff, could help small farms like yours keep going."

"Okay, okay, you win. I'm going back with the boys tomorrow. I don't think they'll get a great education, but, as you say, if they can learn how to read and write, that'll make it worthwhile."

Smiling, she added, "and all the poor farmers in the world will suddenly be rich. How could I say no?"

They both laughed.

The next morning Mahret woke the boys up early and informed them they were going to school.

Neither was thrilled.

"Ah come on *haadha*, we've got a football game going today," Berhanu protested. "All the guys are gonna be there. I planned the whole thing."

To no avail.

Mahret made them wash up and then she marshaled them down the road.

When sitting in Monica Akinye's office she expected some difficult questions.

She was pleasantly surprised.

"Yes, Milka told me all about you. You're just the type we're trying to help here. Have the boys both back tomorrow, 9:00 AM. Berhanu will start in classroom three and Gamado in classroom one. If you can find something for them to write on that would be helpful."

Mahret got each of them a notebook, pencil, eraser, and pencil sharpener.

The next morning, she took them both back to the MVCC.

"Make me proud," she told them.

"Ah *haadha*," Berhanu said as he started off to his first-ever class with the air of a convicted felon heading to the gas chamber, "I hate you."

"No, you don't."

Chapter 29

BARISSO

It had been a very long time, more than a year and a half since Mahret had heard from her husband. She could not write to him because she did not know even which part of the country or which city he was living in—or if he was still living at all. Barisso, on the other hand, had the same basic address for the Western Union office on the edge of Mashimoni that she did, but he had no way of knowing how to contact her by mail.

Barisso had, however, managed to stay both alive and in Ethiopia during all this time. After sending Mahret and the two boys off on the bus so many months ago, he had headed on foot from the farm toward the city of Shashamane some fifty kilometers west, in hopes of finding a means to get to Kenya. He had picked Shashamane for a reason. The men who bought his land had boasted that the Ethiopian people would benefit. The farms would see their leather, coffee, bamboo, natural gum, and flowers marketed in Kenya. Barisso figured that a lot of the trucks transporting these goods would have to stop to gas up at Shashamane, the closest bigger city to the farm on the main connecting road to Nairobi. He figured that if he could bribe a trucker to take him along as an ostensible back-up driver, the Ethiopian People's Revolutionary Democratic Front would leave him alone. The government supported the companies, so it must support their developing trade.

On foot, the trip to the city was a long one—four or five hours if he walked as quickly as he could. Barisso followed the paths until he got to the main road and then headed west. He knew he was taking a chance. The EPRDF was stepping up its vigilance. It would be looking for any man approximately of military age to arrest for supporting the OLF, or to recruit for its own forces. Neither was acceptable to Barisso. The first would obviously mean certain death, and the second, send him back to an existence he now knew he was unsuited to, and on the wrong side.

At this point, however, he was reasonably confident he could avoid detection as he walked along. It was still dark, and there was very little traffic. When the occasional vehicle did approach from either direction, he could hear it and see the lights before it got close. When possible, to be safe, he would duck out of sight behind a bush or any other vegetation on the side of the road.

At sun-up, the traffic grew heavier, and Barisso no longer had the same advantage. There was no point in diving to the sidelines anymore. There were so many vehicles, and they could see him clearly enough at the approximate moment he could see them. He kept going, however, and just at the point when he could make out the outlines of buildings in Shashamane, a jeep coming from the direction of that city pulled up and stopped in front of him.

The driver jumped out.

"Hey you, where do ya think you're goin?"

Barisso's heart sank. It was the same guy who had challenged him several weeks ago.

The guy recognized him too.

"You spending your whole life on the road?"

"No, sir; just going to Shashamane for supplies."

"I don't believe you. Something's wrong here. What're you up to?"

"Nothing sir, nothing, just getting supplies."

The guy pulled out his revolver and pointed it at Barisso.

"You're up to no good! This is too much of a coincidence. Turn around. I'm taking you in."

"No sir, please sir, I have wife and kids; they will starve."

"I think you're heading for the OLF. You're a volunteer, I can tell. Turn around, hands on the jeep. Do it now, or I'll shoot."

Barisso did as instructed. The man took his arms, twisted them behind his back, and slapped handcuffs on him.

Then he pushed him into the back seat of the jeep behind a screen.

"You stay still; one move and you're dead. I'll shoot you out here in the wilderness and leave your body to rot on the side of the road. We've had enough of you guys."

The next thing Barisso knew, three men in uniform at an EPRDF army headquarters were interrogating him.

Two of the men held him while the other did the talking.

And the beating.

"You're one of those crazy OLF insurgents, right? You guys all quit and ran the moment the fighting started. Now you think you can just pretend you're regular people, get off free after turning against your country. You're traitors, and you think you don't have to pay for it."

"No, sir, I don't know what you're talking about. I ain't no traitor. I love my country. I'm a farmer [...]"

The interrogator hit him in the face hard with the butt end of his rifle, knocking him to the floor.

Barisso moaned and rolled onto his back.

"Stop," he said, "I'm no traitor."

The man hit him again with the butt of his gun, this time on the chest.

"Aaaaah, Aaaaah. No, no, help me, farmer, just farmer."

The man kicked him in the side of the head.

Barisso blacked out.

When he came to, he was lying in the lower deck of a bunk bed, his entire body racked with pain. A man in uniform was bandaging his head.

"Where am I?"

"You're in the barracks; you're a soldier now, for the EPRDF. You're gonna be fighting for your country."

They gave Barisso little time to recover.

The next day they got him out of bed and led him back into an interrogation room. His face was badly bruised, and his body ached with every movement. He was terrified too, but this time they didn't question him.

A man in full uniform, white shirt and tie, gave him a pep talk instead.

"You say you're not a traitor. Then you must want to fight for your country. We want you too. You must make sure you understand how important our fight is. You must learn our objectives so you can fight with your heart.

The following will help you. Read it closely, memorize it, and embrace it. When you can repeat it word for word, we'll make a soldier of you. If you refuse, you're a liar and a traitor. You will be executed as an enemy of your country."

He handed Barisso a piece of paper with state propaganda on it.

The Ethiopian People's Revolutionary Democratic Front is determined to ensure the building of a strong, popular defense force that is fully knowledgeable of and loyal to the Constitution, which stands for popular sovereignty, and protects the country against external aggression. It wishes only to ensure that arrangements are in place to enable popular participation in defense, and to encourage continual enhancement and improvement of popular participation. Our armed forces must be firmly united based on knowledge of and allegiance to the Constitution, its ideals as well as its glorious mission.

The man said, "the government is recruiting the best young men the country has to offer to achieve these objectives in the magnificent cause of a free and independent people."

Out of fear, Barisso memorized the statement as required.

No one ever mentioned it again.

What amazed Barisso as he recovered over the following few days, was how well equipped the EPRDF was in comparison to what he had experienced when fighting for the OLF.

The canteen, which they introduced him to right after they gave him the propaganda sheet, offered a great variety of foods. There were heaps of rice, freshly baked chicken, lamb and beef, every type of fruit he could think of and delicious, freshly baked pies and cakes.

They also issued him a uniform consisting of jacket, shirt, trousers, and boots (which he was to keep polished and clean). And he was subjected to an extensive training program, involving hours of physical fitness exercises, as well as classes on combat strategy and instruction in gun handling and maintenance.

They provided him with an assault rifle as well, but in the first three weeks, no ammunition.

"We don't get that till they trust us," he thought. "They're not that stupid."

Barisso shared the barracks with nine other men. They communicated little with each other, a polite "akkam" here and there and stifled conversations about the weather, the condition of the land, family background… but very little in the way of thorough and relaxed conversation or comradery.

"They're just like me, they don't know who they can trust, and they know some of us wouldn't support the cause if we weren't being forced.

It's hopeless too. They're ordering us to fight with love in our hearts for something we hate."

Chapter 30

A *SLIGHT* GLIMMER OF HOPE

Eventually, after a couple of weeks, the EPRDF issued Barisso and comrades ammunition and sent them for target practice in a field outside the barracks.

Barisso took the target practice seriously and found he still enjoyed it. He particularly liked competing with the other men, and he could see that compared to them, he had a genuine talent. He was pleased too that the instructors consistently commented on his ability to hit head and heart.

Finally, though, he could see things were about to get more serious when the sergeant in charge announced they would soon be involved in real combat.

"Get ready; tomorrow you show your love for your country."

When tomorrow came, four days later, Barisso and a dozen others were issued ammunition and pack sacks and loaded onto the covered back of a big army truck. After traveling for several hours in a line of trucks and other vehicles, they disembarked in bush land in the eastern plains region. They loaded their weapons and then, led by their sergeant, went on a march through the wilderness for several hours.

On this day, they did not encounter any OLF forces. They camped just as night was setting in, erecting tents and then eating some of the rations in their packsacks. Barisso was one of the men first posted on guard. After three hours, he was relieved by one of his fellow soldiers.

He slept in a sleeping bag that night. The next day, after breakfast served by cooks and servants in a hastily erected cook tent, the men packed up and went back on march.

This time they met some enemy forces.

There was a lot of shooting. The EPRDF soldiers clearly had more power mainly in the form of fully automatic assault rifles, and they had little trouble gaining the upper hand. Some of the OLF soldiers were killed or wounded. Barisso kept his head down, firing intermittently over the heads of the "enemy," making sure he didn't hit anyone. Thankfully, in short order, the OLF troops gave up the fight and retreated. Barisso and his comrades gave chase, but they didn't catch anybody. When they returned, their sergeant told them to shoot any wounded OLF fighters.

When Barisso came across one lying on the ground, he shot into the earth. He wanted to do as commanded.

"Surely, the poor bastard must be in pain."

But he couldn't.

During several weeks after that, Barisso experienced combat numerous times. He continued to go through the motions, constantly trying not to hurt anyone.

Barisso hated his life during this period, and he kept watching for ways to escape. When he realized there were none, he suffered bouts of deep depression. Sometimes at night, while he lay in his bed, he would contemplate suicide. He also experienced bouts of severe pain in his arms and chest to the point where he had difficulty catching his breath. On those occasions, he thought he came very close to blacking out.

"I can't stand this, I have to get away. Please, *Waqaa*, help me."

Mercifully, after the OLF troops all retreated across the line back to Somalia, Barisso's unit was ordered to return to the barracks. Some days later, the sergeant announced that several units, including Barisso's, would be going on a mission for several weeks to the Ilemi Triangle far to the south near the Kenyan border.

In a briefing with notes, the sergeant told them that the Ilemi Triangle "is a region just east of the southeastern corner of Ethiopia. Kenya claims it. A dispute has been ongoing for centuries between several semi-nomadic tribes for control of the region. They include the Turkana from the Lake Turkana region, most of which is across the border in Kenya, the Didinga and Topasa of South Sudan to the east, the Nyangatom of South Sudan, and Ethiopia, and the Dassannech from Ethiopia. All these people inhabit the Triangle at various times throughout most years, they all claim it as their own, and they sometimes get into armed conflicts with each other.

Our leaders fear losing some of the territory west of the Triangle and north of Lake Turkana that these tribes sometimes encroach on. They want us to go to the border area and prevent any of the people who approach from the south or southeast from crossing into Ethiopian territory."

Barisso felt that this could be the the opportunity he had been looking for to rejoin his family.

"Maybe, just maybe, I'll get a chance to sneak away from my unit when we're on patrol. The EPRDF has no authority in Kenya. They can't touch me if I can just get across the border."

He figured the EPRDF administrators must have been interested in staking a claim to the Triangle. From a geographical point of view, they could claim that it was at least partly on Ethiopian ground.

The thought of attempting an escape scared the hell out of Barisso. Still, he figured he would have to try if an opportunity presented itself.

"I can't go on like this."

He prayed for help.

On the second evening after the sergeant's announcement, one of the soldiers named Hershi unexpectedly started chatting with him on the way back to their sleeping quarters from the mess hall. The discussion gave him a little more confidence in the possibility of escaping.

"So Barisso, you're a farmer from Oromia too?"

"Yeah."

"You have a family?'

"Yeah."

"They still on the farm?"

"Not now. Why?"

"Just wondering. Mine had to leave. I sent them to Kenya."

"Crops no good?"

"Not good enough. Is that the same with you?"

"Yes, my wife and kids went to Nairobi too."

Barisso was cautious.

"Who is this guy? Is he a spy? Is he trying to interrogate me? Trying to find out if I'm a traitor?"

Hershi took Barisso by the arm and turned him to talk face to face.

"Okay, I'm gonna take a chance on you because me and some others here are desperate. If your family like mine and others fled to Kenya, then you must want to see them again. And the only way that's gonna happen is if you can get outa here, right?"

"So?"

"So, the latest word is the EPRDF is never gonna let us go until we're too old to serve. That might as well mean forever."

"Yeah, I s'pose."

"Okay, I'm just gonna trust you. Here's the plan. You can join us or not, I don't think you'll give us away since we're all in the same boat."

"I won't say nothin."

"Okay, three of us are gonna try to find a way to slip across the border from Ilemi into Kenya while we're on patrol."

"Why do you need me?"

"We figure the more men we have, the more guns we have on our side and the fewer we'll have against us if they go after us; also, a better chance one or two of us at least will get through. If we have to run, we can all head off in different directions, so they don't get us all."

"Makes sense."

"Yes. Are you with us? We are all Oromo, two farmers like you and a vegetable merchant."

"Yeah, I'm in."

"Okay, we'll coordinate when we get there. The government wants us to stop the Turkana people from crossing into Ethiopia. So, there must be a time when we'll be going close to the border. We figure we can get across then. We might go separate ways to confuse them; or, if it seems to work better, we might stay together. It all depends [...]"

Hershi stopped talking in mid-sentence as the two of them drew close to the barracks and other men.

"Yeah, okay," he said, suddenly raising his voice. "I still say I can beat you on the range, I've been practicing, and I've been hitting the bull's eye almost every shot lately. I'll win the money this time."

"We'll see about that, I gotta tell ya, I've been practicing too."

The next day Hershi introduced Barisso briefly to the other two potential escapees. They could not talk things over a great deal with so many other soldiers and officers around. They just agreed that when the time came, they would do the best they could to help each other escape.

Barisso decided then and there, he was going to find a way to escape on this trip. He would do it with or without the others.

"Or die trying."

Chapter 31

NOSTALGIA

Barisso woke up one morning with a powerful urge in his heart to see his ancestral home one more time. The urge almost certainly sprang from the conviction that he would soon be leaving Ethiopia for good.

"Whatever happens," he reasoned, "from the time we head south, I will never see the farm and the life I loved there ever again."

He found himself trying to tell his Sergeant how he felt.

"Sir," he said that afternoon, "I care about the army, and I like being part of a force that defends our lands. I would gladly give my life for Ethiopia."

The Sergeant abruptly cut him off.

"What is it you want, soldier?"

The words poured out of him.

"I want to see my farm just once before we go to Turkana. The government compensated me to give it over to a big, modern company that's going to turn the land into huge open fields with modern equipment and thousands of laborers. I support this, it will make the soil productive again, and it will provide many jobs. I just have a terrible empty feeling knowing I will never again be able to live the life I used to love. On the land I grew up in, I worked the fields and planted and harvested the crops year after year. It's hard to give it up, to go on without something that's so big in my heart. It's in my blood. I want to go back before this happens, before my farm, my birthplace, the home I grew up in disappears from the face of the earth. If I could see it one more time, I would be able to let it go, become a professional soldier for good, no regrets."

To his astonishment, the Sergeant's response sounded like this was not totally out of the question.

"How do I know I can trust you? I could requisition a jeep and driver if I knew you were trustworthy. But you Oromos, you only care about Oromia. How do I know you're not going to defect while you're out there?"

"I would never do that. My farm is gone, I can't go back. There's nowhere else to go even if I wanted to. I'm a soldier now. Remember, I was the best shot of the new recruits. I love this life, for a man it's natural. If you let me go, I won't even carry a gun. The driver can shoot me if I try anything; I promise, I won't."

The Sergeant's expression softened.

"You know what soldier, I was a farmer as well. I sold out a long time ago. I've heard about the changes, but I haven't seen them up close either. Where's your farm?"

Barisso told him.

"I'll tell you what, you can come with me. We'll go tomorrow. I'd like to see it too. Used to be a farmer myself.

I'll have my driver take us."

Smiling, he added, "if you try to escape, one of us will put a bullet in your head for sure."

"Galatom, sir, Galatom. I won't try to escape, I promise."

The next morning a soldier intercepted Barisso as he left the mess hall after breakfast. "Corporal, follow me."

A jeep was waiting for him. The Sergeant was waiting inside.

"As it turns out, we haven't got time to go all the way to my place," he said. "It's way up north of Addis Ababa. We'll go to yours since it's so much closer."

He told Barisso to give the driver directions.

Two hours later, they pulled over on a hillside off the road above where Barisso's family home had been.

It was gone.

"It's too late," Barisso mused, "there's nothing left, of our neighbors too!"

He saw great open fields and powerful tractors plowing up the earth where oxen had done the job.

A man came chugging up to the jeep on a bright, green and yellow John Deere tractor.

"Hi fellas," he said after climbing down. "Hanumantha Rao is my name. I was a sugarcane farmer in India. I'm the head of the company, Karuturi Global. It's leading the revolution sweeping through Ethiopian agriculture. We're gonna bring about a miracle."

"How many farms have you taken over?" the Sergeant asked.

Hanumantha reached out an arm sweeping it across a huge swath of the land.

"We're leasing it from the government, as far as the eye can see. The impoverished little farms are no more. We're planting 11,000 hectares here, to grow rice, maize, and oil palms.

Boreholes are being sunk for irrigation too. We're building roads, and an airstrip will soon allow for crop-spraying from the sky. Besides this new tractor, there are thirty more on-site."

Hanumantha insisted that this was not a very big farm, "relatively speaking.

Further west in Gambella, my company is bringing in 1,000 new tractors to work 300,000 hectares. It's one of the biggest farms in the Horn of Africa, maybe on the continent, 120 kilometers wide, three hours to cross by jeep."

"Can the company make a profit with all the costs," the Sergeant asked, "tractors, irrigation, airplanes? These things are expensive."

"Karuturi Global, the world's largest grower of roses, has negotiated an unbelievably good deal with the government. For its farm in the fertile Bako region, we're paying no rent for six years and then only 135 birr (fifteen dollars) per hectare per year for the remainder of the fifty-year lease. In Gambella, which is more remote and sparsely populated, the rent is only fifteen birr per hectare.

"So, you're basically robbing the country?"

"No, not at all. We're producing more food than this country has ever seen before and jobs for thousands of workers. The company believes the potential is so great that it plans to invest nearly a billion American dollars in Ethiopian agriculture. Ethiopia is a food importer. That will soon stop. In eight years, we will be producing 3,000,000 tons of cereals yearly, mostly maize and rice but also palm oil and sugar, from the Gambella farm alone."

"That's impressive," the Sergeant said as he shook his hand. "We have to get back to barracks, but I wish you good luck. I hope you're able to live up to your ambitions for the sake of Ethiopia as well as your company."

Sitting in the back seat on the way back to the barracks, Barisso cried silently.

"They've wiped out everything? Everything is gone. Cleared off the face of the earth. It hurts!"

He was still sure of one thing only.

"I'm getting out of all this, this whole damned country.

Feet first, if necessary."

Chapter 32

IT TAKES GUTS

The next afternoon, Barisso found himself sitting once again with a group of soldiers in the covered back of a large army truck. Theirs was one of several trucks hauling three units the two hundred plus miles to the northern edge of Lake Turkana along the Kenyan border.

With restroom stops, the trip took most of the day. The last two or three hours, they drove along a rough road that paralleled the Omo River, which flows southward into the big lake. When they were within a few miles of the lake, the truck pulled over and stopped.

Once unloaded, the troops marched several kilometers inland and set up a camp like those they had utilized for battles with the OLF.

Barisso was both excited and very anxious. Now would be his one and probably only hope. Would he have the nerve? Would they kill him?

He felt the pain threatening to return to his arms and chest.

His first chance to escape came on day two.

Barisso's unit went out to intercept scouting tribesmen spotted moving in their direction from below the border. The men followed their Sergeant through parched grasslands dotted with low-lying bushes and the occasional tall tree. Eventually, they saw people heading slowly toward them from the south herding livestock—cattle, camels, and goats.

The Sergeant ordered the troops to stop, climb a few meters up the side of a rise, and make themselves highly visible.

"Stay on your feet so they can't miss you. I want them to see the power behind our words."

When the Sergeant with three guards went down to talk to them, Barisso recognized that the critical moment had come.

While all the other troops had their eyes trained on the negotiations, he and his three conspirators glanced and nodded carefully at each other. Then they quietly backed away from their unit. They got out of sight behind bushes and spread out. Eyeing each other when they could, they moved northward bush by bush. Once what seemed far enough away from the other troops, they pushed west and finally south again toward Kenya.

They came together and then, with Hershi in the lead, crept along until they found themselves next to the Omo River.

All four sat down in the grass to rest and contemplate their next move. While they talked, a shot rang out, and then another. The four dropped down behind foliage.

There was another shot and then two more.

"It's the unit they're coming after us," Hershi yelled. "We have to swim for it guys, they're getting too close; it's the water or death."

They all dropped their rifles, took off their boots and jackets, and bolted for the river.

As Barisso ran, the ground disappeared below his feet. He was in the air; then, splash, he hit the water. Everything went dark. He reached for the light above. At the point when he was about to lose his breath, his head popped out of the water. He gulped and gasped and breathed in the precious air.

Barisso was not much of a swimmer, but as a boy, he had learned to tread water and do a sort of "dog paddle" in the stream that flowed into the Ter' Shet' River.

That was sufficient to enable him to ride the current as it swept south.

A bullet splashed beside him. He put his head down and let the river carry him just below the surface until he ran out of air.

This time when he resurfaced, he heard no more shots.

He paddled along in the current for quite a long time—enough, he thought, to put him out of range.

"They must've given up by now."

He paddled his way toward shore, grabbed the branch of a low-lying bush, and pulled himself to the water's edge.

As he crawled onto the narrow strip of land between the river and the bank, he heard a call.

"Help, Barisso."

Taking hold of the branch again, he waded into the water, grabbed Hershi's hand, and pulled him to shore.

"The others are behind me if crocodiles haven't taken them."

They waited as the two men floated in one at a time.

"This river flows into Lake Turkana," Hershi told them once they managed to make their way up the side of the bank. "The lake is huge. If we can get to it, we can easily cross the border into Kenya, and we should be able to find a road heading down from there to Nairobi."

"How will we make it that far?" One of the other soldiers asked him. "We can't walk all that way."

"I think we can hitch a ride with truckers. There is a lot of trade going on; once we get to the African International Highway, there will be all kinds of trucks doing the trek south."

"That's right," Barisso said. "That was my plan too."

They all tore off most of both sleeves of their shirts with hands and teeth and wrapped them around their bleeding feet.

On such a dark, moonless night, travel was difficult. First, they had to navigate marshlands with swamps and streams. Once they were beyond the wetlands, they decided to stop and rest until daylight.

They gathered pieces of dry wood to start a fire to keep the wild animals at bay.

"We just have to keep throwing the wood on so the fire stays bright," Hershi told them. "Then even the lions won't bother us."

"Lions!" Barisso said. "Are there lions here?"

"There sure are. I've heard of such a thing as man-eating lions too. Most of them are apparently afraid of us and shy away, but I've heard that some get the taste of our flesh somehow and kind of get hooked on it."

"Do ya think that's true?"

"Well, I heard about a lion dragging a ranger from his tent by the head. But I think those things are rare. Maybe just the odd starving lion sometimes comes across some guy sleeping. We'll be fine as long as we keep the fire going. One of you guys watch while I pick up some more wood. If any of us fall asleep, somebody better keep watch and keep the fire stoked."

The men were relatively relaxed now and feeling very pleased with their escape. They did not realize the smoke would actually attract the attention of the lions. They also did not know that the personality of the lion changes dramatically at night when it becomes the true king of the bush and a fearless hunter.

And they did not realize that a pack of six lions was watching them from just outside the circle of light created by their fire.

When they heard the cracking sound of a foot on deadwood, they stared into the darkness around them.

Two big cats stepped into the light and started straight for them. The men yelled and threw burning pieces of wood at them. The lions stopped momentarily, but they did not retreat. Another four animals stepped into the light.

Barisso quickly scaled the big tree sheltering the campsite. The others followed. As the last man started up the tree, a lioness sprang out of the pack and caught his foot with her teeth. She pulled him to the ground and immediately put an end to his cries.

The other three men watched the lions ripping the body of their comrade apart. Once the lions had nearly finished their meal, they began to look up at them.

Barisso thought they were safe because lions do not climb trees. To his horror, the same lioness jumped up on her hind legs, dug her front claws into the bark of the tree, and started up toward them. Barisso climbed as high as he could on the treetop; the two men below him crowded as close to him as they could.

The lioness reached the man on the lowest branch and sank her claws into his leg. He screamed as she dragged him down to face his fate.

To Barisso, the big cats appeared to be basking in the delights of a vile game. Those on the ground looked up, almost smiling as another lioness started to climb the tree. Hershi pulled himself up higher until his head was just below Barisso's waist. The lioness reached for his foot. He screamed and kicked at her. The lioness caught his foot in one of her claws and then clamped down on it with her teeth. Hershi screamed again as she started pulling him down. He grabbed a branch with both hands and held on as tightly as he could. The lioness pulled harder; the branch broke. She jerked her head, flinging Hershi into the air. The instant he hit the ground below, one of the other lions jumped on him and crushed his neck in its teeth.

The big cats chewed on the remains of the three soldiers while Barisso prayed. Soon only a few pieces of the larger bones and some bloody scraps of torn clothing were left.

The lioness started up the tree for the last catch.

As she drew near, Barisso edged a little higher on the thinning tree trunk. He screamed at her and tried to hit her on the nose with a branch. It made no impact. As the animal stretched out a paw toward him, Barisso stood on the branch he'd been sitting on, moving his feet out of her reach. She climbed closer.

The trunk of the tree cracked loudly, threatening to break.

The lioness stopped as if afraid. She backed down a few steps. Then she started up toward Barisso again. The tree cracked again. The animal growled an angry, disappointed growl. This time she backed all way down to the ground.

The fire was nearly out, but daylight was starting to break, and Barisso could see the six animals surrounding the tree and looking up at him.

He was terrified they would try again.

Finally, they gave up and left their would-be prey sitting there, frozen to the treetop. After all, their stomachs were full.

Chapter 33

HELP ME OR KILL ME

Soon after daylight, Barisso was surrounded again by what to him were alien beings. Several strange looking, very dark-skinned men came upon the remains lying on the ground at the foot of the tree and poked at them with sticks. One of them looked up and pointed at Barisso.

The man yelled to Barisso in an alien language.

Still, he could not move. His arms would not let go. The man climbed up to a branch just below the one he was sitting on. The tree cracked as it had before. Still, the man stood up on the branch, reached over, and helped him loosen his fingers, one at a time. Then, staying below him, he guided his feet from branch to branch until they were both on the ground below.

Barisso's legs were not strong enough now to enable him to stand. He collapsed. Two of his rescuers put his arms over their shoulders, lifted him, and then joined and crossed their hands to make a chair. They were strong. They carried him while the others followed.

When they got to their village, Barisso was beginning to regain his senses. He made out his rescuers' small grass-roofed huts. They made him think of home. The men themselves wore cloth shrouds over knee-length smocks. A number were carrying poles like those some men used on the farms back home for herding livestock. Some were carrying spears. Others, amazingly, were holding guns, not just regular rifles or handguns, fully automatic assault rifles like those Barisso had got acquainted with "fighting" for the EPRDF.

"The battle for the Ilemi Triangle must be fierce."

When the men carrying him let him stand on his own Barisso did so for a second or two, and then he dropped to his knees and bowed his head to the ground, signaling surrender. One of the gunmen motioned for him to get up.

"If they kill me, they kill me. I don't care, I really don't care."

They did not kill him. Perhaps they pitied him, or they found him curious, a light-skinned man appearing from nowhere subjected to horror beyond belief. And, just maybe, they recognized him as one who must have defected from the hateful military force that had turned their kind away from the Ethiopian border.

The men handed Barisso over to two women who were wearing row upon row of brightly colored beads around their necks and had half-shaven heads. They gave him some fruit he had never tasted before and some fresh drinking water from a wooden gourd.

They left him to rest in the shade of one of the huts.

When Barisso woke up, it was still daylight. He was still in shock, but he knew he had to take control, or he would never see his family again. He found the strength to get up and then to utter the word "Nairobi" to one of the women.

She shook her head affirmatively and pointed down a dirt and gravel road emanating from the village. She also gave him a pair of what looked like hand-made sandals for his bleeding feet.

He bowed his head in thanks once again and then strapped on the sandals and set out.

Gradually, as he began to feel somewhat better, Barisso was able to pick up his pace. About two hours after he started out, the road turned west through some hills and then jagged mountain terrain. He eventually came to a town, which he would learn was called Lokitaung.

On the outskirts of the town, he made out huts like those he had seen in the tribal village, except most of them had sheet metal roofs instead of grass. Beyond the huts, the town looked reasonably modern. It had houses and stores with glass windows, tile roofs, and pre-manufactured doors, and it had buses, red passenger buses.

As he entered the town, Barisso still had to wrestle with the traumatized state of his mind.

"Come on now, concentrate."

Most of the people in the town were quite dark-skinned like the tribal men and women. But they were dressed in what back home they called modern or western clothes; men wore shirts tucked into trousers; women wore dresses, skirts (and a full head of hair). There was a small general store on the main road. Barisso took out some of the cash he had stashed in the money belt around his waist and bought himself a T-shirt and some shorts.

They were very cheap.

Further down the road at a bus stop, he spoke to a man in Swahili.

"Is there a bus to Nairobi?"

"No, sir, they don't go that far. You have to go south to Lodwar, and then take the public transport on the Trans-African Highway from there."

"How do I get to Lodwar, how far is it?"

"The only way I know is a company that puts people in the box of a truck, standing room only. They do it for 500 shillings. It takes about an hour."

"Five American dollars?"

"I don't know, never seen American money."

"Do they have a good record?"

"I don't know; I'm pretty sure they get to Lodwar safely. The bus from there to Nairobi should be okay, it's regular."

Barisso got some *daabo* in the gas station store after that, and that night, he slept on the ground leaning against the side of a building behind the main street.

In the morning, he went to a gas station on the outskirts of Lokitaug, where he thought, truckers might stop to fuel up. Before long, he saw what he thought would be just about perfect. It was an old truck that pulled into the station. From the sound, the engine seemed to be running fine.

"The driver will need money."

After it stopped at the pumps, the driver got out and went inside the station. Through the railing on the back of the truck, Barisso could see sheep.

"Hi, are you heading to Lodwar by any chance?" he said to the driver when he came back out.

"Yes. Why? I'm going all the way to Nairobi."

"Great, I want to go to Nairobi too. I know a lot about sheep. I could act as your swampier."

"I don't need no swampier."

"I think you do. You have to pass inspection, and if one of the sheep is sick, the inspectors could stop you. Then what're ya gonna do?"

"What I always do."

He made a gesture like handing out money.

"Sure, but you'll be a lot better off if you don't have to. It will cost a lot more if you're dirty than if you're clean and you'll lose the sick ones anyway. Those guys get in too much trouble if they let them through. I can look them over and pull any of them that aren't gonna pass before they see them. We can just shoot them and leave them at the side of the road."

The man thought for a moment.

"Okay, I'll tell you what I'll do. You give me 500 shillings and you pay half the money if the inspectors still ain't satisfied after you sort out the bad animals."

Barisso was in no condition to haggle.

"Okay."

"Alright, it's a deal. But if the Kenyan officials or the police stop you because your papers aren't in order, you pay them yourself. You look illegal to me."

Barisso had figured on having to pay in that case, so he had little difficulty with that stipulation.

"Fine, you get your money when we're on the way. When do we leave?"

"In a few minutes. I just want to get some snacks. Throw your bag in the cab and wait for me."

Ten minutes later, they were on the road. Inside the cab, the two men looked like any other truckers working together to get a load to market in Nairobi. The police and other officials did not like to interfere with commerce for fear of a backlash by business owners and, indeed, the government. They usually just let the truckers alone.

The health inspectors were not quite so understanding. They liked to be paid. When the truck was about ten kilometers from the inspection point at Lodwar, the driver pulled over, and Barisso jumped up on the box to survey the sheep.

"That one there," he said. "It's old and its eyes and nose are running. It's probably got IBR."

"What's that?"

The English name is Infectious Bovine Rhino [...] something or other. It's in the lungs, and it's very infectious. They probably won't let you by no matter how much you pay them. If it's like home, they'd get into too much trouble. If that animal stays, they'll reject all the rest in the load too. They could all have the infection from this one."

"What're you talkin about? 'Bovine,' that means cows, not sheep?"

"That's right it's known as a cow disease, but sheep and goats get IBR too. I know; I had an outbreak a few years ago when I still had sheep. Had to kill them all. Broke my heart. I didn't have the money to buy more."

They pulled the sick animal out of the bunch, but the driver did not have a gun, so they just left it.

"Won't last more than a day or two."

The driver gave 500 shillings to the health inspector anyway just to be sure he didn't look too closely at the rest. When a Kenyan official asked to see Barisso's documents, he handed him a twenty-dollar bill.

From that point, it was straight into Nairobi.

As they got closer to the big city, they witnessed the same sort of highway chaos Mahret had observed two years earlier.

"Crazy bastards," the driver said.

"Yeah, crazy and rich."

"Nothin else to do but kill themselves."

"And each other."

Chapter 34

FAMILY REUNION

Hours later, when Barisso got through to Mashimoni the streets were almost empty. People were staying inside this evening out of the torrents thundering down on their tin roofs.

The rain had been so heavy that Mahret had not gone to the communal stove today. She was cooking tomorrow's *marqaa* over a kerosene flame in the middle of the floor.

She had not heard from her husband in nearly two years and had largely stopped thinking about him. Perhaps he had taken a new wife. Or, possibly, EPRDF forces had arrested, imprisoned, and even executed him. Either way, she had learned to navigate Kibera on her own.

Suddenly, he appeared in the doorway. She was truly stunned. Here he was without warning, right in front of her. She screamed his name though she did not have an emotion prepared for the occasion.

She hugged her husband, sort of, and told him she was overjoyed to have him back with the family.

But she felt stiff, almost robotic.

"Come boys. Look! Your father is here, at last. Come give him a big hug."

Berhanu and Gamado seemed to be in a similar mental state as their mother. They went to their father, and he embraced them. But they both looked hesitant like they were trying to relate to something unfamiliar, almost alien.

He spoke.

"How are you all doing?"

"We're getting by; the kids have enough to eat. But it's not easy. I'm always afraid the money will run out. I go to the churches all the time."

"I don't know how you've done it. This place is like hell. The smell, the dirt, the filth. And what a terrible house. How do you stand it?"

Mahret was surprised to hear herself defending something she usually condemned, at least in her mind.

"You get used to it. It's not so bad. The kids like it here and the people are nice, they help us. I'll show you around tomorrow. We'll get a better place as soon as we can afford it."

She told the boys it was time for bed.

"You can talk to *abbaa* tomorrow. We'll all have lots to talk about. Now *abbaa* and *haadha* have to talk."

Barisso hugged them, again.

"I'm so happy to be back with you guys. I dreamed every night about you, about us being together again. We're gonna have a lot of fun together. We can get a football."

"Already got one," Gamado told him.

"Okay, there are all kinds of things we can do.

Night boys."

Mahret and Barisso sat at the little wooden table Mahret had bought at Toi, and talked for hours about everything, or almost everything, they had been through while apart.

They amazed each other.

Finally, Mahret said, "maybe now you can get a job."

"I will try. Let me settle first."

"There is no time to settle. You must understand; our needs are now! How did you find us?"

"I had the directions to the Western Union. It said near Mashimoni. So I asked people how to get to Mashimoni and then just walked around looking for you. Finally, I saw Dawit on the street."

He told me you were here. He's an asshole, wasn't nice at all. I wanted to punch him in the face, but I didn't."

"He's angry at me. I got uncle to send me half the cash. He's really mad about that. Who cares?"

"You're getting twenty-five dollars a month?"

"Yes, it helps a lot."

"It pays the rent?"

"It does more than that."

"We have lots of money then. How much have you got left from what I gave you at the farm?"

"I have most of it, enough for now, but it won't last forever."

"How much have you got?"

"Most of it. I need to know exactly how much you have too. I have to plan."

"I've done all the planning necessary. I'll explain it to you tomorrow."

"I want to know everything; I've come through a lot to get here. I will need to have all the money back."

"Listen Barisso, we can sit down and talk everything out later once you've had a chance to look around and feel comfortable in Kibera. Tomorrow, I'll show you and introduce you to everyone. Then you can look for work."

"Okay, but don't forget I have to know where we stand so I can make decisions for this family."

Mahret felt suddenly that this could turn into an argument. But, unlike in previous days, she was finding it difficult even to sound like she was giving in.

"Now, I know these things too," she said. "I have done very well to settle here with the boys. But, again, we can talk later."

They went to bed. They made love very quietly with the boys asleep across the room on the other bed Mahret had set up for them. The lovemaking was mechanical rather than passionate. Mahret thought maybe she and Barisso just did not know each other well enough after so long.

"Or could it be that we know each other too well?

Oh *Waqaa*, I hope not!"

Chapter 35

RESETTING THE MIND

In the morning, after they'd had breakfast with the boys, Mahret diverted Barisso's attention away from her financial state by keeping him busy. She first took him on tour around the compound and then to the Toi market. She introduced him to everyone she knew. In the afternoon, she also got him to go on a food trip with her to the Jehovah's Witnesses church.

Then, she was able, through great good luck, and Milka, to help him get a line on paid work. Milka was seeing a guy, who had a job in a leather factory within walking distance but just outside of Kibera. He, Carden, was an Ethiopian Jew whose wife had died, leaving him with two little girls now aged five and seven. Despite their religious differences, Milka and Carden had a lot in common. They were both well-educated single parents. He had an engineering degree, and he had previously also had a professional job in Nairobi and got fired.

Carden told Milka that when some technical equipment went missing, his boss "didn't know who to blame, so he fired four of the workers who could have done it. Three Muslims and me; I had nothing do with it, and I don't think the others did either."

Now, when Carden went to work, Milka took responsibility for the kids.

"They can come over to my place," she told him. "You shouldn't be leaving kids that young on their own for so long. Hilani is twelve years old now. She'll keep them out of trouble. She can call on Evra too if she has to. He's a little older, but he's also a teenaged boy."

"I hear ya."

Carden worked in a leather factory. At first, his job had been carting and disposing of the scraps that dropped to the factory floor as the cutters carved out all the various pieces for jackets and coats from tanned goat and cattle hides. His foreman was impressed with his energy, his punctuality, and the fact that he had an engineering degree. So, when a vacancy occurred, he promoted him to a better position servicing the sewing machines.

Carden took an instant liking to Barisso, and shortly after Mahret introduced them, he asked him if he wanted his old job.

"I'm pretty sure I can get it for you," he said, "these people like guys like you and me with brown skin. They don't like the real dark ones and they tell us the carts are too heavy for women. They're not, but that's what they say."

Carden got Barisso to accompany him to the factory the following morning. The foreman hired him on the spot. The job paid fifty shillings an hour, a trifle, but a substantial contribution to the family budget nonetheless.

The work was relatively easy, and it kept Barisso busy. For now, any struggle with Mahret lapsed.

She continued to carry on as before.

"Maybe he will learn, things are different here," she thought, "it might take some time."

Two weeks later, the foreman announced that he was laying off a third of the workforce. He needed Carden's skills, so his job was safe, but Barisso was out of work again. He did not mind. Taking some time to relax a bit seemed fine to him. Mahret, though, wanted him back out there. She let him rest with the family for two days, and then got on his case.

More than anything else, Barisso resented her presumption.

"You stop it," he snapped when she pestered him while they were sitting at the table in the morning after breakfast. "I'll decide when to go back. Like I said, I've lived through hell. I need time. You back off."

"We've both lived through hell. Nothing you've had to do is any worse than what I've had to do. I saved your kids and started a new life, a decent life for the kids, in a horrible place. You must understand that. I will not go back to the way we were."

At that, Barisso got up as if to leave.

"This life is not so great. You got us into a slum. How good is that?"

Uncharacteristically, Mahret raised her voice.

"You accept the way things are or leave for good, don't come back."

Barisso was upset. All through the last two years, he had dreamed of very little else but being back with the family. He had yearned to live like before, with the respect of his wife and children. But everything was different now. His wife didn't bow to his authority, and his children seemed more respectful to her than to him. He didn't know them anymore, and they didn't seem to care.

"You think you've been through so much," he shouted, "I'm gonna tell you a story that will shock you. A story I've kept inside because it's so horrible. But I think now you have to know."

He shocked Mahret as he recounted the story of the lions devouring his soldier companions one at a time and then trying to do the same to him.

"That beast climbed back to get me too. I thought I was dead. She was close enough I could smell her breath. I couldn't believe it when she backed down and left me sitting there."

As he spoke, Mahret could see the fear in his face—something she had seen once before.

"Oh my gosh," she said. "I had no idea. You poor man. I'm sorry. I didn't know. You must be hurting terribly."

She then gently proceeded to tell him the one story she had held back.

"I guess we've both been through so much," she said when she finished. "Isn't this the reason we have to work together now?"

Barisso was speechless. Instead of replying, he left the house.

It was Sunday and the first person he met in the street was Carden.

"What's with you?" Carden asked, "you look terrible."

Barisso found himself pouring out his heart to this man he hardly knew. He told him all about, not lions or killing, but his relationship with his wife.

Carden turned out to be the right person.

"One of the things you have to understand here," he told him, "is that women have to be strong. It takes two to ward off everything from disease to sexual predators, drug dealers, disease, and starvation. They're the ones who keep the kids out of trouble while we're looking for work, and most take their turn bringing in the food. Just think of how much both Milka and Mahret have done, going to the churches, finding schools for your kids where they actually get fed, washing their clothes by hand with dirty water, and the dangers they've faced when they have to go outside the compound. You know Mahret herself was nearly raped, just doing her job to bring in money. A lot of women are forced to beg on the streets too."

"Yeah, I know but…"

"Barisso, it's different here, it will never be the same for any of us; and it's a damned good thing too. In this place, no family would be half as secure without the women carrying a huge share of our load."

"But…"

"No buts Barisso; it's different. You better adjust to it, not the other way around. Get used to it. You're still a man; nothing's changed in that way. The difference is you have a more or less equal partner now. Believe me, you need one!"

What Barisso was starting to understand was that his former life was gone. Mahret would perhaps be more understanding knowing what he had just told her, but she was never going to be the person she used to be. His own nightmares, like hers, would, hopefully, let up in time. But for now, he, like her, would just have to deal with them himself.

He realized too that Mahret was not going to relent about the work thing. The next morning, he got up early and walked to a potential job site Carden had mentioned. He joined a group of twenty or thirty other men huddled together in the rain outside a construction site waiting for the manager to come out and pick the workers he needed for the day.

A Chinese boss appeared.

He shouted at them in a mixture of Swahili and English:

"I need six men for about three hours to unload boxes from the railway cars. The pay is ten birr per hour."

He smiled:

"Anyone interested?"

The boss walked back and forth in front of the men like an auctioneer at a cattle market. He picked and chose as the men in their eagerness, clamored for his attention. They all waved their arms in the air. Some climbed on the backs of those in front of them.

"Me, me, me," they called out.

The company administrators wanted to have lots of men available for work. But they did not want to pay them between jobs. Only the lucky few were selected; the rest were sent home with empty pockets and empty stomachs. Barisso was one of the chosen few.

He had got in early and stood in the front of the crowd. His skin color was still a bit lighter than that of the average African too.

It was also closer to the Chinese color.

He noticed that the three other men picked had similar complexions.

There was no ethical dilemma for the lucky few. For whatever reason, their family would be secure for longer.

Barisso worked hard, and as they finished unloading the last of the railway cars that afternoon, the foreman approached him.

"Hey you, you want more work?"

"Uh, yes sir."

"Fine, take the piss pails those guys are using over there at the construction site to the latrine outside the train station, empty them and take them back again. And keep doin this as the pails fill. If you do well you can come back until they finish the job; it could be a week, maybe two."

"Yes sir."

It was hard work; the rain did not let up. Barisso carried two pails at a time each trip across a muddy path of some 300 meters. Some of the pails he carried had more than just urine in them. The construction men worked late into that night and Barisso stayed with them, making sure they always had pail space.

It was late when he got home. Mahret was waiting for him.

"Are you okay," she said, scanning him as closely as she could in the dim light. "I've been worried. There are so many bad people out there."

"I know, but I got more work, we'll have money, so it's good."

Barisso felt just a little less bad about pretty much everything.

Chapter 36

ADJUSTING

Gradually, Mahret and Barisso learned to live more satisfactorily together in their little shack. This home consisted of two rooms, but it was significantly smaller than their last one, and it did not have a wood floor. They made the best of it. It would do for now. Barisso found an old tarp at the dump, which he tied to the ceiling to make a kind of wall separating their bed from the boys'. Barisso also picked up a transistor radio in the marketplace, like the one they had on the farm. It provided the lone source of household entertainment and news.

"You should consider us lucky with our own water supply, Mahret told her husband; "lots of people can't afford to buy fresh water. They use dirty water from the Nairobi Dam or the river flowing through Kibera. Both are disgusting."

Mahret took the risks of water contamination seriously. Even though the family had their own tap, she used the kerosene burner every day to boil all the water before anyone drank it. There was a latrine pit behind the house that was usually more or less full. They had to pay three shillings each time they used it, so Barisso and the boys, like other males, normally urinated in one of the garbage piles in the street. During the rains, the piles became waterborne and flowed along the footpath all the way down to the Nairobi Dam Reserve.

Mahret paid the price and used the communal toilet during the day. Still, because she and the boys were justifiably afraid to go out into the streets at night, they relied on the throw toilets when caught short.

Mahret also found an answer to one of Barisso and the boys' most immediate challenges—their need for adequate footwear. The sandals the boys had been wearing were in bad shape and, while Barisso liked the ones he had got from the Turkana woman, they were starting to go as well. He had to reinforce the strapping on all their sandals with a fine rope he found in the street. That was not very satisfactory, however. They had to tie the rope around the soles and their feet every time they put the sandals on. Moreover, the ropes made uncomfortable bumps under the soles, which they felt almost continuously as they walked.

Mahret came across a man working a stall in the marketplace who sold sandals of all sizes he made out of old truck and car tires he got from a garage outside Kibera. He paid from eighty to 150 shillings for the tires depending on how big they were and then cut them with a knife to make not only the soles but also straps that he attached to them with small nails.

When Mahret told Barisso about the sandals he went to the market and purchased a pair for himself and each of the boys.

The man had a great little business. The sandals worked fine; they were somewhat heavier than others they had had before, but they seemed very durable, and the man told Barisso that if the nails pulled lose or wore through the straps, he would replace them for ten shillings.

Barisso and Mahret both tried diligently to maintain their existing supply of cash. As they told each other when they reunited in Kibera, they had managed to keep most of the money from the sale of the farm. And, with twenty-five dollars a month from Mahret's uncle in Australia, the food from the churches, and the kids' school, their costs were at a minimum. However, every time they had to spend any of their own money on anything, they both felt very uneasy.

Barisso's job at the construction site brought in a few extra shillings a week, but, unfortunately, it lasted only three weeks. After that, Barisso took anything he could get from the Chinese foreman who liked his light skin.

But he found himself unemployed a good percentage of the time.

When he could not find work, Barisso experienced periods of depression.

"Emptying the piss pails was a pretty humbling experience," he told Mahret, "but at least it was work, honest work. I wish I could find something like that now. I don't feel like a man. I was a man on the farm; now I'm nothing, I'm no longer the head of this family. Just another mouth to feed."

Mahret had little patience with that kind of talk.

"No, no, you're a member of a little team here. It's not a bad team either. This we know, because all its members are still alive and healthy, and they're eating well."

In other words, toughen up.

One thing that really bothered Mahret about her husband and other Oromo men was that during the periods of unemployment, they tended to indulge their taste for alcohol. They all maintained the brewing skills they had developed back home. They did not have all the same ingredients here, but they had enough to keep themselves and their buddies supplied with at least a rough approximation of their original homebrew.

Their *daadhu* wine was just as powerful too. Among other things, Mahret realized it could be dangerous. A neighbor, Wilmana, told her that thirty-four men had just died in two Nairobi slums on a single night from drinking their home-made alcohol. She said that a newspaper reported that they started dying the morning after partying. Over a hundred who did not die were experiencing paralysis and extreme bouts of diarrhea and vomiting.

"Apparently," Wilmana said, "the problem is that they make this cheap alcoholic drink Kenyans call 'changa,' incredibly strong. It's over fifty percent alcohol. After a couple of drinks, they get pissed out of their heads. The booze turns poisonous because they don't know what they're doing.

That hasn't happened here, so far," she said, "but it certainly might. And, of course, those guys that don't get sick get dangerous. They fight with each other or their wives, and they commit crimes. My friend Sacha tried to stop her husband from raping her friend, Milly, and he beat her up bad. She could die."

When laid off, Barisso was attracted to the booze, in Mashimoni just as he had been on the farm. Only now more of his friends were always close by, and they, like him, when out of work, had few responsibilities to absorb their time and energy.

Barisso often smelled of alcohol when he came home late at night. Mahret feared his mood swings as much as anything. So far, while he could be rude to her and the kids, he had not been even a little violent, like sometimes on the farm during the pre-harvest celebration. She suspected this was in part at least because he had more respect for her authority here. But she feared he might get too drunk one night and lash out.

One night when Barisso came home, he was sporting not just the standard bloody nose but also some red stains on his shirt, and a large tear in the knee of one of his trousers. He woke Mahret up as he tripped coming through the door and landed on the ground by their bed.

When Barisso did not get up, she turned on the lamp to make sure he was okay. He was breathing fine, just passed out. When she got him to a sitting position trying to get his shirt off, she noticed there was what looked like lipstick on his one cheek.

"Damn you Barisso!" she said, pushing him back down. "You can sleep in the dirt tonight."

She went back to bed.

By the next morning, Barisso had managed to crawl in beside her. He slept until quite a long time after she and the kids were up.

When he did come to, the boys were outside playing with their friends.

He knew right away he was in trouble.

"Were you playing around with the prostitutes last night?" Mahret asked him.

"What are you talking about? Of course not."

"I'm talking about the lipstick on your face. Where did that come from?"

"I don't know; I can't remember nothin."

"Well, you better figure it out. I want to know what's going on."

"Okay, okay," he said. "Let me think."

She gave him a minute.

"Well?"

"Uh, yeah, what I can remember is there was a young girl. She looked like a teenager."

"I thought so!"

"Yeah, but I didn't do nothin. One of the guys tried to do somethin, and I stopped him. She thought I was her hero. She kissed me to say thanks.

I didn't do nothin."

Mahret was unsure she could believe him. If he was lying, he might have the disease. She thought she could never let him have sex with her again.

When she confided in Milka, however, she got confirmation of his story—to a degree.

Milka told her that Carden had been talking to some of the guys and found out all about it.

Yes, Barisso had rescued the girl when one of them was trying to molest her.

"She screamed at her assailant, he stepped in, and she kissed him out of gratitude. I should tell you, though, that in his drunken state, he seemed willing to accept a bit more than just that. He apparently lingered, if you know what I mean. She's the one who pulled away."

"I don't exactly know what that means," Mahret said, "but I can kind of picture it."

Milka then showed a side of her personality that Mahret had not observed before.

"Men!" she said. "You see why I took so long to find a new one. Most of them are like animals. They do anything to satisfy their urges in any way they can. Booze is just another outlet for their unrelenting, and never properly requited sex drive."

Mahret wasn't sure what "requited" meant, but she thought she generally understood what Milka was saying. She also believed her friend was partly right.

Oddly though (to her), she found herself defending Barisso.

"I know, I guess I'm just relieved Barisso didn't do much. Him and at least some of the other men's drunken sessions are from boredom and a feeling that here in the slums, they're no longer living up to their duty. They can't provide the way they think they're supposed to. They're depressed."

"That may be," Milka replied, "but we have to put up with life here too. It sure isn't any easier for us. We don't go out boozing it up. And we don't go fucking anything we can find either."

"I don't think Barisso would have done anything if he wasn't drunk. I know those guys are way more sexed than us. They have to fight it all the time. I guess we should allow for that. I don't think Carden screws around, does he?"

"Not so far, anyway. If he does, he's out!"

"Yes, and Barisso too. I won't put up with it either. But I understand the problem a little bit."

Luckily, farming of sorts appeared in the urban jungle to help Barisso overcome some of his growing fondness for alcohol. One evening after the lipstick incident, Mahret, on Milka's advice, got him to accompany her to a street presentation by a man named Joshua Otieno from an institution called the Kibera Community Empowerment Organization. Otieno demonstrated that people could grow vegetables such as onions, spinach, and kale in meaningful quantities in the home. They could plant the vegetables in plastic bags using compost manure from the streets for fertilizer.

"If done right," he said, "one bag could contribute significantly to the food supply of up to six people. More bags could bring in extra money for the family from sales."

The thought intrigued Barisso. Within a week, he had six "sack crops" growing next to the house. These he would bring inside every night and on days when storms threatened. He and Mahret told their neighbors that they would sell some of their vegetables to them at a low price as long as they didn't pilfer their crops.

No one did.

Barisso put quite a lot of his energy into the venture. Within weeks he was spending much of the time he had previously spent with his friends, tending to his crops.

Then Mahret showed him that other Mashimonians were now growing all kinds of vegetables between the garbage dumps in the green space along the Nairobi River.

Barisso was very impressed.

"How would I get a space?"

Mahret, of course, asked Milka.

"You go to a woman named Elizabeth. You'll find her on most days working the riverside area tending to her own piece or working with others who need help or advice on theirs. She knows how to grow almost everything, onions, sugar cane, corn, watermelons, pumpkins, plantains, and lots of legumes."

"How does she know so much?"

"She learned from an NGO group called "Solidairite." They taught her everything, and she's a fast learner."

Mahret asked Carden to tell Barisso about Elizabeth.

"If you tell him to ask a woman who leads a farming movement here, to help him get into it, he might just listen to you. I don't think he'd listen to me."

Carden agreed. He told Barisso about the enterprising lady, and advised him to go right away and talk to her.

He buttered him up too.

"She can give you an allotment and then show you how to grow plants you've never seen before. Then, you can use all your farming skills and do a better job than anyone, including her."

Barisso looked hesitant.

Carden figured old values were resurfacing.

"Remember, this isn't the Oromia countryside. Women do all sorts of things here that they wouldn't do at home. They're a big part of everybody's strength. Let her help you, my friend. No one here will think any less of you."

Barisso then mustered all his courage and went to the riverside field to find Elizabeth.

She agreed to give him an allotment.

"It will cost you 500 shillings a month, but you can make profits selling the produce at the Toi market. I'll sell you some plants and seeds to get started, and I'll show you how to plant and look after any you're not familiar with."

"I'm a farmer, you know, and a good one too."

Elizabeth had met men like Barisso before.

"That's what I hear. I'm sure you can show me some good things."

"When do I start?"

"I'll meet you here tomorrow, and we can stake out your ground. I should just tell you that while the ground is very fertile from all the garbage rotting in it over the years, there are drawbacks. First, the sewage and garbage can cause contamination, and when the river floods during the big rains, it can wipe out your entire crop."

"What do you do about it?"

"Are you growing crops in bags at home?"

"Yes."

"You can do that here on a much bigger volume. The bags help prevent contamination and flood damage, too, as long as you plan around the really heavy rainy season when the flooding water can carry the bags off. You can keep them elevated till then by mounding the dirt and rocks under them."

"How do you keep people from stealing the produce?"

"It's a problem, but not a huge one. Hungry people might take small amounts of vegetables or fruit from time to time. But real thieves normally go after bigger prizes than that."

"Alright," Barisso said, trying not to sound too excited.

"I'll see you tomorrow, and we can talk about improving your crops too."

"Okay, Barisso, see you tomorrow then."

She had one more word in mind as he left.

"Men!"

Chapter 37

STILL, WE GOTTA GET OUT OF THIS PLACE

Barisso was suddenly a farmer again. In the days ahead, he spent a great deal of his time planting, weeding, and harvesting. In time he was able to contribute significantly to the family's food supply and a small but much-needed bit to its financial security as well.

He did not stop drinking, but he cut back on it a lot.

The boost to his morale made it somewhat easier for him to accept some of Mahret's presumptions.

This also brought Mahret a more relaxed period in her life.

However, that period ended abruptly.

One Saturday morning, a few weeks after Barisso got his allotment, she went to the market where she expected to meet her friend Milka as usual. But Milka did not appear. There were a lot of people there, so Mahret thought she must just have missed her in the crowd. She decided to drop by her place on the way home. When she got about fifty meters from it, she could see a crowd of six or seven women standing by her doorway. There were sounds like someone crying. As she got closer the sounds grew louder. Inside the house, she found Milka sitting on a chair with her face buried in her hands. Two other women were trying to comfort her.

Mahret embraced her.

"What's wrong, Milka, what's happened?"

"They killed him. They killed him."

Mahret looked at one of the other women.

"What's happened?"

"Her son has been killed—shot."

"What, who shot him? Who would do such a thing?"

"It was the police; it's always the police."

"They shot Evra? How do you know that?"

"He came home late last night riding a motorcycle and told Milka he had just taken his sick friend, Makor, who owned the bike, to Makina clinic."

He said he was going to tell his friend's parents and would be right back.

That was the last time Milka saw him alive. The cops shot him dead."

Milka suddenly fainted in Mahret's arms. As she fell forward, Mahret tightened her grip on her and guided her to the bed a few feet away. One of the other women got a wet rag to bath her face and forehead.

Mahret stayed the rest of the day. She felt useless. When Milka came to, she tried to talk to her, but it was for naught. Nothing she could say was of any help. Nor could she get her to eat or drink. Mahret mainly just saw that her best friend was not alone while it was still light outside.

Mahret gave some money to Hilani so that she could buy some food.

In the early evening, Milka finally slipped into an involuntary sleep.

Mahret kissed her on the cheek.

"You sleep now, and I will be back first thing tomorrow morning. I will do anything to help you. *Sin jaaladaha!*"

In the next few days, Mahret looked into the killing as much as she could. She questioned everyone she could find who had witnessed at least some part of it.

Gamechu, who was at the schoolyard when his friend died, said the police stopped Evra and pulled him off the bike. When Gamechu went over to see what was going on, one of the cops slapped him and told him to go away unless he wanted to share his buddy's fate.

"The police arrested Evra, handcuffed him, dragged him to the schoolyard, and beat him. One cop shot about six bullets into his body while he was still in cuffs. Three others were standing close by. They all had rifles.

While Evra was lying on the ground, one of them put one last bullet in his head. I guess to make sure he was dead."

Gamechu said that Milka heard the shots herself and went out to see what happened. She saw Evra lying there in pools of blood. When she tried to get to him, one of the policemen grabbed her and held her back.

"The cops told her that he had been part of a gang that shot and killed a policeman a few weeks ago. They even said Evra tried to get away, so they had no alternative but to shoot him. They're a bunch of fucking liars."

The police did not let anyone examine the body. Instead, they covered it with a shroud and hauled it away.

"Everyone knows they're killing our kids!" one of the women told Mahret. "Last week it was Moyra's boy, and the week before that it was those three other kids in Kisumu Ndogo. No young men are safe."

"Can you believe it?" Mahret said to Barisso at home the one evening. "The police, the cops, they killed Evra like a bunch of gangsters, no trial, no nothing. They don't even know he did anything wrong. And he was unarmed. They don't care, but it's like they drove a knife into Milka's heart. She'll never get over it. No mother would."

And this was just the first of the two lessons she learned from the episode. The other one shocked her too, though not quite on the same scale.

The police took Evra's body to their headquarters to put it in cold storage.

The next day, when two officers came to talk to Milka at home, it was Mahret who met them at the door.

"Yes? What do you want?"

"We need someone to arrange to get this bandit's body out of our hands. Get it to burial."

"He's no bandit. I'll look after it."

"Okay, come to the station and get the body. But come by the day after tomorrow before nightfall or we'll have to dispose of it ourselves. We have no room."

"Alright, I'll see what I can do."

Mahret went to Langata Cemetery the following morning.

When she saw a man out in the graveyard digging, she approached him.

"Good morning," she said. "Can you help me?"

"Yes, what do you want? Got another one for us?"

"My friend's son, will you make a place for him?"

"You must talk to the boss. See that building through those trees? He's in there."

She followed a rough cement sidewalk through the small grove of trees and entered the front door of a gray stone building in the little clearing beyond it.

A man was sitting at a desk in the center of the room.

"I just want to inquire if you can bury my friend's son."

"We can if you pay?"

"Yes?"

"How big is the body?"

"What do you mean? I don't know."

"He is two years old, ten, nineteen? How big?"

"He's sixteen."

"Full size then. For a burial plot in the virgin area, it will cost you 30,000 shillings."

"What are you saying? We, that is the family, can't pay that much."

"Sorry, lady, we're awful full here, that's the price."

"The mother can't afford it; it's way too much. What can I do?"

"Okay, I make you a deal. You bury it over there where you see those men digging, where there are no gravestones. Someone else is resting down deep, and they are flattening the one who's buried shallow."

"What do you mean?"

"There is someone buried six feet down for many years and another on top of that one, three feet down. The shallow one has been there not so long but long enough. The body turns into dust when chopped up with the diggers' shovels. Then you can bury yours where that one is buried."

"You mean we bury our boy in someone else's grave?"

"Yes, lady, that's right. Actually, in two other's graves, if you count the one down deep. After at least three years, we flatten the shallow graves again and bury someone else there."

"This is not a grave; it's a 'temporary grave.'"

"Yes, cost you only 8,000 shillings. Big savings."

"That's awful."

"Up to you. Throw the body in the dump if you like."

"Your price is so expensive. We don't have money. Can't you do it for less?"

"Take it or not, up to you."

"Okay, I will give you American dollars. I will give you sixty American dollars when we bring the body in the morning. I will bring some men too to do the digging. Find us a spot not there where those guys are digging but in a new place, one that looks untouched even if there are already at least two graves there."

"Okay, lady, sixty American dollars. You bring it with the body. You dig where I show you. No other place. You tell the men they have to chop up the earth with their shovels as they dig. We've already done that once, so the body already there is dust. They won't even be able to tell that it's a body, and it will mix in with the dirt. No one will know it's there, not even the diggers. Tell them only go down three feet, that it's normal."

"Unbelievable! Okay, you show me the spot now. The body will be here in the morning. You tell them to put it by the spot. My husband and his friends will do the digging tomorrow at night, and we will have the funeral after that. Whatever you do, do not tell the diggers someone has already been lying there. You will scare them away."

The next day Mahret had the police transport Evra's body to the cemetery where the employees placed it by the gravesite as directed. Barisso and two of his friends arrived that evening.

To dig at night during the funeral process was a tradition. The men were getting together to honor the deceased. They were expressing their sense of brotherhood and their Christian values. The three men, two of whom had lived in Kibera for years, also brought traditional drinks, the homemade bhang—the "changa," —to chase away evil spirits.

"It makes our blood go faster and gives the energy to dig and escort our young brother to his grave," one of the men told Barisso.

He did not argue.

Mahret found a minister from her own Jehovah's Witnesses Church to conduct the funeral. She also made sure that all the people in the compound knew Milka's son would be buried at the cemetery two days later at two o'clock in the afternoon.

She was relieved when the time for the funeral came, and a good size crowd assembled at the graveside.

She spread blankets on the ground for Milka and Hilani and sat with them through the ceremony. The minister did a good job too. He asked Waqaa to embrace this wonderful young man and accept his energy in heaven.

"We believe that Waqaa is the indestructible Energy that appeared at the origin of the world's creation. Human beings live thanks to that indestructible and divine Energy. We also know that when one dies their material body and energy separate. At noon the next day, when the sun is at its zenith, the energy of the dead fuses with that of the divine. It joins Waqaa. Our young man, Evra, will dwell in Waqaa's Energy for eternity. He will then be waiting to embrace the energy of the people when they die who showed and taught him love."

Mahret found the ceremony uplifting and, at the same time, practical and realistic. She hoped it brought Milka some small relief, though she was unsure whether her friend's sophisticated education allowed her to believe in the basic concepts the good pastor conveyed.

Milka sat stone faced through the whole ceremony, her arms around her sobbing daughter. When it ended, she bowed to each one of the guests as they filed by her.

After the burial, there was food neighborhood women had brought. And, of course, the men got back into their homemade wine. Out of respect for the deceased and the family, they tried to speak to each other in hushed tones. They also tried to avoid laughing (or fighting).

They were not overly successful, but they did their best.

It didn't matter; Milka and Hilani were in no state to take even the slightest notice of them.

Chapter 38

HELL HATH STAYING POWER

In the days after Evra's funeral, rumors swirled through Mashimoni about a similar incident involving a young man named Silas and two of his friends in Kambi Muru. They were sitting near a tenement building relaxing over a cold soda in the warm late-afternoon sun when two police officers emerged from the crowd, raised their guns from under their waistcoats and shot them. The police officers then walked over to them lying on the ground and casually put another shot into each of their heads. They then planted knives and other weapons on the bodies and stood guard over them. They allowed people just close enough to see the evidence of the boys' criminality, until a van arrived to haul them off.

To Mahret, whether or not this event actually happened, or was in part at least the product of gossip, it was another mark on the wrong side of the ledger for Kibera. The fact that people thought it was true to life told her that what had happened to Evra was not all that uncommon.

She and Barisso had two young sons. They must not be subjected to even the possibility of a fate like that.

One of the things that bothered Mahret was that a lot of people seemed to think such killings were a form of justice.

One old man standing in line at the bakeshop told her that police "death squads" had been working with local informants more and more in recent years to kill criminals.

"It's not such a bad thing, the kids are out of control, and the cops get tired of seeing the corrupt judges taking bribes for letting them off."

Mahret was irate.

"Evra was not a criminal!"

"They're all criminals. The kids today are just a bunch of criminals. They have no sense of right and wrong."

"Obviously, you have no youngsters in your family, or you wouldn't say such a thing. All young boys are not bad!"

Several people she talked to had stories to tell about other killings. In most cases, there seemed to be little attempt by the young victims to resist arrest. Could it be that many were innocent and, therefore, felt they were not at risk? Did the police simply assassinate them for the sake of appearances to show the public they were doing the job of crime-fighting?

What convinced Mahret that they were, in fact, assassinations, was a *Sunday Nation* reporter named Otsieno Namwaya who came up to her at Toi a few days after the funeral.

Otsieno claimed to have undergone a major research project about police killings and to have done extensive interviews with people in agencies involved in protecting human rights.

"I understand," he said, "that you are close to this Evra's family, and you know some details about what happened to him."

"Yes," she said, "that's true. I guess I know as much as anybody."

After she told him everything she knew, she asked him if some of the rumors she had been hearing about other kids were true."

"No question about it. Police are arresting unarmed people and then gunning them down. Neither the police service nor its watchdog agency is doing much to stop it.

Human Rights Watch claims that no fewer than twenty-one men and boys in Nairobi's low-income areas were shot down in recent times with no apparent justification. The police offer no evidence. They just say these guys were criminals."

Mahret wanted the details.

"Can you give me some examples that you know are for real?"

"Yes, I'll read you just a few from my notes. These, believe me, I have researched as thoroughly as possible. Each case was summary justice; you know execution."

"Tsuma Mumbo, twenty-five, succumbed to gunshot injuries after a bullet hit him in the head. It was fired by a police officer who said he had been pursuing drug peddlers and users who were on the run.

Jamal Ochieng (Sisqo) was shot one Sunday night as he left Sky Villa Club in Ayany. He had gone there to watch Benga artist Dola Kabary perform. His wife, Akinyi Odera, who was two months' pregnant, was with him when they shot him. She told friends that one officer had accosted him and told him, 'before you kill me, I will kill you first.' She said she didn't believe it 'until he fell down beside me after I heard five shots. I can still hear them in my mind.'

Police tracked down Bernard Otieno (Bobo) and Hillary Owino (Chinjo), and pulled them out of Otieno's house in Kambi Muru in the middle of the night. They handcuffed them before shooting them. Both were players at Uweza Football Club. Otieno's girlfriend, Shamin Sheila, insists they were not criminals.

Last April alone, and in just three days, police in Mathare shot dead seven men who they said were involved in crime. The men were not armed and they did not resist arrest.

On the fourteenth of April, police shot dead Kevin Gitau, twenty-five, who was due to travel out of the country to take up a job offer in the Middle East.

On the seventeenth of April, police shot six men in the Mlango Kubwa area. Staff at a community rights organization in Mathare, who have been documenting the killings and offering support to relatives of victims, said that one of the six was a seventeen-year-old boy.

In May, the community organization in Mathare documented police killings of fifty-seven men and women, allegedly for links to crime, in Mathare alone in one year."

Otsieno stopped at that point.

"I have several more pages of notes on police killings," he said, "but you should hear the interview I did with a self-proclaimed young thief. He claimed the police often collaborated with him and others like him to identify some of the worst criminals."

"Yes, please go on."

"Okay, these are his exact words."

"It's risky business for the police themselves. But if they think they're about to be found out, they just shoot their collaborators to protect themselves. Remember, the police are criminals too. They're into illegal booze and drugs for sure. Many who execute criminal suspects are well known, but investigations never find the evidence. The police threaten the families and friends of the victims who they think might 'rat them out.'"

An interview Osieno claimed he had done with "a businessman who is also a police informer," scared the daylights out of Mahret.

Again, it was word for word.

'The police have a long list of people they plan to kill, and they add to it all the time. The list includes petty thieves and, in a few cases, men and women who have had disagreements with individual police officers."

When Mahret got home that afternoon, she told Barisso, "we can't stay here much longer. If the police shoot young men just because they suspect them of crimes, all young men who live in Kibera are in danger.

The time will come when we won't be able to keep our two boys off the streets."

"You know," Barisso said, "I doubt the police would kill innocent young men. All they're doing is taking out the bad ones. Those guys need to be taken out. The police are doing us all a service. We should thank them. Evra was no saint. God knows what he was into. He probably deserved what he got."

Mahret lost it—again.

"You're just wrong; when the police kill kids without a trial, they are a huge threat to the lives of all young boys, you know, like ours, especially in Kibera. At best the cops make mistakes and kill innocent kids; and if you read about them, you find out they don't much care whether they're innocent or not. The cops are more dangerous than the criminals and lots of them are criminals too. We're not gonna live in a place where there's a constant danger from the very people who are supposed to be protecting us. I know that now, and I'm not allowing our boys to be victims."

Mahret felt desperate to find a way to bring Barisso up to speed, to get him to understand, so he would be a help rather than a hindrance in planning their escape.

"Here, here's a newspaper report I found at Milka's. Read it closely. We have got to get the kids out of here before it's too late. You told me when we had to leave Oromia. Now I'm telling you, we will find a way to leave Kibera. And we will do it as soon as we possibly can. We're leaving Mashimoni, but one day we're gonna do more than that. We're leaving Africa; we're going to the 'new world' just as soon as we can."

"New what?"

"'New world,' that's what Milka calls it. Places that haven't been around that long. They have newer economies and lots of resources and good laws. They even have something called 'social services' to help the poor. Nobody starves."

"When do you think you wanna go?"

"We can't make that move yet. We have to apply and then wait for the government of one of those countries to accept us. But first, and I mean right now, we gotta get out of this neighborhood and into a better one here in this city where life is surer.

We can find it too—we just need to look harder."

Barisso still would not openly admit it even to himself, but deep down inside, he now understood that his wife's status in his family had changed. She was his partner rather than his subject. She no longer hesitated to suggest new ideas or strategies for survival, and he, himself, was rebuking her less and less when she did.

And, as much to the point, she could be right in many of her views. She had thought this one through better than him. She knew what she was talking about.

That did not mean he had to be subservient.

"Okay Mahret, first you look for a place for us all to go to here in Nairobi. Then, maybe later, we can think about other countries. Just make sure you know the place you pick is better than the one we're in now. I think such a place where poor kids who break the law don't get killed by the police will be difficult to find, and a country without poor people too. But we'll all go when you can tell me you know for sure that you've found such a place."

Chapter 39

MORE OF THE SAME

At nine fifteen on Monday morning, Berhanu and Gamado came running in through the doorway they had only just left a few minutes ago.

"*Haadha, haadha*, it's gone, it's all gone!"

"What do you mean, 'all gone.' What's all gone? You boys get back to school."

"No *haadha*, the school, it's all gone. It's gone. They knocked it down with a bulldouser."

"You mean a bulldozer."

"Yeah, a bulldozer. That's what they said, a bulldozer."

Mahret and Barisso hurried to the school site with the boys. And that was all they found—just a site, with a bunch of boards and pieces of boards, sheets of tin, smashed up desks, and books scattered in the mud. All were being scraped into piles and loaded onto trucks by tractors with front-end loaders.

Other parents were standing watching with their children too. When Mahret and Barisso looked down the street, they could see similar equipment doing the same work where a host of shanty houses had stood.

"What happened?" Mahret asked one of the other parents.

"They knocked all the buildings down. The school is gone, and so are the homes of all the people living along here. Dozens of people have lost their places."

They could see people shivering in the cold morning air with blankets wrapped around them. Most were standing beside a scant few of their possessions. They must have got little warning to get out before what was about to happen, happened.

Mahret approached one of the workers standing in the street with a shovel in his hand.

"Tell me, what's going on?"

"Don't know, lady. They just told us to come here and help the bulldozers. That's all I know. Just doin my job."

"This is terrible," Mahret said to no one in particular. "Why would they do this, the authorities, why would they do this? It is so shocking. My kids have lost their school. And where will all these people go? They're out in the cold!"

As it turned out, the authorities (no one seemed to know who they were) decided they needed a new superhighway through Kibera. It was to be a commercial link, which they said would stimulate trade and help Nairobi into the twenty-first century. They could have got the land for it by cutting into a small piece of the edge of the golf course running between Mashimoni and Nairobi proper. However, that facility was the plaything of the city's wealthy elite, who paid its fees. So, the decision-makers decided to build it through the very heart of Kibera. They sacrificed Berhanu and Gamado's school, along with seven others that happened to be in the way, and the charitable Egesa Children's Home that served some 200 orphans.

They also tore down hundreds of homes. When teachers told the children who turned up that day to go home, some found they had no home to go back to since they lived along the route of the new highway.

"We had 800 kids," the principal told Mahret. "We housed them and educated them. I don't know what to do because I don't have any other place to take these children. I have helped the government for all those years by taking children from the streets, but they can't see that. We were relaxed because they told us the learning process would not be changed. We are shocked; they have reneged on their promise. They were just lying to keep us from rebelling."

Mahret went to Milka, hoping that if nothing else, anger might help to extricate her from the quagmire she was in over her son's death.

Temporarily it did, in part because she had special and intricate knowledge of the situation.

Two years previously, the World Bank and the Swiss Agency for Development and Cooperation (SDC) joined forces with the national government to rehabilitate a part of the city's infrastructure, housing, and economy. They formed a planning committee that was to work on providing clean drinking water and proper wastewater and garbage disposal systems along with public schools and health care centers. A bureaucrat who knew Milka from when she and her husband were respected and known to support charitable projects, got her appointed to the committee.

Through red, swollen eyes, Milka told Mahret that "this was to be a truly 'integrated urban project.' As it developed, however, the other eight members of the local group (all migrants of rural origin), and I, were progressively eliminated from decision-making. They relegated us to the status of passive onlookers.

There are only two government schools for more than 50,000 children, but more than 350 informal schools like ours in the poorest areas of the city. The government has sacrificed one of the best ways for kids to get out of the slums, for the short-term pleasure of the wealthy."

"Who's to blame?"

"The planning committee and the city council, that's who. Initially, the planning committee just sat by and did nothing while the city council continued to allow the road reserves to be swallowed up and turned into slums by greedy developers in richer areas. Then people were made homeless to make way for road and railway expansion. People originally saw an empty space. They set up their huts and then found out they'd built on a road reserve and had to stand by while the government destroyed their homes."

"How do they, the government, justify this?"

"The government advertised that it was building 'decampment sites' or 'giant holding areas' where the thousands displaced could go until new homes were ready for them along the new roadway."

"Doesn't that make a big difference? I'd have thought many people would be glad to take advantage of that."

"No, it doesn't. The decampment sites have decent living conditions, but most are too far away from people's original communities. For societies where life depends on social capital, bartering, and community support and protection, this completely disrupts everything.

I could show you many examples.

For instance, Simon, a man Carden knows, is a skilled carpenter by trade. He came back to Kibera after moving to one of these human holding areas a few weeks ago. He told us that the new quarters are fine, but being so far from Kibera, the loss of a market is ruining his business. Now his only trade is with other residents of the decampment site who, in their newly built temporary homes, have very little need for his skills.

He said, 'I'll starve to death if I have to stay there any longer.'

In the days following the demolition, many people took refuge wherever they could find it closer to where they had been living before the government destroyed their homes. Some moved in with friends or relatives. One woman, along with her six orphaned grandchildren, moved in with her sister. They all slept on the floor in one room. Ironically, others went back to homes in the countryside they had originally left for Kibera. They had left the farm because they were unable to survive there, and now it turned out to be their only refuge."

Mahret got Milka to accompany her and their kids, in a protest march by hundreds of other parents and children. Some carried cardboard signs with slogans demanding the right of every child to get an education. Others in the same way appealed for the homeless.

They wasted their time.

"It's so awful," Mahret later told Barisso, "our rotten little school with its terrible toilets and dark rooms was the one thing I thought might give the kids a chance for a future. It's hopeless here!"

Barisso could not argue. He did not feel Mahret's sense of urgency, but he did also think that it was unfair for the government to think it had the right to prevent the boys from getting an education.

This time, he was not prepared to defend the authority's actions.

From this point on, Mahret and Barisso had to stop concerning themselves about the demolitions only because a more immediate and even more frightening issue came to the fore. It had the potential to destroy all hope they had of any sort of life in Kenya.

Two afternoons after the kids' school disappeared, both parents were out on the street talking to some of their neighbors when one of Barisso's friends, a man named Markime, came running up to them.

"Quick, they're coming," he shouted, "they're just a few minutes away. You better get off the street!"

"Who's coming, what're you talking about?"

"I'm talking about immigration. Two officers were just at your house. They went inside and looked around. Now they're looking for you guys. You have no papers. You're not the only ones around here by a long way, but somebody must have told them about you guys. If they find you and find out for sure, you'll end up in Dadaab or even shipped back to Oromia. You better hide."

Barisso and Mahret went straight to the street behind Milka's house where the boys were playing soccer with their friends.

"Berhanu and Gamado, come with us now," Mahret yelled.

The boys could hear the seriousness in her voice. They did as told.

Barisso picked up Gamado and headed down the street with Mahret and Berhanu following. When they got to the end of the block, he put Gamado down and told Mahret to take both boys for a walk. He would stay close to the house to watch and see what the officials were doing.

"Go to the marketplace; I'll see you there once the coast is clear."

"Okay, be careful they don't see you. We need you here."

"Just go, quickly. I'll catch up in a few minutes."

Barisso went back to about a hundred yards from the house and watched as two suits questioned their neighbors.

"Obviously asking if they know where we are."

The suits went back to the house and went inside again. This time, when they re-emerged, they left the area.

"Obviously, somebody told immigration that we're here without papers. They knew something, or they would not have come straight to our house."

"It could only be Dawit," Mahret said later. "He's never gonna get over me writing uncle and getting half the money. He's bitter."

"Yeah, I think you're right. He's the back-stabbing son of a bitch."

Barisso and Mahret kept the kids away from home the rest of that afternoon for fear the officials might be hanging around.

That evening they sort of snuck home, but they were tense. They did not light the lamp. When they spoke, they spoke in whispers. They froze with fear every time they heard someone walking by their doorway.

The next day other people in the compound kept watch for them.

It was Milka who lent them the critical hand.

"You come and live with me," she told Mahret. "There are only two of us now that Evra is gone. You can stay as long as necessary. We will love to help you."

Mahret was reluctant to take her up on it, but she did not know what else to do.

That evening she and Barisso left the kids with Milka, went home and got some belongings, including two cowhides to sleep on, and then moved in with their friend.

"We won't be here long," Mahret told her, "I will spend all the time I can to find a new place for us in another area. We need to get the boys a new school. Gamado is seven now and Berhanu ten. If they were girls, it wouldn't be that important, but boys need a proper education. We'll get a place where the government won't find us too."

Milka repeated her invitation for them to stay as long as necessary. She also told Mahret that her "acceptance of gender inequality is terribly outdated."

Like Mahret, Barisso now also believed they had to move, though, perhaps, his priorities were not exactly like hers.

"We can't wait. Oromia would be a death sentence for the whole family, and Dadaab is hell on earth."

Chapter 40

OFF TO SCHOOL AGAIN

The family was relatively safe living with Milka. They had moved approximately just two blocks from their old home, but Mahret and Barisso knew that if the men who were looking for them came back, their neighbors would not give them away. So many people in Kibera had escaped from somewhere, and lots did not have the proper documentation. Anyway, for whatever reason, everyone felt at risk whenever officials of any kind came around.

"Mum" was the one word everyone in the compound understood and respected.

However, finding a new home now became the central priority for both parents. Six people crowded into Milka's two little rooms was not going to work in the long-term.

After they both spent the bulk of several days looking around without success for an empty shanty, Mahret came up with a new strategy.

"We should stop looking in Kibera. Instead, we should see if we can locate a good school for the kids somewhere outside this terrible place first. Do it now instead of later, and only then see if we can find a home close by. It should be an English-speaking school too because all the new world people Milka tells me about came from Britain. And it should be Christian since that's the only religion the kids know."

Barisso had no problem with that.

"You've been talking about moving for a long time," he said. "Go ahead and do as you like. I'll go back to tending my garden while I try to find other work."

Several Christian schools were advertising on street poles, bus shelter benches, and construction fences—Muthaiga Primary School, Eden Annex Primary School, Valley Bridge Primary School, Our Lady of Fatima Secondary School, and so on. The one that intrigued Mahret the most was the Harmony Child Rescue Center that Rekik had told her about when she and the kids first arrived in Kibera. Along with instruction in English, it promised agricultural training within Nairobi. Mahret thought it would be wonderful for her sons to experience something of the country life they had once enjoyed on the farm.

"Harmony Child Rescue Centre is a Christian facility too," she noted, "though it accepts all children. As a rescue center, it must also be charitable. Maybe it won't charge."

The ad for the school gave an address in Kasarani, a phone number, and the name of the Australian founder and director, Caroline Ellingson. It also boasted much better than average facilities. It had eight classrooms for 290 students, a student–teacher ratio of about one to twenty-five and, almost as important, a toilet to student ratio of about one to twenty-two. Its outdoor cook house looked very basic and small on one of the ads, but the ad also claimed the school was in the process of constructing a big new kitchen in a separate building.

Mahret thought that the agricultural component could be a selling point with Barisso, and she mentioned it to him.

He was duly impressed.

"Maybe they'll hire me to teach them," he joked.

"Okay," Mahret said, "then we agree. Let's go to Harmony Child Rescue Centre and see if they'll accept the kids and if they will, help us with the costs."

"No," he replied, "you go ahead and do it yourself. If it looks okay, I might come to see it later."

Mahret went to Milka for advice.

"We are trying to find a new place to live so we can get out of your hair," she said, "but we want to find a place close to where the boys can go to school. I saw an ad for one that has a farm in a place called Kasarani, but where is this Kasarani? Is it close?"

"Don't worry about getting out of my hair, but, yes, I do know where it is. We, my husband and I, once lived in Dandora, about five miles from there. We left because the part of Dandora we lived in was close to the biggest garbage dump in the world. It's Nairobi's only major dumping ground, and the Dandora Oxygenation Pond, which is a big part of it, is the city's main sewage treatment works. It discharges processed water into the Nairobi River."

"Is the dumpsite awful?"

"It's an environmental hazard. The burning of the waste during the night sometimes makes you choke. They said it was poisoning the air and making people sick. A lot of people were dying from diseases, malaria, tuberculosis, and simple diarrhea. We felt desperate to get away, so we moved."

"So, the school would be too close to it?"

"Not really. Dandora is divided into five phases extending out from the dump. Kasarani is on the south end, beyond the fifth stage. It won't be affected any more than most of the neighborhoods in Nairobi. To get there, you go about ten kilometers past the dump. It's worth it to take a bus. Take one of the big ones. You'll be out of Kibera so they're more dependable. If you walk that way (she pointed down the road) to just beyond the fence and wait at the first bus stop, you'll eventually see one with a sign that says 'Kasarani.' It is very cheap, about a shilling, and then if you have an exact address, you should ask the driver to tell you when you get as close to it as possible. It will take about an hour on the bus."

Mahret determined to try to convince Barisso that they should both visit the school.

"Maybe you actually could get a job on the farm. Who knows, they might just need someone with experience to work in the field or something."

But Barisso was shy in front of people who had a better education than him. He resisted.

She kept at him.

"Listen, I know it's a long shot, but we have to move, and wouldn't it be nice if we could find a job for you at the same time and a good place for our children to get an education and learn English?"

He continued to resist.

"Look, I told you to do this yourself. You're the one who's so insistent the kids have to get back to school so soon, so you're the one who should handle it. I have other things to do."

Mahret threatened to apply for the farming job herself.

"I did just about as much farming as you. I helped with harvest and planting and the animals. I wouldn't have a problem talking about any part of farming in Oromia. I even know what's wrong with the soil, that it needs rest, and more dung. This Miss Ellingson is a woman; she's the headmistress. And she's educated like Milka. I'm pretty sure she'd be willing to hire a woman to do farming."

That did the trick.

The next morning after breakfast, Barisso followed his wife down the road, to the bus to Kasarani.

By this time, they had an address for the school.

"Do you know," Mahret asked the driver, "where Kwangura Estate is?'

"Yes, that is on our route. We go right past it."

"Will you let us know when we get there?"

"No problem."

Forty-five minutes later, the driver pulled up alongside a small park.

"Just walk across the open area until you come to the buildings you see there. That's Kwangura Estate."

It was hot, and the wind was blowing. As they walked along, their feet stirred up the dust.

"I hope we don't look too dirty when we get to the school," Mahret said.

"Who cares? We're trying to convince them we're farmers, aren't we?"

"Barisso, happy up, this is for you too."

Chapter 41

HARMONY CHILD RESCUE CENTER

This day, Mahret and Barisso would later agree, was to be one of the luckiest of their life together. Little did they know as they approached the school that by the end of the afternoon, everything they had dared hope for, would come to pass—including a new farming experience.

When they got to the other side of the field, they came to a wall that was about ten feet high with a great solid wooden gate.

"I don't see a sign," Mahret said, "but this could be the entrance to the school."

Barisso knocked on the gate; it swung open. They heard what sounded like children playing.

"Can I help you?" A man asked.

Mahret found her voice first.

"Uh, we have two children."

"And you would like to enroll them in Harmony?"

"Yes, I think so."

"Well, we are quite full, but you can talk to Miss Ellingson, our headmistress. Please follow me."

As they walked across the school grounds, Mahret looked closely at the facilities. The buildings looked a bit warn, but they had real glass windows, and the roof was tiled—no tin. She also noticed that the playground had swings and teeter-totters, and there was a small playing field beyond them.

When they got inside the school, they walked down a hallway to a small office with a large glass window on one side and a desk in the middle with two chairs in front of it.

"Take a seat," the man said, "I will find Miss Ellingson and let her know you're waiting to see her."

They waited nervously for a few minutes until a very ordinary-looking white woman entered the office and sat down behind the desk.

"*Akkam* folks," she said, "welcome to Harmony. My name is Caroline Ellingson. What can I do for you?"

"Well, we have two young boys," Mahret said, "one is seven years old and the other is ten. We want them to go to school."

"This school?"

"Yes. Well, that is, we would like to know more about your school. We think it should be the best, but we wanted to talk to you."

Miss Ellingson was clearly very proud of what her Harmony had to offer, and its accomplishments under her direction.

"We support nearly 500 children at Harmony, providing school fees, uniforms, books, supplies, and meals. We enable all the children to attend celebratory events at the school too, like our annual Christmas party. We also see to their medical care at Mercy Hospital, and we prepare students to take tests in all the core subjects so that we can place them in the proper grades.

We have a family care program as well for approximately a hundred children.

They all require a higher level of support, either because they have been placed in foster care or because their family situation is extremely vulnerable.

On top of that, we help students who complete secondary school to apply for a Promise Scholarship to attend a vocational/technical university when they graduate from Harmony. These scholarships are highly competitive and awarded only to top students."

"That sounds wonderful," Mahret said, "perfect for our boys. Will you take them?"

"The problem is we are full; we set up for 290 kids but now have nearly twice that many. On top of that, our farm manager just quit. He is very old, and he told me just this morning that he can't do it anymore. It is difficult to get a good farmer in the middle of this city who can relate to children. We grow so much of our own food supply here. We need the vegetables and fruit and the wheat for flour, and we teach farming to the kids too, we always have."

"My husband, Barisso, is a farmer! He was an outstanding farmer. He can do everything, planting wheat and corn, looking after animals, everything!"

Mahret looked at Barisso and nodded.

"Yes, I, that is, I am, a farmer. I farmed all my life until just a while ago."

"He has grown lots of wheat and maize and almost every garden food you can think of. He was a terrific farmer. Everyone in our neighborhood said so. He's been farming even here in Kibera, you know bag farming. He just can't give it up."

Ms. Ellingson smiled, "you're quite the spokesman for your husband. I like your spunk. Maybe God sent you to us today. We really are desperate. Could you start work tomorrow?"

She looked at Barisso.

"Yeah, I, I think so."

Mahret cut in again:

"He can for sure. It's no problem but will you pay us, I mean him?"

"It depends; I assume you do not have money to pay our tuition fees for your children, or uniforms, textbooks, and supplies?"

"No, we don't."

"How about if I let your boys come to the school without charge and I pay you a small sum, say 6,500 shillings a month on top of that? Would that work?"

"Yes, that would work. We could move close, where would we live, is there some houses close?"

"Well the best might be Dandora. It's about three miles from here. It would be a bit of a walk for the kids, but it is doable."

"But Dandora has a terrible garbage dump that poisons the people."

"Yes, the people who live close to it, but if you move to this end of Dandora you will be miles from the dump. We are basically in the same area, and we have had no problems here. We have a connection in Dandora in an area they designated "stage four" when they upgraded it. It is to the east and north of the dump. The Kaskazi monsoon winds from the north, and the later Kuzi winds from the south, push the odors and pollutants away from these areas. The only time you should be bothered by the smell from the dump is during the transitional periods when the winds stop blowing.

Then the smell settles on the entire city. I am sure you've noticed it before. But it is no worse in our areas than anywhere else."

"Maybe it would be okay then. What do you think Barisso?"

"Uh, yeah, should work, I guess."

"I can give you people an address where you will find a man who will help you find a home. The area is considered poor, but the government has done quite a lot of work on it, and the housing is better than in most other such districts like in Kibera. I think you would like it there. What do you think?"

Mahret looked at Barisso again.

"Okay," he said, "I think that would be okay, but what all would I do?"

Mahret wanted to hit him.

"Basically, in the spring, you would plant the corn and wheat, then fertilize it, irrigate it, and harvest it when ready. We leave about half the land in summer fallow each year so you would have about an acre all told. You would also plant and look after the garden and bring in the vegetables when ready: Lemons, onions, cilantro, peppers and tomatoes, and leafy greens, spinach, kale, or collards.

We also grow fruit: oranges, lemons, and mangos, pears, papaws, bananas, and pineapples."

"That sounds fine," Mahret said, "Barisso is a wonderful farmer. You will really like him."

Ms. Ellingson smiled again:

"Your enthusiasm is impossible to resist. We will give you a three months' probation period, and if we are both happy after that, we can make our arrangement permanent."

"Great."

"We have a deal then. Bring the children to school as soon as you find a place to live. They will be starting at least two weeks late, but we can get them caught up. Mr. Barisso, you get the family moved and report here as soon as you can. Perhaps tomorrow is too soon for you, but please come as soon as you can. We are trying to do our best with the crops and garden, but we really only sort of know what we're doing."

"He can come tomorrow morning. Don't worry, he will be here."

The headmistress took their names and the names and ages of the children. She also gave Barisso a card for an agent in Dandora stage four who, she said, would find them a rental property at a fair price.

Miss Ellingson walked them back to the school gate and shook each of their hands.

"Goodbye for now. The sooner you can get the children here, the better for them; and, Mr. Barisso, the sooner you can get here, the better for all of us."

"He can come tomorrow for sure. I can find a new place by myself."

"Are you sure?" she said, looking at Barisso.

"Yes, okay, I will."

They tuned and headed back down the dusty street.

Mahret took the card for the rental agent from Barisso.

Suddenly, the future looked more assured than it had for some time. The family would move, the two boys would go to school, and Barisso would have a job, a good job. Mahret would spend her time buying food with what would be left from the money the Uncle in New Zealand sent and from what Barisso brought in after they paid the rent.

Barisso was happy too, though he tried to hide it.

"You don't do that ever again," he lectured Mahret. "You don't talk for me like that. You don't speak for me."

He, of course, recognized the futility in such a statement. And the thrilling thought of being a fulltime farmer again, a real farmer, tempered his anger.

Anyway, Mahret had done the right thing overall.

Moreover, she apologized.

"I know Barisso, you're the head of the family. I'm sorry. I was just so happy for you and for us. I couldn't hold back. I always get carried away."

"Hmm."

Chapter 42

STEPPING UP

The next morning, Mahret left Barisso to report to work, and she took the bus system again to get to Dandora stage four. Unlike most of Kibera, it had real streets, and the bus got her close to the address on the card Caroline Ellingson had given her.

When she got to the address, she found a sign marked "Mohammad Asarbajany, rental agent." The sign was on street level in what appeared to be a relatively new three- or four-story apartment block.

She knocked on the door.

"Hello, my name is Mohammad. What I can do for you?"

"My name is Mahret, I uh, that is, Caroline Ellingson, gave me your card. She said you might help me find a home here in Dandora."

"Yes, I help Caroline's families. What kind of home? How much you can pay?"

"I was thinking maybe about 2,500 shillings a month."

"I have a nice place available, but it's three times that much."

"Can you show me?"

Mohammad led her to a two-story building on the other side of the street. They entered and climbed the stairs to the second floor.

"This building is only five years old," he told her; "it is in good shape, and it has a toilet on each floor and a washroom beside it. There is a water tap on each floor too, and the apartment has a kerosene cooker.

But can you afford it?"

Mahret was thrilled.

"It's all so new and seems so clean," she thought, "it doesn't smell like Kibera, and the paint on the walls looks good. It isn't marked and scratched very much. And three rooms all to ourselves!"

"Would you take 6,000 shillings?"

"No. I'll tell you what; I will let you have it for 7,500 a month."

"How about I give you seventy American dollars?"

"You drive a hard bargain. But, okay, if you can pay me the first month's rent now."

"Yes, but that's all I can afford."

"Okay."

Mahret had brought two fifty-dollar bills with her. Do you have change?" she asked as she pulled them out of her satchel.

Mohammad smiled, "you're a business lady; you could have paid what I asked. Yes, let's go back to my office, and I will get you the change, but it will be in shillings."

On the way home in the bus, light tears once more clouded Mahret's eyes, but this time happy tears.

"At last, a nice place. All our own and the boys can go to a real school. We will be clean and safe, like on the farm. We don't have much extra spending money, but with the churches, it will be enough. Life will be better now."

The same day Mahret and Barisso got the kids to help them move all their smaller belongings over on the bus. Then, they left the kids in the new home and made another trip to Mashimoni to get their beds.

On the ride back, an older lady was most annoyed that she could not sit down because the cumbersome cowhides and mattresses took up two full seats.

"Silly bitch," Mahret whispered.

They both laughed.

The first thing the following morning, Barisso went to work at Harmony, and Mahret registered both boys.

The government, with help from the World Health Organization, had started upgrading the Dandora districts as long ago as 1977. However, the area still had slum-like qualities. As Mahret was to learn, while, percentagewise, more people seemed to have a job, lots also mixed and socialized on the streets during the day. Sexually transmitted diseases were well-known, and young girls were also liable to sleep with older men for one reason or another. At nights, lots of suspicious-looking characters prowled the streets.

Still, the housing Mahret, Barisso, and the kids now had was much better than before. Also, the streets were streets and did not have a little stream flowing down the center full of a variety of wastes. Moreover, people who lived in the immediate area were as neighborly as those in Kibera. Cohesion was largely unaffected by a similar mixture of races, religions, and languages.

There were thirteen families (consisting of one to six members) in the new compound. Six of them were Oromo, who had originally fled persecution and/or poor harvests. Four were Kenyan Christians. One was Ethiopian Jewish. And the other two were Muslims who were escaping the violence they had faced in the region they inhabited along the Kenyan/Sudanese border.

Here too, all worked together. As needed, and when they could, they fed and looked out for each other's kids, and they shared information about anything that might have a significant impact on their lives.

"Dandora, like Mashimoni, has its problems," Mahret told Barisso, "but at least people pull together to survive just like they did in the old compound. I remember when I walked through Kibera for the first time, what struck me most were the smiles. I couldn't believe it, they were everywhere, relieving the nervousness I felt about being in a new country. I saw more friendly faces in Kibera than I had seen in a long time, and it made me feel less like a stranger. They were nice and accepting of each other. It's the same here."

People helped each other to educate the children on civilized behavior too.

"My new friend, Dallia, whose husband is dead, told me that when her son got in a fight with one of his friends from school, a guy from another family on her street took both boys aside and gave them a firm lecture. He told them that fighting is unacceptable here; that all the boys are brothers; and they all have a sacred duty to help each other. The boys shook hands and apologized. Dallia says they're friends again."

Dallia told Mahret that the community was even starting a fund that young girls would be able to go to for money to buy sanitary pads.

"I promised to give them fifty shillings a month if they get enough overall to make the plan work," she told Barisso. "That is so little, and someday it might help protect young boys from a disease. They're trying to get the government to match our money."

The local security gang did not have control of public utilities or housing. It, therefore, made a living almost totally by providing security. For that reason, its members tended to do a very good job. At first, Mahret accompanied her two boys to and from the school. They crossed the Nairobi River over a footbridge less than a half-mile from home and then veered north until they got to the Kasarani Mwik Road, which they then followed to Kwangura Estate. They managed the walk in about thirty-five minutes.

Mahret saw some of the gang each trip monitoring the kids closely and, consequently, figured they could accomplish the walk just fine without her.

Berhanu and Gamado soon got to know other Harmony students who lived in their area, and they started to make the journey with several of them.

Berhanu and two other bigger boys made sure that all the kids—large and small, boys and girls—stayed together in a group.

Normally, they would get to school early enough to play in the yard before the bell rang.

Both Berhanu and Gamado loved their school uniforms.

"So wonderful," Mahret told Barisso. "They all feel they come from a decent home; and they all feel the same, no rich, no poor, no lording it over other kids by some who have more money."

No one in the family was happier than Barisso. He loved the feeling of being part of real farming again. He so enjoyed the job that from the beginning, he made a habit of going to work well before school started and coming home well after it ended.

He asked Ms. Ellingson to get a van and driver she sometimes hired for school outings to haul several his plants from the river allotment in Mashimoni to Harmony. After he explained the advantages this would provide to low-income families, Ms. Ellingson was fully supportive.

"I can show the kids how to grow food in their own homes. If they do it properly, they can even bring in a small income, " he told her.

"What a good idea," she said, "God's speed."

"I can keep the plants by the cornfield and bring them inside at night when the weather is really bad."

"Wonderful!"

Chapter 43

DISCIPLINE: WHAT'S THAT?

Mahret woke up one morning thinking about the time, now more than a year back, when she had gone to thank the man who saved the boys' little friend on that frightening occasion when an evil man tried to carry him off. She had known then that the boy's savior was an immigrant from the Gambella region, a part of Ethiopia she had never even seen. She knew he was Muslim, too, as his daughter was wearing a hijab. Yet what stuck in her mind was not his origin or his religion, but that he was witty and funny, reminding her of a neighboring farmer who had made her laugh at times back home.

"I do what I can," he told her when she praised his quick action and concern for the child. "I try to help even Oromo when I think maybe there's the slightest chance they're worth it."

Mahret was startled by the remark, until she saw the glint in his eyes and laughed with him.

"If we ever get the chance, we will help you too," she told him.

"I might be beyond hope, but great."

When they said their goodbyes, she actually kind of hugged him.

Mahret thought a lot about social relationships. On the farm, they had lived daily with Oromo Christians who spoke the same mother tongue, celebrated the same festive occasions, concerned themselves about the same things, such as the condition of their land and crops, and also worshipped at the same local church. While there were jealousies amongst them, expressed mainly in the form of gossip, there was also a certain understanding, a sense of comradery. What reinforced this was a feeling that any people who did not share their way of life were outsiders; they were "others" and, therefore, worthy of a good deal of suspicion, even contempt – Tigrans who monopolized the Ethiopian government, Somalis who were Sunni Muslims, city people from Addis Ababa or even Shashamane, misguided Christians who were not of their denomination. Each of these groups, they had always viewed as a large, at least slightly evil lot, rather than as individual men, women, and children with their separate ways and daily concerns.

Now, as they found themselves pulling together with such a great diversity of cultures, real personalities kept peeking out from them. They seemed so real to her in part because they all shared most of her own concerns. They too wanted most of all to keep their families together, safe, sound, and healthy. And most wanted their children to get an education. Also, so many in Mashimoni had helped her family so much, keeping watch for immigration, feeding the boys when Dawit turned on them, protecting them from the predatory outsiders, or taking the kids to the field beside the river to play football. They, like her, were all just human beings living through a difficult life and knowing full well that if they could help to make it better for others, it would be better for them too.

"They were me, and I was them. It's the same now. Nothing has changed."

Yes, there were bad people in the compounds who refused to meld with the rest, like Dawit, for instance, but they were a small number.

"*Waqaa* knows, back home, there were Oromo I didn't always agree with. Some men drank way too much. And what about the one, what was his name, who beat his wife till she almost died? There were others I didn't like, too, in our own neighborhood. What about Sammy who killed our sheep because it strayed onto his field?

But most we knew were decent human beings, and it's the same here, only in this case they come from such a wide range of races, religions, and ways of making a living. I've been amazed to see good ones that aren't Oromo, or Christians, or even farmers. How could I have been so ignorant?

I will never be like that again."

Mahret had not lost her pride in Oromo or Oromia. She would always have fond memories of her home and neighborhood back there. It was still the best. But praising whole groups and condemning others outright, she knew, she could no longer do.

Mahret suspected that her boys must also be becoming more forbearing than people back on the farm as they played with all the different kids in their school and community. Berhanu and Gamado never seemed even to realize that their playmates came from all over Africa and from families with different backgrounds and cultures. Matters of race and religion never made their way into the playground. To them, all these "others" were not others at all. They were kids like them, and they judged them on little else than personality and playability.

A few weeks into their time at Harmony, Mahret would have been surprised to learn that if asked, both boys would have said that what impressed them the most about the new school had nothing whatever to do with their friends.

It was, of all things, the importance of punctuality.

Most weekdays, the boys were left on their own to get to classes.

Barisso was so enthusiastic about the farming job that he left for work each morning as the sun's rays were beginning to peek over the horizon. And on three mornings during the week, *haadha* would leave at about the same time to go to one of the churches in Kibera for food.

Meeting their group on time for the trek to school was not always that easy for Berhanu and Gamado as they did not have a device like a clock or watch to tell them precisely what time it was. What they figured out was that classes started about an hour after sun-up. Usually, that worked well enough, as those kids who got to the meeting place first would normally wait a few minutes for stragglers. One morning, however, Berhanu and Gamado were more than a few minutes late. The previous evening, they had stayed out until after dark playing street football. They got up late and made their way to school alone, and about ten minutes after the bell had rung. The big gate was closed, and no one answered their knocks and calls until the first recess.

It was Mr. Headly, the vice-principal who finally let them in.

"Why are you late?" he demanded.

The boys did not recognize the depth of the gravity in his tone and, thus, did not even realize they were in trouble.

Presumably, this was in part at least because left on their own so much of the time over the last few years, they had learned very little in the way of discipline. It was just not part of a life that left them unsupervised so much of the time.

"I dunno," Berhanu replied.

"Dunno? What do you mean by that? We do not allow this! You have missed your early morning classes. We admitted you two when all sorts of other kids would have done anything to have your places. This is unacceptable."

He took them into his office, raised a pipe with a strap attached to the end of it over his head, and slammed it down on his desk with a loud "thud!"

"This does not tickle when you feel it on your behind."

He made them lie across the desk one at a time and gave them each a good thrashing. It hurt.

Gamado cried. Berhanu just managed to hold back the tears.

"Way you go," Mr. Headly said, "Berhanu, you're in arithmetic, down the hall on your right. Gamado, follow me, you're in printing."

The boys were impressed.

From that point on, they did everything they could to get to their meeting place and into school with their friends.

This experience may at least in part have been the reason why they were soon doing well academically.

The atmosphere in all the classrooms tended to be both serious and intense. Kids were classed according to the education they had when they first arrived at the school. That meant the classes served a multiplicity of ages. Berhanu and Gamado had taken no Math or Science in their last school. Therefore, they attended the same classes for those subjects. But they had both learned to read and write more or less appropriate to their age levels. For Literature, Gamado was in grade three and Berhanu grade six. Their teachers reported that both boys could progress appropriately through all the subjects.

What the boys, themselves, liked the best was phys. ed. The school had a proper kinesiology program with an instructor, who supervised them in the important team sports—football, cricket, and basketball—all with the correct rules and a referee. Weather permitting, they played in the schoolyard as Miss Ellingson had not been able yet to build a proper indoor gymnasium.

On the days when it did not rain, Berhanu and Gamado were in no hurry to head home after classes. They often stayed behind for an hour or so to play one of the sports they were taking in class with the other boys. Normally, the kids played well together.

There were, of course, exceptions.

The games always included some of the orphan kids who lived at the school. One, Jonah, was big and seemed to have a chip on his shoulder. He could be rough with the other kids and, at times, tried to push them around. One afternoon when Berhanu and Gamado were leaving for home through the big gate after a game of football, Jonah came up behind them and slapped Berhanu on the back, hard.

"Hey," Berhanu said, "what'd ya do that for?"

"I'm just bein friendly. Sayin how are ya?"

"That hurt, don't ever do that again."

"Oh, tough guy, you threatening me?"

"I'm tellin you, don't do that again."

"And if I do, you gonna do something about it."

"I might."

The two kids were now facing each other. Jonah slapped Berhanu on the shoulder from the front.

"I warned you!"

Berhanu hit him in the chin hard with his fist knocking him down.

"If you know what's good for ya, don't get up. I'll beat the hell outa ya."

Jonah jumped up and grabbed Berhanu in a wrestling hold. Berhanu just managed to stay on his feet, pushing him back and away. When Jonah came at him again, Berhanu ducked down, twisted his torso, and flipped him into the air. He hit the ground hard and headfirst.

Berhanu pounced on him and started hitting him on the back of the head with both fists. Gamado yelled at him.

"Stop Berhanu, you're gonna kill him."

Berhanu kept hitting him.

Gamado jumped on him from behind, wrapping both arms around his neck.

Berhanu stood up, reached back with one hand, and pulled Gamado over his shoulder. He landed on Jonah.

Gamado rolled to one side and lay on the ground, trying to catch his breath.

Berhanu was shocked at his own actions.

He had always been his brother's protector.

"You alright?"

Gamado let him have it.

"Berhanu, what's wrong with you? One day you're gonna kill somebody. They'll put you in jail. The police'll kill you."

"I don't fucking care. Let's get out of here."

Berhanu grabbed Gamado by the arm and pulled him back up onto his feet.

Two other boys helped Jonah to a sitting position. He had a vague look on his face as though he couldn't comprehend what had just happened.

"Everything's spinning."

He struggled to his feet.

"I'm gonna go to my room and lie down."

Gamado knew his brother was quick to temper. He had seen this type of behavior in him before, in Mashimoni. But he had never felt he had to try to stop him from hurting someone badly.

"Jeez" he said, "you could get in trouble for this. We better don't tell nobody."

Gamado was shocked too when he thought he saw a tear trickling down his brother's cheek.

Berhanu told Gamado he didn't "give a shit" about getting into trouble.

Nonetheless, he was relieved the next morning to see Jonah on the playground looking his usual self.

From that point on, he treated him with some respect and, eventually, the two of them found they had quite a lot in common. On one level, this might have been a natural outcome of the fact that they both had lived relatively traumatic lives.

One of the characteristics they shared was a natural affinity for physical challenges. They liked to show their prowess at throwing, kicking or dribbling a ball, doing push-ups or chin-ups on the bar in the playground, and feats like arm-wrestling.

It was Berhanu who came up with the idea of a "fight club."

"You know what?" he told Jonah one day, "we could have a lot of fun and find out who's the toughest kid at school at the same time."

"What're you talkin about?"

"I was thinking, we could take all the boys and make them fight each other until we figure out who is the best in each age level. We could hold the fights on the other side of the cornfield after school, where nobody can see us. We'll start at grade three and work our way up to grade six.

It'll be a lot of fun."

"Yeah but we'd get in trouble?"

"Nobody will get hurt. It'll be just like football or any other sport. Me and you will be there for every fight, and we can make sure they stop before anyone gets hurt bad."

Jonah was not hard to convince. He figured if he had another chance, he could even take Berhanu. He would win for the grade six, and everyone would see that he was the real boss around here.

Berhanu, of course, figured he would win and secure his present stature.

"I'll get Gamado to fight for grade three," he said. "You pick a kid you think will give him the most trouble."

"What if they won't fight?"

"We'll make'm fight."

When Berhanu told his brother that he was going to be in the first fight, Gamado told him to "go to hell."

"If you wanna fight so bad you fight somebody your age. Take on Jonah again. Leave the rest of us alone. Let's see how tough you are."

"Good idea, I can beat any of the guys around here. I'll fight anybody in grade six, and I'll beat the hell out of 'em. But we're starting in grade three. That's you. You're gonna go first. Jonah's finding some kid to fight you. We'll bring him in tomorrow, and I bet he cleans your clock."

"Just leave me alone."

Berhanu did not leave his brother alone. The next afternoon when the boys would normally be heading home, he grabbed Gamado by the arm and used a combination of flattery and coercion on him.

"Hey Gamado, I really do believe you're the toughest kid in your class. You're one of the biggest, and I know you're really powerful. Sometimes when you get mad, I can barely stop you from beating me up. How'd you like to prove yourself? The kids'll really look up to you."

"No," Gamado told him, "I don't wanna fight. What if I'm not the toughest? I don't want no black eye."

"Nah, that's not gonna happen, no one can hurt you. This is just wussy wrestling. You'll just beat the hell out of them all anyway, and then they'll really want to be your friend. They'll do anything you say."

Jonah appeared dragging along another boy.

"Hey, you guys, this here is Malto. He says he's the toughest kid in grade three."

"No, he's not, Gamado is. Gamado could take him with one hand tied behind his back."

"I don't wanna fight," Malto said.

"And I don't want to too," Gamado added. "Leave us alone."

Jonah might have let it go at that point, but Berhanu persisted.

"You guys stop being babies. One quick fight. It'll be over in a minute, and one of you will be the hero."

When Gamado tried to pull away, Berhanu yanked him back.

"Come on don't be a baby; get out there and show us you're a man. You're embarrassing me."

A crowd of kids had gathered around them, and the two boys suddenly felt they couldn't back down. Gamado was scared of Malto and he was shaking a little as the fight began. But he fought as hard as he could.

The boys grabbed and struggled with each other, and then Malto hit Gamado in the face with a clenched fist. Gamado fell, but he jumped back up quickly and ran at Malto with his head down. He hit him in the stomach with his shoulder, knocking him hard to the ground.

"I give up, I give up!" Malto cried, holding the back of his head with both hands.

"That's enough big guy. You're the winner," Berhanu told Gamado, "we'll have another fight for you soon."

"If there's a lump tomorrow, Malto, just tell Mr. Headly you fell down the stairs. Don't let him find out you were in a fight."

Thereafter, Berhanu and Jonah held a fight whenever they could line one up. They would pick out two boys at a time from one of the grades three, four, five, or six who were more or less the same age and size. Some wanted to fight, others not so much.

Boys will be boys. There was always a sizeable audience. The kids jeered and cheered, and a couple of them would usually lift a clear winner onto their shoulders and parade him around a bit when the fight was over.

True to their predictions, Berhanu and Jonah proved to be the toughest two kids in the grade six group. They had little difficulty with the opponents each of them got to fight the other. Twice challenged by kids a little bigger than him, Berhanu came out on top in part because he was as aggressive and determined mentally as physically. He just would not quit no matter what, and his adversaries eventually gave up from exhaustion if nothing else.

Berhanu made them articulate the words "I give up" before he would let them go.

"Jeez Berhanu, you guys are gonna get in trouble," Gamado warned him. "When Mr. Headly finds out, you and Jonah will get strapped for sure."

"Who cares?"

And, of course, the vice-principal eventually did find out. The day Berhanu and Jonah were scheduled to fight each other, Mr. Headly saw one of the other combatants sporting a black eye. He took him aside and interrogated him. It didn't take long to break him down. The kid naturally blamed it all on Berhanu and Jonah.

After school, Mr. Headly grabbed both of them by the scruff of the neck as they were heading out to the open area behind the cornfield.

"There will be no more fighting at this school," he said. "Jonah, you get back to your room, and Berhanu, you go straight home. I want to see both of you in my office first thing tomorrow morning. Do you understand?"

Both boys shook their heads in the affirmative.

"Okay, remember, first thing tomorrow morning!"

"It's not my fault," Jonah blurted out, "I was being friendly, and he punched me without warning. He started it all."

"That's a lie, he hit me first. I had to fight back."

"I don't know what you guys are talking about. It sounds like there's more to this than the fight club. We'll have to get to the bottom of it in the morning."

Neither boy slept well that night.

Chapter 44

NICE CLUB

When Berhanu got to school the next day, one of the kids told him he was supposed to go straight to the vice-principal's office. There, he saw Jonah sitting on a chair beside the big desk looking paler than usual.

The vice-principal made them tell him all about their club and about the fight they had with each other. As they talked, they kept eyeing the strap lying across his desk.

"I sense," he said, "that you two were going to have to finish your battle once you got all the other kids over theirs. You're not going to do that. Your club is disbanded now. Do you understand?"

Jonah said, "yes, sir."

Mr. Headly took both boys to one of the empty classrooms down the hall and pulled two desks together.

He whipped Jonah first. He came away from it, looking like he wanted to cry. But he did not cry.

"You can go now," Mr. Headly said.

"Okay, Berhanu, your turn. I don't know what we're going to do with you. You seem to be a real problem. Is there something that we should know about?"

"No, sir."

"How is it that you are back here waiting for the strap a second time in such a few days?"

"I dunno. I didn't mean to cause trouble. We were just having a little fun."

"But you knew it was wrong. You snuck over to the area behind the cornfield to stage your fights, like a bandit. Explain that."

"It was just a good place. We weren't really trying to hide."

"Do I look that stupid?"

Mr. Headly then put him through the same ordeal as before. But this time, the whip hurt more. Such physical pain Berhanu had never felt before.

But again, he refused to cry.

"I know you have never had to face anything like this before," the vice-principal said. "But we have to teach you here about civilized behavior, and we can't do it with nearly 500 kids unless we're serious about it.

This better not be necessary again. It won't will it."

Berhanu got up off the desk.

"I dunno," was all he said.

"Well, I can tell you, next time you're out, of the school, that is. Is that what you want?"

"I don't care."

"Really, you don't even care? I don't know what to say to you. Get out of here."

Berhanu went home, but the episode was not quite over.

The afternoon following the strapping, Miss Ellingson sent a note home with Gamado in a sealed envelope, asking Mahret to come to school as soon as possible to talk about her sons. Miss Ellingson told Gamado that the note was for his mother only and that no one was to see it before she did.

He carried it inside his notebook.

The following morning, Mahret told the boys she was going to school with them.

"What for?" Berhanu asked.

"I just want to talk to Miss Ellingson to see how you guys are doing."

"Ah Jeez," Berhanu thought, "bet Miss E wants to tell *haadha* about the fight club and the strapping."

"How embarrassing," he said, "what if somebody sees us walkin with our *haadha*? They'll think we're a couple of wusses."

"A couple of what?"

"Wusses."

"Yeah, wusses."

"Well, you just tell them you're not wusses, whatever that means."

Mahret found Miss Ellingson in her office.

As previously, she was very friendly.

"*Akaam* Mahret," she said.

"*Akaam*. Your note said you want to see me. Is everything okay?"

"I think so. I'm just a little concerned because we have had a lot of cases here of children abused at home. I just want to be sure that Berhanu isn't one of them."

"Of course, he's not one of them! My children are safe in our house! No one would ever abuse them. We love them, and we protect them. Everything we do is for the children. Why do you say this? Why you worry with Berhanu? You have a reason?"

"Well, we watch all the kids closely here. Some who show signs of aggressive behavior have had very trying incidents in their lives."

"Aggressive, what you mean? Is Berhanu aggressive? Has he done something?"

"I don't want to suggest anything, it's probably just a regular boy thing, but he was in a fight with one of the other kids, and then he and one of the boys started what they called a 'fight club.' They made other kids fight with each other. From what we understand, Berhanu was the main instigator."

"Really?"

"Yes, and sometimes we find out that with some kids like this, there is a problem at home, a father or step-father or uncle or whatever has been abusing them."

"There is no trouble like that at our home. My husband would never abuse the children. He loves them like I do."

"Then your Barisso is not violent or anything like that; he doesn't hide things he does with the boys from you?"

"No, I lived alone with the boys for two years. Barisso has only been with us for eight months. There is no chance he would do anything like that. He loves the kids. And they love him. They would tell me if anything […]"

"Okay, are you aware of the sexual abuse that goes on here in some of the homes? Because you spent so much of your life on the farm, I doubt if you are aware of a lot of it. As a mother, you need to be."

"What do you mean? What has this got to do with Berhanu?"

"See, some children who show aggressive behavior are reacting to sexual abuse. The fighting your son was involved in might be normal. Boys will be boys. However, I think I better paint you a complete picture just in case there is a problem that could be affecting Berhanu and even Gamado. I'm not saying there is, I'm just telling you this in case there could be. I think you should know about it anyway. Some of your friends and neighbors are facing it almost for sure.

Please listen to me. We can talk about your personal situation in more depth when I'm finished."

Mahret was feeling angry at the suggestion of even the possibility of abuse in her home. Still, she thought she better listen, or Miss Ellingson would think she was hiding something. She let her go on.

"A lot of boys in the informal settlements are sexually abused. They call it sexualization. Here are some signs. Some show preoccupation with their own private parts or interest in the private parts of other kids. Some want to have a good wash more than usual, as if trying to wash away the experience. They might also show signs of being afraid, or they feel guilt, and they might go into a panic at times without knowing why. They might be afraid of men, of strangers, of being left alone, and of going to school. They might have nightmares and wake up in the middle of the night, shaking and afraid.

A lot of kids like that are reacting to sexual abuse, and many by their father. Some of the fathers are just pedophiles. They're mentally ill. Others have AIDS, and they believe that the one way to get rid of it is to have intercourse with a child—boy or girl—usually, they will go after somebody else's kid. But some will go after their own if they can't find another one. They don't care who they hurt as long as they get rid of their disease."

"What? Do it to a child to get rid of AIDS? How could they believe that?"

"I'm afraid that's the 'urban myth' here. People also call it the 'virgin cleansing myth.' It's that having sex with a virgin is the only way to cure sexual diseases, oh, and to prevent them if you don't already have them. This is ironic considering that there are antiretroviral drugs available now to treat AIDS. The problem is people are afraid to admit they have the disease or just plain ignorant. They don't seek proper treatment."

The orphan children are the victims more than any because they are the easiest prey. Many will get AIDS, and they will die long before they have a chance to grow up."

"That's terrible, don't they have [...] I mean, isn't there a church or something that can help the orphan kids?"

"The churches are overwhelmed, trying to care for those who have a chance to survive. They know that most kids like the ones you see begging won't be around long. Most concentrate their efforts on those they think will be."

"There's no answer, then?"

"No, we're trying to do our share to help these kids. We have taken some orphans at Harmony. We give them three meals a day and a clean place to sleep, but we're only scratching the surface. What else can we do?"

Perhaps trying to discount the possibility that Mahret could, herself, be part of the problem, Miss Ellingson also told her that some of the single mothers desperate for cash succumbed to sexually exploiting their own children.

"Many women who have lost their husband sell their own body if they can. Others sell their children. They can get a few shillings by selling an evening with their daughter or even their little boy. They're desperate, it doesn't make it right, but they're desperate, and they don't have another way to get money for food or rent. They don't have work. A man comes into their area who's willing to pay more money than they can get any other way, and the mothers see their children are hungry. They give in. They give their child to some man, and they turn their back on it as if it didn't happen. They go out and buy some food with the money and treat their child to a good meal and feel they've rewarded her (or him) enough to make it okay. They've paid them back, they think, and in a moral sense too."

"Oh my!"

"Yes, it's awful. Of course, some of the girls who are just a little older but still really just babies sell themselves to men who believe the virgin myth."

"I have a good husband!" Mahret said. "When our boys are older, he'll help me keep them away from all the young girls with these terrible diseases."

"For many women, that doesn't work."

"Why not?"

"Because the mothers don't have a good husband and they aren't always in a position financially to defend their kids against their fathers. A lot of fathers mess around, and many believe the virgin myth. They get so scared of the diseases. They take it out on their own children."

"How do you know this?"

"I've seen the evidence. For instance, I have a friend, I won't tell you who she is, but let's say her name is Mora. She's forty-two now; a few years ago, she allowed her ten-year-old daughter to go upcountry for a few days with her husband. When they returned, she noticed that (I'll call her Amy) was acting strangely. She was walking very slowly and looked as though she was in pain. Mora confronted her about it, and Amy told her that her father had hurt her by shoving his thing into her private parts. Mora rushed her to see Mr. Otieno at the pharmacy.

He's not trained, but he sells all sorts of medicines and disinfectants cheap, so everyone sees him sometimes when they get sick.

Anyway, he examined Amy and told Mora that her vagina was swollen and torn. He said, "she must have been raped."

"My Gosh, her husband, he must be an animal. How could he do such a thing?"

"Unfortunately, too many of them are like that here. Mora pulled a knife on her husband and told him that if he ever did that again, she would kill him. But that didn't work. He just kept doing it after Amy healed."

"Couldn't she leave him?"

"That's the problem. She didn't have any way to support herself and Amy. 'How was I to feed my children?' She said, 'and where was I to have left for without a single coin in my pocket?' She did the only thing she thought she could. She stayed and tried to protect her girls."

"She had other children?"

"Yes, she had an older daughter. When Amy died, her sister committed suicide. Finally then, Mora killed her husband with a knife and left him in the dump. No one knows about it, but me, and no one cares. She came to me after that and asked for help.

She's bitter now about life, but she's okay. Maybe she'll eventually get over it; I hope so. She looks good for her age, and she makes good money now selling herself to men. She works with a group of women, and they have a youth gang that protects them; she only sleeps with men who use a condom.

Mahret, I hope I haven't shocked you. Pedophilia is not just a problem here. It happens everywhere. We keep hearing about it in the biggest and most modern cities in the world. Men stray and molest everywhere. The biggest problem in Kibera and in other societies like it is the weakness of law enforcement and, of course, destitution. Desperate people, hungry people, mothers who can't feed their children properly, turn to desperate measures. I feel only sympathy for them.

You seem sure your husband is not abusive to your kids. When I've found this sort of thing in other homes, the women have usually not been able to deny it so vehemently. Some just break down and cry. I'll take you at your word. But if you ever suspect anything, you do need to get help."

Now it was Mahret who could not just let the conversation drop.

She had worried about possible repercussions for Berhanu especially from that incident on the road. Miss Ellingson was genuine; she was concerned. Mahret also thought she was smart, so she decided to let her in on a long-hidden secret.

"There is only one thing I would like to ask you. It has nothing to do with Barisso."

"Yes, go on."

Mahret told her all about what had happened two years ago when she and the boys were on the bus to Kenya.

"It was terrible," she said, "and the one devil came close to raping Berhanu. He was right there when a woman knifed the guy to save him. Then he watched the guy who had raped the one woman lying on the ground bleeding after his senior officer shot him. It was all so ugly for a young boy to watch."

She also described Berhanu's later reaction when he woke up in the night and cried.

"He talked to me about it and then told me he was okay. And I don't think he has acted in any of the ways you've told me about, but I have no way of deciding for sure if he is over everything."

"Since then, there has been nothing?"

"No, nothing. I'm worried about him, and I watch him as closely as I can. But he has never done any of the things you talked about."

"I think the fact that he was able to talk to you at that one time is a good sign that he is recovering. The only thing I'm a bit concerned about is what they call 'oppositional and conduct disorder.' From what I understand, the fight he had with Jonah, he seemed very angry and didn't want to quit hitting him when he had him down, as if he was letting something out of his system, anxiety that he had been keeping to himself."

"Anxiety?"

"Yes, you know the pain inside that he was trying to get rid of by expressing it physically. Some abused children will try to void the aggression that was perpetrated on them by hurting others."

"I don't know for sure," Mahret said. "But mostly he has played okay with other kids, you know, at home, in the streets. He has always been the leader with the kids. When there's trouble, he is sometimes involved, but maybe mostly because he's the leader. Other kids look up to him."

She told Miss Ellingson about the time he tackled the man who was trying to take the little boy in Mashimoni.

"But," she said, "maybe what you say is a little bit true. Maybe there is some anger left; maybe he feels, what you say, violated. He was too young to watch me knife that man right there in front of us."

"So, it was you?"

"No, I shouldn't have said that. It just slipped out. Please forget it."

"Your secret is safe with me. I don't blame you at all. What else could you do?"

"Okay, then, I did it. Maybe that bothered him as much as the threat the man wanted to rape him. At that time, he didn't even know what the man wanted to do to him. He was so young. He had never heard the word rape. Now he knows, and it scares him, but I think he can deal with it. The killing maybe was worse."

"I think you're right. You are a good mother and an intelligent woman. You've thought it through. I think we should continue to watch Berhanu—and we will here at school. We will talk to him, too, and try to help him wherever we can. It will take a little more time. But I don't see a sexual problem and normal young boys do fight. We put a stop to it fast.

The fact that he was not actually raped, also makes me think his mental scars are not so deep they won't heal."

Miss Ellingson paused for a moment.

"You know, Mahret, what I think you should do is talk to Berhanu. Ask him if he ever has bad dreams about the incident. Try to get him to tell you what exactly is in his heart. What is he keeping to himself that he doesn't tell others? Tell him how much you love him [...]"

"Okay, I will. Maybe too, it would help if I tell him about my own problems?"

"What do you mean?"

"Well, I have had bad dreams myself since that time. I screamed in my sleep. Berhanu had to wake me up. I didn't know what to do. I went outside and cried."

"You know what I think. I think you had something like what they call PTSD."

"What's that?"

"Post-traumatic stress disorder; it's what happens to a lot of people after traumatic events. The events keep coming back in their sleep.

Did this happen again?"

"No, I think maybe because I was so busy trying to start us over again living in Kibera, I didn't have time for it. I had to put it out of my mind to survive, to keep us safe and together."

"Yes, well, if you had a dream like that, I would think Berhanu, who is so young and has had a lot more time in his day, maybe has had a similar dream and more often. I know that's what they say about PTSD. The dreams keep coming back."

"Maybe."

"I'll tell you what Mahret, we have a psychologist here who tries to help children with these sorts of problems. I will have her talk to Berhanu. Maybe she can help him. If he has such dreams, maybe she can get him to talk about them, vent them, and unburden his mind a bit. That might help."

"*Galatom*. When can she do it?"

"Right away. I'll get her to talk to him after school next week. I'll get her to talk to him, and we will get back to you."

Mahret was overwhelmed. Finally, some help for her oldest baby.

She cried.

"I've worried so much about Berhanu, and I always feel so helpless because I don't know how to handle it. *Galatom*, you are a wonderful person, and you have a wonderful school."

As she walked home that morning, Mahret felt so much better. Now Berhanu would get professional help. She would watch him more closely, herself, in the future, but she had back-up, people trained, who knew what they were doing.

"If I see Berhanu has more problems, I will be able to go to a good person, a very smart one, for help.

Miss Ellingson is another Milka! Another blessing from *Waqaa*."

Chapter 45

ON THE MEND

The psychologist, Alvera, was a young Kenyan woman with degrees from the university in Nairobi. After her initial session with Berhanu she was to realize he was intelligent, and also stubborn; and that it would take a lot more than one meeting to get through to him.

"Hi Berhanu," she said, "please have a seat."

"Why'd you call me here?"

"I just wanted to ask you if you are feeling anxiety about anything here in school or with your friends."

"What do ya mean by that? What's anxiety?"

"Berhanu, sit down. I won't keep you for more than a few minutes. I just want to know if you have anything on your mind that I can help you with. I'm trained to do that."

"What're ya saying, like I'm crazy?"

"No, not at all. It's just that sometimes when we have been through something traumatic, we feel better, sometimes much better, by talking to someone about it. This is normal. Many kids at this school have been through something like that. We've been able to help them. Miss Ellingson told me about the fight club, and I just want to be sure you're not mad at the world about something that made you want to fight with other kids. Sometimes that is the case."

Once she explained what she meant by traumatic, Berhanu referred to seeing someone who tried to hurt his mom, but that was as far as he would go.

In the following weeks, she called him out of class to meet with her several times under the pretext of helping him learn how to get along with his peers.

Berhanu at first resented her interference in his life.

And he told her so.

After a few sessions, however, he started to relax a little and to kind of enjoy talking to someone who seemed to care and not to be judgmental.

Finally, on their fifth meeting, he broke down and cried. Then he poured out his heart.

He told her how hard it was to stand the nightmares. He had been waking up two or three nights a week with images of a man coming after him with his clothes off, or his mother knifing a man or men and leaving dead bodies bleeding on the ground, and, as fearsome as any, his mother getting into a jeep with a strange man and taking all her clothes off.

He told her, "it's making me crazy."

And she told him that what was happening to him was normal. If he kept coming to talk to her, the images would stop.

"*Haadha* had nightmares too—about the same thing. You will conquer them, as she has. She's a grown-up, she's more mature than you, and it's a little easier for her to control her mind. But she has suffered. And if you and I keep talking, no one else will know. It will just be the two of us. Eventually, you will get control too."

The psychologist was right. After a few weeks, Berhanu told her the nightmares were not as consistent as they had been.

"I haven't had one for a while. I think I'm starting to get better."

"I think so too. You've been through a lot. I'll tell you what; let's get together every two weeks. I'll ask Ms. Ellingson. Your bad dreams will probably come back once in a while. We can talk about them if they do. And maybe someday they'll stop coming back all together; then we can just be friends. I will be here if you need me.

Okay?"

"Okay."

"Also, if the dreams do come back you can come to see me the very next day, even if it's not our regular meeting day, and we can talk."

"I think Berhanu is a lot better," she told Ms. Ellingson. "He can talk openly to me, and he knows he will have my support in the future whatever happens."

She also asked her to authorize their agreement.

"Yes, of course. Wouldn't it be wonderful to actually help even *one* of our kids back to something like normalcy whatever that is?"

Keep it up, please, just keep on doing what you're doing."

Chapter 46

HEALING

What Miss Ellingson did to help end all the boys' fighting at and after school was to speak through the school priest, Vicar Jasmin. The kids were all required to attend a service once a week, and, during one of them, the good pastor delivered a sermon on brotherly love.

He started by quoting from John 13:34.

"A new commandment I give to you that you love one another:

just as I have loved you, you also are to love one another."

Then he told the kids that brotherly love is "sacrificing and serving others! We are taught by God to do this through and by Christ's example. We ought to be willing to lay down our lives for one another. If we say we want to be like Christ, then let us realize that that is exactly what He did. He died for each one of us, and He expects us to be willing to do the same. He expects us to love each one of our brethren just as He does. Sometimes dying for our brethren means living for our brethren. It means serving them, helping them, ministering to them. In other words, putting each other first in all things."

The priest also told the kids he had heard that some boys had been beating each other up.

"God would not approve; you must not give in to the devil, whose only interest is to see us all burn in hell through all eternity."

When he ended by telling the kids that "eternity" meant "for ever and ever," his sermon seemed to hit home.

It also helped that for the kids, themselves, something came along just in time to replace the fight club.

One morning when the grade six boys arrived at the playing field for their physical education class, the instructor, Mr. Holmes, told them, "I have a surprise for you. Today we're going to switch from football to dance. It's time you boys learned some of the finer things in life. It's time you learned to do the proper steps and moves for some of the dances you will need to socialize properly when you get older."

Berhanu immediately protested:

"Eee, yuck, no way! We don't wanna dance; we wanna play football. Come on coach, this isn't fair."

"Wait until you see what I'm talking about before you complain," coach told him.

"Nah, come on coach, we don't want no damn dance. Dance is for sissies."

"Watch what you say young man, keep your mouth closed and just watch now."

"Ahh coach."

Mr. Holmes turned to a group of six athletic-looking young men and six athletic-looking young women waiting behind him.

"These young people are called swat dancers, S W A T. They've come to school to show you something new. Let them show us their stuff."

The group formed two lines—two males with a female between them in the front, and two females with a male between them in the back.

What then took place was one of the most amazing scenes the boys had ever witnessed.

Some very modern hip music filled the air. Then, in perfect time, the dancers performed incredible steps. Their arms and legs seamlessly coordinated, moving in all directions, they danced separately and then joined hands and danced together. They performed some amazingly athletic moves too—forward and backflips, roles, and summersaults without touching the ground.

It was all just too hip.

The boys were dumbfounded, and when the swat crew leader asked them if they would like to come up and try some basic steps themselves, Berhanu was the first on the stage. All the other boys followed.

Suddenly was born a whole new dimension in the kids' lives. They practiced hard during the three successive phys. ed. classes that their new heroes supervised. Then, after school, Berhanu started up a new club. He got Miss Ellingson to allot him and a number of both boys and girls a room with a music player. They pushed the desks to one side and practiced as many moves as they could remember. The more athletic, the more Berhanu and his friend, Jonah, excelled. They were cool, like the swat group, and the other kids looked up to them.

"This is great. It will keep them all busy until something else catches their attention," Miss Ellingson told Mr. Holmes.

The dancing kept Berhanu both enthused and pre-occupied, and, along with his discussions with the psychologist, it helped him keep other matters out of his mind for longer periods.

He truly began to heal.

Chapter 47

ATTENDING TO BUSINESS

Mahret did watch Berhanu as closely as she could in the weeks following her discussion with Miss Ellingson. But she was more at ease now knowing that someone much better qualified than she was working with him. And she felt she saw a change in him. He laughed more, he was less moody, and he stopped taking his anger out so much on Gamado.

Mahret told Barisso, "he seems much more like any other twelve-year-old boy. He's the old Berhanu. I think we're getting him back."

This and the fact that Miss Ellingson and the psychologist were on the job gave her a chance to deal with other important concerns.

The best way to help Berhanu and the rest of the family, she still believed, was to leave both Nairobi and Africa forever. The secret to that, obviously, was money. She now had enough to pay the bills for this new and better home in Dandora without digging further into their savings. But she had no illusions—if her family was ever to manage to seek a better life in what Milka called the "new world," she would have to do better than that.

Unfortunately, in this, she was largely on her own.

Barisso did not share her sense of urgency about getting out. He was quite content with the life they had.

"Relax," he would say, "we have it good now. I have a great job; the kids are happy. Be thankful for what you've got."

Mahret was Berhanu's mother, and this was one of the times when it showed.

Instead of giving in, she developed her own plan.

Having spent so much time watching all kinds of people eking out an existence based on a multiplicity of tiny businesses, she believed she had to become an entrepreneur. She would just have to be a better entrepreneur than most of them. To do that, she would have to pick out a business that could work exceptionally if handled well.

The more she thought about it, the more she kept coming back to one idea.

Tourism.

Mahret had noticed the number of visitors coming into Kibera, not just from Nairobi and other parts of Kenya, but from all over the world. Many of them, it was impossible not to recognize, were white. They were of European origin, some from America, some from Britain, and, as one of the tour guides told her, some from places like Germany, Denmark, and France.

When she and Milka took a day trip into central Nairobi, Mahret saw posted signs advertising the tours for forty-five American dollars per person.

"In other words, one fee could pay our rent for over three weeks."

Mahret decided she could run such a business, too, except for one major problem. She could not, herself, conduct the tours. Firstly, she was too shy and, secondly, she did not have the confidence in her English.

A guide she talked to told her that he had to show that he was fluent in both Bantu Swahili and English to get his job. That, he said, was adequate as "most of the tourists we bring to Kibera have at least a basic understanding of one or the other."

Swahili was no problem for Mahret, but her English was very basic. It would not do. She did, though, know someone who had the necessary linguistic ability. And on top of that, she had lots of nerve and a greater general knowledge not just of Kibera but of Kenya and the entire world than anyone she had ever met. That person also needed the challenge to help her find a reason to live. Mahret had only to talk her into becoming her partner.

That proved more difficult than she hoped.

One morning after Barisso and the boys had gone to school, she went back to Mashimoni to find Milka. She took one of the big buses to Kibera and then went to the marketplace. Milka was there doing her usual Wednesday morning shopping.

"Hi, how are you?" Mahret said, hugging her.

"I'm okay, I guess. One part of me wants to die, but I have another child to look after. I can't let her down. It's ironic, I can't see any purpose to be in this world, but I must help my daughter make some sense out of this life. I must try to give her reasons to believe in what I no longer believe in myself."

"Milka, I'm so sorry," Mahret said. "All I can tell you is that when my sister's baby daughter died so many years ago, she felt just as you do. But in time, the wounds heal enough to make it possible to go on. She found the strength, and you will too."

Standing there amid the market crowd, Milka broke down and cried. Mahret put her arms around her and cried with her.

Then she sat her down at one of the tables and got her a cup of *shaayii*.

"Listen, Milka," she said, "I have a plan that I think would be good for you, for both of us. It would give you something to do, help you go on, and it could make both of us some money. It might even get us both out of the slums."

Milka replied through her tears.

"I could sure use some extra cash. I want to leave this place too, now more than ever before. What is it?"

"It's like this: I want to start a tourist business where we bring people to see Kibera, who wish to see what it's like to live in such a place."

"Oh, I don't know about that. A lot of people here hate the way that kind of business exploits our poverty. We would be unpopular with a lot of people."

"Yeah, well, I don't have a problem with it. If people are so curious about our plight, why shouldn't we make them pay for it? I don't see the problem."

"But others are already doing this. How could we compete?"

"We will do it better than them. We work together, we don't hire nobody, and we charge thirty-five American dollars for each customer; that's over 3,500 shillings. If we get one customer each time, great, if we get two or three or four, wow, it's so much money and no costs but our time. We don't pay no workers and you can do the talking. I can't but you can, your education, your uppity language."

"But we know nothing about business. We don't know what you're missing; what other costs? We're two women; the men will try to rip us off. You know they will."

"Listen Milka we have to be strong. That's one thing you and I have both learned together living here. We've got to fight for what we want. If we end up fighting the men to run a business, then so be it. And we will!"

"How would we get customers? Have you thought about that?"

How do we share the work?"

"We both go to the fancy hotels, one hotel at a time, with signs that advertise. We do that together. Then you take the inquiries because your speaking is much better than mine. I will be an example of slum life. I will dress poor, like always. You will dress in your best clothes, one of the outfits you brought with you to Kibera from when you were rich. You will look professional. I will look poor. If they ask you, you will tell people that I'm a real slummer. We won't tell them that you are too. They'll see you as the business manager, the professional. We will both take the people to Kibera; we will both be guides, but you will do the talking. People will be impressed with your ability. You know the right words."

"Oh, I don't know. It scares me."

"I'm telling you, Milka, 4,500 shillings is the lowest price anyone is charging. We will beat the competition because we do all the work ourselves; we don't hire nobody, and then, when the others are gone, we can charge more."

"I don't know. We aren't businesspeople. We don't know what problems can come along. I'd sure like to make some money, but this is very scary."

They spent most of the day together.

"I can't do it alone," Mahret kept telling her, "If you don't come with me, I can't do it at all. But together we can do it better than anyone else. In a while, we'll be the only ones in the business. It will be ours to do as we want. Then we can make a lot of money.

All we have to do is show both the good and bad sides of Kibera. Rich people want to see the children happily playing so they can say, 'ah isn't that lovely, look how happy they are even though they have so little.' But they also want to see sewers flowing down the middle of the street, the poverty, the filth, the misery. They want to love us, but they also want to pity us. They want to see our pain."

"How will we work it? I mean like how do we get them here after they sign on?"

"We'll get them to meet us on the corner where the main road crosses into Mashimoni and then take them on a walking tour."

"Where will we get the signs for advertising at the hotels?"

"We make them out of cardboard this weekend. There's lots of that around. The dump is full of it."

"They'll look cheap."

"Yes, and that will just say to people that we're genuine."

"I think maybe too genuine. They'll be afraid of us."

"Some will maybe, but a lot will see me as a true slum person, and you as a rich person all dressed up in some of your rich clothes. You can talk to people in your posh voice and tell them that you're proud of our signs because I brought you the cardboard from the dumps of Kibera. They will pity me and trust you. They'll see we're the real thing. It's perfect."

"Yes, but this is scary."

"You keep saying that! Listen to me Milka. We have to get out of here. This business takes no money. We just get people to meet us, and then we take them on a tour. That's what the others do; we've both seen them showing rich people around; they're making those people pay them real money to show how we live here. That'll be your job once we get them signed up. You don't only know more about Kibera and all kinds of stuff than anybody else, but you can talk really good English and Swahili. They will be very impressed.

You can tell them you're doing this to help me and others like me survive and feed our children. They will love that. Their money will be going to help the poor. We have nothing to lose. The others are charging forty-five dollars for each customer. Do you know how much that is? 4,500 shillings each for three hours work. What if we get ten people? We have nothing to lose."

"I guess," Milka said. "I'm scared, but you're so confident. Maybe it's rubbing off on me.

When do you want to start?"

"Tomorrow!"

"Really?"

"Yes, let's get started. We can't wait, or we'll never do it."

"Okay.

Oh my God, I'm going along with this.

I'm starting to share your dream."

Chapter 48

THOUGHT TO ACTION: TWO ARE BETTER THAN ONE

The two ladies met at Mahret's home the next morning to iron out the practicalities of starting their new business. Milka had by then come up with some ideas of her own.

"Listen," she said, "from what I can see, there are two difficulties we must overcome. The first is advertising. I think going to the hotels with signs is problematic."

"Problematic?"

"Yes, I mean, it won't work very well.

What we should do instead is make up business cards to take to the hotels. We can have hundreds made for very little money. They're cheap. We could give these to hotel employees and pay them a small fee for every customer they get. We pay them after the tour, so there is no risk to us. Hotel clerks and baggage handlers, cleaners, and room servants aren't paid very well. They can just leave the cards in the rooms, by the telephone. They will jump at the chance to make a little more particularly as there would be no risk."

"But how will we know which worker left the card that our customer found?"

"We'll use just one hotel employee on each floor. When our customer signs up, we will ask which floor they're staying on in which hotel. Then we pay accordingly."

"How will that work? Customers will see our business, but how will they contact us. Will we just be standing outside on the street?"

"No, that would look unprofessional. They wouldn't do it. You know, I have an old mobile telephone and an M-Pesa account. M-Pesas are new around here, but they work. They're very cheap too. Lots of people in Kibera have them now. They use them to send or receive money to or from their family when they can. I need mine anyway, so the little I pay for it, we don't have to charge against the business. For the business, it will be free."

"How will it work?"

"I'll register the phone again and keep it charged up, and then I can carry it around with me from place to place. All the people who might want to tour the slums already carry mobile phones with them wherever they go. They always have them on them.

They would be able to contact me anytime to register for the tour."

"Yes, of course. You're right. We can make sure the hotel workers have our card, and then customers can call you and sign up."

"It's even better than that. The M-Pesas take deposits. People can use their phones to pay us. They can pay us before the tour. The M-Pesa will deposit it and hold it like a bank, and then we can get the money anytime we want. We just go to their office and get them to change the online money into real money."

"I don't know, Milka, what if they steal our money?"

"They are perfectly trustworthy. They have no choice. They're so good and cheap that they're putting the banks out of business. They're making a name for themselves, and all sorts of businesses are starting to use them. They can't cheat. They have an impeccable reputation, or they will be gone. They know that."

"Are you sure?"

"Yes, I've sent a little money this way to the kids' school. It's a very small amount, but it works. Much bigger businesses are using this system, and they trust it totally. It's not a worry. I will put the account number on the cards. Foreigners are all used to online payments. People can pay us a small amount to sign up for the tour and the rest when we meet them to begin the tour. There is no risk for us or, indeed, for them. It's perfect. If some people want, they can just pay us in cash too, of course, but I think the vast majority will pay online. They're accustomed to doing that."

"How much for the cards?"

"Probably about 5,000 shillings."

"Okay, you supply the phone, and I'll pay for the cards?"

"Deal, we'll put my phone number on them, and I will set up a deposit account with both our names on it. Rich people will be able to pay with their credit card numbers. They are accustomed to doing that too. These days they live on their credit cards."

Milka explained about credit cards.

Mahret was even more convinced than she had been that she needed her best friend in the business.

"This kind of know-how is what I don't have, but you do, see why I came to you?"

The next day they made up the advertisement for the cards they would need and then went to an M-Pesa office just outside of Kibera and started up a new account. They put Mahret's name on it too and fifty of her American dollars on deposit.

Milka also called a company that made a card a salesman had given her years ago to advertise his dress shop. She had held on to it as a fond reminder of the time in her life when she could afford such things. The company was still in business, and Milka ordered 500 cards. She then transferred ten dollars of her own money to the M-Pesa account.

"We have nothing to lose except our time and, of course, about forty American dollars," Mahret told her. "We better make this work, or I'm going to feel terrible about throwing all that away. We won't tell Barisso what we're up to.

But we can do it – we will do it. Let's not doubt ourselves.

Think positive."

A few days later, Milka went to the post office on the edge of Mashimoni and picked up the business cards.

In English the cards read:

"Tours of Kibera, see one of the world's largest slums and help the children. View the poverty, the harshness of life against the vitality, the craftsmanship, the children at play, the hope."

"Call: XXXXXX."

That evening she called on Mahret.

"I've got everything."

"Okay, it's time to start. Let's get entrepreneurin.'"

The ladies agreed to meet the following day at the train station beside the nearest Hilton hotel in Nairobi.

Milka was familiar with the hotel, and she was able to give Mahret exact instructions on how to take the train to the appropriate station.

"If you get there first, just wait for me. I will wait for you if I'm first."

Mahret went dressed in her everyday clothes, the only kind she had.

She arrived at the station first and a few minutes later saw Milka get off the train dressed in a skirt, blouse, and jacket that Mahret figured she must have worn a few years earlier to the university.

"Wow, there's a woman who knows how to look uppity."

They had to be very discreet. They knew the hotel management would not look positively on a business from outside trying to exploit their clientele. But they also knew that many of the lower hotel employees were poor like them, and that, in fact, most would be slum dwellers too.

In her respectable outfit, Milka looked just like one of the hotel guests. None of the management level people even noticed her. She decided to approach the woman she found supervising the cleaners on the third floor instead of the cleaners themselves.

"Supervisors are the last to check the rooms before the guests arrive. She can leave the cards without worrying about another supervisor finding them. She sees a lot of rooms each day too."

She first approached the supervisor on the third floor.

"I have a business deal I would like you to consider," she said. "It will make money for both of us. All you have to do is see that hotel guests get these cards. My company will give you a hundred shillings for everyone who signs up for our tour."

The woman did not even look up.

Milka persisted.

"I mean it. You will be able to make some real money. You have nothing to lose."

The woman was scared even to talk to her.

"Quiet, there might be someone listening."

"No, no one is listening; I don't want them to know either. They'd want to shut me down. They don't like outsiders."

"How will you know if someone got the card from me? How will you pay me?"

"This is the only hotel we are doing this time, and this time you are the only one we are contacting. You can hand these cards out to all the rooms you're responsible for, and we will know it's you. I will come back the day after the tour and pay you, or if you have an M-Pesa, I will deposit the money in your account. All you have to do is leave one card in each room. If one person takes our tour, you will get 100 shillings. If ten, you will get 1,000 shillings."

"I don't have what you call M-Pesa, and this could get me fired."

"Okay, we will meet you the day after our showing and pay you in person."

It won't get you fired. Look at all the business cards by the phone on the desk. The hotel lets companies it likes, do this. Our card will just be one of six or seven others. They won't notice it, and even if they did, they wouldn't know who was responsible.

It could be the room service guy or a cleaner or even the last patron who stayed in the room. There's no way to connect it to you."

"Okay, I'll do it if you give me 500 shillings now as a fee and then a hundred for each person you sign up."

Milka wanted to consult her partner.

But that was impossible.

"Here you are. I'll give you 200 shillings now. If this works, I will bring the rest of the money to you tomorrow.

And you will be able to earn more after this, many times more.

Do we have a deal or not?"

"Yes."

Milka paid her and went back down to meet Mahret on the street.

Mahret had had another experience that seemed to auger well for the future.

When she grew tired waiting for Milka, she sat down on the sidewalk beside the hotel. To her surprise, a wealthy-looking white man walking down the street reached into his pocket, pulled out a ten-dollar bill, and handed it to her. A few minutes later, a black lady dressed uppity like Milka, gave her 500 shillings.

"*Galatom*," she said to each of them.

When she saw Milka coming out of the front door of the hotel, she went over and showed her the two bills.

"We already got lots of our investment back! Looks like we really can't lose."

"Where did you get that?"

"I was sitting on the sidewalk over there, and these people just handed it to me."

"Really?"

"Yes, there's good in looking bad. They want to feel good about helping."

"I had to pay out two hundred as bribe money. Is that okay?"

"Yes, we are more than covered already. Everything looks good! Let's take this as a sign from *Waqaa*."

"I'm trying. I really am trying! If this business does work, you're a genius."

"If it doesn't, I'm a fool."

"No, you're not; you're the smartest person I've ever met."

"No, you are."

"Oh my God, we're in business.

Hey partner! Gosh, I'm scared silly."

"Now I am too.

Call it scared and itchin to go."

Chapter 49

OFF WE GO

Mahret and Milka decided to do only the one hotel this first time so they could see what bugs there might be in their system.

On the way home, Milka told Mahret the cleaning supervisor, "was suspicious at first, but she wants the extra money, and I'm sure she'll be willing to do it again."

"I hope you're right. I think you are. She would be awful short-sighted to just keep our two dollars when she could make a lot more."

"Actually," Milka said, "at this point, it all looks pretty damn good to me. What will tell us for sure if this is going to work is the number of calls we get. I'm terrified we won't get any."

"Don't think that way. Remember, we agreed to be positive."

"Okay, you're right, I'm positive again. I have no doubts, we're about to become millionaires."

This time neither laughed. It was just too close to the moment of truth.

They went straight to Milka's place after that to wait for calls. It was an agonizing wait. None came in until evening.

The first was a man's voice:

"Hello, ve vould like to see Kibera, I have read about the place so much. You will take us there tomorrow?"

"Yes, we can take you at ten o'clock tomorrow morning. Does that suit you?"

"Yes, that vould be fine, if you vould give me a goot price."

"How many people in your group?"

"Ve are five with the baby."

"Uh, okay, five tickets would normally be $150.00. How about $140.00?"

"Oh, I think you can do better than that. I give you $120.00. Our baby shouldn't count. He von't even know vhat's going on."

"One moment." Milka turned to Mahret.

"Family of five, one's a baby. Offers a hundred and twenty."

"Dollars?'

"Yes."

"Take it."

"Okay, sir. I'll take it. As long as you pay before we start the tour."

"Yes, of course. How much deposit?"

"Ten percent."

"Okay, I send you twelve dollars right now. Can you take an e-transfer?"

"Yes, here is our M-Pesa number. Just call it, and you will be provided instructions. In the morning, take a taxi to Kambi Muru produce market on the Sheikh Mahmoud Road. This is right at the entrance to Mashimoni from the north. We will meet you there to start the tour."

"Yes, that is goot."

"*Galatom*, sir, we'll see you tomorrow at ten."

In relatively short order after that, Milka had another three paying customers signed up.

"We're doing great," she told Mahret, "our business really is looking fine!"

She got more confident with each customer. When one tried to bargain down the price, she told him "we are already the least expensive tour in town. This is not because ours is second class. It's the best of them all. We guarantee that much. It's because we own and operate our business ourselves. We have both actually lived in Kibera. You can't get closer to it than that."

The man relented.

"We better make sure we're ready," she told Mahret. "I've been thinking about my presentation for the start of the tour. How about I practice on you now?"

"Good idea."

Milka's practice talk took about ten minutes.

"It's good," Mahret told her, "I think you should just do less happy talk. It's realistic, a lot of the kids are content with life as you say, and some adults too. But I think a lot of people come here for the misery. Maybe just tone the happy talk down a bit. They probably don't admit it even to themselves, but one of the things these people want is the poverty and hardship. Maybe tell them about the orphan kids too."

"Mm, yes, you're probably right. I'll include a little more about the poverty, and what about some of the crime outside the compounds?"

"Yes, good. It's fine. Don't talk about the sex crimes. Rape, child prostitution, and all that; it's too much, it'll turn them off. When that sort of thing happens in their own areas people just overlook it as much as they can.

Otherwise, your talk should work out just fine. Great practice run, next time it will be even better. "

"I wish I could find your confidence."

"You *will* find it because you have to. We both will. We are going to make this work. This could be the only way out.

For both of us."

At nine oclock the next morning, the two ladies met again, this time on the Sheikh Mahmoud Road in front of the Kambi Muru market. Mahret wore the same clothes she had worn the previous day, and Milka wore another expensive jacket, skirt, and blouse.

All their customers turned up on time. Milka gave each a simple "Galatom," when they paid up the rest of what they owed.

She wanted to kiss them.

Milka turned out to be a natural. She showed her clients everything, the sewage stream, the local dump, the shanties, and the children playing in the streets.

People listened attentively.

"They look so happy, and they have so little," one of the gentlemen remarked.

Mahret remembered her own reaction when Rekik conducted her through the same sort of area nearly three years ago.

At intervals, Milka would stop walking along the street to allow everyone to gather around her and hear her speak spontaneously on a particular subject. She spoke in an officious voice as if she had done this many times before.

"The kids you see playing are the children of the slums," she told them. "Many of them get only one meal a day at home, usually in the morning, and then scrounge for anything else they can find. They get handouts from good folks like you and fruit and baked goods people in the marketplace throw away as it gets old. It's not enough, but most of the kids survive if they make it to the age of five. Many kids go to school too, and they might get an extra bowl of porridge there in the morning."

"What about the schools?" one lady asked. "Are there any good ones here?"

"In Mashimoni there are several schools, but these are all for nursery, primary and elementary education only. Most are informal, backed by charities and religious organizations, but they are in private facilities. The quality of the education is not regulated. The schools suffer dreadfully from poor basic infrastructure. They all lack adequate desks, lighting, books, and even proper toilet facilities."

"It must be hard for kids to learn."

"Yes, and for teachers to teach. There is only one government-supported school. But it doesn't have the room for nearly all the children in Mashimoni. It's not much better than the informal ones. They pack forty-five students into inadequate spaces for both study and play. The school is located right below a cliff and in an area that vagabonds frequent for their drinking sessions. The paths leading to the school are dirt paths with open sewage streams. Sewage pours over the cliff into the children's' play area too. Anyway, the playground is far too small. The children never get as much exercise as they should."

Mahret hovered around the outside of the group, trying to help anyone who needed any sort of assistance. One white woman dropped a handkerchief without realizing it, and Mahret picked it up and handed it back to her.

"Oh, thank you so much."

The little girl in the Norwegian family fell and scraped her knee. She cried loudly, and the father picked her up and tried to console her. Mahret quickly bought a small package of jellybeans at a candy stand, took one out of the package, and held it up to the little girl. It did the trick. She stopped crying and opened her mouth. Mahret popped the jellybean in and gave the rest of the package to the father.

"Thank you so much," the man said. "I'm going to tell all my friends about your business."

Later, as the group walked along the street, he handed Mahret a twenty-dollar bill.

"Oh, sir, she said, taking the bill, "this is not necessary."

"Yes, it is, I'm sure you can use it for your own family. You people are so thoughtful."

"You are very kind."

He looked pleased.

Several minutes later, a Japanese woman in the group handed her a ten-spot.

This time, Mahret just said *"Galatom."*

When Milka led the group to the market, everyone stopped to buy locally produced crafts, paintings, ornaments, and trinkets of various kinds. Some also bought clothing.

"Look at this shirt," one Kenyan lady said to her husband. "Only 400 shillings. Jocko will think we got it at Macys."

One of the clients was a German man, a forty-five plus tourist named Lotte Rasmussen. He had lived in Nairobi for some years, and he told Milka he had toured Kibera more than thirty times, often with friends visiting from abroad.

"I bring friends to see how people live here. The people might not have money like us, but they are happy, and that's why I keep on coming. I think what you do to show people Kibera is admirable. I know you support local initiatives like children's homes and women's groups; I do not see an ethics problem."

However, others living in Kibera came right up to Mahret to vent their anger.

Awino, a Mashimoni mother who had at times assailed other tour groups was one

"It is morally unfair that tourists keep on coming to the place we call home. This is terrible, barbaric even. Think of the opposite. What would happen to an African like me in Europe or America, touring and taking photos of their poorest citizens? People would say that's not France or Germany, that's just a small part of it.

When I lived in Mombasa, I used to see families from Europe and the United States flying in to enjoy our oceans and beaches. Now they come here. Seeing the same kinds of tourists in this filthy broken-down neighborhood to observe how we survive is shocking. To them, we're just objects. We satisfy their curiosity. That's all there is to it. When they tried to photo me, I wanted to yell at them.

You make money doing this. You should be ashamed of yourself."

A local man told Mahret, "this is not a national park, and we are not wildlife. The only reason why these tours exist is because a few of you people are making money out of it. Showing a handful of wealthy people how the poor are living is morally wrong. People like you should be ashamed of yourselves."

Mahret stood her ground. She simply told them that this was just another business and that if they made any money, they would be giving generously to the children's organizations.

"The tourists give handouts to the kids too and look at all the things they're buying. Anyway, what's wrong with showing the world how bad conditions are here? We don't cover up anything. We show them the filth of the running sewers, the dirt, the smell, and the poverty. The world should see it all, and maybe something will be done at last to make it better. We are not the enemy. We are part of the hope."

Whether or not that was what stopped anybody from making an open scene, is debatable, but none did.

The tour ended after about three hours as planned. Milka got their clients back to the place where they had met them earlier and they said their goodbyes.

Then the two partners walked to a cafe in greater Nairobi to split up their dough.

"This is unbelievable," Milka said once they were seated at one of the outdoor tables. "We have all this money. We can keep on doing this. We will be rich. Mahret, you're a genius."

"Stop saying that, I'm not a genius. I'm just like you, desperate. And anyway, what you added with the cards and phone makes a big difference. I think you're the genius."

They agreed to wait a week and then try it again at two or maybe even three of the big hotels.

Milka at least had something to hold onto for the first time since losing Evra.

And Mahret had renewed hope that one day she, Barisso, and the two boys would leave this place.

Chapter 50

DOWN IN THE DUMP

Mahret and Milka did operate their business again a week later. They continued to take it slowly and thus went to two hotels. It worked well for them once again, and this time Mahret got three generous tips while Milka was bartering and two later. They made about the same amount of money. Afterward, they made up advertisements for their tour on some white cardboard they got from the dump. They put their M-Pesa and Milka's phone number on them and taped them to lamp posts near some of the bigger hotels in the city.

"They'll tear them down," Mahret said, "but we'll get some good coverage in the meantime. We can just put them up again next week."

After conducting the tours to Mashimoni for the first several weeks, Mahret got the idea that they should try to vary their destinations.

"We should have the ability to reach out to other areas of the city so that people don't get bored with us. Some of these people will like to go more than once. We should expand to new areas for them. The more we offer, the more they will be satisfied, and they will stay with us."

"Where do you think we should go?"

"One place that might be really good is the dump at Dandora. People would see a lot there to satisfy their curiosity. It must be really ugly."

"You know what, that's a brilliant idea. Dandora dump is famous around the world. It's been in the news almost everywhere—newspapers, radio, television, the internet. You name it somebody has reported on it."

The ladies had a separate set of cards made up with the address of the entrance to the dumpsite on them.

Twelve people took the tour.

Milka had done her research.

She kept their clients well entertained.

"More than a million people live around the site. It was declared full more than a decade ago, and yet it continues to take more than 2,000 tons of new garbage every day. The twelve hectares of land hosts an informal recycling economy feeding nearly 3,000 families in surrounding slums. You see all the people picking through the garbage. They're looking for anything they can sell in the marketplace—or eat. Many, as you can see, are just children. Some kids skip school regularly to get food from the back of the airport trucks as they come into the dump with leftovers from the food services of the airlines."

"These people must all be suffering from the pollution," someone commented. "The air stinks awfully, and the smell, my God, it's terrible."

"Yes," Milka told her, "the United Nations sent hygienists in to try to determine how much living around the dump was affecting the kids' health. 154 of the 328 children tested were suffering from heavy metal poisoning directly associated with this site."

Mahret spotted a lady working in the mounds of garbage with her three children. She offered her a hundred shillings to let them introduce her to their customers and answer any questions they might ask.

Milka acted as her interviewer, and, for those in her audience who did not understand Swahili, she translated to English.

"This is Raja," she said. "She lives here at the dump and works here every day with her children. She has what looks like a chronic lung infection. Three years ago, she lost her newborn baby to an infection. Still, she is afraid the site might close down because that would take away her only means of support. She says if it moves away, she and her children will move with it."

Milka asked Raja if she was worried that by continuing to work here, she was risking her life.

"Yes," she said, "I am afraid. But what can I do? I still have two children, a ten-year-old boy, and a twelve-year-old girl. This is the only way I know to support them. They work with me too. I know it's very dangerous for them, but each day we need food, we need a bit of money for that, we can't survive without it. What else can I do?"

"Would you take a job outside the dump if you could get one, something that has nothing to do with all of this?"

"Yes, of course, but what is there? I have no training. My husband was a bus driver. It was only when he died that I started to go to the dump. I couldn't get anything else."

"Your husband, what did he die of?"

"It was a disease. We lived too close to this place even then. I think it caused him to get the cancer."

Three of the men in the audience handed the woman money.

On a much lighter note, the tour came to a crowd of men playing pool on a real pool table.

"The table is owned by a man who retrieved it from the dump and fixed it up," Milka told the crowd after a brief discussion with one of the players.

"He charges them to play."

"How can they afford it?" someone asked.

"They can't, but the charge is very low, and most of those who play are probably single young men who don't have a family waiting for their daily bread."

"Then, they'll never be able to leave here?"

"No, that's true, but playing pool isn't the problem. The problem is that all these people have become dependent on the dump. They likely are never leaving anyway."

They came across another young woman carrying potatoes.

"Where did you get those?" Milka asked her in a voice loud enough for everyone to hear.

"I found them over there," she said, pointing.

What are you going to do with them?"

"I'm gonna get my daughter to peel them. We're having fries for lunch today."

Mahret got another woman named Margitu to agree to speak.

"This is Margitu," Milka said. "How are you Margitu?"

"I am not good. I have constant chest pain. It hurts me all the time."

"I'm so sorry; it must be a constant burden. Will you ever do anything else but work here?"

"No, I tried other things. When I first started working at the dump, I collected used plastics, electronics, and metals to resell. After two years, I opened up a little restaurant, mainly for the people who work here.

I used to make twenty dollars a month. I was running away from recycling, thinking this will be better for my health. It wasn't, and it was a lot more work and a lot more worry, trying to keep customers and all. I closed my restaurant after seven years. Now I'm back picking through the garbage.

It's the only thing I know."

She also said she was getting desperate. Her health kept deteriorating and yet, as the sole breadwinner in her family, she had no choice but to go back to the dumpsite each day.

"You must be anxious all the time?" a lady in the tour asked.

"I get depressed. This is because when this pain gets into me, it means I have to limit my days of working. But this is hard since I need to pay my bills. My sister took me in with my children. But I look for money to feed them and pay school fees.

I don't have any choice."

Tourists rewarded her with generous handouts.

Milka told her audience that "the people who pick through the garbage develop chronic infections because of the unrestricted dumping of domestic, industrial, hospital, and agricultural waste. It is the city's main dumping site, and it has a terrible impact on the environment and not exclusively here. It reaches as well into the more prosperous districts of Nairobi too.

The city understands that before the trucks dump the garbage, they should separate it into recyclable, biodegradable, and non-biodegradable products. The recyclable should be recycled, and the rest should be kept together and burned. This way, the dumpsite would be cleared, and the amount of air pollution reduced. The problem, as you have now witnessed, is that too many people are economically dependent on it the way it is."

Based on crowd satisfaction, the outing at the dump appeared very successful. Both Mahret and Milka felt they had made a good impact on their audience.

"I'm sure everyone went home with a new attitude toward life in Nairobi. It will never be the same for them," Mahret said.

However, they were not sure how often they would repeat this tour since all the on-site handouts went to people living and working there. Mahret got none.

They decided they should go there every fourth or fifth outing.

"We have to consider the help the poor people living at the dump get from our tours," Milka said, "otherwise we're just getting caught up in our own greed."

"Yes, that's true. Isn't it the shits, though?

I can't believe I said that. All it takes is a little money, and some of us start getting awful wicked."

"Yes, you're a bitch, and I'm afraid I'm becoming one too. In a way, though, superciliousness is kind of enjoyable."

"I have no idea what that means, but I'm sure you're right."

They both laughed.

"This is so good for Milka," Mahret told herself later. "She'll never totally get over the death of her son, how could she? But I can tell, in enough time, she'll be more like her normal self again.

"And me and my family, we'll be able to get out of here."

Chapter 51

GIVE US A BREAK PLEASE!

Times were suddenly good for Mahret, and better than before, for her partner. They could, they thought, both look forward to someday leaving Kibera. In short order, however, their ability to produce profits was curtailed by the interference of the local gang to which Mahret had twice donated money.

After their fifth outing, the two women were sitting at a rickety table at the Mashimoni marketplace when Hashu himself appeared, pulled up a chair, and sat down beside them.

"*Akkam* ladies, how are you?"

"We're fine," Mahret responded, "you?"

"I'm great. My guards tell me your new business is doing very well."

"I wouldn't say very well," Mahret responded. "It's okay, but we won't get rich."

"That's not what I've heard. Thirty-five U.S. dollars for each of your clients and very low costs. That's a lot of money."

"But we do have costs," Milka told him. "We have to advertise; we have to pay for our M-Pesa and travel expense. We work so hard, too, not just showing the people around, but also to get the clients."

"Yes, yes, but the return is awfully good. I can see you're taking home 200 dollars to twice that much every time. And that doesn't count the tips."

His guards obviously had been watching them closely.

They both now easily foresaw what he was about to spring on them.

"As you realize, this is my organization's area. We protect all the people and the businesses here too."

"Yes, we know that, and we appreciate it, I have contributed to you in the past."

"Yes, and that is the point. You contribute because you know how important our protection is. Life here would be almost impossible without us. But we can't survive either, without financial support. For that reason, I ask the best businesses here, like yours, to contribute to our well-being, a tax so to speak for the protection you couldn't operate without. Does that seem reasonable?"

"Yes, I guess, so long as you don't charge too much."

He cut to the chase.

"I will make this as clear and fair as I can. I want you to pay my organization 8,000 shillings for each outing. That is equitable, and you can easily afford it."

"But, sometimes we'll only get two people, that's more than what we make."

"Hasn't happened so far, and sometimes you get six, eight, even a dozen people. You will get more, too, as you get better at it. This is a small amount in comparison to your returns."

"What if we quit, then you will get nothing!"

"That is your decision. I will let you think about it until your next showing, but at that point, I will stop offering protection unless you pay my guard on the street 8,000 shillings. That's it, that's my final offer. We all have to help keep the peace around here, that's my job, but I need more than your goodwill. I need real cash, or anything might happen to you."

He got up then and left.

The partners now had a serious discussion about the future possibilities for their business. They conceded that they wanted to keep going, but this would put a top on what they could make. They might even lose money on some outings.

Mostly, however, they figured they could still make enough to improve their lives. They resented the intrusion, but they realized and agreed, that Hashu had helped to keep their children safe in the past. As he said, his protection for the business was essential.

So, for now, they would continue on, though without quite the same grand hopes they had before.

Mahret summed it all up.

"There is little point trying to expand very much, if we get too big, we'll have to hire people to lead some of the outings just as the other tours have done. If we make more, Hashu will insist on more too. There is no end to what he can demand."

Mahret started an M-Pesa deposit account of her own, in which to save as much money as possible after each tour.

She eventually told Barisso about the business:

"I didn't tell you before because I was afraid it wouldn't be successful, and I didn't want you to worry. But it is actually pretty good. Along with your job, it can be our future. Our next life will be in a better place where Berhanu and Gamado will be safe and someday bring up their children without the constant fear and worry we've had. It is going to take a while, but we have to keep going. We'll just have to put the money aside a little bit at a time until we have enough."

"That's great," Barisso told her, "we have lots of time."

"No, we do not have lots of time. Berhanu is about to turn twelve. This is no place for a young man to grow up. As soon as possible we have to find a country for him, and for Gamado, where young men can get good work and find a decent life. The slums condemn people to poverty on top of all the other risks.

We must never start feeling content here. Maybe it could be good enough for you and me. But it will never be nearly good enough for our boys!"

Barisso had no answer [...]

Once again.

Chapter 52

THE LAST STRAW

Quickly on the heels of her conversation with Barisso about her business, two frightening events augmented Mahret's erstwhile impatience with life in the slums.

The first was the 2007 Kenyan general election.

This was a national election that saw incalculable violence and bloodletting. What made it so horrific was a decade's long rivalry between the two dominant political parties in Kenya, one originally centered on the Luo tribe and the other around the Kikuyu. Their rivalry now gained fuel as their respective leaders, Raila Odinga and Mwai Kibaki, competed for the presidency.

Immediately after Kibaki was declared the winner, men on the Luo side charged electoral fraud, and Odinga appealed to his supporters for a million men to join a great show of strength in Nairobi's Uhuru Park. During the gathering and then in the weeks that followed, men stormed and burned Kikuyu homes and assaulted people in the streets. Kikuyu supporters fought back, and, eventually, many on both sides were hurt or killed. Thousands were left homeless.

Even skin color (or at least shade) became a spur to the violence.

George Onyango's lips quivered as he described what a gang of young Kikuyu men said to him before they beat him with sticks and opened two gashes in his head.

"You are black, too black. We don't like your black skin."

The shooting of legislator David Kimutai Too added to the distrust of police. People in three western towns targeted police stations. In Too's home village, 3,000 people armed with bows and arrows, spears, clubs, and machetes killed a police officer. The mob accused the officer of wounding a civilian when he and his fellow policemen opened fire on a crowd protesting Too's death.

The police were part of the problem.

On several occasions, police officers opened fire indiscriminately. In one incident, they killed six people and wounded at least ten.

They brought out tear gas, water cannons, and batons to quell the unrest, and they engaged in running battles with the people. A young man was shot and killed in Dandora. They claimed he was a dangerous criminal and a member of a notorious gang in the area. Nairobi County Police Commander, Japhet Koome, said the man and an accomplice had robbed a woman of valuables before escaping to the Dandora dumpsite. However, residents claimed he was deaf and did not hear the gunfire. They also said the bullet wounds were in his back. Youths from the area took his body and hid it. When police officers attempted to find it, they stoned them. The resulting clash left two men dead on Dandora Bridge.

"When will this end?" asked Alfrank Okoth as he nursed a bullet wound to the chest in the Massaba Hospital. The 28-year-old said police had shot him at the gate of his house.

Pastor Francis Ivayo said he was shielding a group of children near his church when police fired from a train going through the area, hitting him in the lower back.

"They killed my daughter," a woman screamed. "Our new prime minister is a killer. He must die."

She and her little girl were washing dishes on her doorstep when police opened fire.

Many people who escaped the violence suffered in other ways.

"We have no food; there is no water," a man in Kibera said. "We can't make a living in all the chaos. People here are dying."

Most of the violence occurred in Nairobi, but it also spread across the country. In the city of Eldoret, rioters burned fifty-nine members of the Kikuyu tribe alive as they worshipped in their church. Some forty bodies, many of them displaying what looked like machete wounds, were left in the streets.

Outside the towns and cities, people looted farms. They also blocked off the roads, making it impossible for many farmworkers and commuters to get to work. Countless people lost their job. Many fled the violence to Uganda and other countries. Tourism in Kenya came to a complete stop.

Like a lot of people living around them who wanted to avoid the conflict, Mahret and Barisso stayed home for days to allow the violence to subside. They kept the kids home as well.

Now and again, however, it was necessary to go out into the streets for provisions. The Dandora marketplace was open to some extent partly because so many of the people selling meat, garden goods, and *daabo* were desperate. They needed an income from sales to sustain life.

And, of course, many others needed food.

Mahret was caught short when the violence first broke out.

"I know it's scary out there," she said to Barisso three days after it all started, "but it's worse for women than men. We need some flour so I can at least keep the boys from starving. I guess you better plan on heading to the market. If you go early tomorrow morning, there shouldn't be too much going on in the streets."

Barisso did go the next morning. He had no problems.

Then, several days later, he had to go again.

This time he was not so fortunate. He got to the market easily enough, but when he was heading home with groceries under his arms, he saw six young male members of what he would later find out was a Luo political group assaulting a dark-skinned man in the street. The youths had circled the man and were taking turns kicking and punching him.

They were heaping obscenities on him.

"You, dirty, worthless, *haadha rawu*. We gonna kill you."

The fighting was directly in Barisso's path, so to avoid it, he ducked into a small open space between two of the shanties. As he peered out at the fighting, he suddenly realized that the guy being attacked was a friend of his. It was Horval, a man he had shared some changa with on many occasions back in Mashimoni.

"Hey," he yelled. "Hey, you guys leave him alone. I mean it.
Six to one, that's not a fair fight."

They paid no attention.

One of the men grabbed Horval from behind to hold him so the others could get better shots at him. Barisso's instincts took over. He ran headlong into the fray, knocking one of the assailants to the ground and kneeing him hard in the face with both knees

The guy didn't get up.

Barisso turned and punched the guy who was holding Horval.

The guy fell. He got up holding his face and limped off.

Barisso stood next to Horval as the four remaining assailants circled them trying to throw punches and kicks. When one moved in on Barisso, Horval dropped him with a crushing right. That was it for him.

"Okay, now," Barisso yelled, "three boys left to fight two men. How do you like them odds fellas? Do you think you're up to it? Try it again, and we're gonna make sure you don't ever pull this kinda shit anymore. If I was you, I'd stick my tail between my legs and get the fuck outa here, while ya still can."

One of them turned and ran; the other two traded looks and followed their friend.

Horval was bleeding from the nose and had a cut on his forehead.

"Are you okay?"

"Yeah, I'm okay. I'll probably feel it more when I get up tomorrow.
Thanks for helping me. Those guys were cowards, but I couldn't beat them by myself."

"How did it happen? How come they attacked you? What're you doin in Dandora?"

"I was talkin to Milka, and she told me where you're living. I had nothin to do today, so thought I would come over to your market for groceries because ours hasn't been very good since the fighting got real bad. Thought I might bump into you. I think they attacked because they hate Jews. I didn't think it would be like this. I owe you."

"You'd a done the same for me. Come with me; I live just up here. Mahret will doctor up your face, so you don't scare the kids when you get home."

When Mahret saw Horval, she hugged him.

"What happened to you? You got caught in the fighting, didn't you?"

"Yeah, Barisso helped me, saved me actually."

While the two men talked about the fight, Mahret cleaned Horval's wounds. And then they all sat down together over a cup of *shaayii.*

They caught up on all the latest gossip.

Finally, Horval said, "I better get home, Marsha will be worried. Thanks for everything. I won't forget this. Come visit when you get a chance. We miss you guys."

"We will. You and I can tip a glass or two again."

"Yeah, for sure!"

Shortly after he left, Mahret laughed out loud.

"Barisso!" she said, "do you remember how we used to hate the Jews that were farming about twenty miles down the road from us in Oromia. You used to say that if you had a gun, you'd go over and shoot a couple for taking up land we figured good people like us should be using. We called them 'dirty Jews.'"

"I know," he said, "the world's not as simple as we thought."

For Barisso, the one positive aspect of the episode was a renewed sense of self-esteem—of his manhood. He felt he had stood up to be counted when called on. He had fought like a warrior to defend a friend.

He was a man again, in the old-fashioned way.

That night when he lay in bed with Mahret, he experienced a gratuitous erection.

Under the covers, he quietly pushed his loins over against her body. She was asleep and pulled away from him. He reached over, pulled her back, and slipped his penis under her nightgown, entering her from behind. The erection was strong and trustworthy. He pumped quietly and methodically.

Mahret woke up. She could tell Barisso was excited. Audaciously, for her, she pulled his penis out with her hand and gently rubbed it against her most sensitive part.

For the first time in months, man and wife came together.

"What kind of a mother am I?" the wife thought. "I'm just like a prostitute.

But oh, that felt awful good!

It just felt so good!"

Chapter 53

THE LAST LAST STRAW

Much of the chaos during the 2007 election occurred in the most deprived areas of Nairobi. People who lived in those areas were astounded by it. They had been accustomed to, and ever so proud of, the incredible cohesion that had characterized their compounds. Kibera was a flashpoint of violence. In a pro-government Kikuyu quarter, angry young men roamed the streets with machetes and bows and arrows, eventually hacking ten Luos to death. In an opposition stronghold, young Luo men half-drunk on local brew carried machetes and nail-studded sticks and massacred any Kikuyus who came their way. "People had those tribal feelings," a man named Mahura said during the election, "but they didn't want to express them before. Now they don't want to stop talking about them."

It should be noted, on the other hand, that there were also numerous attempts by men living in Nairobi slums to stop the violence.

"Block by block, person by person, and often at the risk of death," some people in Kibera tried consistently to bring the two sides together.

There were cases of Luos hiding Kikuyus in their homes to protect them, and of Kikuyus stepping in at the crucial moment to save Luos from being murdered. There were reports too, that "small gestures of trust and urgent conversations between friends" were instrumental in preventing large-scale tribal clashes that almost certainly would have seen a great deal more bloodshed.

In the weeks after the new government took office and calm returned to the country, a welcomed reaction set in throughout the country against all the partisanship. Kiberans were among the staunchest advocates of reconciliation. The most obvious manifestation of this was a campaign by a variety of religious groups to show openness and tolerance toward each other by painting their places of worship the same bright yellow color.

On three separate occasions Mahret, Milka, and Barisso pitched in to help a group from the Jehovah's Witnesses Church in Kibera take part in this campaign. Ultimately, the group painted not only their building but a variety of other churches, Muslim mosques, Hindu temples, and Jewish synagogues.

Mahret was no doubt heartened by this. She also realized, however, that the commotion that erupted during and following the 2007 election was simply a repeat of what had happened in the past— the same lawlessness, the same violence, the same killing, the same police criminality.

And it would happen again and again in the future.

"Everything seems nice and peaceful and friendly now," she said, "but give us another few years, and we'll do it all again. Let's not forget that."

Then, something even more threatening occurred that she deeply feared would ultimately also be repeated. It was more alarming to both her and Barisso than anything they had been through to that point.

One morning, Gamado got very sick. He developed a fever, quit eating, and had several bouts of vomiting. Mahret put him to bed and went to the closest thing to a health clinic she knew of, the well-known pharmacy near their former home in Kibera. Despite his lack of training, the thirty-two-year-old owner, John Otieno, had years of hands-on experience prescribing cheap drugs he sold in the store.

Otieno prescribed amoxicillin for Gamado. It was a first-line antibiotic often used for a broad range of infections from bacterial pneumonia and chlamydia to salmonella, strep throat, and lyme disease.

The drug proved ineffective, however, and Gamado's fever and vomiting quickly got worse. He developed severe diarrhea as well. Mahret returned to the pharmacy for one prescription after the other.

None worked.

"Please," she finally said to Otieno, "there must be something else you can do. Our son is so sick; we're terrified he's dying."

"I have two more drugs that I can prescribe," he told her, "but I warn you they are costly, completely out of reach for most here."

"How much?"

"1500 shillings."

Mahret reached into her purse, pulled out the money, and handed it to him.

He got two small bottles out of his cabinet and gave them to her.

"If I had known you had that kind of money, I would have suggested them earlier. See if these work. Try this one first. If it works, see that he takes the daily directed dosage until the entire bottle is gone, even if he gets well right away. If you don't use the other bottle, you can bring it back, and I will return your money."

Gamado's condition did not change much during the first day of treatment, but he did not get worse, and by evening he seemed to be resting a little easier. Then, when Mahret got up and checked on him in the middle of the night, she could tell the fever had subsided. The next morning, he was sitting up in bed looking tired but much better. By noon he was demanding food.

Mahret went back to the doctor to thank him.

"He's okay," she said, "I think he's going to be okay. The fever is gone. Thank you for the powerful medicine and thank *Waqaa*."

"Yes, thank the Almighty, it's too bad, it's so expensive. Usually, I don't mention it until the situation is desperate because people here don't have the money. They beg me to give it to them, but I can't afford it. I'd be out of business here very fast."

Mahret asked him why the cheaper drugs were so useless.

"The problem is that antibiotics, the miracle drugs credited with saving millions of lives worldwide, have never been more accessible than they are to the world's poor. We have so many cheap antibiotics here thanks mainly to the mass production of generics in China and India, and so much sickness from the filthy conditions of the air and water that the drugs are losing their ability to kill the germs they were created to conquer.

Many bacteria have evolved to the point where they're outsmarting the medications. They mutate and gain resistance. It's an endless cycle. A lack of sanitation leads to more diseases, which leads to higher antibiotic use, which leads to greater resistance."

"Where will all this end? It looks like a disaster is in the future. The germs will out smarten the powerful medicines eventually too, and then everybody dies."

"Yes, I worry about Kibera, but also about my own family. One day I could go home and infect my children with one of these dangerous bugs and find that even the best of the drugs don't work.

I feel guilty for prescribing the drugs, but who am I to deny people what they believe is their only hope to get well? The other problem is that most can't afford to buy more than three or four pills at a time, an amount that is one-third or less of the recommended course for most antibiotics. So, they get a bit better, but they do not completely eradicate the bug from their system. It comes back.

And even when I manage to sell them the whole box, my patients rarely take them all because they think it's just too many pills. They want to save the rest for next time."

"So, what you're saying is that because we can't deny people the drugs, our main efforts should be to clean up the poor districts, so we don't need all of them?"

"That's right, epidemiologists and public health experts who have studied Kibera say there is a direct correlation between poor hygiene and the infections that stalk nearly every household. Harmful bacteria in feces that are allowed to seep into the surrounding soil can survive for months. In densely populated settlements like Kibera crisscrossed with dirt paths, they easily find their way into food and water. And they're all over the stray dogs and chickens that people touch. Often people unknowingly carry the pathogens into their homes on shoes or unwashed feet or hands."

"Is there any hope for places like Kibera?"

"I don't see any. In my anxiety, I picked up a study by the Center for Disease Control and Prevention. It shows that cases of typhoid fever among children in Kibera are fifteen times higher than among those living in a rural area west of here. Infections in Kibera were the highest in low-lying areas where sewage tends to pool and provide breeding grounds for pathogens like E. coli. Every disease known to man is on the rise—typhoid, malaria, tuberculosis, cholera—you name it, we have it, and it's getting worse. Diarrhea kills almost one in five children before their fifth birthday."

"Thank *Waqaa*; our son is going to be alright," Mahret later told Barisso, "I've never been so frightened. The slums face what Milka would call an insoluble problem. I've heard her say that a lot. I believe this is *Waqaa*'s way of telling us we must get out of here. And we must go to the new world, as soon as we can find a way. Dandora is not as filthy and crowded as Kibera, but it is far from perfect, and the germs don't stop at Kibera's borders anyway."

"Where exactly do you think we should go? What do you mean by the 'new world'?"

"Milka talks of going away to a better place where everyone has money, and the law protects them. I want to go to one of those places. I told you, she keeps telling me about New Zealand, Australia, Canada, America, these she says are the 'new world' countries. She says almost everyone has money in those places, and those that don't can get support from something she calls 'social welfare.' There is much less disease, and you can go to a doctor whenever you need to and get medicine too, almost free. They have lots of hospitals for kids who get sick or hurt. Police don't shoot the kids, gangs don't rule the cities, and political violence is not allowed. We must find a way to get to the new world."

Barisso shook his head in bewilderment:

"Just when I was beginning to love it here, you know, with the farming job and all. Just when I'm feeling like a man again."

"Barisso, we'll get you a great job in the new world, and for once, our kids will be safe. They won't be joining any gangs when they get older, they won't get shot in the street, they won't contract deadly diseases without doctors, and they won't get AIDS from dirty girls either."

"Yes, Mahret, I know, I know! We'll be happy forever."

Chapter 54

THE FINAL LAST STRAW

It was early in the morning, Mahret was heading for the Dandora market intending to bake some muffins on the cooker when she saw a woman sitting on the edge of the road with her head resting on her knees.

"I wonder what's wrong with her. She must be sick."

As she tried to step past her, the woman raised her head.

"Mahret!" she said. "Help me, please help me!"

Mahret thought she had heard this woman's voice before, but she did not recognize her face. It was unnaturally black and rather blue, there was an open wound and dried blood on the one cheek, and both eyelids were terribly swollen.

"What's wrong with you, you've been beaten?"

"Mahret, it's Rekik, Rekik! Please help me!"

"Oh, my goodness, Rekik!!"

Mahret knelt beside her and put her arms around her, very carefully.

"What happened to you?"

Rekik didn't answer. She seemed to be running out of strength.

Mahret helped her to her feet and half-carried her back down the street to home.

When they were inside, Mahret shouted at Barisso to get up. At the same time, she sat her friend down on the edge of the bed.

"It's Rekik, the one I told you about, who saved me and your kids. We must help her!"

Mahret put her hand to the back of Rekik's head and gently helped her stretch out. Then she got a rag, soaked it in cold water, and began dabbing her face and forehead.

Rekik closed her swollen eyes and fell asleep—or lost consciousness—there was no way to tell.

After Mahret fed Barisso and the kids and got them off to school, she paced the floor keeping an eye on Rekik. Finally, after several hours, she watched her come back to life.

When Rekik's eyes were open, she looked a little better, or at least more with it.

Mahret stroked her forehead.

"Oh, my *Waqaa*, you look awful. What happened to you?"

Rekik replied with some difficulty.

"A gang came in to take us over. Some of us resisted. They killed two of the young guys who were protecting us and chased the rest away. They brought their own men in with big guns to take over, and they beat me up, killed one of my sisters, and made the rest cooperate with them and pay them for protection. They hate me because I tried to stop them. I can't go back. I don't know what to do."

"Don't worry. You can stay with us as long as you need to. How did you know where to find me?"

"I had sources. I asked a couple of girls we knew who work nights in Mashimoni to keep an eye out for you. They said you went to Dandora. I went to the market; I knew you would be there regular. I thought you would help me. There was no one else."

Mahret and Barisso let Rekik have their bed. They got another mattress and cowhide in the market for themselves and laid it out on the floor beside her.

They allowed Rekik to rest during the next few days while the swelling in her face went down, and the bruises and cuts faded.

On the fourth day, Rekik told Mahret she would soon be ready to leave.

"What will you do?"

"I don't know, go back to work I guess, maybe in a new district."

"No," Mahret said, "you are not doing that. We are going to the new world, and you are coming with us. You are my sister. We will get passports for all of us, and you will come with us. Life was okay for us here for a while, but lots of bad things still happen, and this is the final test. We are all going to apply for papers, and we will go together. You are no longer a prostitute. You will never do that again. You are my sister. We will get real jobs in a new country. We will find a new life."

Rekik was in no position to argue. They had pulled her world out from under her. And she did not relish the thought of returning to it.

"*Galatom*," she said, "you're a good person. I must tell you, two of the guys who beat me up raped me, and I don't know if they used a condom."

"Two out of how many? You made your clients use protection for all those years. *Waqaa* won't forget that; chances are you're okay; you should be alright. If you start to feel sick, tell me. I know where to get the medicine that will make it better."

"The pharmacy, right?"

"Yes, it has very strong medicine that cures everything."

"Only if you have the money, right? A sick slummer doesn't often have it."

"I know, but you will."

"How will we get out of here? I don't have papers, and I'm pretty sure you don't either."

"No, we don't, but I will ask my friend Milka. She knows everything. Then we will leave Nairobi for good and find a new life. You saved me and my children when we first came here. We'll help you now. You will be my sister forever. You must just get that into your head. And keep it there. If you believe it, the people who give us papers will believe it too.

In a week or two, or three, our family is going to start a new life, the whole family together, and that includes you."

Chapter 55

A VERY BAD PLACE WITH GOOD TEACHINGS

The next Sunday, Mahret called on Milka so the two of them could go to the church together. Milka had promised Mahret she would go with her once in a while for the companionship. Mahret harbored hopes that her best friend could find something that along with their new business might help her deal with Evra's death.

As they walked along Mahret told her all about the fight Barisso and their friend had with the Luos. Then she told her about Rekik.

"What continues to amaze me," she said when she finished, "is that now we help protect people like that, people we used to think we hated. We not only live and work with all these different people, we trust most of them. I let a prostitute into our home, and I'm not even afraid to let her sleep in the same room as my boys. Barisso risked his life for a Jew."

"You've changed; we've all changed."

"Yeah, I'm more amazed at us for hating so many different people in our first life than I am about accepting so many now. Do you know what I mean? Why did we think we had a right to hate so many? What's wrong with us humans? We're instinctively hateful creatures."

Milka, of course, had a sophisticated explanation."

"To understand it properly, I think you need to consider first the reason why we're so naturally inclined to miss-understand each other. I just read a book about people who commit genocide. The author explains that human beings learn to view human beings of other cultures as vile and killable basically by just separating from them, the other human beings I mean."

"I don't understand?"

"Yes, well you see, we keep to groups based on race, religion, or nation; the author calls them 'compartments.' We identify with one group of people, who are all the same in important ways, and we push other groups away; you know both physically and mentally. That makes it so we just can't recognize the other groups as composites of individual human beings. We see them instead as sort of distant, foggy, inhuman masses. And then it becomes easy to kill them—men, women, children, it doesn't matter. They all blend together. In our minds they become monolithic."

"That's terrible!"

"Yes, it's not very nice. It just seems to be a form of tribalism. One tribe thinks it's better than another, or, indeed, all others. Whole nations even become tribal mainly by beating it into their peoples' heads that they are separate from and special in comparison to other nations. It's called nationalism. The people teach themselves to care only about themselves, their own group or society. Everyone else becomes a mass that absorbs all individuality in human beings. Then we make up negative images of them—'lazy, stupid, evil, crazy, hateful, inhuman or even black.' I mean, honestly, it's crazy. You know as well as I do, that we even compartmentalize not just skin color but shades of skin color. We've learned better but look how some people prefer light blacks over dark blacks. It's madness. Dark blacks have been pushed away—you know compartmentalized—people don't want to kill them, but they lump them all together in their minds. They're all the same and somehow, they're all inferior."

"Hmmm, I think maybe we were a little like that on the farm in Oromia. We were all the same in some ways. We celebrated together too. We were separated from everyone else in the world. And we thought we hated or at least looked down on all sorts of people."

"That's exactly what the author was trying to explain. He looked at many cases of genocide—the Nazis and the Jews, mass murder in the Balkans, the Rwanda killings where the Hutus and Tutsis tried to annihilate each other. You must remember that?"

"Yes, we heard something about it."

"The point is that separation from other societies, or even other types of people, encourages us to judge them as monoliths."

"Yes, you said that. What does it mean?"

"As monoliths, you know, as if they are all one big unit like a huge stone that has absorbed all the little stones—no individuals, no people. And because we assume they're not only alien but also not like us, we judge them to be all bad. So why not kill them?"

"Can this apply to people in certain careers?"

"What do you mean?"

"Like prostitutes. We don't normally see them as people; they're all the same and all bad. And that's all there is to it. There's no possibility that any of them could be different from all the rest. They're just the same sinful group."

"Yes, exactly, I think that's right, another perceived monolith.

What's happened to all of us in Kibera is just the opposite of compartmentalization. Here, as you and I recognized a long time ago, we have had to mix with all sorts of different types of people to survive. The fact that they come from every race, religion, and walk of life we have ever heard of forces us to temper our judgment. Because we have to depend on them, work with them to protect each other, our children, our old people, we start to overlook differences. We can't help it. We automatically start to see people whose motives and aspirations are like ours. Men, women, and children stand out from their different customs and beliefs; yes, and looks. We eventually find that we have much in common with many we thought we should spurn. It's mutual too."

The more Mahret mulled all this over in her mind as they walked along, the more she was sure Milka was right. She remembered once again the Muslim guy who saved the little boy in Mashimoni. She also thought of the time Barisso put his life on the line for the Jew, Horval, and then the women who had kept the rapists at bay. As her own church came into view, she thought about the painting campaign she and Barisso had both got involved in after the last election.

Mahret thought the black, black people who saved Barisso from the lions might also be a case in point.

"They didn't live with him, but when they saw him clinging to that tree, they understood his pain, they had seen lions kill their people; Barisso was suddenly one of them, a man. They overlooked his light skin, and they couldn't just think of him as part of some strange, foreign [...] what's that word Milka uses? 'Mono [...]' something. No, he wasn't that. He became a person like them.

That's what happens to everybody in places like Kibera. They share each other's pain over a period, and they have to help each other; they do it first for survival, but once they see others as themselves, they learn to give a damn."

"It's just for our own sake, this pulling together," she said to Milka, "in a way, it's kind of an accident?"

"Yes, it is. It's self-interest. As we try to secure life for ourselves, we all have to help and protect each other. Then as we work together, we actually see that 'others' are people too. We automatically grow more broad-minded, more understanding. We don't necessarily want to, we just do. We have to."

"Okay, then, what about women. Don't you think that we have learned to rise above race and religion a bit too, all of us? That's why we help each other so much. I saw this happening a long time ago—on the way to Kibera; on the bus, a woman stopped the driver from leaving me and Berhanu at the side of the road. And I helped that woman who got raped.

And what about Rekik and the other prostitutes she used to work with. They came from different places all over Africa, but they called each other 'sister.' That's the word they used. They helped each other with everything: their children, their business, their housing, their lives.

But there was more to it than that. Rekik took me in even though she knew I wasn't a prostitute. She just saw me as a woman in trouble. She had learned to think like that from cooperating with the other prostitutes. To her and her sisters, all women became people. What about that?"

"Hmm, yes, you're a very perceptive person Mahret.

And, I agree, women do join forces to overcome compartmentalization. The incident you had with the rapists is probably the best example. The Kenyan government has compartmentalized a cultural group in that area known as Nubians. It has never accepted their property or citizen rights though Kibera has been their home for an entire century. The government keeps insisting they are squatters on our land, and they refuse to provide any utilities or public services for them. They leave these people in an enclave of poverty, marginalized from the rest of society. From your descriptions I am quite sure the women who helped you were Nubians. And yet a sense of gender clearly overcame everything. They had worked so closely with other women to try to deal with all their terrible hardships. They saw you and Anna as their sisters. That to them made you people instead of Oromos or whatever."

"Yes, they saved us from being raped. They didn't share our religion, or even our race or skin, but they saw us as their sisters in a way, and in trouble. They had to help us."

"They saw you as them because they had learned to identify with women generally. They had taken on life's greatest challenges in league with all the other women living around them. And they learned to see all of us as people.

Incredible."

For a few moments, both Mahret and Milka were silent.

Then Mahret spoke.

"I guess at least we've learned somethings here that we wouldn't have learned anywhere else. We've lived in a very bad place with the rape, the killings, the filth, the diseases, the poverty, but it's a very bad place with good teachings."

"Yes, I suppose that's one way of looking at it."

"Why is it that some people are so bad and yet some living in the same place are so good? Some steal, some are high or drunk most of the time, some murder other people and yet, some help others, feed their kids, protect their kids, share what they have even with African people they used to hate. What is it about this place [...]?"

"Listen Mahret, I long ago decided that there is no such thing as free will. People are doomed to be themselves. There is no good, no bad, and no in between. Just people. They're not to blame for their own actions, they go through life just doing what they have to do in given situations because of the way their brains are constructed, technologists would say 'programmed.'"

"I remember you telling me those guys who shot the men at the bus station weren't bad.; those guys who wanted to rape little boys were going to heaven."

"That's not really what I said. All I said was that we are born with a certain type of brain that makes us who we are—that makes us a certain type of person. Under the right conditions it makes some of us subject to alcoholism, some to short-term gratifications of various kinds, some unable to think or worry about the future, and some deeply thoughtful, empathetic and caring; and some able to pull together with others—even other races—when it's important. We have no control over which type we are. We are just one or the other."

"You think then everyone is innocent."

"What I'm saying is the terms 'good' and 'bad' are irrelevant. They're meaningless because we cannot be blamed for being who we are. We face all kinds of situations in life, and we react to them in ways that are predetermined by forces over which we have no control; forces that are built into our brains at birth. There can be no good and no evil because no one can be blamed for who they are. They just are who they are."

"But that means *Waqaa* is to blame; we're like animals, like trees blowing this way and that way in the wind. It all depends on which way the wind is blowing. We can't escape it!"

"Precisely."

"Oh, Milka, you're wrong. This can't be right. You've taught me a lot. You're the smartest person I ever met, but you're wrong about this."

"Well think about it Mahret; your husband, Barisso, for instance. You know he has a hard time making decisions. You told me how hard it was for him to react to your problems on the farm, and I know you had to drag him out to the good school and the new home. But you overlook his ways, his shortages, because you know he has no choice but to be himself with everything that entails. He has good points and bad ones, and you accept them all because deep down inside you realize he has to be him. That's the way it is with all of us.

And you, you're the type of person who is patient and understanding. You were born that way and you will always be like that. That's why you accept Barisso's flaws."

"But [...]"

"No! You Mahret, you are also the type who takes control under difficult situations. You drag your husband and the kids along. You start a new business. You talk to Miss Ellingson about Berhanu. You're the one who gets help, not Barisso. That's the way it is with everybody. We're just people—a great mass of individuals beating away on the drum we were born with. You know that's true.

Evolution over thousands of years formed our brains, just as it formed our bodies."

Mahret was suddenly stunned. What if her best friend, the smartest person she ever met, was right?

She knew that Barisso and she were in ways not like each other. And they would always be like that. Just as Milka said. And the boys too.

"I have to think about this, how, how did you come up with such an idea? What makes you so sure you're right? Aren't you making up conclusions, without proof?"

"Yes, that's what I thought at first. But it seems to me that the people who are so sure we are in control of ourselves, that we have free will, are the ones making assumptions. Nobody questions free will. They just instinctively believe in it—without evidence, without even giving it any thought—they just know it's true. And I just feel I know they're wrong."

"What made you think this?"

"Life. I watched my husband, and I knew he would always be a cheater and untrustworthy because he couldn't help giving into his impulses. But most of all it was coming here to Kibera. I've seen so many people reacting in so many ways to so many situations and I've seen patterns. They're all predestined to pick a way that satisfies the brain they were born with. To me this is one of your 'good teachings.' I've gained a greater understanding of the human race here than I ever had before, and to me it's an important lesson even though it does not provide a very positive picture of people. To me it's important for the human race to understand itself even if we conclude that we are basically robots. It's the only way we can be more realistic in our judgments, in our expectations. We have to learn to understand ourselves. If we eventually do that, we will see that we are all in this together. Hateful judgments are irrelevant. Understanding will teach us that there must be a rational way to overcome our shortcomings. Punishment alone is not the answer, neither is violence."

"Even if you're right about this, it isn't something people will take to while you and me are still alive."

"I know."

Mahret felt a bit overwhelmed. While she might not accept Milka's interpretations she also would never see things in the simplistic terms she had in the past. Ultimately, to her the good teachings were that the world is way more complicated than she ever thought.

For the present she had one clear thought still in her mind. She had to find a way to get the family out of Kibera.

As they began the trek home after the service, she asked Milka what she knew about the possibility of emigrating to one of the new world countries they had talked about.

"Legally, I mean."

Milka told her that after her son's death, she had looked into it herself and concluded that for her family, it would at this stage still be too difficult.

"I think I have enough money, but the only way to do it would be as a refugee. And just as I feared, the problem is that you need to be able to show that you qualify as a refugee. Kenyans do not. We haven't had to take refuge from anywhere."

Milka thought for a moment.

"But you know what? You probably could. You and Barisso and the boys are refugees from Ethiopia already. If you apply to the UNHCR, I bet you would be accepted."

"What's that?"

"It's the United Nations High Commission for Refugees. They decide if you can get the status necessary to go to one of the countries that accept refugees."

"Are we, the family, I mean, are we really refugees, like legally?"

"Yes, I'm pretty sure you are. I think because you had to flee persecution in your original country, you would qualify.

You can get financial assistance too.

I'll tell you what; I know where the UNHCR is in Nairobi. I'll take you there, and we can ask what exactly you have to do. We might even come across something that could help Hilani and me find a way out."

"Really, could you come with me? I'm so scared of officials. I never know how to talk to them. I'm sure I would just freeze up."

"Don't worry; we'll do this together, like so many other things over the past few years. How about tomorrow? We can do it after we go to the hotels."

"Great, yes, thank you."

Chapter 56

A WAY OUT FOR GOOD

The next day, Monday, after they took the big bus into the city to advertise their weekly tour, Mahret and Milka walked over to the UNHCR. By this time, Mahret had begun to think America would be their refuge. American dollars were always sought after by people here, and time after time, she had listened to American news and pop music on the radio.

At the UNHCR, however, they found that the easiest country to emigrate to might be Canada because its rules seemed quite straight forward.

"What you have to do to get to Canada is simply get the agency to refer you to Canadian immigration as an officially approved refugee," Milka told her after reading the rules. "And I think you meet the requirements. If you are outside your country and cannot return for fear of persecution because of your race or religion or politics or nationality, they will give you refugee status. It says that right here. I don't see any reason why you wouldn't qualify."

A few minutes later, they found themselves sitting in front of the big desk of an UNHCR official.

"Hello, what can I do for you?"

"Hello sir, my friend here, Mahret, wants to apply for papers."

"Okay, you have to apply. Go down that hallway right over there and tell the clerk in the office with the open door what you just told me. She will tell you what you have to do to apply for refugee status."

"Thank you."

When the two women came to the office at the end of the corridor, they went in and approached a woman sitting behind another large desk.

"Hello," Mahret said, "please, I need to apply for refugee papers for my family."

"Don't you have any papers?"

"No, ma'am, we're from Oromia."

"You came to Nairobi from Ethiopia without papers?"

"Yes, ma'am, the government in Ethiopia was persecuting us. We had to leave."

"Why didn't you get papers first?"

"There was no time. They were rounding up our neighbors. We had to leave or go to jail or die with our children."

"Why didn't you go to Dadaab?"

Suddenly, Mahret was afraid she had made a mistake coming to this place.

"Oh, ma'am," she said weakly, "that is a death camp. Please don't send us there. My children [...]"

The woman interrupted her.

"Do you work? Do you have a husband, does he work?"

"Yes ma'am, my husband works at the Harmony Child Rescue Centre. Our children go there for school."

"What does he do there, your husband?"

"He is the farmer; he raises crops and looks after farm animals and helps the kids learn about farming."

"Well, at least that's something. Now listen to me, I am going to talk to my superiors about this situation. Kenya is a developing country, and you people keep coming here and becoming a charge on our resources. I think you should be sent to Dadaab before you apply.

You take my card and show me on the map where you live. I am going to talk to my superiors and see what else we can do. Someone will come to you."

"Yes, ma'am. Please don't send us there. We will die, my children […]"

"Just go home; we will talk to you in one week. Do you understand?"

"Yes, yes, one week. I will wait."

"Why," Mahret asked Milka, "didn't I leave well enough alone? Now she knows where the school is and will be able to find us whenever she wants. I should have left it alone. I should have left things as they were—they were pretty good, and I had to cause trouble. I know I won't sleep well now. Barisso was right. I should have listened."

Milka was more optimistic.

"You'll be alright. People like that lady just try to show you their authority. They're there to help you, not send you away to horrible places. Don't worry you did the right thing."

The following week went slowly for Mahret. She kept expecting immigration officers in uniforms to come to the house. On Wednesday and Thursday, nothing happened. On Friday, however, a man who looked like a Kenyan did come to the door. He was a short, stocky suit type with a balding head. Mahret was outside talking to her friends when she saw him heading toward the house. She considered hiding in hopes he would just go away.

But she remembered what Milka told her.

"No," she thought, "I can't do that. He'd come back. I want to face this now anyway. If I avoid it, it'll worry me to death."

She left her friends and walked over to head him off.

"Hi there," she said, "I'm Mahret, were you looking for me?"

"Yes, I was. I'm from the United Nations Department of Refugees."

He had a clipboard in his hand.

"I want to ask you a few questions."

"Okay."

"You are Mahret, is that right?"

"Yes."

"Your husband—what is his name?

"Barisso, B-a-r-i-s-s-o.."

"Your children and ages?"

"Gamado, G-a-m-a-d-o. He's seven turning eight.
Berhanu, B-e-r-h-a-n-u. He's eleven."
Is that all?
"No, I have a sister. Rekik, R e k I k. She is thirty-two."
"You are all from Ethiopia?"
"Yes."
"And you do not want to go to Dadaab?"
"Yes, I mean, that's right, we don't want to. Please, sir, we are good people. We only came here because of persecution in Oromia. They were going to kill us if we didn't leave."
"I don't believe you. Anyway, that's not our problem. You are the problem, and I am afraid you are going to have to go. We can ship you to Dadaab tonight. When will your husband, children, and sister be home?"
"But you can't do this. We are good people. We will die in the death camp. My husband has work. Please, isn't there another way?"
"Look lady, this is not my call. You people are just too expensive. And you have not made any contribution to the state system that's supporting you. You take from us, but you give us nothing back."
"But we do contribute. My husband has a good job at Harmony Child Rescue Centre. He helps the kids learn farming. He helps them a lot. And they don't pay him much."
She did not bother to tell him about her business for fear he would think it exploitive.
He glared at her.
Mahret was frightened, but she thought she possibly detected some hope in the man's last statement. Just maybe he was saying that there was a way out in the same way she had got them all here.
She knew, however, that there was a lot of risk. If she offered him money and she was misreading him, he would almost certainly have her charged for corruption.
But she had to take the chance—just be very careful.
"Uh, sir, I'm sorry we have cost your country money. I don't have very much but I could offer to pay back somehow about 500 shillings. Would that help to release some of the pressure on the state?"
"Of course not! What do you think this is—a shakedown!"
"No sir, I'm sorry, I know it's not much, I just thought you might see it as goodwill. I didn't mean to insult the government."
She was sure he was about to put her in handcuffs.
But he did not.
"I, I mean we, that is my organization, needs twice that much money. Nothing less will do."
"Oh, *Waqaa*," she thought, "what amazing good luck, this really is just another shakedown."
"Listen," she said, "I am a poor woman, but I do have a little bit of cash left over that I brought from home. I need some for survival, but I can give you 600 shillings. I'm sorry, that's all I can spare."
"It's not enough. I'm going to send you to Dadaab right now."

"Okay, then, we will go to the camp. Maybe it's better anyway. Is it possible for me to see your supervisor or someone high up to apologize for not being able to offer you more money? I feel really bad about this, and I hope the department will understand. I will go to them and apologize in person."

The man lowered his eyes.

"All right, I guess the 600 shillings will have to do for now. I will tell the department that's all you have for now. They might send me back, though."

Mahret didn't think so. Now that she had shown her willingness to expose his demands to his betters, he wouldn't push his luck again.

"Just a minute," she said. "I'll be right back."

She went inside the house. When she returned, she had 300 shillings in her hand.

"I will give you half now. My husband has the rest, and after we get the papers, you can have it all. I hope that is okay."

"It's not okay," he said, "I want, that is, our policy is, that you pay the full amount upfront."

"Oh, I'm sorry, that's all I have. My husband has the rest. I guess we can't apply. I'm sorry if I wasted your time."

"Oh, alright, I guess I better take this now and the rest later. I will come back when I have the papers. It will take two or three weeks to get them ready for you. I hope once you have them, you and your family will leave this country. We don't need people like you around here. I will need the names, ages, and place of birth for all of you. You will have to fill out this application form for the whole family."

Mahret filled out the form with his help.

He left after that, and she never heard from him again. Three days later, another man appeared.

He showed her his official United Nations card and his government-issued identification card with a proper photograph on it. The other guy, he told her, must have been a scam artist.

"There are men around who make their living cheating desperate people whenever they can. We've had a lot of complaints."

He asked her basically the same questions as the first guy. And he made her prove she had enough money in her M-Pesa account to sustain them for several months in the new country.

He told her she would need about 200 American dollars more to make the minimum required.

"Can you manage that in about six weeks?"

"Yes, I can do that for sure. We will just be very careful. My husband has a good job, and I work for a tour company. We will do it for sure."

He asked her for money too, fifty shillings, and he gave her a receipt.

"The United Nations Refugee Agency (UNHCR) will, I think, process your request. It will take three or four weeks. There is no reason to think we can't go ahead and provide the documents you want. We get a lot of people like you, and we want to help as much as we can."

That evening after Barisso and the kids got home from school Mahret told them and Rekik, "I think we're going to the 'new world.' We're gonna get out of this place after all."

It was another six weeks before the man appeared again with the papers. She had, by then, put away every cent she and Rekik could spare. It was nearly 1,000 dollars more than required.

In the meantime, the boys continued to go to school, and Rekik helped Mahret and Milka with their business. She would go with them to show people around, and she set the standards for handouts.

"You do better than me," Mahret told her. "You look poor too when you put on normal clothes instead of the sexy ones, and you're so young and beautiful the men can't resist you."

The UNHCR made her, Barisso, and Rekik attend some classes on how to get started in a new country (and how to use modern conveniences including a flush toilet with actual toilet paper).

Then the UNHCR gave them tickets for a flight on an airline called Air Canada to a city called Toronto in a province called Ontario. Mahret's intention at that time was that, once there, they would work for six months or a year and then most likely make their way across the American border to New York City.

Mahret did one more good thing in the meantime. She found a way out of Kibera for her best friend.

The day she first went to the United Nation's offices in Nairobi she had seen an advertisement in several languages, one of which was English, for United Nations employees.

It read:

Kibera needs land/tenancy rights, housing, water, electricity, health clinics, education, employment, security, plus much more. All these issues are being addressed to a lesser or greater extent by many organizations including the Churches, UN-Habitat, MSF (Médecins Sans Frontières or Doctors Without Borders) and AMREF (African Medical and Research Foundation). Money is finding its way through from many international organizations, including Gates Foundation, Bill Clinton Foundation, all the well-known charities, and several churches both in Africa and internationally to this cause. However, money cannot help without people to direct it. All the organizations require assistance. They all need intelligent, keen, willing, and compassionate people to help.

The ad also called for people with education, preferably a university degree. It was printed on a large pad of tear-off pages.

Mahret took one, and a couple days later, she went back to Mashimoni and found her friend.

"It describes you, Milka, it's perfect for you. You have an education. You speak their language. You have to apply."

Milka did apply. She had to tell them about her husband's indiscretions, his fall from grace at the university, and the effect it had on her. The people at the UN did not seem to be concerned about that sort of thing. They were more interested in Milka's struggle to survive, her courage in adjusting to Kibera, the help she had extended to other mothers in similar situations, and, ultimately, her successful business.

Milka was one of a number of the people hired.

She thanked Mahret, "with all my heart."

She told her, "you're the best friend I have in the whole world."

"Don't thank me," Mahret said. "They're so lucky to have you. Now you can help so many the way you helped me, with all your knowledge, your advice, your caring. You can help people help themselves. The one thing we learned in the slums above all else is that we're all in this together. That's a lesson I will never forget. And you more than anyone else taught me by your example."

"Well, okay, maybe. *Galatom* for saying so, but you and I have lived an adventure together. We are two women of diverse origins who joined forces for both stamina and durability. We overcame so much together. We found strength in numbers even if we only numbered two. Together, we found food, we found schools for our kids, we helped our mates find work, we started up a business that made it possible for us not only to feed our children but even to put money aside for a future we would otherwise not have. And now we've managed to get you to the new world and me into what might well turn out to be a respectable career. We accomplished a lot."

"All that's true. We got together to overcome the harsh world we lived in, and we learned that we could be strong, that women could be strong."

"Yes, we took up the ways of the ghetto; we worked with each other and with all sorts of people from all sorts of countries and all sorts of cultural backgrounds. We overcame compartmentalization and in a very small way we helped to make the world a better place."

"I guess so, not much better but a tiny little bit better."

"Now we must not let distance separate us. We will write to each other. We are both going to be able to move now, but you can write to me by sending letters to the Mashimoni post office. I'll get your address from the letters and write back with my new address. We will be able to talk to each other all the time. We will be friends for life. We'll grow old together."

"Yes, someday we'll see each other again, in the new world."

"There is no doubt about that."

"*Galatom!* I will always be close to you even when we are oceans apart."

"Me too."

EPILOGUE

In the next stage of their life, Mahret, Barisso, Berhanu, and Gamado were to find themselves in a major North-American city. Before moving to that city, Mahret, in particular, imagined they would quickly establish a secure life. What she was to discover, however, was not exactly what she expected. For linguistically challenged, relatively uneducated, and impoverished people like them, making the necessary adjustments was to prove much more complicated and difficult than she had anticipated. Her experiences in the slums of Nairobi were to be instrumental in helping her understand why.

Remembering what Milka had told her, Mahret figured that one of the main barriers to achieving a better life in North-American cities was a societal proclivity for compartmentalization. This, she surmised, was mainly based on the widely varying physical traits of the people. In Nairobi, almost everyone had been black-skinned (all be it with shade variations) and had curly black hair and dark eyes. Looking back, Mahret concluded that under normal circumstances (excluding elections in particular), this must have helped to soothe cultural, religious, and linguistic differences. In North American cities, by contrast, the white-skinned mainstream stood out from several minorities tagged "visible" mainly because their physical features were distinct from those of the majority. Mahret noticed, as well, that the people in each minority group looked different from those in most of the other minority groups. Moreover, they and all the groups tended to cling together in neighborhoods populated mostly by their own kind. Thus, the white suburbs in the cities had readily identifiable Filipino, Latin American, Arab, Asian, and black neighborhoods around them.

Mahret realized too that her family conformed to this pattern. When she and Barisso first came upon black people in their new city, they were instantly drawn to them. And as soon as possible they found housing near a number of them. From that point, they and both boys socialized almost entirely with other blacks. It mattered little to them whether their friends came from Kenya, Ethiopia, Botswana, the Congo, Nigeria, or, indeed, North America. As long as they were black, they were comfortable with them.

Mahret also thought that unlike in Nairobi, this must be hardening rather than tempering cultural differences. She believed that as ethnic communities became more and more cohesive, the people in them increasingly drew away, mentally as well as physically, from other racial groups. That is, they compartmentalized. In so doing, they augmented tensions, which not only occasionally exploded into violence but also seemed to underlie ongoing disparities in employment, education, and wealth. Ironically, this, at times, would induce Barisso as well as Mahret to look back with some fondness to the shanty towns in Africa they had fled.

Oromo Words and Phrases Used in the Text

Waqaa (God)
Marqaa (a large, baked, ring-shaped breakfast staple often shared by family members)
Abbaa and *haadha* (father and mother)
Haadha rawu (mother f**ker)
Shonkora (sugarcane)
Lubaa (priest)
Qamis (dress)
Shaayii (tea)
Daabo (bread)
Shashi (head scarf)
Goraa (berries)
daadhi (wine)
Nagaa Jirtann (good evening)
Galatom (thank you)
Waaqayyo galatom (thank you)
Akkam (hello)
Akkam jirtuu (how are you)
Sin jaaladaha (I love you)
Akkam waaritan (good evening)
Berele (hand-made Ethiopian glass bottle)
Shallee (woman with low morals)
Tambo (penis)